BEWICCHED

The Sea Wicche Chronicles

SEANA KELLY

Bewicched: The Sea Wicche Chronicles

Copyright © 2023 by Seana Kelly

Ebook ISBN: 9781641972345

KDP POD ISBN: 9798391799573

IS POD ISBN: 9781641972659

NYLA Publishing

121 W. 27th St., Suite 1201, NY 10001, New York.

http://www.nyliterary.com

*For my brother Pat Kelly
who invited me into his room when we were little to read the poem Annabel
Lee to me,
thereby assuring my love of reading, Poe, and him*

They Weren't Kidding When They Called Me, Well, a Wicche

U rsula, a villain who did not deserve to be considered one, was my favorite Disney princess. She's a working woman, offering a service, and was vilified for it. The payment was obvious. The whiners knew the score. They just thought they were special, that they could get magic for free. That's not how magic works. You always have to pay. Plus, octopuses are incredible, so I refused to support fairy tales disparaging them.

The Little Mermaid aside, I was calling my Monterey seaside art gallery and tea bar The Sea Wicche because I, Arwyn Cassandra Corey, am a sea wicche, or at least I really wanted to be. The wicche part is true enough.

It was a perfect day, with clear blue skies and a cold, salty wind on the California coast. I went out the back door of my art studio to the deck that ran along the ocean side of a small, abandoned cannery I was having renovated. The deck gave a little with each step. Strangely enough, rotting wood was a bit of a safety hazard. I loved this place, though, even when it had been filled with standing water and rusted machinery.

I used to break in and run around here when I was little. Mom worried I'd hurt myself, but Gran said she'd seen in a dream it would be mine and to leave the poor child alone. In wicche families, the older you are, the more powerful. No one messes with the crones. I was, consequently, looking forward to getting old. The crones do not give a fuck. They've seen and done it all and have lost the ability to be polite about it. They'll tell you what they think to your face, because what are you going to do about it? That's right. Nothing.

I couldn't wait. Anyway, Gran said the cannery was mine, so it was mine. Even at seven, it was all mine. The deck sat on tall posts that were mostly submerged at high tide. Now, though, at low tide, the barnacles, oysters, coral, and algae were visible. There were even a couple of gorgeous orange starfish that had made my posts their home.

I sat on the edge of the deck and leaned over, holding on to the weather-warped wood with my ever-present gloves. The two starfish were still there. One was clinging to a post covered in a carpet of purple and green algae. I needed photos. Tourists snapped them up for a good price, especially this close to the Monterey Bay Aquarium.

Tipping back, I rolled over onto my stomach and took my phone out of my back pocket. Dangling over the deck edge, I framed the shot and took it. Perfect. Yes, my DSLR camera would be better, but the light was magical now. The colors were so vibrant, they'd pop out of the frame. If I ran back in for my camera, the light could change and I'd lose the shot. I'd made that mistake too many times. I had a phone with the best digital camera on the market and I could tweak the image once I got it on my laptop.

I wear special gloves all the time, not just when touching rotting wood. They're a thin, soft bamboo fabric with connective threads on the fingers so I can still use my smartphone. Touch is a problem for me; clairvoyance is not for the faint of heart. I see too much, hear too much. You try shaking someone's hand and hearing he thinks you're a money-grubbing fake taking advantage of his mother, bilking her out of her last dime, and he wants you to drop dead. All of that and more the moment his hand touched yours.

Or, even better, how about finally getting a kiss senior year from the guy you've had a crush on since sixth grade, only to learn that he really wished your ass was smaller and he hoped Rachel heard about his kissing you because he was trying to make her jealous. Oh, and he actually thought you were a weirdo, but groping was fun, so...

Yeah, dating sucked when touch meant picking up every stray thought and emotion. For a while, I self-medicated with booze. That wasn't a sustainable plan, though. I hated drunk Arwyn and hated even more the predators who moved on me when they saw I was wasted enough to dull the voices. So, new sober me wears gloves and has sworn off dating and sex. It's a modern world. There are electronic alternatives that don't close their eyes and think about someone else.

I took a few more photos as long as I was hanging here, none as perfect as that first one, though. A text popped up on my screen and I flicked it away. It was my mom again, reminding me that Gran expected me at dinner tonight. They'd been trying to get me to join the Council since I was in my teens.

Maiden, mother, and crone, the Council oversaw all disputes, heard pleas for help, and granted magical aid, usually for a fee. Now that I was back from England—and my chess set was finally in the hands of the werewolf book nerd it was intended for—they were pushing hard for me to join. It wasn't that I wouldn't help when they needed me. I just didn't want to be tied to the regularity. I had my work and really did not care about the day-to-day petty crap. If they needed me to power a spell, fine. The rest of it, not so much.

Mom and Gran knew the toll it took on me, knew I lived through the worst horrors the people petitioning us carried with them, but they didn't experience it, so it was easy to forget the price I paid for my magic. I hadn't had a full night's rest in ever. The nightmares haunted me as though they were my memories.

So gloves, isolation, and my ocean buddies it was. There was movement in the water below. A tentacle almost broke the surface. Yes, my octopus friend was still hanging out below the cannery. "Hello, Cecil! I hope you have a lovely, watery day!" The way he moved was mesmerizing to watch. So much so, it took me too long to realize what was happening. Damn it! I was going to end up in the ocean.

Throwing the phone over my shoulder, I gave it a magical push to get it to the deck and then hoped for the best. My vision went dark. *Snarling.* I heard that first. Often the sounds and scents came to me before the images. *Growling and the scent of the forest. Two yellow eyes, huge, staring into me, before the scene formed. Large wolves circling one another, one jet black, the other tan.*

The tan lunges. The black meets him, clashing tooth and claw. Blood flies as they shake off the pain, circle, and charge. It's vicious and violent. I don't want to watch, don't want new nightmares. The tan one, bloodied and limping, cringes away when the black one howls. The black wolf is set upon by others as they drive him into the dirt...

My body tipped as I watched the wolves tear each other apart. Damn it, I knew it. I was about to get dunked, watching wolves kill each other.

Yellow eyes stare into mine, waiting.

I wasn't in the water, wasn't wet. What I was, though, was hanging in the air. A very tall, very strong man was holding me a foot off the deck, a hand gripped around the back of my neck. I stared into warm brown eyes and shouted, "What the fuck? Put me down!"

He dropped me like I was on fire. Thankfully, my balance was pretty good and I kept my feet under me.

He cleared his throat and pointed toward the water. "You were sliding in." He handed me my phone.

"Thanks," I said, "for picking up my phone and grabbing me before I went in. I'm an epileptic." Not really. I just needed a cover for my habit of hitting the ground. "This is private property, though. You shouldn't be here." I shaded my eyes. Oh, my. He had to be six and a half feet tall, a perfect muscular specimen, with dark hair starting to curl around his ears and a full, dark beard. He wore faded jeans, sturdy work boots, and a t-shirt topped with a flannel. I might not be able to touch, but I could look.

"I'm on the construction crew. Phil asked me to stop by to take measurements on the deck." He stared at me as though he was pretty sure I was insane but was too polite to say it.

Ha, joke's on him. People have been calling me nuts my whole life. It didn't even register anymore.

"So you're okay?" He had a deep growly voice that I liked. "You threw your phone at me and then just flopped over the edge, like dead weight dropping into the ocean."

I checked my phone. "Seizure. I'm fine now." No scratches on the screen. Score! "Go ahead," I said, gesturing to the rotting deck. "Do your thing." I started back into my studio and stopped. "Why are you working today? It is Sunday, right?" I checked my phone for the date.

"I wasn't doing anything, so I figured I might as well get started." He shrugged one beefy shoulder. "Plus, I need the work." He pulled a measuring tape off his belt. "Do you want the deck any different, or am I replacing this one exactly?" He took an old receipt and a pencil from his shirt pocket, starting to take notes.

"You can do it without dropping planks into the ocean or pounding on the posts so hard you disturb the ecosystem, right?"

"Ecosystem?" He walked to the edge and leaned over, peering down. "Is that what you were looking at?"

"My starfish Charlie got a new friend." I peered over the edge and saw the guy's arm move, like he was ready to grab me if it looked like I was about to go in. "The friend kind of looks like a…Herbert." I slid the phone back in my pocket, brushing the dirt from my gloves. I owned many pairs in a rainbow of colors, all washable.

"Herbert and Charlie, huh? Which one is which?" His balance was amazing. He'd been leaning out past the edge of the deck for a while and not a bobble or tremor in sight.

Wicches can tap a part of our brains that allows us to see a person's aura, essentially to see what kind of person we're dealing with. The brighter and shinier the aura, the more trust-worthy the person. The smokier the aura, the more we needed to watch our backs. Yes, I was a strong wicche who could take care of myself, but six and a half feet of muscle on a psycho was probably something I should prepare for.

Letting my vision relax, I sized up this guy who wanted to work here while I was alone in my studio. Huh. No aura. Well, hell, that's why I had the vision. Fingers twitching at my side, I readied a spell, just in case. "Werewolf?"

Poor guy looked like he'd been smacked in the face with a shovel. "What?"

"It's okay." I pointed at myself. "Wicche."

"I know, but how did you?"

"You knew?" I'd never laid eyes on this guy before. How did he know?

He tapped his nose. "You have a scent."

I felt my face flame. I'd showered this morning, hadn't I? *Shit.* When I got involved in a project, I lost track of time and personal hygiene.

Chuckling, he clarified, "Wicches as a group, not you in particular. *You* smell like plaster and paint. And the ocean."

"Oh." Well, that was okay then. Not all werewolves were psycho killers. In fact, very few of them were. Still, I let the spell dance between my fingers in case I'd read the situation wrong.

He wrote something on the paper in his hand. "What kind of railing do you want?"

"None."

He raised one eyebrow. "You'll need some pretty good insurance to cover all the lawsuits from people falling off this thing."

"The plaster and paint you're smelling are from the tentacles I'm building. They'll be thirty feet tall and come up from below the water, curving this way and that to keep people from falling in. It'll look like a sea monster is pulling us into the ocean."

His eyes flicked from the ocean to the edge of the deck. "Nice." After pausing a moment, he asked, "What about kids? The curves will leave holes, the perfect size for little heads. Plus, you're not going to want the tentacles crowding out the view, right? There'll be gaps."

I bit off the automatic denial and thought about the design I had in mind. I waved him in the back door of my studio. It took up about a third of the cannery building and was the first section remodeled. I needed a place to work. The gallery could wait. I sold my work in other galleries around the world.

I stopped him before he stepped over the threshold, though, my hand on his chest. "Wait. What's your name?"

He stared down at my hand until I moved it. "Declan."

"Declan what?" I'd be texting all the cousins first chance I got to see if anyone knew anything about this guy. Then again, my cousins were assholes. Maybe I'd chance it.

"What's it to you?"

"Maybe you're a serial killer." I doubted it, but it was possible.

He stared at me, his intense brown eyes making my stomach flutter. "You're the wicche," he said, leaning in. "Am I a serial killer?"

Damn, he was potent. Instead of answering, I just waved him in. I was pretty sure he was safe. Being a werewolf, I couldn't read him easily, but I had a spell at the ready if he gave me trouble.

"You know, I'd like to know your last name too?" A second man's voice made me jump.

Who the hell was that? I ducked my head through the open

door and found another muscular guy on my doorstep. Unfortunately, I'd met this one before. He was Logan, the Alpha of the local pack. Six-four, tawny hair, tanned skin, blue eyes, he was the golden child of Monterey. Women flocked to him, and he'd never met one he hadn't liked.

"Arwyn." His gaze traveled from my out-of-control curls down to my paint-spattered sneakers. "Good to see you again, although I can't say much for your company."

My cousin Serena had dated Logan in high school when he was the star athlete on every team. She was head over heels, but he was working his way through the female student body, so it didn't last long. She said he wasn't a jerk about it. He was just a guy who loved women and couldn't rest until he'd bedded all of them. Everyone needed a hobby, I supposed.

When he turned to Declan, the physical change was extraordinary. Relaxed and flirtatious morphed into clenched jaw, puffed chest, tightened fists. "You know the rules. You can't come into my territory without meeting with me and getting my approval. I'm Alpha." Logan crossed his arms over his chest and glared at Declan, eyes going wolf gold.

Declan didn't flinch, didn't seem the least bit concerned. "I'm not in *your* territory. Pack grounds are in Big Sur. I live and work in Monterey. Eve is the Master of Monterey."

Logan growled, "Bloodsuckers don't rule us. You want to stay here, you meet with me."

"Gentlemen," I interrupted, "I have reason to believe this won't end well. What do you say you just shake hands and walk away? In fact," I added, glancing back in my studio, "I can offer you both a freshly baked fudge brownie with a layer of caramel in the middle. Can you smell them?" Being werewolves, they'd never back down from a fight, but it was worth a try.

Declan studied me a moment, lifting his head to scent the air, and then grinned. "I'm in." He stuck out his hand and waited.

I did *not* expect that.

Logan smacked Declan's hand away.

Yep, totally expected that.

Declan blew out a breath and leaned against the doorframe. "Where and when?"

"Pack grounds. Full moon. And since I had to track you down, you'll join our hunt instead of meeting me in my office. You think you can handle that?" Logan sneered.

Declan's expression was priceless, like he was dealing with a toddler having a tantrum. "I'm sure I'll be fine. Thanks for your concern, though."

I had to bite my lip not to laugh. Laughing at a pissed-off Alpha was a good way to get bitten.

"We'll see what happens when you're on pack lands and whether or not I allow you to stick around." When Logan grinned, for just a moment his teeth seemed too long, too sharp, but it could have been a trick of the light.

And then his eyes were back on me and all the aggression was gone. "You Corey girls sure do have the biggest, prettiest blue eyes."

"Green," Declan corrected.

"Right. So, I've been meaning to ask you, there's a new Mexican restaurant in town I'd like to take you to. What do you say?"

"Well, I'll have to think about that, won't I?"

"You do just that. And I'll see you again real soon." With a warm grin, he sauntered off.

Logan had been doing his damnedest to seduce me since I was fifteen, bragging about what a powerful couple we'd make. When I turned back to Declan to discuss railings, though, he wasn't watching the threatening Alpha depart. He was watching me.

2

Chocolate Makes Everything Better. Mostly

"I believe you said something about a brownie," Declan said.

I blew out a breath, shaking off the weirdly charged, testosterone-fueled moment, and went for the baked goods. When I realized he was still standing in the doorway, I beckoned him forward, saying, "Come on in."

I could use a brownie too. The way this guy blew off impending werewolf trouble for baked goods made me want to classify him as a decent guy. Of course, that might have been because I couldn't hear his shitty thoughts. Trusting, I was not.

I put two brownies on a plate for him and one for me. "I have coffee, tea, milk, soda, or water. Do you want anything to drink?" I grabbed myself an orange soda and a fork. Wearing gloves meant I almost always ate with utensils. Try eating chips with chopsticks. Go ahead, I dare you.

"I'll take an orange soda too, if you've got another." His voice was closer than I'd expected.

I turned, trying to decide if I needed to drop the baked goods and get that spell ready again. Nope. He was just studying my paintings. That was a relief. I didn't want to have to drag his huge unconscious ass out of here after I'd put him down.

My studio was part workroom, part apartment. I had an

oversized worktable in the center, with cabinets against the far wall for supplies, finished pieces, whatever. There was a door in that wall that led to the Fire Room. I did glass blowing and pottery in there. Opposite that wall was the door to the gallery space, which was double the area of my studio. I also had a couch and a chair in a small living room area.

Along the back wall was my kitchen. I had an industrial-grade stove because when the nightmares woke me, I baked. A lot. My gallery—when she finally opened—would have an area where I sold baked goods and my mom's tea. She ran a very popular tea shop.

I had a small toilet downstairs and a full bathroom upstairs in my bedroom loft. Stairs ran along the wall in common with the gallery and led to a huge loft that served as my bedroom. My bed was soft and inviting, with water-colored bedding and a mountain of pillows. Over the years, I'd tried everything in an attempt to sleep through the night. As that never actually happened, I also had a comfy reading chair. Above the bed, there was a new skylight. When I lay awake in bed, I was now able to watch the stars, the movement of the moon, the shifting of the clouds.

I brought his brownies and soda to the worktable. I could have put them on my coffee table, inviting him to sit down, but I didn't know anything about this guy. He could stand and eat.

He was leaning in to examine something on my *Deep Ocean* canvas when his head snapped to the windows overlooking the deck and ocean. "A tennis ball just dropped on your deck." His confusion was hilarious.

"Be right back," I called, jogging to the door. "Eat your brownies."

Once outside, I shaded my eyes from the sun, looking for the little scamp. Wilbur was a gray speckled harbor seal who liked to play catch. And hide-and-seek. I grabbed the wet tennis ball. Looking for the telltale ripple, the quick surfacing of his rounded head, I searched the water.

"Where are you, you little punk?" I muttered, pacing across the deck. Giving up—that brownie wasn't going to eat itself—I pulled my arm back to throw it as far as I could and then stopped, remembering I had access to a werewolf's arm.

"Declan!" I shouted, turning back to the studio door and bouncing off his chest.

"Yes?" He was leaning against the doorframe, watching me.

I handed him the wet ball and pointed out into the ocean. "Throw that as far as you can, please."

He did and I loved that he didn't ask questions first. Just threw. I walked past him to change gloves and get my brownie when I heard him say, "Look at him go."

I ran back out, searching the water. "What did you see?"

"A seal. He came shooting out from under the deck, racing after that ball."

"You're a cheat, Wilbur!" Shaking my head, I stared through the slats of the deck. "I know you were hiding him, Cecil! I'm not happy with you either!" I stomped back into the studio. They were ganging up on me.

Declan stayed in the doorway. "Got beef with a seal, huh?"

"He knows what he did. I don't have to explain it to you." Sneaky little bugger, hiding where he knew I couldn't find him. "Hey, how long will I not have a deck?" Some days, it felt like half my time was spent out there.

"You going to eat that brownie?" Declan was staring at the brownie I had left on the plate with the fork.

I stared him down, laughing on the inside. It made me happy when people enjoyed my baking. It took the edge off all those sleepless nights when I baked instead of slept. "Depends. How long will I be without my deck?"

"Do you want it fast or do you want it good?" He walked over to the plate and slid it closer to himself.

I hit it with a spell, sliding it back to my end of the table. "I want both." I lifted the plate and forked up a huge chunk, stuffing it in.

"Talk about cheaters," he grumbled. "I can do it in two or three days. Since I need to be careful during demo, making sure nothing drops in the water, it'll go a little slower."

"Hmm." I slid the plate back across the table. With my finger. "Okay. And as an act of goodwill—something a cheater would never do—I'll have baked goods at the ready for you to urge you along faster."

He rested his hands on his hips and gave me back the suspicious stare. "How do I know the rest of what you bake is any good?"

"You don't." A knock sounded in the gallery space. I checked my watch. "I have an appointment. Go away." I waved my hand toward the open studio doorway before heading through the gallery door.

Crossing the floor felt like walking on water. As the contractors had to level the floors anyway, I had them pour deep swirling blue-stained cement in the gallery and studio. The gallery portion of the cannery was still wide open and empty. The cannery had a forty-foot ceiling, with exposed metal beams and a wall of windows looking out over ocean.

The workmen had made all the repairs, painting the walls a dark midnight blue and replacing all the broken windows. The window washer bill was going to be astronomical, which was why I still took on random clients for readings. I needed to keep the money coming in. And as the windows rose almost as high as the ceiling, I needed to have them UV treated. I didn't want my art pieces fading in the sun.

I pulled open the dented metal door—the last thing that would be replaced once all the work was done—and found a nervous-looking man on my doorstep. Short dark hair and sad brown eyes. He wore jeans and a light blue button-down.

"Hello." I knew this was the guy I was waiting for, but I could tell he wanted to run, so I gave him a chance to make up a story and take off.

"Hi. My sister Lili said I should come see you." He stuffed

his shaking hands into his pockets and waited for me to put him out of his misery.

"Sure. Come on in." I opened the door wide and waved him in. "How is Lili? I haven't seen her in a few months."

Some of the tension in his shoulders loosened. "Oh, you know Lili. Working her way up that corporate ladder. Mom and I joke she'll be their youngest CEO."

"I don't doubt it." Lili was actually good friends with my cousin Cat, but I knew he needed comfortable small talk. "Hey, I just made brownies. Would you like one?"

He pulled a fist out of his pocket to wave off the offer. "I don't want to be a bother. I'm fine."

"Nonsense. How am I supposed to explain to Lili that I left her brother hungry when I have a tray of brownies in the next room?" I gestured to the table and chairs while making my way to the studio door. "I'll be right back. What would you like to drink?"

"Uh, water's good."

I ducked back into my studio and found Declan leaning over the table, drawing. "What are you still doing here?" I hoped this wasn't a feeding-a-stray-dog-and-they-never-leave situation.

"I can get started today. I'm sketching my plan for the deck. I want to make sure you approve before I begin."

"Oh, smart. But in general, if a woman tells you to go away, you should." I grabbed a couple of paper towels and then plated a brownie for Rob, who had yet to introduce himself, and a lemon square for Declan. I wasn't rewarding bad behavior. I was demonstrating my awe-inspiring baking skills. After pouring a glass of water, I pulled beer from the fridge. I couldn't stand the stuff, but I had friends and family who liked it, so, you know.

"How come I wasn't offered a beer?" Declan glared at the brownie and beer and it was so hard not to laugh.

"I have my reasons." Let him wonder. I left him the lemon square, which softened his expression, and then headed out.

Rob was staring out the window. "I'm not sure, but I think a seal just tossed a ball onto your deck."

I left his beer and brownie on the table and then took off out the back door. Declan was already there, picking up the tennis ball. He raised his eyebrows, waiting for the go-ahead.

"Chuck it!" I knelt at the edge of the deck, waiting. Declan could throw three times farther than I could. Okay, fine. It was at least ten times farther than I could. Shut up.

The ball hit the water with a splash and gray streaked out from under the deck. "I see you, Wilbur!" The seal had been arrowing through the ocean, but at my shout, he rolled over and over before doing a flip. I won that round and we both knew it. "Thanks for the assist." I nodded at Declan before returning to Rob.

"Sorry about that," I said, closing the back door.

"You have a pet seal?"

The wonder on his face finally made those tense shoulders come down. "Not a pet. Just a friend." I walked to the table and sat down. "I know you said water, but I thought you might want a beer." I pointed at the plate. "And if chocolate isn't your thing, I have lemon too."

"Uh, no. Chocolate's good. Thank you." He sat down and some of the wariness returned.

"Go ahead and eat. We can get started in a minute." I paused, waiting for him to pick up the brownie. When he reached for it, I began to ramble. The poor guy was wound so tight, I'd never get anywhere with him.

"Did Lili tell you I lived in a converted cannery?"

He shook his head.

"Yeah, I used to play here all the time when I was little. You could smell the fish a half mile away..." He didn't look bored as I droned on. He seemed genuinely interested in my story about the cannery. Nice guy.

When he finished, he wiped his fingers off on the paper

towel and tipped back the beer bottle. "Thanks for all this. This psychic stuff makes me uncomfortable."

Something dropped in the studio and poor Rob flinched.

"That's just the construction guy who's rebuilding my deck. Let me just check nothing was broken while you finish your beer." I stood up.

"Oh." He shook his head, laughing. "I thought the place was haunted."

"Nah. No ghosts here." My sneakers were silent across the floor. Nonetheless, when I opened the studio door, Declan was staring at me. Closing it behind me, I stared right back. I knew that look. It was the look of disbelief and disgust. Whatever. "Can you please go sketch in your truck or something? You have excellent hearing and his business isn't yours."

"You're a psychic?" The flirty interest in his eyes was gone. "I thought you were an artist."

"I am." It shouldn't have hurt. I barely knew the guy. "But what I am or am not is none of your concern. I've asked you nicely twice to go." I wriggled my fingers. "If I have to ask again, it won't be nice."

He ripped a page out of my sketchbook and tossed it across the table. "I'll be back in the morning to get started. If you want changes, you can tell me then." He walked out without a backward glance.

I let out a breath, watching him go. They always go, don't they? Didn't matter. Rob needed my help. What Declan thought of me was irrelevant.

3

Dealer's Choice

I went back and sat, pushing my wild hair over my shoulder and folding my gloved hands on the table. "So, what are you thinking? I can do palm or Tarot reading. I also have psychometry abilities, if you'd just like me to hold your hand and tell you what I see." There was more, but I wasn't looking to scare the poor dude.

He shook his head, the nerves returning.

"Okay, how about this? You tell me the question you want answered and it'll be dealer's choice." I was pretty sure I already knew the question, but for his own peace of mind, he needed to say it.

He scratched the stubble on his cheek. "I'm having a hard time with something."

"Okay. Why don't you tell me about that." He was struggling so hard, my stomach began to knot.

"I guess my question is if I should be a father." Shame underlaid those words.

Mentally, physically, this was going to take more out of me, but I knew the cards weren't right for this situation. I pulled off my gloves and rested my hands, palms up, in the center of the table. After a moment of hesitation, he placed his on top of mine.

I felt it almost immediately, the sharp open-handed smack across the face. I flinched, trying to absorb the pain. A shove jolted me in the back. My hair was yanked. In that moment, it was happening to me. I breathed through the hurt. I knew of ways to block my empathic side, but creating that barrier made me far less effective as a psychic. Self-preservation dictated I fuck that noise and create the buffer, but I struggled, knowing the horrible guilt that sometimes accompanied putting my own needs above the person who was hurting.

My family didn't know the half of what it was like for me. I believed—I really wanted to believe—that if my mom knew, she wouldn't be hounding me to be on the Corey Council. She had, over the years, given me hell for not blocking more. I said I didn't because I'd built a reputation and had to deliver in order to make money to fund my art. And while that was true, it wasn't why.

I'd gone to school with a girl. Quiet. Skittish. She wasn't in my class. I was two years younger, but I brushed past her in the halls and lunch line. The darkness and pain in her overwhelmed me. I blocked hard—as much as I knew how at that age—and tried to stay away from her. We found out later her uncle had been molesting her. Third grade and she'd tried to kill herself. If I hadn't blocked, hadn't avoided, maybe I'd have been able to tell someone, do something. Anything.

This was why the psychics in the Corey family had dark, horrific lives. One of us is born every couple hundred years, and all those before me went insane and died young. So, you know, I had that to look forward to. As I was twenty-eight, already twice as old as most of the others when they shook off this mortal coil, I couldn't help but feel like I was on borrowed time. As far as magical gifts went, mine blew.

All of which is to explain why I was holding this man's

hands and allowing the punches to land. Guilt crushed the soul. "How long did your father live with you?"

His hands flinched. "He left when I was seven."

His mom took the kids and ran when he was seven. What kind of evil pushes adults to prey on the helpless? "And how was it with just your mom?"

"Mom's great. She's over the moon. Can't wait to be a grandmother." His voice had lightened, as had his memories.

The ring on his left hand brought him joy and love. I tried to hold on to that feeling. "And your wife? How is she reacting to the pregnancy?"

"She smiles all the time." He shook his head in wonder. "I mean, not always, except kind of always. She throws up in the bathroom and then comes out, rubbing her belly, full of plans for the baby's room."

"What color are you painting it?" Swatches of color raced through my mind.

"I don't know. She showed me colors, but I walked away. Whatever she wants, you know?" He shrugged, misery written all over him. "I'm hurting her. I can see her disappointment, but I never wanted kids. I'm just—I don't think I'd be good with them. Isabella wants me to be a part of the planning and preparation, to take the class and read the book, but I can't." He stopped and gave his head a little shake, as though arguing with himself. "I don't like talking about this. Besides, this isn't why I'm here. I just want to know"—his hands fisted in my palms—"will I hurt it?"

I gave him time to settle after asking the real question. I could have led him through it, try to get him to see it himself, but I could feel his exhaustion and self-loathing.

"I can't tell you that you'll never raise your hand to your child. The future has yet to be written. I can remind you that there have been many people in your life that have pissed you off and you never hit them.

"Your first job—fast food? I smell oil, hear sizzling—there's an older man who's being creepy to a teenager you were working with. He scheduled her late or kept her after. Something that got her alone. You stayed, though. Your shift was done, and you came back or stayed late. You knew she was scared and so were you, but you were there when he ran his hand down her back, grabbing her ass."

"I shoved him against a wall. Hard." His face fell, as though I was confirming his violent tendencies.

"You protected an innocent from a predator. You, Rob"—he hadn't given me his name, but I needed him to hear me—"are a protector, not a monster. You're nothing like your father. You've been enraged plenty of times in your life, just like the rest of us, and not once did you take it out on someone smaller and weaker."

I paused, giving him time to think, to run through those moments in his life that supported what I'd said. His hands in mine were already feeling lighter. "Don't let him take this away from you. He's done enough damage. Be a part of the planning. Borrow some of your wife's joy until you feel it yourself." I squeezed his hands. "You're going to be a good dad *because* you know exactly what it is to have a bad one."

I pulled my hands back and put on my gloves.

He stood, rubbing his forehead. "Yeah?"

"Go help your wife paint the nursery." I nodded, shoving my hands into my paint-spattered overalls.

"Yeah, okay." He nodded, a tentative smile appearing. "I did like that green she showed me."

"I like green," I said, though he'd stopped listening to me. His delight had me tearing up.

He turned to the door and then stopped himself, spinning back to me. "Sorry." He pulled his wallet from his pocket and laid five hundred dollars on the table. I'd told him on the phone my fee was two-fifty, so it was a nice tip.

"Thank you."

"No," he said, "thank *you*." As he left, he pulled his phone from his pocket. "Izzy, honey—" and then the door slammed.

I shook out my hands and jogged in place before bending forward, stretching, palms to the floor. I straightened up and pulled an old-fashioned scrunchie from my pocket. I swear, they were the only things strong enough to take on my hair. I tied my hair up and then headed for the back door. I needed my friends to shake off the melancholy of a beaten little boy who grew up, saw his father in the mirror, and began to fear himself.

The clouds had rolled in, the wind almost knocking me back through the doorway. I went to the edge and knelt, as I had before. Pulling off my gloves, I stuffed them in my pockets and then lay down, my head and shoulders over the edge, my arms hanging down.

Charlie and Herbert were still with me. "Hi, guys! Looks like the tide is coming in. I won't be seeing you for a while. Is Cecil still here?" A tentacle rose and splashed the water at the surface. I waved back.

I'm only half wicche. My father is water fae. I'm not sure what flavor. I've never met him. Mom didn't want to talk about him and my empathy for her discomfort meant I mostly kept my questions to myself. One of my more assholish cousins questioned if I should really be considered a Corey wicche, given my questionable parentage. My aunt Sylvia shut that shit down fast, smacking him upside the head and making him apologize. While it was nice in the moment, that stuff never works. It just taught him to be sneakier in the future, which he was.

From my father, I inherited an affinity for water, particularly the ocean. I held my hands over the waves and pulled, willing it to rise gently toward me. Much like my octopus friend Cecil, I could direct short bursts at a target. I'd mastered that by the time I was ten. And believe me when I tell you that my little shit cousin Colin got blasts of saltwater in the ear whenever he dared to go near the ocean.

It was slow, measured control that had always been difficult for me. I drew two narrow towers of water up, slowly pulling them to my palms. They were almost there, a foot away, when Wilbur shot up out of the ocean and dove through both lines of seawater, splashing me in the face and flinging the tennis ball onto the deck.

"Wilbur!" I wiped my face on my sleeve. "You little—fine," I muttered. "You won that round."

A tennis ball flew over my head, far out into the ocean. I reared back to find a certain dark-haired werewolf sitting on my deck, leaning against the doorframe of the studio. "Oh, it's you." I sat up, not liking a potential enemy at my back. "I thought I told you to scram."

"You did. I came back to apologize. I was out of line."

Huh. Another unexpected reaction. Interesting.

"Psychics." There was that look of disgust again. "You seem nice enough and that water trick was cool, but I just don't believe in psychic abilities." He shrugged one big shoulder. "My aunt believed in that stuff and got taken by a never-ending chain of frauds, making vague predictions, rephrasing what she'd already told them to make it seem like they'd heard the info in the great beyond. It's all smoke and mirrors, and then hand over the money. But what you do is none of my business, like you said, and I really want this job. So, I'm sorry for being rude earlier." He stood, nodded once, and walked around the Sea Wicche to where he had no doubt parked.

When I looked down at the water, I found Wilbur looking back. He gave an exaggerated shake of his head and dove under.

Yeah, right there with you, buddy.

4

Yes, Mom. I Know, Mom

"Arwyn?" My mom's voice floated through the open door. What was she doing here? I gave Cecil a last wave, stood up, donned my gloves, and brushed the rotting wood dust from my clothes. Internally sighing, I headed in.

"Really, dear, is that what you're wearing?" She swatted at the dirt on my knees. "I thought you said you had a reading today." She gave my grubby gloves a shake of her head and pulled a clean pair from her bag. It was voluminous and carried all manner of things. "Here. Throw those things away."

"They can be washed, Mom." I wadded up the dirty ones and stuffed them in my pockets before carefully taking the new ones from her. I already knew that my mom considered a lot of what I did a waste of time. I didn't need to brush her fingers and hear it again. Don't get me wrong. She loved me and was proud of my art. She just thought I should prioritize my magic, that I would be using my skills to better advantage if I took my rightful place on the Corey Council.

"You saw a client like that?" The judgment was clear. "Sylvia and the girls are right behind me."

"Okay." My aunt Sylvia was great. Mom was the oldest of seven siblings, five girls, two boys. Sylvia was right in the middle of the seven and the one who never looked at me sideways because of my mixed parentage. I mean, it wasn't like the aunts and uncles ever said anything to me directly, but I knew through the cousins that they took shots at me in private, too scared to take on my mother. As an adult, I can see how younger siblings, even those who were in their thirties and forties, could be resentful of their oldest sister, my mom, who held the Council position, had the strongest skills, and lost no power or privilege after giving birth to a question mark like me.

So, yeah, I understood why there were grumbles as my mom seemed like the perpetual golden child. What I didn't understand was why any adult would let their annoyance and jealousy for a sister bleed into derision, even momentarily, for a child. Life was tough enough without my cousins feeling justified in any rotten stunt they pulled or cruel remark they made. Whatever. It taught me very early in life who was to be trusted and who was to be avoided. I guess that wasn't a bad thing.

The front door swung open, and my aunt Sylvia and her daughters Serena and Calliope walked in. Serena, of the dated-Logan-in-high-school fame, was gorgeous, but not a dick about it. She had long black hair, Corey green eyes, pouty lips, and cheekbones for days. She was a stunner, like her mom. And my mom, for that matter.

Coreys had a look, one I didn't, for the most part, share. Corey green eyes were a dark, mossy color. Mine were a light sea green. Coreys had straight black hair and slim builds. My hair was a wild mix of brown, red, and gold colors that people had been accusing me of dyeing since I was in elementary school. Also, I was more curvy than athletic. Still, no one came close to my power, so they could shove the rest.

Calliope, or Cal as she was often called, was a pale imitation of Serena, not as tall, not as beautiful, not as popular, but she was mostly fine. She wore her hair short in a pixie cut that complemented her waifish looks. I'll say this much for her, when the cousins were making jokes at my expense, she didn't join in.

I could see the glee in her eyes, but she never said anything, which I appreciated.

"Oh, Arwyn, it's coming along so nicely!" Sylvia pulled her gaze from the windows to study the floor. "They did an excellent job on these. Sybil, look. Maybe we should do something like this at the teashop." She glided over the floor. "It's like walking on water, isn't it?"

My mother glanced down, nodding. "They did a good job. There's depth and movement." She surveyed the whole empty space. "And don't be ridiculous, Syl," she said to her sister. "This works for the gallery. Our floors are warm and cozy, which is perfect for us."

Serena fake shivered. "It's beautiful but cold. Don't you think?"

Mom walked to the wall in common with my studio. "Are you planning the tea and sweets over here?"

"Yeah." I followed her over. "Not by the back door, though. Over here, where the two steel struts meet. See? It creates a kind of alcove that helps set this area apart from the gallery."

Mom nodded. "I trust your eye, darling. Now," she began, clapping her hands together, "Serena has a wonderful idea that will benefit you both." She gestured to my cousin. "Go ahead. Tell Arwyn."

Serena brushed her long hair over her shoulder. "Right. Okay. You have a huge retail space here and while you have completed pieces ready, it won't be enough to fill this whole gallery. My shop does great business, but it's small."

"That close to the Aquarium, the monthly rent is astronomical," Sylvia added.

I didn't like where this was going.

"You need to fill up this huge space and I could use a secondary retail spot, so I thought you could have shelves installed—maybe over here, near the tea since this already breaks with the rest of the gallery—and this could be a satellite shop, filled with my most popular soaps, lotions, fragrances. I'd be willing to split the profits—for just what's sold here—with you."

Calliope looked on expectantly. It was so kind of them to spring this on me. I'd be having words with my mother later, not that it would help. Once she'd decided something was a good idea, trying to dissuade her was pointless.

"Interesting idea. Let me think about that." The only reason I was adding the tea and baked goods was because I baked everyday anyway. I might as well make some money selling them, and my mother's teas were the best. I was more than happy to send customers her way.

It wasn't that Serena didn't make excellent products. It was if I said yes to her, soon other Coreys would come knocking, looking for a spot, and then I'd no longer have an art gallery. I'd have the Corey Consortium Mercantile.

My mother patted my shoulder as she walked by me. "It just makes good sense. Your grandmother gave you this Corey building for a reason. If you'd—"

"I *said* I'd think about it and I will." I glanced at the women, who appeared shocked that I'd interrupted my mother, except for Calliope, who nodded her encouragement. "You all know that Gran didn't *give* me this building, right? I paid for it with my art, with my readings. All the remodeling has come out of *my* pocket. I have a very specific plan for my gallery, and it doesn't include a collection of smaller retail spaces." I shifted my attention to Serena. "I said I'd think about it, and I will. I'll let you know if I decide it makes sense for me."

"It could go both ways," Calliope said, moving to stand beside her sister. "Serena could display your art in her shop with the address of your gallery."

The earnestness in her eyes almost swayed me. Almost.

"What a lovely idea, Calliope." My mother nodded in approval.

"Serena's shop gets a lot of foot traffic, given it's on Cannery Row," Calliope continued. "Your gallery is going to be amazing, but it's a bit off the beaten path." When I raised my eyebrows at that, she went on. "You're very close to the Row and on the ocean, but people driving down this road are watching the water or taking pictures. They're not shopping."

Pulling the scrunchie out of my hair, I stuffed it in my pocket with my dirty gloves. "So, by that logic, it doesn't make sense for anyone to want to use my gallery as a satellite shop as this is going to be a huge failure and a financial pit. Okay, good talk." I moved to my studio door. "Anyone want a brownie? I made them this morning."

"Arwyn, you know your cousin didn't mean anything of the sort." Mom was ticked.

"Oh my goodness, no. I'm sure people will come from far and wide to visit your gallery. We all know how talented you are." Calliope blushed and my mother ran a hand down her arm in comfort.

"Thanks. I *will* think about it, but right now the topic of brownies is on the table. Who wants one?"

Serena ran her hands over her slim hips. "I couldn't possibly. I don't know how you bake those kinds of things all the time and aren't the size of a house." She shook her head. "I suppose overalls are good for hiding a multitude of sins, though."

"I'll have one," Aunt Sylvia said. "And overalls are perfect for what Arwyn does. She's an artist, darling, as the paint spatter should tell you." Sylvia nudged my shoulder and winked. "If I'd had your figure, I'd have laid waste to the male population of the entire central coast."

My mother rolled her eyes. "You did just fine on your own, Syl." Mom turned to me. "You're coming to dinner at your grandmother's tonight, aren't you? She expects to see you."

I was sure she did. Gran was the matriarch of this coven, the crone on the Corey Council. One did not blow off a summons from Gran.

"Ladies, I need to speak with Arwyn alone a moment. Please go on ahead and save me a seat."

I ran to get Sylvia a brownie and walked them to the entrance, saying my goodbyes to Serena and Calliope. Once they got in their car, I closed the door and leaned back against it. "Okay, Mom. What is it?"

She strode across the huge empty space, her sensible heels echoing. "You can't keep putting this off. The petitions for intervention and help are becoming more frequent, the problems more serious. Your grandmother and I can't handle it all anymore. We need you, Arwyn. There's something evil wending its way through this town. We both feel it. Have your nightmares been getting worse?"

Yes, damn it.

I hadn't responded, but she nodded, knowing. "Come tonight. Let your Gran explain." She opened her bag and slid on a glove before cupping my face. "My darling girl, we're not going to force you. If you refuse, we'll need to find another to take your place. Either way, we need our third. We've been weakened for too long." She air-kissed me. "Come tonight, have dinner, and make your decision. All right?"

I nodded. "I'll be there."

"Good," she said on a nod, pulling the glove off and returning it to her bag.

The crash of the door closing as my Mother left had me wincing, not because she'd slammed it, but because my sensitivity was heightened. Another one was coming. *Damn it!*

I'd already had one vision today. When they came this hard and sudden, I knew I'd be down before I could make it to my studio. My head pounded painfully and the vision hadn't even started yet. I sat where I stood and lay back. If I didn't do it myself, the vision would drop me and I'd have a lot more bruises.

Staring up at the ceiling, blackness encroached, my eyesight contracting to a pinprick as the pressure had my head in a vice. The pain was excruciating. And then I was in it.

A child screams, his little voice like a nail to my skull. Lost and scared, he tries to run. He's scared of the dark. Footprints in mud, leading into the forest. A shadow emerges, beckoning the child forward. Terror overwhelms me.

A woman in the moonlight, laughing, staring up into familiar eyes that turn distant and cold. The smile drops from her face as she starts to run. Cold. Freezing cold. Hands push her down, keep her under. My lungs burn as she chokes on seawater.

A dark mansion looms in the fog. Faint light flickers in empty windows. I shiver, my breath escaping like a fog. Black eyes bore into me, a hypnotic voice in my head pulses and persuades. Blood drips from the walls and cascades down the stairs. A wolf howls in pain as a courtyard fills with blood.

A man, vaguely familiar, hunches over a great leather tome. A shadow comes to him and whispers in his ear. The man looks up from his book, maniacal grin on his face as the darkness invades him, laying claim to his soul.

Fire. An inferno roars to life and consumes my heart. I'm gasping in pain, a voyeur to my own immolation. A towering wave of black water rises, breaking over a wall, washing away my ashes.

Wolves tear at one another, claws rending flesh and sinew. Howling, terrible howling pierces the silent night. A shot rings out, tearing through flesh. Blood soaks the forest floor as a predator hunts his prey.

A woman barely clings to life in a hospital. I can't see her face, but I know her. I love her, but I can't get to her, can't find her through the fog. A familiar voice summons a demon. No! Following the voice, I run into the hospital bed and see the foul thing crouching on her chest, sucking out her soul and gobbling it down. I'm the one screaming now as a silhouette stands in the corner, gold dripping from its mouth as it gleefully watches the horror.

The demon turns his head, his eyes piercing what's left of me as he stares into my soul. I throw my hands up, cast a spell he waves off. Leering, he springs, knocking me to the hospital room floor. A ton of rocks lay on my chest as he leans forward, inhaling my life.

5

It Doesn't Pay to Piss Me Off

I startled awake to a deep voice.

"Shhh. You're okay."

Blinking, I looked up into concerned brown eyes above a thick, dark beard. I started to get up, but he held me in place. I was still on the floor, but Declan had pulled my head onto his lap.

"Take a minute. You're safe." He glanced around the big empty gallery. "Do you have somebody here who can take care of you?" He tilted his head a moment. "I'm picking up three or four distinct wicche scents. Four. I think four." He looked down, studying me again. "Do you take any meds for these seizures?"

"What?" My head pounded horribly from the lack of oxygen. That demon sitting on my chest, crushing me, left me breathless.

He gestured to my back door. "I was on the deck, making some changes to the plan, when I heard you whimpering. I came in and found you here. I was afraid you'd bash your head against the floor or something."

"I'm fine, really." I sat up and my head swam. I only had a second before my stomach rebelled. *Shit!* I hopped up and almost lost it, listing to the right like I was trying unsuccessfully to keep my feet under me on the deck of a ship in a storm, but Declan was there, holding me steady.

Hand over my mouth, I ran to the studio and barely made it to the toilet in the far corner before my stomach contents came hurtling up. I tried to hold my own hair back, but there's so damn much of it. I grabbed at stray curls falling forward, unable to stop the cramp and reflex, the bile.

Two big, warm hands pushed mine away and pulled my hair back.

"Go away," I gasped between heaves. My stomach was empty, but my body couldn't stop trying to rid itself of that vision.

"It's okay," he soothed, going down on one knee beside me. He still had my hair clasped in one hand but placed the other one on my stomach. Like a heating pad, it helped to settle my spasming muscles. "Slow, deep breaths. You're okay now."

I wiped the tears from my face and held my head in my hands. What had happened? I'd had nightmares and visions for as long as I could remember, but none had even been so vivid. Caused sleepless nights? You bet. Caused retching? Nope. First time. My body felt like it had been in a car accident. Everything hurt. The vision had reached down my throat and throttled me from the inside.

I closed the lid, flushed the toilet, and pushed up to my feet, ignoring the hands on my hips holding me steady. "Sorry you had to see that, but thanks for helping." I went to the sink, removed my gloves, cupped a hand under the water, and then brought it to my lips, swishing it around my mouth. My stomach was still unsettled, but I thought I was safe for the moment. Rather than drying my hands, I brought them to my face, closing my eyes against the cool wetness.

Dropping my arms, I stepped around Declan and went back into the studio. "Listen, I can't talk about the deck now. Show me your plans tomorrow. I need to shower and"—I checked my phone for the time—"and go to my grandmother's for dinner."

"Are you sure you're up to that?" The concern in his voice was a far cry from the disgust earlier, but I hadn't forgotten.

"No, but I have to go." I checked the time again. "I'll need to call a ride-share. There's no way I'm riding my bike tonight," I mumbled to myself. That'd give me a little extra time too. Maybe I could lie down for thirty minutes before the shower.

"Don't you have a car?" He stood, hands on his hips, seemingly reluctant to leave until I had a clear plan of action.

"Well, as I'd prefer not to kill myself or others by driving heavy machinery and then having a seizure, no. No car for me. My bike is usually fine, but when it's not, I call for a ride." I waved him toward the back door. "Thank you for helping, but I'll be fine. I want to lock up and get ready."

He ran a hand through his thick, dark hair, not moving. Eventually, he shook his head. "I don't understand why I came back or why this bothers me so much." He stilled. Brows furrowed, his gaze turned to flint. "Are you spelling me?"

It took my brain a moment to make sense of what he'd just asked. *Am I...* "Fuck *you*. Get out." I was about to collapse from that damn vision. I couldn't deal with this too. "I don't spell people to care about me, you asshole." I pointed at the door. "I take back every nice thing I said." I waved my hand and cast a spell shoving him back a few feet.

"I thought you said you don't spell people." Eyes lightening to wolf gold, he was pissed now too. Good.

I shoved him in the chest because his jaw was too high to punch. "I don't fucking use my magic to manipulate people's emotions!" Who the hell was this bastard to accuse me of something so low, so pathetic and underhanded? "But I am more than happy to use it to kick narrow-minded dicks out."

Holding up a hand, I pushed the air in his direction, a spell jumping to my fingertips, ready. My magic was always ready for me. He hurtled out the door and off the deck with an angry shout and a huge splash. I waved another hand, locking all my doors and dropping the shutters over my windows. Asshole!

I stomped up the steps to my loft, glad I'd agreed to the shutters when the contractor had recommended them. They cost a ton and it wasn't like we got hurricanes along the Monterey coast, but the night before I'd met with the contractor, I'd had a dream about something hideous with long nails scratching on the glass, trying to get in.

Locks and shutters would never keep out a determined werewolf, but hopefully the cold water would snap him out of his rage. I didn't need his shit. I had too much of my own to deal with, not the least of which was dinner with my mother and grandmother.

After I'd cleaned up and changed, I was feeling steadier. I called my contractor Phil and asked him to take the new guy off my crew. The work was being done to my home and I didn't want him in it.

I wore black jeans and boots with the light green sweater Gran had given me for my birthday. After locking the front door, I dropped my keys into my black leather backpack and sat on the front stairs, waiting for my ride.

I knew what my mom and Gran wanted. It was what they'd always wanted: Me on the Council. I got it. I did. But I also had to do what was right for me. Maybe it was selfish, but—

A small car pulled up in front the gallery. I checked the license plate against the info on the app. I also took a pic of the front of the car, license and driver visible, and texted it to my mom. Could I have taken him on? Sure. As long as I was awake and alert, that is. If I dropped into another vision, I had no control over my body.

I opened the back door. "What's your name?"

He half turned, giving me a friendly wave over the seat. "I'm Dan."

I checked the info on the app again and then slid in. When he pulled out onto the road, heading farther from downtown, I leaned forward. "Hey, just so you know, I'm epileptic. If I have a seizure, just leave me alone. I'll be fine.

When we get to the address, ring the bell and my mom will come get me, okay?"

"Uh." He glanced nervously at me in the rearview mirror.

"But nothing's going to happen. We're only going a couple of miles. We're fine." Hopefully. The poor guy looked spooked.

Luckily, we were only driving for a few minutes. Mom had a rambling Queen Anne historic home near the water in Pacific Grove, the next seaside town down the coast. Gran, however, was quite close to me.

The road south veered away from the water and into a wooded area. Tall trees popped up on either side of the car, along with a few houses between the road and the ocean. Gran had one of these rare old homes, mostly hidden from view.

"Slow down."

The driver's eyes shot to the mirror again. "Are you okay?"

"Sure. The driveway's here on the right. Slow down or you'll miss it."

Dan turned into Gran's drive, through a narrow break in the foliage. Pacific Madrone and Monterey Pine created a canopy over the hidden driveway, with white camellia bushes, elderberry, hostas, and hydrangea filling in the pockets around the circular cobbled drive.

"Wow. I never even realized this was here." The driver ducked his head under the visor, trying to see as much of Gran's home as possible.

I pulled a ten out of my wallet, adding a memory charm to the bill. I'd already paid for the ride through the app, but I offered Dan a cash tip with the charm because I really needed him to not be so interested in Gran and her place.

I had barely gotten out of the car before he started to drive away without a sidelong glance back. Perfect.

The glossy wooden door, carved with protective sigils, opened. My mother stood in the doorway.

"There you are." Her smile dimmed as she reached for my hand. "What's happened?"

"Nothing. I'm okay." I tried to walk past her, but she barred the entrance.

"You're not bringing that darkness into your grandmother's home. Stand out there. Let me get the sage."

She closed the door on me, so I went back to the center of the small circular drive. There was no point in arguing, and if Mom felt a darkness lingering on me, I wanted it gone too.

Mom and Gran emerged a moment later, both with sprigs of smoking sage. They walked in circles around me, wafting the sage head to toe, as they each recited purifying incantations.

Finally, Gran handed Mom her sage and pulled me into a hug. "My angel, come in and tell us what's happened."

"I didn't realize I was carrying evil. I never would have come."

"Hush now." Gran batted away my apology. "That was a nasty one clinging to you. Come in and tell us what's been going on today."

6

In Which Arwyn Learns the Conditions Put on Love

M y grandmother's house was like a bag of holding. It appeared to be a tiny forgotten stone cottage, clinging to the edge of a cliff. When you walked in, though—over polished wood floors, laid in intricate patterns mirroring the sigils on the door—the ceiling rose higher than the roof. A one-room hovel became a three-bedroom, three-bath showplace.

Every room had huge windows overlooking the ocean. Gran didn't have a furnace or heating system—certain technology she just didn't trust—so each bedroom had its own fireplace, with a huge one—always lit—in the great room. She kept a cauldron hanging over the fire for nostalgia, as she actually did her potions work in the kitchen. She had two pantries: one for food, one for spell ingredients. The latter was, of course, the much larger one.

"Sit with your mother. I'll bring the tea." Gran headed to the kitchen.

"I can help," I said and got a hand wave in response.

Mom, already wearing the gloves she always kept in her bag for when she'd be seeing me, took my elbow and led me to the couch by the fire. "That sweater looks lovely on you."

"I told you!" Gran called from the kitchen.

Mom rolled her eyes. "I like you in purple and blue, but your grandmother was positive this was the one for you."

"And I was right. As usual," Gran said, wheeling in the tea cart. "Okay, honey." She waved me over. "Your turn." She sat in her favorite rocking chair by the fire and waited for me to pour her a cup.

Having performed this ritual countless times in my life, I got Gran, Mom, and then myself a cup of my mother's loose leaf tea before I sat again.

Since both were waiting expectantly for the story, I took them through my day.

"Two visions?" My mother's brows furrowed in concern.

Gran shook her head. "The first one was normal. A strange wolf was coming. Her magic told her what she needed to know. That one's not the problem." She sipped her tea, ruminating.

"Do you think this wolf brought the demon with him?" Mom looked like she was ready to go hunt down Declan. What Mom could do to Declan was a lot worse than a swim in the ocean.

All of a sudden, the fire tripled in size with brilliant blue flames engulfing the cauldron for a moment. Gran nodded, as though agreeing with the fire. "Walk us through the second vision again."

So I went back over it, trying to explain each moment of it in detail. Reliving it for them had my stomach twisting anew.

"Drink your tea," Gran said to me. "Sybil, do you think the drowning woman…"

Mom nodded. "Yes, I'm afraid so."

"What?" I looked between the two for some clue.

"Your aunt Hester called a few minutes before you arrived," Mom began. "Her daughter didn't come home last night. Hester woke with a start a little before two in the morning, worried about her."

"Pearl's an adult, isn't she? She's got to be in her early twenties by now." Hester was the sister of Aunt Sylvia's husband.

While she was a wicche, she wasn't terribly powerful. I felt sorry for Pearl. She was younger than me, so it wasn't as though we hung out, but she had it rough. The cousins—some of them, anyway—could be real shitheads about magical gifts. If Pearl had inherited any magic from her mother, it hadn't emerged yet.

"She's twenty-one now and has been seeing a new young man. According to Hester, who hadn't met him, he went to school with Pearl. Your aunt might not be the strongest of wicches, but she knows in her heart something's happened to her daughter."

I took another sip and closed my eyes, trying to bring back the face of the woman on the beach. Shaking my head, I opened my eyes. "I can't see her clearly. It's been years, but the woman in my vision had blonde hair. Pearl's a brunette."

"Not anymore," Gran said.

"She went blonde a few weeks ago, when she started dating this guy," Mom added.

"Do you have a picture?"

Gran and Mom exchanged glances. "Yes, but—" she shook her head and pulled out her phone. "That doesn't matter." She scrolled through a few and then tapped an image, handing it to me.

My stomach dropped. I zoomed in, just to make sure, but I already knew. That was the face I'd seen. "She looks so different. I remember long dark hair that she hid behind while she stood silently in corners." Granted, it had been years, but this was a huge transformation.

"Hester was so happy that Pearl was finally coming out of her shell," Mom said, her voice weighed down with grief. "She was a sweet girl." My mom stood, taking the phone back from me. "Her mother's going out of her mind with worry. I need to call her." She walked down the hall and into a guest room.

"This is why you need to join us."

I turned from the hall to Gran. "What?"

"You have a gift, Arwyn. A prodigious one." She leaned

forward in her chair. "It's your gift. We know that. But our gifts are handed down from generation to generation, to every wicche in this family. Responsibility comes with that gift." Gran gave me the look that made the strongest amongst us wilt.

Gran had always been in my corner. Through all of the petty backstabbing bullshit among the cousins, the side-eye from the aunts and uncles, the nightmares and depression, my Gran has stood beside me and dared any to come for me while she was around. I loved and respected her, but…

"Do you understand what you're asking me?" I knew Mom and Gran loved me, but asking me to do this felt like my whole life had just been a fattening of the lamb for slaughter.

"Of course I do. I'm asking you to finally step up and take your rightful place on the Council, to help us stop these tragedies before they happen. How can you choose inaction when it means the loss of an innocent like Pearl?"

"No, Mom." My mother emerged from the guest room, swiping a hand down the front of her sweater set. Even delivering horrible news, every hair was in place. "No one is to blame for Pearl's death but the man who killed her. Don't lay that at Arwyn's feet."

"We can't do anything after the fact. We need to know beforehand," Gran pushed back, rocking angrily while staring into the flames. "I defended your excursion to England," she said to me. "You had to go. You needed to create your chess set for some werewolf and vampire. Why you had to go there to do it is beyond me."

She shook her head and then turned back to me. "I defended you to the family. We needed you but you wanted your art. Okay. We waited. Finally, you're back now. You have your studio and gallery. All we want is your help."

She stopped rocking, the anger draining out of her as she set her empty teacup aside. "I never thought you were a selfish girl. I'd never have believed that of you. Until now."

My vision blurred. Standing abruptly, I blinked away the

sudden tears. "You can say this to me when you know there have only been a handful of wicches like me in all of Corey history. We live short, miserable lives, usually dying by our own hands. You know this."

My grandmother turned back to the fire, her jaw set. My mother held out her hand to me, but I stood alone, separate from both.

"I know I told you this when I was little, curled up on my bed, too sick to move, but perhaps you've forgotten. I don't just see the visions. It isn't as though I lie down for a nice nap and have a scary nightmare. I mean, I have those too. Every night of my life. But I live the visions. I'm the one pushed under the water, my lungs bursting, gasping water. I'm the one lost in the woods, scared and alone, being lured from home. I'm the one on fire. My skin bubbling and blackening. I live through the most horrendous experiences imaginable and then I come out of it and am expected to pick myself up and carry on like everything's okay.

"And you sit here in judgment of me because I don't want to end up like all the others before me, trapped in the horror and pain, looking for any way to make it all stop." I exhaled slowly, needing them to understand.

"You want me to join the Council, knowing you're asking me to *invite* the visions that will ultimately drive me insane. The visions that torture me. You want me to have more of them if it will benefit others. My pain isn't important, only how I can make myself useful to others, is that it?"

The women were silent, my mother's gaze willing me to relent while Gran stared into the fire. I went to the front door and picked up my backpack. "Ask yourself this: Would you be so cavalier with my sanity and my life if both my parents were wicches?"

Gran turned to me then.

"Am I expendable? Disposable because of the fae blood?"

"Arwyn, you know we love you." Mom stood tall, but her right hand trembled.

"Sure." I swallowed. "But you love what I can do more." I walked out, closing the door with a quiet click.

I don't really remember the walk home. It was long and cold, the wind whipping over the ocean and tearing at my clothes and hair. My chest hurt, my stomach hollowed out. I couldn't get Gran's expression out of my mind. I'd thought she was the one person firmly on my side, no matter what. It wasn't that, though, was it? She'd been biding her time until my gifts could be put to her use.

A truck blew past me, almost hitting me in the dark. Stumbling into the sand and tall grass by the road, I stopped to think. I was only a quarter mile from home. I'd paint tonight. I had images in my head I needed exorcized through the canvas. First, though, I'd fix a shitty thing I'd done. I pulled out my phone and placed a call.

"'ello."

"Hi, Phil. Can we pretend I didn't call earlier? I was in a really bad mood"—a demon-fueled one—"when I called. Declan's fine."

"You sure? I've got another deck guy I usually use. He won't be available for a couple of weeks, though. If you don't mind waiting, I can call him."

"It's fine. I'd like the deck redone as soon as possible. I'm out there all the time and I'd prefer it didn't disintegrate beneath me." Declan had said he needed the work, and I felt the truth in that. He'd be out there. I'd be in my studio. I wouldn't even need to deal with him.

"Okay, great. I haven't gotten a hold of him yet, so we'll pretend the call never happened."

"Perfect. Have a good night and I'll see you tomorrow." I lifted my arm to block the headlights coming up the road.

"Sounds good, honey. Good night."

Phil was my Uncle John's good friend, one who often still

thought of me as the odd little girl who wore long sleeves and gloves and would, when we met at the beach for holiday picnics, tell him the areas that were *bad* and he should keep away from. Even then, the echoes of violence upset me and I wanted to keep him safe from them.

Phil would laugh off my warnings, but my Uncle John would pick me up and hug me to him, carrying me on his hip. He knew.

When I finally got home, I changed into sweats and pulled out a fresh canvas. I mixed the paints and lifted the shutters, watching the moonlight play over the waves. Sometimes I sketched first, but tonight I just wanted my brushes and the paint.

As Pearl was on my mind, I painted her last moments. Under the dark churning water, a ghostly silhouette holding her down and waiting for her to choke out her last breath. The ocean surrounded her, accepting her. It was the shadow lurking above the waves that held true menace.

I knew it was the wee hours of the morning when I put aside the canvas, but I couldn't sleep. I wasn't done. One more image wouldn't let me rest.

7

Wanna See My Fort?

W hen the workmen arrived, I was just putting down my brush. Bone weary, I went through the gallery to the front door. Phil and three guys, one of whom was Declan, were laying down tarps and hauling in their tools.

"Morning." Phil patted my shoulder. "You look tired. Pull another all-nighter?"

I nodded, zombie walking back to my studio. Maybe if I drew the shutters back down on the studio side and put on headphones to block out construction sounds, I could get some sleep. Probably not—let's face it—but it was worth a try.

"Oh, hey, Arwyn," Phil called.

I ducked back through the adjoining door. "Yeah?"

"There's a woman out here to see you." He glanced over his shoulder out the front door and then shrugged, going back to spreading out tarps.

I shuffled back, rubbing my hands over my face, trying to wake up. When I made it to the open front door, I stared at the woman in khakis, a button-down, and a blazer, leaning against the side of her car. I knew that face. Why did I know that face?

The woman moved to the base of the stairs. "Ms. Corey, I don't know if you remember me—"

"Sofia?"

A bright smile flashed, her warm brown eyes crinkling at the corners. "You remember. I'm Detective Hernández now."

"Oh, yeah," I said, coming down a step and sitting. "I think one of my cousins mentioned you'd become a cop. And a detective now, cool. So what can I do for you?"

Detective Hernández watched the workmen moving in and out of the gallery. "Do you have somewhere private we could talk?"

"Sure." I stood, started to sway forward, and caught myself on the newly installed railing.

"I told you that'd come in handy," Phil said as he walked back to his truck bed.

"We'll go to my studio." I waved Detective Hernández in.

"Wow."

I turned to find the detective staring at the shell of my gallery. "It will be. We're still mid-transformation."

She tore her gaze from the high ceiling and wall of windows, taking in the deep, swirling blue of the floors. Tapping a foot, she said, "These are amazing."

I was able to muster a smile for that. "I know, right?" I waved again. "My studio is through here."

After Detective Hernández followed me in, I closed the door and went straight to the kitchen area. "I have brownies, lemon bars, and some dark chocolate and almond lace cookies that turned out great." I turned back to find her standing directly in front of my most recent painting, leaning in as though trying to look through the trees.

She stepped back, her mind obviously preoccupied, before she blinked and smiled. "Um, they all sound great, but how about a cookie?"

"You bet," I said, grabbing a grape soda from the fridge. "I can make you a cup of superior tea, excellent cocoa, decent coffee, or any of a number of cold beverages." I carried over a

44

plate of cookies and left them on the coffee table, inviting her to sit.

I pointed to the canvases. "Sorry. I'm kind of out of it this morning. I was working on those all night, so I haven't slept."

"Is that grape soda?"

"Yes, ma'am," I said, nodding.

"If you have another, I'll take one of those." She reluctantly moved from the paintings and sat on the edge of the couch, picking up a cookie and taking a bite. "I hate to bother you— oh, my God," she said, staring in wonder at the cookie in her hand. "This thing is amazing."

Chuckling, I placed the grape soda bottle on the table beside her and then dropped into my favorite chair. Could I have poured it into a glass with ice? Yes. But she's a cop. She might have to leave right away. This way, she can take it with her. Plus, I didn't want to go to the trouble of putting it in a glass. Sleepy.

Hernández took another bite and savored it. "Sorry. I was saying I came here because I'm working on a case and hitting dead ends. I'm wondering if maybe you can help."

"Me? What can I do?" Other than not-dinner at Gran's last night, I hadn't gone anywhere in a couple of weeks. And before you wonder, groceries can be delivered. It's not lazy. Someone needs that job, just like I need to be here doing my job. And balancing groceries on a bike sucks.

"I ran into my brother-in-law Roberto this morning." She shook her head. "He was like a completely different guy. He and my sister Izzy are expecting their first child. Rob's been struggling. We all saw that. Today, though, he was waiting for the hardware store to open so he could buy paint for the nursery."

"Good."

"I called my sister and she said Rob's sister Lili recommended you to him. She said you were a psychic that helped him put his worries aside." She took a sip, eyeing me and the studio warily. "Have you ever worked with the police before?"

Shaking my head, I pulled up the hood on my sweatshirt,

suddenly cold. I set the bottle aside and stuffed my gloved hands into the kangaroo pocket. "No."

"Okay. I can see the idea makes you uncomfortable. It's just, this—" She pointed at the second painting. "I've walked there. That's the path the missing boy disappeared from."

My scalp prickled. "I can't. You need to go." My vision contracted on her surprised expression. Not again…

"Shh," he whispers. "Don't wake your mom."

Dark. It's so dark, but I hear the urgent whisper in my ear.

"Come on. You said you wanted to see my fort."

No longer in complete dark, the dim bedroom has a Spider-Man night-light by the door. A dark silhouette leans over the small boy.

"Now? But—" The child looks at the darkened window and shivers. "It's nighttime." The tremor in the little voice breaks my heart.

"Hey, if you don't want to see it, that's fine. I have better things to do than hang out with a little kid." The shadow moves. It's almost at the door when he hears what he's been waiting for.

"Wait."

The shadow smiles and beckons the child to him.

I woke with a start, something cold and wet on my forehead, and Detective Hernández leaning over me.

"Hey. Are you okay?" Her voice was gentle, but I could tell she wasn't sure what to think of me. Her sister Isabella and Rob's sister Lili had both said I was the real deal, but she'd never consulted a psychic before and my passing out on her wasn't inspiring confidence. She'd called her girlfriend on the way here to get her opinion, and while Andie was more of a believer than Sofia, she was hesitant too, mostly because women in law enforcement already had challenges without throwing a psychic into the mix.

And how the hell did I know all of that? "Did you touch me?"

Detective Hernández stepped back. "I put a cold cloth on your forehead." She cleared her throat. "You passed out and were in distress, crying in a high-pitched voice and then choking. I was just about to call the paramedics when you came around."

"Sorry," I said, sitting up in the chair and taking the wet rag off my head. "I appreciate this. I would have warned you not to touch me if I'd realized that was going to happen."

I stood and took the cloth back to the kitchen. "I'm just so tired. My defenses are low."

"Warn me about what?" Detective Hernández stood with her hands on her hips, looking ready for whatever I threw at her.

"I pick up on things through touch." I held up my gloved hands. "I don't touch people because I don't want to hear their thoughts."

"Oh." She moved farther away, glancing to the side at the painting that so interested her. "What did you hear?"

"Um." I went back and sat, gulping down my grape soda. "Izzy and Lili think I'm the real deal, but Andie isn't sure. She's more of a believer than you, but she worries how the guys at the station will react to it, especially as a Latina detective in a mostly white male precinct, there's already some pushback."

The color drained from her face.

"Sorry. It's why I'm always so careful with long pants, sleeves, and gloves. I don't want people's private business in my head. Since it's there, though, I don't want you *not* to know what I heard."

Nodding, she finally said, "I see." She glanced back at the painting. "My mom says we have *brujas* in the family, but I've never met any."

"We're everywhere," I said with a laugh. I hated that I was making her so uncomfortable. We weren't friends in high school or anything, but it was a small school and I remembered her being one of those rare cool kids who was a really nice person.

"Okay, well." She moved toward the door, ready to shitcan this psychic idea.

"He was lured out of his bed." If I had to live through the vision, she might as well hear what I had learned.

She stilled and then grabbed a small notebook and pen from her tweed blazer and started writing.

"It was in the middle of the night. The person—male— woke up the child, offering to show him his fort."

"Fort?" Brow furrowed, she studied me. "He said a fort? Was this an adult?"

I shook my head. "I don't think so, no. I'm not positive, but I got the impression he was a teenager. The little boy—Christopher!" I finally got his name. "He didn't want the bigger kid to think he was a baby, so when the kid started to leave, Christopher asked him to wait. The little boy was afraid of the dark but wanted to see the fort the big kid had been telling him about."

"What's the big kid's name?"

I shook my head again. "I don't have it. He's harder to see. I don't know if my mind shies away from the darkness or what." I finished the soda while she scribbled. "I've had a lot of years of visions and nightmares to come up with theories, but they're just theories."

I paused, waiting to see if she wanted to hear it. When she nodded, I continued, "I'm not a black wicche or a sorcerer. I think as people move further down the evil spectrum, they move further from my grasp. I see them, feel them, but I can't know them the way I can the Christophers or Robs of the world." I shrugged. "It's a work in progress, but it feels right."

She looked down at her notebook and then back up at me. "Black witches and sorcerers?"

"Things you don't need to worry about." I was going to give this poor woman a nervous breakdown.

"Until I do," she said, one eyebrow raised.

"Until you do."

She gestured to the painting with her notebook. "If I took you there, right there in the painting, could you tell me more? Because I have no teens on my radar. Christopher was abducted two nights ago. Their property butts up against forest. The mom has said that Christopher liked to go for walks and play in the forest. He never strayed far from home. He just liked taking his superhero dolls into the forest to play."

"Spider-Man," I murmured.

"What?"

"He has a Spider-Man night-light by his bedroom door." I didn't want to do this. I really did not want to live through that child's death, and I was almost positive he was dead.

"Please." The detective looked spooked but resolved.

I opened my mouth to say no, but she cut me off.

"Please," she said again. "And may you never have to look into the eyes of a desperate parent whose child is missing."

I sat with my elbows on my knees, my head in my hands. I didn't want this. I'd never wanted this. The poor kid was already dead. I was sure of it. I couldn't get his bedroom out of my head, though. Avengers dolls lined up on his desk, T-ball trophies, school pictures, drawings tacked up on a bulletin board, ticket stubs to Shakespeare in the Park. His mom thought he was finally old enough last summer and took him to see *A Midsummer Night's Dream*. She prepped him, explaining the story and all the characters. And he'd loved it. She'd gotten weepy watching him watch the play. He'd been mesmerized and she'd vowed to take him back every year. Only now, there would be no more summer Shakespeare, no more anything.

"Yeah. Okay."

8

Spider-Man, Ironman, and Wile E. Coyote

I heard wooden boards being pried up outside. "Give me a minute."

"Sure." Hernández watched me walk across the studio but didn't say anything more.

I opened the back door and stepped out onto the deck.

"Hey. Get back in," Declan's deep growly voice sounded especially cranky.

Oh, yeah. I'd shoved him in the water yesterday. "In a minute." I crouched at the edge and looked over. "Good morning, Cecil!"

A tentacle rose, breaking the surface.

"Charlie, Herbert, you're both looking especially handsome today. I just wanted to warn you. There's a big, growly guy up here who's going to be making a lot of noise. He's promised not to drop wood into your home." I turned and gave Declan my squinty, suspicious look. "Soon we'll have a beautiful new deck, and I can start installing the sea monster tentacles." Cecil slapped the water again.

I stood. "If Wilbur comes by, tell him I'll be back soon." I glanced around the deck and found the tennis ball wedged under the doorframe to the gallery. I pulled it out and threw it as far as I could. "Bye, guys."

I was just turning to walk in when I heard, "I have a tarp strung up under the dock to catch any boards that get past me."

Oh, well, jeez, that was nice. Especially after yesterday. Ugh. I was going to have to do it, wasn't I? *Shit.* "I'm sorry about chucking you in the water yesterday. I was in a bad place, and you wouldn't fricking leave!" Arwyn, not helping. "Anyway, sorry I did that."

"It pissed me off." He shrugged. "But it was effective. Sorry I didn't leave the first time you asked."

"Okay." I gestured to the studio door. "I need to go now."

"Uh."

I stopped and looked back.

"Do you want me to go with you?" He scratched his beard, looking distinctly uncomfortable.

The question confused me until I remembered his wolf hearing meant he'd heard our entire conversation. "No, thanks. I'll be fine. And can you put in earbuds or something?"

He shook his head. "Sorry. I can't." He glanced at the studio window, no doubt trying to determine if Hernández was listening.

"See? Right there. You'd hate it." No one enjoys being eavesdropped on.

"I would, but I have to be able to gauge threats." He shimmied his prybar under another plank and pushed slowly. The boards were rotting and he was trying to get a full board rather than crumbling pieces. "Good luck."

I went back in and closed the door before looking down at myself. Eh, paint-spattered sweats seemed fine for a walk in the woods. I went to my worktable and pulled open a drawer. Dropping the dirty gloves on the table, I pulled out a fresh pair of green gloves. My hands would blend with the forest. I grabbed my phone and wallet, stuffing them in my kangaroo pocket. "Ready."

Detective Hernández looked out the window, no doubt wondering about my talking to sea creatures, but she let it go with a quick nod, leading the way back through the gallery, out the door, and to her car.

"Arwyn," Phil called. "When you back?"

Shrugging, I said, "Soonish." I pointed to Hernández. "She says I'm not being arrested this time, so that's good."

The look on Phil's face was priceless.

Once we were strapped in, she pushed the ignition button while studying me. "*This time?* I checked your record. It was clean or I wouldn't be here. What do I need to know?"

"That I'm easily bored and fucking with people is fun." I stuffed my hands in my pocket. "Let 'em wonder and whisper."

Hernández nodded and pulled out onto the road. "It doesn't bother you when people talk about you?"

"Not really. People have been telling tales about me my whole life. People like to gossip. What are you going to do?" I stared out the window as she turned off the main road onto a narrow lane, away from the water.

"I wish I didn't care," the detective said, turning down an even narrower road. Mailboxes dotted the lane between trees. For some of the homes, they served as the only marker that a house was hidden somewhere behind the trees and bushes crowding the road.

"Look at it this way. You're interesting enough for people to gossip about. That's probably better than being so boring no one even notices you, right?"

She tilted her head, thinking. "I'd rather be ignored."

"Fair enough. Me too, to be honest." It was a pretty drive and one I didn't want to end. "Hey, did you know that somewhere between thirty and fifty percent of the population don't have a running inner monologue?"

She glanced over, brows furrowed. "What?"

"Their thoughts aren't in words. They feel emotions or whatever, but they're not constantly thinking in words. They have to translate their feelings into words when they have conversations." I shook my head, lifting my hands palms up. "I mean, how? How are you just walking around with silence in your head? I wonder if they're good sleepers. I'd love to shut off the shit in my head for awhile."

"Really? Everyone doesn't have a voice in their head?" Hernández looked as shocked as I'd been when I'd read the article.

"I know!" I shrugged to myself. "I mean, is that an introvert-extrovert thing? Is that why some people have earpods in all the time? Or some people can read with music playing and a TV on? I don't know."

Hernández was silent for a while. "I need to ask my friends."

"Thinking is such an isolated, individual thing. It's fascinating when we learn how others do it. Like—" I smacked the detective's arm without even thinking—"some people can't picture things in their head. They need to see the thing. They can't create its image in their mind. They know what the thing is, but they can't create the visual in their heads."

"This is it," she said, pulling into a driveway.

Oh. It wasn't that I'd forgotten where we were going so much as I was hoping to stave off the inevitable with random brain trivia. When you're different, you're often looking for the explanation as to why.

It was an adorable little cottage in the woods with an abandoned bike laying on its side on the small lawn near the front door. Just that was enough to make my throat tight. I didn't want to do this. Wasn't there enough horror in my head?

"Let me go talk with Nancy, his mom. She hasn't left the house in case he comes home."

Nodding, I lagged behind, not wanting to get hit with the tsunami of grief that woman was no doubt carrying. I flicked a spoke of the tire that was tilted up in the air and watched it spin. Unable to stop myself, I took off a glove and stopped the wheel, holding on to it.

Joy. Heart-racing joy when he sees it sitting beside the Christmas tree in their tiny living room. His mom put a big red bow on it. Spider-Man again, on the bike this time.

Christopher gets rid of the training wheels quickly. He has his mother's superior natural balance. Soon he's riding his bike up and down the lane. His mom reminds him to be careful. The road is narrow, and he'll be hard for drivers to see. He rolls his eyes and says he knows, but he never tells her about that one car that drives him off the road. He ends up in pine needles, knee and elbow banged up, while the car honks and keeps going. It scares him so badly, he walks his bike home, but when Mom asks how his ride was, he says fine. He knows if he tells the truth, he won't have the same freedom.

It's as he's walking it back, still shaking, that he meets an older kid who takes an interest in him. It's cool. Older kids never pay him any attention. The kid asks him to come help him for a minute. He's making knots with a long rope. When Christopher asks why, the kid says he's practicing for an Eagle Scout badge. The boy doesn't know what that is, but he's excited to help, especially as it keeps him from thinking about that scary car.

The kid asks Christopher to put out an arm, which he does. The kid slips a noose over the boy's hand and pulls it taut. The fibers pinch and hurt the boy's wrist. The kid yanks again, causing Christopher to gasp, but the kid doesn't seem to notice. He's happy his knot works. The boy shakes off the pain, caught up in the big kid's excitement.

"Arwyn." Detective Hernández said it like she'd already called me a few times.

I hadn't passed out or anything. This, I was prepared for. I hadn't been hit with a vision. This was a psychic reading. I remained in control during readings.

Pulling my glove back on, I walked up to the porch, where the detective was talking with a thin, nervous-looking woman who was twisting her hands in front of her.

"This is Arwyn. She's helping us out." Hernández turned to me. "Do you want to see his bedroom?"

I was about to say no, there was no point, but then I reconsidered. Something was drawing me in. I nodded. "If you wouldn't mind?"

The mom shrugged her acceptance, though I doubt she knew what she was agreeing to. She was so far over the edge, she was like Wile E. Coyote, clawing at the air right before the drop. Hernández needed to get her help now.

Seeming to have picked up on the same thing, Hernández walked Nancy to the small kitchen to make some tea. I needed to remember this address so I could send over the good stuff.

I meandered through the small living room and down the hall. It had been a happy house. I could feel that, even below the weight of fear and grief. Pictures of Christopher or of the two of them lined the hallway walls. A few featured a younger version of the boy with an older couple, presumably his grand-parents.

The bedroom on the right side of the hall was the one I'd seen in my vision. Trophies, Avengers, drawings, they were all here. Something felt off, though. What was it? I stood in the center of the room, closed my eyes, and turned slowly in a circle. When my stomach cramped, I stopped and opened my eyes. His desk and bulletin board.

The action figures lined up, a sketch book open to the begin-nings of a drawing, a tin filled with colored pencils, it all looked as it should. Turning my attention to the bulletin board, I studied each drawing, looking for a secret message. Most of the drawing were of superheroes, but a few were of the forest, of a rabbit and a bird. The bird…

Glancing in the corner, where I remembered the ticket stubs, there was now a feather. The oily black feather made my stomach clench.

Pulling off my glove again, I laid one finger on the feather and felt an electrical jolt, the stench of death heavy in my head.

"Hey, want to see something cool?" The older kid is back. They're in the forest behind the house now.

Christopher has Spider-Man in one hand and Ironman in the other.

He's surprised to find the kid right outside his backdoor but thrilled too. "What is it?"

He waves the boy down the dirt path, away from his house. "Look!" He points down at a dead black bird.

Christopher steps back. Spider-Man and Ironman are held tight in his grip, up against his chest like a kind of shield. "What happened to it?" he whispers.

"I don't know," the big kid says with a grin. "Maybe a cat got him. It's all tore up like it's been clawed." He leans down, pretending to get a better look.

Christopher vomits where he stands and then runs, horrified by what he's seen and mortified to behave like a baby in front of his sort-of friend.

"Anything?" Hernández was standing in the doorway, watching me.

"Yeah, but let me wash my hands first." I went into the bathroom next door and did my usual glove and sleeve shuffle that allowed me to clean my hands without touching faucets or soap dispensers with my bare hands. I was sure I looked ridiculous, but it worked for me.

I walked out, drying my hands on my sweatpants and then pulling my gloves back on.

Hernández was waiting for me in the hall.

"Let's go out back and we'll talk," I said.

9

The Woods Are Watching

The detective led the way back through the living room and into the kitchen. The mom was sitting at a little café table by the window, not looking up when we walked through. "We'll be right back, Nancy."

The mom nodded listlessly while staring into her cup.

Once we were out of the house, the oppressiveness lifted. "She needs help. She's losing hope and won't stick around."

The detective looked over her shoulder at the back door, nodding. "I know. She says she doesn't have any family to call. I tried to send a priest or something, but she says she's not religious. I can get her admitted for observation, but I know she needs to be here to wait for her son."

"She's fleeing an abusive spouse. She doesn't want you to call her parents because they live in the same town as the ex and she's worried news of her will get back to him. She's also ashamed she stayed with him as long as she did before she grabbed her son and ran."

"How do you—"

"My glove slipped and my finger grazed the faucet." A wind kicked up, making me wish I had a hair tie in my pocket. I wound my hair into one long coil and then stuffed it down the back of my hoodie collar to keep it out of my face.

I started down the dirt path. "She wants her parents with her but she's too afraid to call. Everything becomes real when she acknowledges it and talks about it, the abuse and now the abduction." I stopped where the dead bird laid.

"What are you—oh." Detective Hernández followed my gaze to the bird. "Why are we staring at a dead bird?"

"This is what he used to scare Christopher. He pretended to just find the bird when Christopher came out to play with his superheroes. He hadn't happened upon it, though. He'd followed the boy after their first meeting and had been watching the house."

I stood right where he had when he'd beckoned the child over. Being this near to evil made my stomach cramp. "He didn't find the bird, or at least not here. He found a dying bird with a broken wing. He cut it open while it was still clinging to life. He was so tickled by the obscenity, he brought it over to share with the boy, as a kind of torture appetizer.

"Christopher was horrified, vomited, and ran. The kid started to pick up his bird to take it with him, because he enjoyed his handiwork so much, but then decided it would be put to better use here, where the boy would be terrified and sickened by it. And perhaps, eventually, move in for another look."

"Do you know who he is? Where he is?" Hernández took out her notebook again.

Shivering, I stuffed my hands in my hoodie pocket. "No." I stared out into the woods around us, wondering if he was out there now. Watching. Listening. I tipped my head toward the trees. "He's out there. He'd been stalking the boy for a while, dreaming of what he'd do when he had someone to play with. No more animals for him. He's leveling up."

"He lives in the woods?" she asked.

I considered. "His passions live in these woods. But, no. He has a home. Some kind of adult who looks after him. No, what's out here is his fort, his hideout. It's where he tortures and kills animals. I think that's where you're going to find Christopher. All the evidence will be there. He can't bear to part with his toys, even as they decompose."

"Well that just gave me goose bumps," Hernández muttered under her breath. "These woods have been searched, in case he just wandered away."

I shook my head. "Not well enough. Not far enough. He knows how to camouflage his workshop. Look for large bushes and…" I closed my eyes, trying to get it. "I feel like he's underground. It's bigger than just a hole, though."

I turned to the detective. "I can't get a clear picture in my head, but it feels underground."

Hernández made a quick note and then dropped her hands. "Thank you. I can see if there's a fee we can pay you for your assistance."

I was shaking my head before she finished her offer. "I can't take money over the body of a dead child." I held up my hands, warding off her words, and stepped away. "I'd like to go now, though. I can't shake the feeling I'm being watched and it's really bothering me."

Hernández fished into her pocket for her car keys and handed them to me. "Go wait in the car," she said, unholstering her firearm. "I need to talk with Nancy before we leave." She walked into the woods, scanning the trees, looking high and low. "Go on. I'll be out in a few."

When the detective emerged twenty minutes later, I was still standing there, waiting for her.

"I thought you were going to the car?"

I handed her back her keys. "I know what he is. I couldn't leave you out here alone."

She nodded. "Thanks for that. I do need to go in and talk with Nancy, though, maybe convince her to let me get her help."

Blowing out a breath, I said, "I'll go with you."

Nancy was right where we'd left her, a full cup of cold tea on the table in front of her.

Detective Hernández sat opposite the mom and talked quietly with her. I moved to the living room, not wanting to crowd them. How had he gotten in? This was not a woman who would forget to lock a door. A window? A woman on the run would lock those too, but would a kid?

I wandered back down the hall to Christopher's room. He had a big picture window looking out over the forest. There were blinds, but unlike all the rest of the windows in the little house, the blinds weren't closed. They'd been pulled up, the view unfettered.

They'd probably already dusted the windowsill for prints, but as this seemed the most likely point of entry, I pulled off a glove and touched a finger to where I guessed he'd have needed to plant his hands to haul himself in. Cops, techs, Christopher, his mom… I felt them all but in the background, there was a darkness.

I pushed open the window and touched the outer sill and my stomach heaved. I just made it to the toilet to vomit. It hurt and sickened me knowing that kind of evil existed in the world, existed and went about stalking children, setting mothers adrift in vast oceans of grief.

When I came out, Hernández was in the hall again. "He came in through the window." My voice was pitched low so his mom wouldn't hear.

The detective shook her head. "They dusted. They didn't find any prints that didn't belong."

I held up my hand. "Gloves. He liked to watch Christopher sleep, to plan what he was going to do. He stood right outside, held onto the sill, and watched."

Hernández turned and walked out. I heard the front door open and close, so I went into the kitchen. I wanted to leave— her grief was like a weight around my neck, dragging me down

—but I couldn't. Taking the seat the detective had earlier, I sat across from the mom. She didn't acknowledge me.

I placed my ungloved hand on the table, palm up. After a moment's hesitation, she laid hers in mine. My head reeled back with the force of the punch. I felt blood trickle from my nose. That was new.

Wiping my gloved hand under my nose, I said a little spell in my head to staunch the flow. I wasn't a healer, but it also wasn't much of a nosebleed. He'd worn her down, tearing away at her self-confidence as soon as they were married. She got pregnant with Christopher right away, as he'd taken her birth control, exerting another form of control.

She hid the bruises, even as he pushed her family and friends further away. It became a relief, really, not having to tell all the lies, not having to hide what was happening. And then she had Christopher, and he was perfect, the only joy she had in that miserable life.

Then it happened. Christopher was so little, just a toddler, when he'd knocked over his father's drink. The boy had been coloring quietly—always quietly—while his father watched a game on the TV. The boy moved his coloring book to start a new picture, not realizing the far edge of the book would push the glass off the table.

Nancy heard the crash and the shout. She was in a dead panic, sweat breaking out as she ran to the living room just in time to see her precious beautiful boy, the only light in her life, get backhanded by his father, his little body propelled through the air.

She screamed, knowing how breakable a body was. The husband said she was overreacting. The kid needed to learn discipline. She was too easy on him. She needed to clean up the mess first…

She did what she needed to, but when he went to work the next day, she ran.

"Your parents miss you so much, just like you miss Christopher. They'll move here for you. They'll help you bring charges against your ex. Whatever you need, they'll do. You just need to call them to let them know where you are."

Eyes haunted, she tipped up her head to look at me. "I can't," she mumbled. "I ignored them. Every time they tried to reach out and help, I threw it back in their faces." She shook her head. "And even then, I couldn't keep my baby safe."

"There's evil in the world. You know all about that. You raised a happy, secure, kind little boy who would have grown into a considerate young man, one who loved going to Shakespeare with you, one whose artistic talents would have grown and become the focus of his life."

She dropped her head to the table and sobbed. I knew the detective was standing in the doorway, but she was silent.

Gasping for breath, she lifted her tearstained face and choked out, "He's gone? My baby's gone?"

I nodded. Maybe I shouldn't have, but it felt like the only way to break her out of this stasis of mourning.

"Can Detective Hernández call your family for you? They miss you so much. Let them help you through this. Also," I began, squeezing her hand, "she's a pretty important cop. She can contact the police in your hometown and warn them about your ex, have them keep an eye on the guy and make it obvious so he knows he can't do anything more. Right?" I looked over my shoulder at the detective and knew Nancy had followed my gaze.

Hernández wore an expression of stoic strength. "Yes. I can and will do that. Let me take care of this."

I slipped out, pulling on the glove, understanding Nancy needed strength to feel safe enough to call. I'd delivered the horrible news. I needed to go away. I headed out the front door, intending to lean on the car and wait, but instead rounded the house for Christopher's window.

Standing in the mint under the window, I couldn't see in. Granted, I wasn't tall, but I figured a maybe eleven- to fifteen-year-old wouldn't be too much taller. So he must have stood on something.

I wandered around the back of the house and a little into the woods, looking for what he could have stood on. Finally, under a bush at the corner of the house, I found a plastic milk crate. I took off a glove and touched it like I would a sizzling skillet. This was it and he'd touched it with his bare hand. It was doubtful they'd have his prints on record, but when they found him, it might help convict him.

When Hernández walked around the corner, I moved a branch out of the way and pointed out the crate, told her about the prints. While she did her cop thing and called who she needed to call, I went back to the car.

"Excuse me."

I stopped halfway across their lawn and looked up to the porch. Nancy was standing in the open door.

"You're sure?" Her desperate desire for me to be wrong, to hold on to any glimmer of hope, made my head pound and my throat tighten.

I nodded.

She wiped her face, walked back in, and closed the door. A moment later, the sound of muffled wails echoed in my head.

"Hernández!"

She jogged around the corner of the house. "What?"

"You've got to take me home now. I can't stay any longer." I needed to curl up in a dark room until the pounding eventually stopped.

"I can't. I have lab techs coming. I need to be here. You can wait in the car."

I shook my head, walking backward toward the lane. "I have to go."

"Wait. I'll get a patrol car to take you home." She spoke into a small radio at her shoulder. "It'll be here in a couple minutes. I need you to wait, okay? I can't leave evidence unattended. You stay, okay?"

I stood in the road, the wails deafening in my head. "Yeah, okay."

10

It's the Balance That Impresses Me

I don't remember much of the ride home. As soon as I saw the police car arrive, I tried to open the back door so I could leave. The door was, of course, locked. I had to wait for the patrolman and Hernández to talk. The wailing in my head was too loud to hear them over it, so I waited, head resting on the cool of the metal door.

The farther he drove from the house, the less ear-splitting the wail. By the time he stopped in front of the gallery, the keening had been silenced, though the pounding remained. I think the officer said something to me, but I couldn't hear it. I got out, trudged up the steps, and walked through the gallery, ignoring the workmen. Once in my studio, I closed the door, turned off the lights, and brought the shutters down.

Exhausted, I dragged myself up the stairs, hit the switch closing the skylight, crawled into bed, and prayed for sleep. Thankfully, the universe listened.

When I woke a few hours later, my headache was almost gone. I showered, washing away the last dregs of pain, and got dressed in my softest loungewear. I wanted a big cup of tea, something to eat, and a book. I checked the time. The workmen should still be downstairs.

I went in search of Phil. I thought he'd needed to ask me something earlier, but I'd left before he could. The lights remained off, but I lifted the shutters. The studio was filled with a soft gray light. Dark, heavy clouds hung over the ocean.

Shaking out my damp curls, I went to the windows and looked out. The deck was gone. Stilts, like candles on a cake, rose out of the water. On top of the post closest to my back door was a tennis ball. I laughed, the sadness finally slipping away.

Opening the back door, I shouted, "How did you do this, Wilbur?"

I'd have to reach out over a ten-foot drop to the ocean to grab the ball. It wasn't like I was worried about drowning. Dad's DNA meant the ocean and I were cool with each other. It was more that I'd just showered and was wearing my favorite cozy clothes. I didn't want to go for a swim.

Glancing out the door, I found no one nearby, so one little spell later, I had the ball in my hand and was throwing it as far as I could.

I closed and locked the back door and then went to the gallery in search of Phil. I didn't see him, but his men were still working, including Declan.

"Hey, guys. Is Phil around?"

Juan and Mike, who were Phil's usual guys, both shook their heads. Although they'd never stated it, I got the impression Juan was in charge when Phil wasn't on site. Juan was a hair shorter than my five foot four. He had dark hair and eyes and wore the most beat-to-shit boots I had ever seen. He should be the spokesperson for that brand of work boot. They were indestructible. Mike, on the other hand, was mostly quiet. He had red hair with a wispy beard. He smiled when he saw me and always tried to help if I asked him for something, but otherwise deferred to Juan. Declan, the newest to the crew, stayed out of it.

"He's at another job. Do you have a question for us?" Juan asked.

"It was more I thought he had a question for me. He said this morning that he needed to talk to me today." Hopefully, I didn't hold up anything important by not being here or by napping.

Juan nodded and pointed to the café area. "The display case was delivered today. We didn't unbox it yet. Phil said you wanted to add shelves. We just needed to know where before we dropped the display case in."

"Oh." I looked back, and there were beautiful gray wood shelves around the café area for my mother's teas, as well as on the back side of the metal strut.

"Your mother stopped by earlier looking for you and said this is what you wanted." Juan looked at Mike. "Normally, we'd wait for the owner to confirm before we did anything, but she was insistent and…" The poor guy looked lost for a moment. "I'm not sure why we did that without your okay. *Is* it okay?"

I knew why. My mother had put a little push behind her words. Spelling my crew? The woman did not understand boundaries.

I nodded, mostly to wipe the look of concern from Juan's face. It wasn't his fault my mother was a controlling piece of work. "Yeah. I'm sure they'll work out just fine. In the future, though, if my mom asks you to do something, please check with me. This is my gallery, not hers."

"Yeah, of course." Juan shook his head as though he couldn't believe they'd done that.

This was exactly what I'd feared when I'd said I'd sell Mom's teas here. She'd try to take over and bring the rest of the Coreys with her. If I hadn't needed something for my customers to wash down my baked goods with, I'd have kicked Mom and the rest of the fam out. As it was, though, Mom's tea was that good. I'd work on spelling the building to try to hinder any undue magical influence.

"We were just heading out," Juan said, picking up a toolbox and tarp.

"Oh, sure. Have a good evening." I walked them to the door so I could lock up.

Declan was the last out the door. He studied me a moment as the other guys jogged down the front steps. "You need more sleep."

"Tell me something I don't know." I waited for him to leave and then turned the lock, adding a spell to the mechanism. A side effect of horrendous visions and nightmares was a hyper awareness of all the bad things that could happen. I did my best to shake it off or I'd be a gibbering idiot, hiding in a closet.

On a night like this, though, when I was raw, the fear was close to the surface. So, doors locked and spelled. No one was sneaking up on me.

I went back to the studio—locking that door, as well—and made myself a cup of calming tea. I considered making dinner, maybe soup to settle my jittering stomach, but decided it could wait. I wasn't ready.

Instead, I curled up in my chair, tucked a soft throw around me, opened my e-reader to the mystery I was reading, and held my tea cup, warming my hands.

I'd just started the who-done-it chapter when there was a knock on the back door. As I was pretty sure Wilbur hadn't grown hands, I went to the light switch by the door and flicked it on. Declan, balancing on a post by my back door, was holding up a bag from a local burger joint.

What the hell was this?

Barely opening the door, I was hit with a blast of cold wind off the ocean. I stared down. He was balancing on one boot on a post swaying with the waves.

"Good. I was hoping you weren't asleep yet." He looked completely at ease. Balancing. On one foot.

"What are you doing?" I held the door mostly closed, trying unsuccessfully to block the wind.

"Can I come in?" He held up the bag again. "I brought dinner."

"But why?" This was unprecedented.

"You looked so tired earlier," he explained with a shrug, maintaining his balance. "I felt bad and decided to feed you." He paused. "But the burgers are getting cold the longer you make me stand out here."

I opened the door wider and stepped out of the way. He leapt in easily, closing the door behind himself.

"Is this okay?" he asked. "I was working out there"—he gestured to the back door—"and I was thinking about what the cop told you. I don't know." He dropped the food bag on my worktable. "You looked shaken when you got home. I'm guessing you didn't find the kid?"

I opened the bag and looked in. Two of everything. Moving the bag to the coffee table, I went to the kitchen for plates, a beer, and a soda. Why not? I was hungry and he had brought food. I did an internal check. I thought my stomach could handle food now. It was worth a try.

Motioning to the couch, I said, "Thanks. I was hungry." I held up the beer. "Okay?"

He nodded and sat, tearing open the bag and distributing burgers and fries on the plates. "I wasn't sure what kind of burger you liked, so I had them put the toppings in a separate container. Except the cheese, of course."

I lifted the bun. "Pepper Jack. Good call."

He grinned, taking a bite of his huge burger.

I opened the container and added lettuce, bacon, tomato, and jalapenos before taking a bite. *Mmm.*

"I had a feeling you'd like spicy." He ate a few fries. "So, did you? Find him?"

I took a sip of soda. "How could I have found him? I'm a con woman, remember? A charlatan." Rolling my eyes, I took another bite.

"Yeah, about that. Sorry." He put down the burger and wiped his hands on a napkin. "That was out of line. The scammers that cheated my aunt—" he shook his head. "Giving her hope about communicating with my mom, dangling the possibilities while taking all her money." He let out a deep breath. "I have a hard time believing all this stuff. I'm working on it, though." He pointed to my burger. "Am I forgiven?"

"It's going to take more than this, but it's a start." I took another bite and swallowed. Detective Hernández hadn't told me I couldn't talk about the case. At least, I don't think she did. It was hard to hear there at the end. "No. I didn't find him. I'm sure he's dead and I have a sense of the killer, but not his face. It's still in shadow right now. And I don't know what he did with the body."

"Oh," he said, brow furrowed as he finished the burger. "I was hoping he was lost in the woods."

I put the rest of my burger down, stomach twisting. "I think we all were."

He stared at my burger and then at me for a beat before shaking his head. "I shouldn't have asked that question while you were trying to eat. Here," he began, pulling a folded paper out of his jacket pocket. "Look at the deck plan—I've been playing with ideas—and tell me what you think. I'll start building it tomorrow."

Walking me through his ideas, he laid out a plan that incorporated my sea monster tentacles. It was perfect, giving the tentacles impact without blocking the view too much. When we were done, he smiled down at my empty plate and then bussed the table.

"I was going to suggest watching a movie or something"—he spun, searching the studio for a TV screen—"but it doesn't look like you have a TV."

"I have better," I replied, grabbing my remote from the side table. I hit a button and a huge theater screen motored down from the ceiling. Another button started the projector mounted above. And then I was scrolling through streaming options. "What are you in the mood for?"

Declan watched with envy. "This set up. That's what I'm in the mood for. Damn, woman."

I vetoed his sports suggestions. He vetoed my cooking show suggestions. We eventually discovered a mutual love for British murder mysteries. I moved to the couch to avoid a crick in the neck, wrapped my blanket around me again, and settled in for a country parish vicar investigating crimes.

I awoke with the sun streaming through the back door. My head was on a broad chest, with a strong heartbeat in my ear. What. The. Hell?

When I tried to sit up, I realized I had an arm around me. The remote hitting the ground startled Declan awake. He blinked and then smiled before leaning over and picking up the remote control.

"Good. You slept." He stood, stretching. "Is it okay?" He pointed to the bathroom in the corner.

Absently, I nodded. I'd slept. The whole night through. All night. Not one nightmare. I checked my watch, my vision going blurry with tears. Seven and a half hours. Depending on when I'd fallen asleep, I was out for at least seven and a half hours! Never in my life had I slept that long.

"I should get home to shower and change before coming back to work. Thanks for letting me hang out. After you fell asleep, I watched a basketball game and it was glorious. Okay," he said, checking his pockets. "I'll see you later."

He walked out the back door, hopping to the nearest post and then leaping to the next out of view.

Seven and a half hours. How?

11

In Which Arwyn Needs to Deal with Creepy Shit Closer to Home

I was feeling better than I had in I didn't know how long. I went to the back door, pushed it open and then lay down on the floor, my arms crossed over the doorsill with my chin on my arms.

"Good morning!" Since my starfish friends Charlie and Herbert were clinging to the outside of the farthest posts, the ones normally right under the edge of the deck, I couldn't see them, but I knew they were there.

"How did you sleep, Cecil?" After a moment, a tentacle broke the surface in what I interpreted as a wave.

"It's a beautiful morning." The air was chilly, the gorgeous greens and blues of the ocean sparkling under a cloudless sky. It was a tentacle day! While Declan rebuilt the deck, I'd finish sealing a tentacle before starting the next.

While I considered the shape and curl of that next one, I saw something green and round out of the corner of my eye. "I swear, Wilbur, you're like a circus seal." There was no way I could reach the post where he'd left the tennis ball, so I either left it or...

I didn't see anyone nearby. There were fishing boats far from the coast, but unless they had binoculars trained on me, they wouldn't see anything. "You're trying to get me busted, aren't you?" I grumbled.

One quick spell later, the cold, wet thing was in my hand and I was winding up for the throw. Unfortunately, I didn't have a werewolf's strength so it didn't go far but Wilbur had never seemed to mind.

Deciding to get an early start, I closed the door, jogged upstairs, got cleaned up, donned another pair of overalls with a green thermal top and my trusty paint-spattered sneakers. When I went back down to my studio, I stopped by the kitchenette for a large mug of tea and a cranberry orange scone.

I had the back door open to vent the sealant fumes and so heard when Declan arrived to begin deck construction. As a good night's sleep warranted gratitude, I grabbed him two scones and went to the door.

Hanging my head out, I'd intended to offer the plate, but something dark caught my eye.

"Hey, those look great." His deep grumble of a voice was oddly comforting. That talisman, though, was not.

When he leapt to the top of the first post, I held up my hand. "Stop. Go back. I need to take care of something first."

I went back in, slid the plate onto my worktable, and opened the cabinet that held my wicchey supplies. I wasn't a potion maker, so my stores were pretty slim, but I knew how to conjure a nulling draught.

Someone had left a curse at my doorstep. I couldn't feel its presence, which scared me more than anything. Whoever had left the cursed fetish meant me harm and was a skilled black wicche or sorcerer.

"Everything okay?" he called.

I finished my silent chanting over the water. "No. That black feathery thing sitting on top of that post is a curse."

Contemplating how to get to it, I looked back out the door and found Declan balancing atop a post beside it, bending over to get a better look at the magical fetish.

"How are you doing that?"

He looked up, his scowl disappearing. "I have good balance. This is a curse?"

I nodded.

"I saw this yesterday. It was nailed under your deck. Found it when I was demo'ing. Carefully." He shook his head, hands on his hips, still balancing on the ball of one foot. "If you hadn't asked me to make sure none of the boards fell on your friends, that would have fallen in the water and been lost."

A chill had gone up my spine at his words. "You found this yesterday? Attached to my home?"

"Yeah." His scowl had returned. "I'm the one that moved it there. I figured it was some wicchey good luck thing."

"You didn't touch it with your bare hand, did you?" *Shit.* Was this why I'd had a vision about wolves tearing into each other? Had the evil seeped in?

He glanced down at his hands and then shook his head. "I was wearing work gloves."

Oh, good. No berserker wolves today. "Meanwhile, how do I get over there?"

"I can bring it to you."

"No way. I don't want that in my house. Plus, you need gloves." I considered a moment. "Do you remember which way it was hanging when you found it?"

He leapt from pole to pole until he was back on land. "Maybe. I thought at first it was a decomposing crow or some seabird that got stuck under the deck. I was about to throw it in the ocean, but then I saw the stone and got a whiff. It smells like homemade catgut was used to tie it all together."

At the sound of trucks pulling up, Declan turned his head and waved. "I need to go back to my truck for gloves and then talk to Phil, as I'm assuming you don't want an audience for this. I'll be back."

Declan walked out of sight while I went for my camera. I switched out the lens for a high-powered telephoto one and then went back and lay down at the doorstep so my body was stable while I leaned out with my camera and zoomed in. Dark feathers, twigs, something that looked disturbingly like shriveled organs, and a stone with a rune etched into it.

I couldn't make it out, but for many rune stones, the position of the glyph dictated its meaning. An inverted, or upside down, rune could have the opposite meaning of a right-side-up one.

Pulling in the camera, I glanced down and saw a cute little seal nose break the surface. "Hi, Wilbur. I'm dealing with some bad stuff right now. We can play later."

He flipped and dove under the water. A moment later, when I was standing up, the tennis ball flew over my head and bounced squishily over my floor.

"Hey! No making messes!" I ran in and grabbed a kitchen towel, mopping up the seawater before picking up the tennis ball. Yuck. We needed a new one to play with. This one was becoming a mess.

When I went to the open doorway to throw the ball, I saw Wilbur circling the post with the curse sitting atop it.

"Wilbur, no! Get away from that thing." I could see it, though. I knew exactly what he was going to do so I threw the tennis ball, hoping to distract him. It didn't work. When I saw him gathering for a jump, I dropped my phone on the windowsill and dove in, arrowing through the water, dolphin kicking to my seal friend.

Thankfully, the minute I hit the water, the game changed. Instead of stealing the fetish, he was now distracted by chasing me. He raced me through the posts like it was an agility test. When I turned and started back, he circled me, beside, above, below. It was like trying to swim through a seal tunnel. This was clearly the most fun he'd had in a while.

As long as I was wet anyway, I swam out to the edge of the posts and surfaced. "Morning, Charlie. Herbert." I waved. They did not wave back. I felt something wrap around my ankle and ducked my head under the water. "Hi, Cecil!" Bubbles rushed from my mouth to the surface as I waved. His tentacle slipped from my ankle with a move that mirrored my own.

Wilbur nudged me in the back, wanting to continue playing. Instead, I surfaced again, looking for Declan. He was jumping from one post to the next when he saw me and almost missed the landing.

"What the hell are you doing in there?" he growled.

"Wilbur was getting too interested in the curse."

He watched the seal swimming around me, nudging me to play, and then nodded.

I gave Wilbur the slip and then raced him to land. Surprising absolutely no one, the seal won. I climbed the rocks and found Declan waiting for me, the curse in his gloved hand.

"I just need a potion bowl and my nulling draught. Be right back." I took two steps and then remembered that I'd come out the back door. I didn't have my keys and couldn't exactly use a spell while Phil and his crew were waiting for me. *Shit.*

Judging by the look on Declan's face, he'd come to the same conclusion. He slipped off the glove, making sure to keep the fetish in the palm of the empty glove and then handed it to me. "What do I need to get?"

"Let Phil and his guys in the gallery and then go back to my studio. Grab the bottle of water on my work desk and in the open cabinet, on the top shelf, you'll find a hammered silver bowl. It's wide and shallow. I need that."

He nodded and leapt to the first post.

"Oh, and my phone is on the windowsill. I need that too."

"Got it."

He disappeared through my back door and I stood in the wind, shivering. I knew it made no sense, but freezing ocean temperatures didn't bother me in the least. Standing here cold and wet, the wind gusting through my sopping clothing, had my teeth chattering.

Looking down at my arm, I tried to gauge the wet fabric's transparency. It was hard to tell, though. I didn't care about my bra being visible. I was wearing overalls and whatever. It was my back being exposed that bothered me. My father's fae blood had left marks on me, marks I'd covered up in an unusual way.

Eventually, Declan came jogging around the side of the cannery, the silver bowl under his arm. When he got to me, he took a good look and then took the glove holding the curse from me, carefully placing it in the bowl before putting the bowl on the ground. He took off his flannel-lined jacket and helped me into it.

"I'm going to get it all wet."

He shrugged, zipping it up for me. "It's just water. And your lips are turning blue."

Some sun broke through the cloud cover where we stood. As lovely as that felt on my face, it was nothing compared to his big warm coat that hung to my knees. It was glorious, having retained his body heat and scent. It felt like a hug.

He leaned in, reaching for my hair and I flinched away, but he was just pulling up the hood while glancing over his shoulder.

"Your, uh, lips aren't the only blue thing."

Shit. I stuffed the curly mass of hair into the coat, out of sight. Also thanks to my dad, my hair reacted strangely to salt water. It brought out various indigo lowlights and green high-lights. I needed to wash it in desalinated city water to return it to my usual mélange of brown, gold, and red.

"And there are dry gloves in the pocket."

Oh, thank goodness. Even though I didn't want to, I pushed up the coat sleeves to peel off the wet ones, dropping them in the scrub grass at the water's edge. I hesitated, not wanting to plunge my bare hands into his pockets.

"Here. Let me." He reached into his right pocket and pulled out new gloves.

I slid my hands into dry warmth and then dove into his heavy pockets for the water bottle and phone. I put the bottle on the ground by the bowl and let out a defeated gust of air, swiping through my phone.

"I have to call my mom."

"Okay."

"No. It's really not, but I have to do this right. I can nullify the curse, but I want her to see if she can trace it to its source first. I don't want to play whack-a-mole with curses around here. I need to know who has it out for me."

While I listened to the ringer in my ear, the sun glinted off the stone tied to the fetish. I hunkered down, the coat completely covering me, as I studied the strange symbol. It wasn't a proper rune—not one I was familiar with, anyway, and I thought I knew them all. This appeared to be an unsacred combination of runes.

"I didn't think you'd call to apologize until tomorrow. Perhaps you're growing up." Oh, good. I was dealing with Snotty Mom who clearly felt *she'd* been wronged.

Declan had squatted down beside me to study the fetish. At my mother's words, he glanced up. Werewolf hearing being what it is, he was following both sides of the conversation.

Rolling my eyes, I said, "No apologies from me, Mom, as you and Gran were the ones in the wrong." I barreled on before she could argue that point. "I'm staring down at a cursed fetish that was hidden under my home."

"What?" There. She'd lost the stick up her ass and sounded concerned.

"One of the guys rebuilding my deck found it."

"Don't touch it!"

"Yeah, I'm not stupid. The guy who handled it was wearing work gloves at the time, so he's fine too." I gave Declan a suspicious glance. He better not have touched it.

"You didn't bring it inside your home, did you?"

"Mom," I responded sharply. What the hell was with her assuming I was a moron?

"I'm getting in the car now."

I heard the engine rev and tires squeal. "Don't get into a car accident. It's outside, near the water's edge. It's sitting on a work glove, inside my silver bowl. I have a nulling draught—"

"No. Don't null the spell. I need to feel it first."

"That's why I'm calling." I stood. It felt like it was pushing me away.

"And don't leave it alone. Whoever set it will feel its discovery. They'll try to retrieve it by any means necessary."

12

See? She's Not All Bad

D eclan stood as well, braced for whatever might be
coming.

"It was found yesterday," I said.

"And if he or she was busy—maybe holds a job—they might
not have realized."

I'd been looking over my shoulder toward the road,
assuming trouble would come from that direction, but then I
heard a strange whistling sound. When I turned to see if Declan
was hearing it too, I was met with his very large back.

"Stay behind me," he growled.

The bowl holding the fetish was on the ground between us. I
tried to peek around him to see what was coming when long,
lethal claws slid from his fingertips.

On the one hand, great. I'm sure we could use those claws
in a fight. On the other, What. The. Fuck? Werewolves couldn't
transform isolated parts of their bodies. It took multiple
minutes, depending on the strength of the wolf, to transform.

A cacophony of seabirds screeching rent the air. Not a
moment later, a dead seagull laid at Declan's feet.

I dropped into a crouch to avoid the birds—I always worry
they're going to go for my hair—and cast a spell. We couldn't

have Phil and the guys, or random tourists watch Wolverine over here tear apart seabirds.

"Do what you need to do," I told him. "Anyone looking in this direction shouldn't notice you now."

"Good," he said. "More birds are coming and this is about to get weird."

I saw movement out of the corner of my eye. Worms. Hundreds of worms were pushing up out of the ground around us. Yuck? Sure. But what the hell was a worm going to do?

"Worms?" he said, sounding more confused than anything. "Pick up the bowl and move. The birds can eat the worms."

With a laugh, I grabbed the silver bowl and ran to the road, heavy footsteps pounding the earth behind me. When I got to the sidewalk, I turned. Declan was standing halfway between the water and the road. Most of the birds had been distracted by the snacks. A few remembered their mission and Declan tore them apart.

My mom pulled up a moment later. Declan walked to us, claws retracted, shaking his head.

"What kind of attack was that?" He sounded both grumpy and offended.

"An ineffective one?" I shrugged.

Mom flew out of the car, looking perfectly put together, of course.

"Darling, really. Why are you so close to the road? People will see us over here." She was pulling the bowl from my hands as she chastised me.

I felt a comforting thump on my shoulder before I responded, "Because whoever set the curse just attacked with birds."

"And worms," Declan added.

I couldn't help it. I just started laughing. All the stress and worry came tumbling out in uncontrolled laughter. When I turned, Declan was wearing an amused grin and watching me, eyes crinkled at the sides.

"Arwyn, this is serious." Mom had the bowl on the hood of her car. After that quick reprimand, her lips returned to moving soundlessly as her fingers twitched in a spell.

While Mom worked, I plopped down on the dirt and grass to wait. I hugged my knees to my chest, the coat covering me completely. Stacking my arms on my knees, my chin on my arms, I waited for her pronouncement.

Declan stood behind me, his legs touching my back, an invitation to lean on him. I didn't, but it was tempting.

Mom lifted her head and held out a hand. I pulled the water bottle from the coat pocket and started to get up, but Declan took it from me and handed it to my mom.

"And who are you?" Mom at her most imperious.

"Mom, this is Declan. Declan, this is my mom Sybil," I said, gesturing between the two.

Mom stared for the briefest of moments and then took a step back. It felt overly dramatic and beneath her.

"Yes, he's a werewolf. Jeez, Mom."

She barely spared me a glance. "Obviously he's a werewolf," she muttered. "I hadn't been told one of the Quinn line still existed. Our family has a connection with the Quinns, you kn—"

"We have a connection? You never told me that. The woman I made the chess set for was a Quinn wolf." I watched her pour water on the fetish, a spell on her lips.

Declan was suddenly crouched beside me. "What Quinn wolf?"

But I wasn't done with my mom yet. "Is that why I was dreaming about her all the time? Why didn't you say anything?"

"There's another Quinn?" Declan asked again.

The urgency in his voice distracted me from my mother and her endless secrets.

"Yes. She's a woman named Sam. She's married to a rage-y vampire. I met him in England. The other vampire said the husband wasn't always like that. Sam had been abducted and they were looking for her." I turned to my mom. "It was connected to those asshole fae who'd taken me."

"Which never would have happened if you'd stayed here. This, however"—my mother pointed at the black, sopping mess —"is why you *had* to go to England to make that chess set."

"What?" I popped up and leaned over the bowl.

"That rune is an unholy combination of Hagalaz—"

"Destruction, cataclysmic change," I muttered.

"Nauthiz," she continued.

"Need. Emotional stability." I leaned in to study the weirdly blended rune.

"And Raidho," she concluded.

"Ooooh, I see."

"I don't," Declan interrupted.

Stepping away from the now powerless fetish, I explained, "Everyone thought I was nuts when I said I *had* to go to England to make this piece. So much pissiness and eye rolling. This," I said, gesturing to the bowl, "was what was pushing me to leave. Horrible cataclysmic destruction if I didn't begin a journey to somewhere far away."

"I smelled sulfur," my mother said, with all the gravity it deserved.

Moving farther away from it, I pulled my arms into the over-sized sleeves of Declan's jacket and hugged myself. "A demon? What the hell did I do to a demon?"

"A sorcerer," my mom clarified.

"Hey, Sybil!"

We all turned to see Phil, my contractor, waving at my mom from beside his truck.

"Hello. It's good to see you." She turned her head and whispered, "This is no place for this conversation. Destroy that thing and go in. I'll meet you in your studio." She walked to Phil's truck. "I was just telling Arwyn that I need to hire you to work on the tea shop's back room. It's awkward for our needs."

While she went off to chat with Phil and give us cover, I

picked up the bowl, walked to the far side of Mom's car, and sat on the curb, the bowl between my feet in the gutter. I said a cleansing spell over it as I poured out the water onto the cement, just to be safe. I knew my Mom had already stripped the curse, but this was my home.

Declan reached down to retrieve his glove, but I grabbed his hand and shook my head. "I'll buy you a new pair."

I conjured a blue flame in my palm and then dropped it into the bowl. The fetish and the glove were instantly engulfed and a moment later, black ash clung in clumps to the inside of my bowl.

"Can you grab the bottle from the hood of her car? I think she left me some to clean out the bowl."

When the mostly empty bottle dangled in front of me, I grabbed it and poured it in the bowl, swishing the ash in circles, trying to dislodge any remnants. I poured the sludge into the street, the silver of the bowl blackened but now curse free.

"It's safe to bring this in now."

Declan gave me a hand up. "I need to get to work or I'm going to get fired. I want to know about that Quinn, though."

I made my way to the front door of the gallery. Nodding to Phil, I tapped my mom on the back. "Come on in and have a cup of tea when you're done."

The men were building the counter and cupboards for the café area. I waved and kept going, pretending like I couldn't hear the squelching squeak my wet sneakers made with every step.

Once in my studio, I closed the door, put down the bowl, and ran upstairs, directly into the bathroom. Leaning into the shower, I turned on the hot water and then stripped off my sodden clothes. I'd had Phil install a washer and dryer in my bathroom, since this is where dirty clothes left my body. I threw in the whole sopping pile and then stepped into glorious heat.

Afterward, wrapped in a towel, I started the washer and then moved to my closet for a soft, warm purple thermal top and another pair of overalls. I still had work to do today. Slipping on socks, I listened to my mother puttering around in my kitchen, no doubt making us tea. I found another pair of paint-spattered shoes and went back to the bathroom, pulling the drying towel off my mass of hair. I squeezed ridiculously expensive conditioner for curly hair out of a tube and worked it through the strands.

"Tea's ready." My mother's voice floated up the stairs.

"Be right down." Whenever possible, I let my hair air dry. After stuffing a hair tie in my pocket for later, I headed downstairs to the sound of hammering coming from the home of my future deck.

"There you are." Mom handed me a cup and sat in my chair. Power move. "Now, tell me why you were in the ocean and all about this wolf."

She took a sip, waiting for me to fill in the blanks, which, of course, I did. She might be a pain in my ass, but she was the defacto head of the Corey family for a reason. She was shrewd, ruthless, and very powerful.

When I finished, she placed her empty cup on the table and considered. "It can't be connected to the demon you did a job for. That curse was placed there long before you located his banshee."

"They have names," I groused.

"I'm sure they do, and those names have nothing to do with this conversation. Why does someone want you gone but not dead?" she mused.

"We don't know not dead." I got up to get us more tea.

"Of course we do. The fetish was spelled to send you far away, not kill you." She nodded her thanks as I filled her cup.

"I was abducted in England."

She pursed her lips. "Don't be dramatic. Wrong place, wrong time in England."

It's always nice when your mom thinks you're neither interesting nor important enough for anyone to steal.

"What's to be gained by getting rid of you?" She stared out the window, thinking. "There's the Council, of course. Someone may want your position."

"They can have it," I muttered.

She *tsked* and put down her cup. "You've never fully appreciated the power and responsibility that comes with the position. Yes, your grandmother and I could have chosen someone else as our third years ago. The fact of the matter is, though, that I don't trust any of them as I do you."

The shock must have shown on my face.

Mom rolled her eyes. "For goodness' sake, Arwyn, you're one of the most powerful wicches this family has ever produced, and that's no mean feat. Plus, your father's fae blood has only enhanced your formidable gifts. I admire strength and power, and you have both—"

"Aww—"

"*But*—"

"Here we go," I said under my breath.

"But," she repeated, "you don't have the arrogance that often accompanies those two attributes, which is what makes you trustworthy. Others, with a more flexible moral code, could easily be manipulated for information or, worse yet, to use the secrets we're privy to on the Council to target others. To prey on them and bleed them dry."

"You think I'm powerful *and* not evil? Mom, you *do* like me!" I pretended to wipe tears from under my eyes while she shook her head.

"The curse could definitely be Council-related," she insisted.

"Or it could just be someone who thinks I'm an asshole."

She stood and brushed off her skirt. "We'll need to hope that's not it. The list of suspects would be endless." She glanced out the window again where Declan was framing the new deck. "I don't like the way that one was looking at you."

"There's nothing going on there." Though I did have the

best sleep of my life touching him. Nah, she didn't need to know that.

"I'm not blind, my darling girl. I know heat when I see it. Remember, the last time a Corey tried to go against the family and marry a wolf, misery followed."

13

This Tentacle Isn't Going to
Seal Itself

After my mother left, I went to the corner where I was corralling my tentacles to grab the one that needed sealant. I unlocked the wheels on my worktable, rolled it out of the way, put down a tarp, and then dragged out modified sawhorses from the kiln room.

The sawhorses each had a long, curved strap of metal attached to the top that went up on the edges to keep the tentacles from rolling off. I placed them about ten feet apart and then moved the thirty-foot tentacle into place. Once I'd turned on a fan, I went to open the back door and found heat. Mom was rarely ever wrong.

Declan stood on a board, his hand poised to knock on the glass door.

I swung it open. "Yes?"

"Can we talk now?" The man was so large, he blocked out the sky.

Stepping back, I waved him in.

He hopped over the gap between the board and the doorsill, and then went to inspect my latest tentacle. "I saw you carry this over. Almost anything this big is going to be heavy. What's it made of?" He reached out to touch it and then stopped, glancing over his shoulder at me. "Is it okay?"

"Go ahead. I haven't started sealing it yet." I collected the tea cups, taking them back to the kitchen. "I use chicken wire to sculpt the frame and then a special plaster all my own." I wiggled my fingers. "It's stronger than typical plaster. It requires multiple sessions though. I can't do it all at once. I need sections to firm and dry before I rotate. I've made a million and a half suction cups, but I really like the effect."

"They're amazing," he said, wonder in his voice. "If I didn't know better, I'd swear this was an actual giant sea monster tentacle. The detail…it's unbelievable."

"Thanks."

He picked one up, weighing it in his palm. Turning, he studied me a moment before replacing the tentacle. "You're stronger than you look. Dad's DNA?"

I shrugged, pulling two sodas from the fridge and handing him one. "Probably."

Opening the can, he took a sip and then nodded toward the couch. "Can we talk?"

I led the way, reclaiming my chair.

He sat on the edge of the couch, his elbows on his long legs, the soda forgotten on the table. "How does your mom know I'm a Quinn? I don't go by that name. And who is this other Quinn you were talking about?"

I glanced over at my tentacle and checked my watch. If I didn't get started soon, I'd only get one coat on today.

"What?" he asked, following my gaze.

"I've got to get started. Can we talk while I work?"

He stood. "Yeah. I'll help you. You take one end. I'll take the other. And we'll meet in the middle."

I hesitated.

"What now?" Hands on hips, his scowl had returned.

"These are really important to me. If you don't coat it completely, water will get in and rot my art."

The scowl deepened. "Are you accusing me of half-assing it?"

"I don't know that I'm *accusing* so much as wary of." I shrugged. "I barely know you. Trust is earned."

He gestured to the window. "I just protected you from demon seagulls!"

"That's true," I said, leaning over to pry off the top of the gallon pail. "And while I appreciate your fighting skills, those don't really translate to precision painting."

He huffed out a breath. "I'm building your deck."

"In theory. In reality, you've torn apart my old deck and nailed down some boards. The whole master builder thing has yet to be proven."

Scratching his beard, he looked down at the floor and then back up at me. "I'm not sure I like you."

I nodded. "I get that a lot." I pulled on my work gloves. "How about this. I'll put in my earbuds, and we'll talk on the phone while we both do our own work. Okay?"

He stared out the window a moment and then nodded. "That's a better idea." He pulled out his phone and waited, brows raised, for my number.

I gave it to him and then waited for mine to buzz. He put his in his shirt pocket, speaker side up, and then buttoned the pocket closed so it didn't fall out into the water. I went to the kitchen where my earbuds were charging. I put them in, tapped the right one, listened to the startup tone and then heard my back door close.

"Can you hear me?" I went to the door, needing it open before I was asphyxiated by the fumes.

"I can, but I could without the phone." He was already back on the bank, picking up a thicker framing board.

"I need this to stay open," I said, "so I don't pass out in here."

He nodded.

"So," I began, walking back to the tentacle, "why don't you

go by Quinn if you are one? From what I've heard, that's a pretty important name in the werewolf community." I slipped on a face mask, dipped my brush into the sealer, and began the process of coating the iridescent purple tentacle. The gradation in color, from deepest eggplant to lightest pearl, along with the sinuous curve, gave the impression of movement, like a real octopus.

"Yeah. It's a loaded one, all right. My father was Alexander Quinn. He was Alpha of the Santa Cruz Mountains Pack. My mom owned a nursery. The story goes that he had a green thumb himself and liked working in the soil. He came in, looking for plants that would do well in the shade, and he and Mom hit it off. They started dating.

"It was all going well and then there was some big blow-up in the family. He apparently never explained what it was, beyond not approving of his son's wife. It was right around then that Mom realized she was pregnant. They were really happy, though. He eventually told her what he was and what I might be. She freaked out, but he calmed her down and moved her into his big home in the mountains.

"I'm told I came early. That's not unusual for a born wolf. Since born wolves are so rare, though, it got people gossiping about whether or not my father was my father. They discussed getting married after I was born but didn't seem to be in a hurry."

"I've always wondered about couples like that," I said, dipping in for more sealant. "It must be hard when one is immortal but the other isn't."

"Yeah, but while wolves *can* be immortal, most don't live that long. Submissives might. The more dominant ones, though, are always getting pulled into fights. Alexander was very strong. From what I've heard, he was hundreds of years old and the original Alpha of the pack. I remember him. Sort of. He's more of a strong, protective presence than a person."

"Do you look like him?" I was picturing a scowling baby

Declan and smiling while I painted.

"No idea. I've never seen any pictures of him. I was about two when he and my mother died."

It came on so quickly, I barely had time to plop my butt down on the tarp. *A man very much like Declan, but with no beard, walked in the forest, along the edge of a ravine, with an attractive woman. She appeared to be somewhere in her thirties, tall and slender, the top of her head reaching his nose. She wore jeans and a sweater, her golden-brown hair pulled back in a ponytail.*

They were laughing and it was lovely. A small boy with dark brown hair scampered ahead, stopping frequently to study the plants and bugs.

"Not too close to the edge, baby," the woman said.

"Not baby," he responded, running ahead again.

"Stay where we can see you," the man called.

The child giggled from behind a tree.

The man and woman shared a look and a smile. And then the woman's eyes flew open as she tumbled over the edge, a thick arrow shaft in her chest.

The man roared, reaching for the woman, trying to catch her when an arrow pierced the back of his head. He followed her over the edge, falling to the jagged rocks below.

Eventually, the boy jumped out from behind the tree, trying to scare his parents, but they were no longer there. He searched, thinking they were hiding as he had. Finally, he wandered to the edge and saw them, broken at the bottom of the ravine.

He giggled at first, calling to them. When neither moved nor called back, fear crept into his voice. Finally, some understanding seemed to settle on him because he crumpled to the ground, curled up, and cried for the mommy and daddy who had fallen and hurt themselves.

"Arwyn? Are you okay?"

I opened my eyes and stared into intense brown ones, dark brows furrowed. The man had very expressive eyebrows.

"Was it the fumes? Did you pass out?" He was holding me outside in the fresh air, balancing on a board.

"No," I shook my head, trying to figure out how to get down. "Listen, put me back inside, okay."

He hopped across the doorsill and then put me down. "Was it a vision?" He crossed his arms over his chest, still clearly uncomfortable with my gifts.

I nodded. "It was the death of your mother and father. I'm sorry you lost them both so young."

"You saw my dad?" He moved closer. "You saw it happen? Who killed him?"

Waving him over to the couch, I shook my head. Declan ignored the invitation to sit and instead paced the studio while I explained what I saw, finally stopping at the window and staring out.

"My mom and I were there? You're sure?"

"I'm sorry." I couldn't get two-year-old Declan out of my head.

He braced an arm against the window frame. "My aunt took me in. She said Alexander had fallen from a cliff and that my mother had died of a broken heart." He glanced over his shoulder, pinning me with a stare. "Yes, I know how that sounds, but to a little kid it makes complete sense." His voice dropped to barely a whisper. "I don't remember. Not any of it."

"That's completely normal, especially at that age and with such a traumatic event. A lot of my clients have stories like that locked inside them." I got up to make him tea and then heard the derision in his echoed *clients* from across the room.

"Hey," I said, marching back, tea forgotten, "I'm sorry you have issues with magic, my type in particular, but I'm not going to accept your contempt while I'm trying to help. For free, I might add. These are my gifts and this is how I support myself. I'm sorry you have a problem with that, but there's the door. You should go back to doing what you do to support *your*self."

I pushed him toward the door, but he didn't move. When his eyes met mine, I saw they'd gone wolf gold. A chill ran down my spine. It was instinctual.

"I'd love to be able to slam the door in your face, but I need the ventilation."

He turned and strode from the studio.

14

Let the Apologies Begin

The sealant was already getting tacky, damn it. I wanted a nice, uniform layer, not clumps—shake it off. It was always the same, though. They eventually showed their true colors. A good night's sleep didn't earn trust. And two things could be true at once. I could mourn for baby Declan and still want to kick grown Declan's ass.

Needing out of my own head, I pulled my phone from my pocket so I could stream loud music through the studio's speakers. It was then I realized the call was still connected. I had tapped on the little green rectangle to open the app and disconnect when I heard something.

"I'm sorry. That was a shitty thing to say and I'm sorry."

I didn't say anything, but I didn't disconnect either.

Bang. I jumped, almost dropping the brush before I realized he was hammering in boards.

"I didn't realize how much I needed to know until you told me. Made me see us as we were. Showed me what my life could have been. Instead, my parents were murdered and I was taken in by my aunt. My aunt only knew some of the story and I've been trying to fill in the rest ever since.

"We didn't know I was a wolf. It came as quite a shock when

I was eleven and shifted for the first time. We were camping. I loved to camp." He let out a gust of breath. "No mystery as to why, I guess. I was keeping my poor Aunt Sarah awake, tossing and turning. My arms and legs were killing me. I'd been going through a growth spurt and the pains were often unbearable. We thought that's what was happening. She'd just turned on a lantern to get me a couple of pain relievers when I watched my arms sprout fur. I was in a nightmare. I had to be. There was a flash of pain and then my eyesight was crystal clear and the scents." He paused while the banging continued.

"Unwashed bodies, mold starting in the tent corner, my aunt's shampoo and the coppery scent of her period, burning wood from the fire we'd doused, the pollen of blooming flowers, the rotting decay of a dead squirrel. It all hit at once and I panicked. I wanted to escape the nightmare and ended up tearing up the tent while my aunt stared wide-eyed at me, horror and fear written all over her.

"I ran then. Just ran and kept going, crashing through the woods, avoiding campsites where people might see me. I knew it was a dream—was almost positive—but I didn't want to chance anyone seeing me. It was like if they saw me, it would be true.

"When I got tired, I realized I had no idea where I was, other than miles and miles away from our campsite. I finally turned around and followed the scents of broken branches and freshly turned soil, hunting for my aunt's scent.

"It was near dawn when I made it back. The tent was gone, though some shreds of nylon clung to the grass. I was so tired, but I followed her scent back to where we'd parked before back-packing in. She was sleeping in the car, doors locked, but she hadn't left me.

"My paws rested on the door as I looked in and then I was standing there naked, freezing and embarrassed. I knocked on the window and she jolted awake. It took a moment for the fear to leave her eyes and that was hard, but she unlocked the door and reached in back for my pack so I could get dressed."

He was silent then, placing boards, hammering, but not talking. Maybe he was waiting to see if I spoke, but I was pretty sure he was just thinking, so I let him.

"Full moon tonight," he finally said. "I've been summoned and that Alpha's itching for a fight. That's the problem with being a dominant. They feel it and the more aggressive or insecure ones take it as a challenge. Immortality isn't really an issue when I have to deal with this shit all the time."

"So you lay low," I said.

He let out a gust of breath as though he'd been waiting to see if I'd speak. "Yeah. I move around a lot, either living where there are no packs or moving out before the full moon."

"Why didn't you do that this time?" I walked around the tentacle to start on the back side.

"I was planning on it. Even packed up my truck and headed out of town. Instead, I ended up parked in front of this place. I don't know why. I just don't want to run this time."

We were both quiet while we considered the reasons for that.

"Are you worried about tonight? The pack?" I had seen Logan's eyes, felt his intent. He wanted to destroy Declan.

"Worried? Not really. I've been dealing with this since my first shift. They hunt me down to challenge me. When I was young, I didn't know how to fight with restraint. It was all so new, and I was terrified. I left dead bodies on the ground. More than I'd care to think about." He paused. "I just want to be left the fuck alone to my woodworking and occasional midnight runs."

"I get that, but sometimes you have to show them exactly who you are and why they should be trembling in your presence to get a little breathing room."

He chuckled. "That sounds like a story."

"It is. For another time. I will say that my cousins no longer try to fuck with me, which was their favorite pastime growing up."

"Now I definitely want to hear——" He paused a moment.

"That detective is back. I recognize the sound of her car. Yeah. She's asking Phil if you're in."

"Thanks for the heads-up and talk to you later." I disconnected the call, pulled out the earbuds, and went to the gallery door. When I opened it, I found Detective Hernández with her hand raised, preparing to knock.

"Oh. Hello. Are you feeling better today?"

I stepped out of the way, inviting her in. "Sorry. I must have looked like a lunatic yesterday. The mom——"

"Nancy."

"Yes. All I could hear was her wailing in my head. I had to get away."

Hernández nodded as though that all made perfect sense. She took her notepad out of her pocket, tapped it against her thigh a couple of times and then put it back in her pocket. "I know you said you wouldn't help us search the forest, but I was hoping after things settled down, you'd reconsider."

I was already shaking my head when I heard, "Sure. We can do that."

I turned to find Declan standing in my doorway.

"I'm sorry," Detective Hernández began. "And you are?"

"Declan. I trained in search and rescue up in Oregon. I can help Arwyn." He moved forward and held out a hand to the detective.

She took it and shook. "That would be great. We'll have our own team, but the forest is quite large, so we can use some help narrowing it down."

"I'll just"—he gestured to the open gallery door—"go tell my boss I have to leave on official business."

Once he was gone, Hernández looked at me, brows raised in question.

I shrugged. "I think he's okay. He's building my deck and seems like a decent guy. I mean, I don't get serial killer vibes off him, so we should be fine."

"That's certainly a relief. Shall we?" The detective moved to the door and waited for me.

All I wanted to do was work on my tentacles, not hike through a forest looking for a poor dead kid. Damn it. "Give me a minute." I capped the pail of sealer and wrapped my brush in cling film. I didn't have time to wash it now and had every intention to get back here soon to finish the job.

When we got outside, Declan was standing by his truck. "I'll follow so you have a ride home."

I nodded before pulling a hoodie over my head and dragging it down, covering the top half of my overalls. "Good idea." I liked having a better escape plan this time.

Detective Hernández hit the key fob and her car chirped. I opened the passenger side door and slid in. The detective buckled up, checked to make sure I was strapped in, and then drove off. I checked the rearview mirror and found Declan's faded red truck following.

"Did the other cops give you a hard time about bringing a crazy psychic to your crime scene?" I'm not sure why I asked this. I was pretty sure the answer was going to irritate the hell out of me.

She shrugged a shoulder. "At first, but when they found fingerprints on the milk crate that didn't match Nancy or Christopher, the smirks disappeared. Then I had detectives with cold cases asking what your name was and if you'd be willing to help."

I wasn't looking forward to that. "I think I freaked out the poor guy who drove me back to the gallery." I didn't like people seeing me in that state.

"Jon? No, not at all. He's a good guy. He actually felt really bad for you. He said it was obvious you were in a lot of pain and he was sorry he couldn't help. He was just trying to be quiet and drive as smoothly as possible so he didn't make it worse."

"Aww, that was sweet of him." I hadn't expected understanding. I thought for sure I'd have been the butt of every squad room joke for a couple of days.

As she drove up the narrow winding roads again, my stomach started to twist. I didn't want to do this again. Glancing in the rearview mirror, I saw Declan was sticking close. Strangely enough, that helped steady me. I wouldn't be doing it alone.

When Hernández pulled up, there were lots of other cars. Oh, good. I'd have an audience.

"They're not all going to be walking with us, are they?"

The detective was just about to open her door but stopped and turned to me. "Is that a problem?"

"I'll do better on my own. All their thoughts and emotions will be crowding me. Can you just—I don't know—give me a walkie-talkie or something and we'll go in and search alone?"

She shook her head. "I can't do that, but I can keep the search party to a bare minimum. And we can walk behind you. Okay?"

"We can try that."

Declan opened my door as Hernández stepped out and went to talk with another cop. "Can you get me into his room?" Declan whispered. "I need his scent."

Nodding, I crossed to Hernández. "Detective, can I see his room again?"

"Sure. Let me introduce you to who we'll be walking with." She gestured to an older man with graying hair and hard eyes. "This is Captain Hauer." Pointing to the woman standing next to him, she said, "This is Detective Rosen. She has medical training, in case we need it." She tilted her head toward the uniformed man standing in the loose circle. "You remember Officer Cross. He drove you home yesterday."

I nodded and smiled at everyone. There were still quite a few people standing around the lawn who hadn't been introduced. "What about—" I looked at all the curious, suspicious, angry gazes not so subtly aimed at me.

"They'll wait here," the captain responded. "If they get a call," he said, voice raised for all to hear, "they'll go answer those calls. If not, they'll wait to see if we need them to join the search. We're all very concerned about this child." He cleared his throat. "Many of us are not believers in psychic ability—"

"At all," someone snarked, earning a look from Detective Hernández. Regardless of what she'd said, she'd probably had to deal with a lot of shit because of consulting me.

The captain continued as though he hadn't heard. "But that doesn't mean that we ignore possible leads. So, you do what you do, and we'll do the same." He paused, studying Declan. "And who are you?"

Declan held out a hand to shake. "Declan Adams. I'm her assistant," he said with a disarming grin.

Detective Hernández waved us forward. "We'll be right back. She wants to see the bedroom again."

I tried to shake off the hostility of the men and woman milling about, but it wasn't easy. Once we were in the house, I said, "Thanks for keeping the rest away from the search. The suspicion and hate rolling off them is hard to block out."

Hernández looked surprised but nodded as though that was a completely normal thing to hear. She waited in the hall while Declan and I walked in. I knew the room probably smelled of dozens of people and fingerprinting chemicals, so I tried to find places where Declan could get a scent. I opened the closet door and looked around, then went to the narrow bed and threw back the covers.

Taking off a glove, I touched the sheet, mostly for cover so Declan could breathe in his scent, but was immediately hit by a vision, a small but powerful one.

When my knees started to buckle, I caught myself and pulled my glove back on. A chill ran down my spine as I glanced over my shoulder at the window. "Christopher saw the kid in his window. Just a silhouette, a shadow, but it scared him. He wet the bed, thinking his father had found them."

Declan leaned into me, his back to Hernández, and sniffed, a strange look on his face.

15

Worst Walk in the Woods Ever

"We can go now," I said, moving around Declan and heading for the bedroom door.

Once outside, we rounded the side of the house, moving into the forest beyond. Declan and I walked a good ten yards ahead of the police, which helped me clear my mind.

"The killer's a kid?" Declan asked, his voice low.

I nodded.

He let out a long, slow breath, saying nothing as we walked deeper into the forest. When the path curved out of sight of the law, he leaned in and whispered, "When you had that vision in the bedroom, you smelled like the boy."

My step faltered and his hand was at my elbow, keeping me steady. I didn't know why that bothered me so much. I was an empath. I felt what they felt. The smell, though, indicated I might have been framing it wrong all these years. Perhaps what I felt in visions wasn't an echo, but a shared experience. How, though, did I share anything with the dead? Ideas to ponder later. I had work now.

Squirrels chittered angrily and a bird squawked before flying off.

"It's me. My presence is getting them worked up." Declan

lifted his head, scenting the wind. "Are you picking up anything —if that's the right term?"

Was I? Who knew? There were too many people, too many distractions. Glancing over my shoulder, I watched the cops talking quietly to one another. "Can you hold up a minute?" I called to them. "I want to try something."

They stopped walking and waited.

"Grab me if I start to go down. I don't want to get all dirty," I said to Declan.

He grinned. "On it."

I took off the same glove I'd removed in Christopher's bedroom and touched my index finger—the one I'd touched the sheet with—to my thumb. I was hit with the panic again, the silhouette in the window. It was like a punch to the chest, but my knees didn't buckle this time. Revisiting a vision seemed to give it less power. That was interesting.

Rubbing my fingers in little circles, I tried to calm the Christopher in my head, thereby slowing my own heartbeat. *Where did he take you?* I got a flash—the briefest of visions—and it had me bolting into the woods, stomach heaving. Gentle hands held my hair back, my abdominals unable to stop convulsing, even though there was nothing left but foamy spittle.

"Is she okay?"

"Don't know yet," Declan said, sounding annoyed that they'd rushed forward, crowding us.

When my stomach stopped quivering, I stood. Declan handed me a handkerchief to wipe my mouth—who the hell carries around handkerchiefs?—and then lifted my naked hand by the wrist of my hoodie, my abandoned glove in his other hand.

My relief at seeing my glove was drowned out as I watched slices cut open on the back of my hand. It stung, but not the way sliced flesh would. At least I didn't think so, never having been carved up. Perhaps it was the adrenaline.

It finally got through the shock that the cops were gasping and muttering.

"I don't—This has never happened before," I said, lifting my head. The four police officers took a step back. Declan, however, moved forward. He yanked his sleeve over his hand before tilting my chin up.

I wiped at my mouth again, suddenly self-conscious. "What?"

"Your eyes are bloody and there's a deep cut down your cheek."

I flinched away, my heart in my throat. I lifted my other hand and Detective Rosen made a quiet noise of distress. Blood was blooming through my glove.

Staring at my hands, my brain froze. What was happening to me?

"Her chest," Officer Cross breathed.

My gaze snapped to my chest and the thin lines of blood staining my white sweatshirt. I held up trembling bloody hands. "I need you to move back. I can't figure out what's happening to me with an audience. I need a minute."

"We need to get you medical help," Captain Hauer snapped. "Rosen, get her bandaged and check both of them for blades."

Declan growled, prompting Officer Cross to rest his hand on his firearm. I stepped in front of the pissed-off werewolf, grateful my own rage was clearing away the terror.

"First of all, fuck you," I said, a bloody finger pointing at Hauer. "You have no right to accuse either of us of lying and staging this. I'm here because you need me. You couldn't find him. Had no idea what had happened to him. In one day, I've given you more information than you'd discovered in weeks of searching. So, again, fuck you."

"Miss Corey," Detective Hernández began.

"No. You, I like, but I'm not going to stand here, out in the fucking woods where this little psycho killer is probably watching me, bleeding from wounds that match Christopher's, and listen to this asshole question my integrity."

"Your cheek," Rosen said.

"What about it?" I rubbed at it with the sleeve of my hoodie, sick of these people gawking at me.

"It stopped bleeding," Hernández said. "There's no cut, not even a scar."

"Because I'm not him. I wasn't sliced by a psychopath experimenting with torture." I blew out a breath and dropped my head, my hair a wild curtain between me and them. Staring at the purple and green paint spattered across my sneakers, I tried to find the stillness and the focus.

I'd seen it before the vomiting. I knew where he was.

I slid the glove back on my bare hand before stuffing both in the kangaroo pocket of my hoodie. "He's in an abandoned bomb shelter. It's about a mile down this path and maybe a quarter of a mile north. When you reach a downed pine tree blocking the path, you cut left."

I closed my eyes and slowed my breathing. "It looks like a mound of earth covered in branches and leaves. On top, half buried in the dirt and pine needles, you'll find Spider-Man, one of Christopher's superheroes. He thought that was funny, Spider-Man sitting on top of the horror and doing nothing. The door on the side is under Ironman."

Rubbing my forehead, I continued. The headache was like a spike behind the eyes. "He has anatomy charts ripped from library books taped to the walls. And knives, lots of knives. He's been stealing them for years, dreaming of using them. The power he'd feel. The control. Life and death were his to grant or deny. All his previous experiments are in there with Christopher.

"He has shoeboxes, cereal boxes, bread bags holding his kills. He's recently graduated to jars, empty peanut butter and jelly jars. He has animal organs floating in water. He hasn't discovered yet that water isn't the right solution to preserve them, but he will.

"He lives with…I can't be sure, but it feels like a woman. Not a mother. Older. Grandmother, maybe." I shook my head. "I can't see her. He doesn't think of her. Barely notices her. And she certainly doesn't see who he really is. Still, I think *she*. It's just the two of them. He's the one in charge. Sick. Maybe she's sick and can't watch him better."

A darkness hung in the air, pressing in on me. "He won't be in the shelter, because he's out here somewhere." The cops started to move. "Get Christopher. The killer knows these woods like the back of his hand. He'll lead you on a chase and then double back to set the contents of the shelter on fire. No evidence. No crime."

Declan wrapped an arm around me. "Let's get you out of here."

"Aren't you staying to track?" I glanced up at him and realized for the first time that his eyes had lightened. The full moon was close and he was a ball of barely contained rage.

"No," he said, looking at me, not them. "You gave them everything they'll need to find the boy. It's their turn now."

It felt like Cross was going to detain us, but someone must have waved him off because he didn't do or say anything else. The captain started shouting orders into a walkie-talkie, but we were already down the path and turning out of sight.

"Assholes," he growled.

"Oh, it bothers you to be called a liar and a fake, huh?" I pulled my hands out of my pocket and pushed down the cuff of a glove to see if the cuts were still there. Thankfully, all I found was blood-smeared unmarked skin.

Declan had dropped his arm from my waist, no doubt because I continued to give him shit. Whatever. While I might have missed the weight and warmth, I didn't need it. I didn't need anyone. I was more comfortable alone. Always had been. Always will be.

"Had that ever happened before? The bleeding? You looked shocked." He moved in front of me, an arm out to keep me safe from the cops running up the path.

"No. I have visions. I feel what they feel, to a lesser degree. I don't bear the marks. I need to think about what happened today and why. I can't do it out here in all these swirling emotions and chaos. Later, in the studio, while I finish sealing the tentacle, I'll think." I moved off the path again as more uniformed police jogged past.

"Will they find him?" Declan asked.

"Which him?" The prickling along my spine hadn't let up; the dark presence seemed to be trailing me.

"Both."

"Christopher, yes. The killer, it's too soon to tell. The future is malleable. It changes with a thought. When something is close to happening, I feel it with more clarity. They'll find Christopher within the hour. The killer"—a chill ran down my spine—"not yet."

We moved aside as men in paramedic jumpsuits with heavy-looking backpacks hurried past.

"You know you're going to end up the prime suspect because you knew where he was," Declan said. The poor guy kept adjusting his long stride to stay beside me.

"Oh, not just me, drifter man. The majority of serial killers are men. By a whole lot. They'll suspect us both, but mostly you. Thankfully, I have two lawyers and a judge in the family. I'll get Mom and Gran mobilized. They'll shut that shit down before it begins."

"Are they going to dangle me in front of the cops to get the focus off you?" The insult in his voice had me smiling.

"Sorry, dude. Family first. You're on your own." When I realized how true that comment was, I elbowed him in the side. "They wouldn't do that. Especially after I tell them not to."

"Your mom seems like she'd happily sell me out to protect you."

"Ordinarily, yes." *Shit.* That's exactly what she and Gran would do. "I'll deal with them. Don't worry. You're in the clear." Probably.

16

When I Said She Wasn't All Bad, It Was Understood She Was Pretty Bad, Right?

On the drive home, I had Declan detour to Gran's house while I called my mom.

"Twice in one day? I'll need to mark my datebook." Judging by the background noise, she was already in her car, which was good.

"Can you meet us at Gran's?"

"Us who?" Thankfully, her blinker sounded. She would come.

"Declan and me. I was helping the police find a murdered child and a darkness followed me out of the forest."

"You'll help the police but not your family. Interesting."

"Mom, cut me some slack, will you? The detective came to me. It wasn't like I volunteered. And the poor little boy was cut to ribbons. But since I told them where to find him—"

"They're going to assume you or your friend had something to do with it." She sighed. "Let me make a phone call. Don't go to your Gran's. Pull over and wait with the windows rolled down. When we're ready for you, we'll call."

I rolled my eyes at Declan. Mom was so damn bossy. "Okay if we stop and get something to drink while we wait?" What was it about her that made me revert to teenaged petulance in response?

"If you don't mind being responsible for a minimum-wage fast-food employee burning himself with hot oil or having the shake machine fall on him, by all means, bring your dark presence to people ill-equipped to recognize or deal with it. What a wonderful plan. Perhaps you should get some fries to go with that drink."

"You made your point, Mom, and I was only joking."

"Quite amusing, darling." *Click.*

"Well," Declan began, "at least I see where you get it." He put on his blinker and pulled into a turnout beside the ocean.

"Hey, I'm nothing like my mom." Stupid werewolf. What the hell did he know?

We sat in silence for a while and then he finally asked, "Why are we going to your grandmother's home?"

"You heard. Something evil followed me out of the forest. We need them to cleanse us and the truck. I'm not inviting evil into my home."

After a bit, he said, "Can you tell me about the other Quinn? I thought I was the last of the line."

"I don't really know much about her. Like I said, she owns a bookstore and bar in San Francisco and she's married to a very angry vampire." I stared out at the waves. "I had nightmares every night about her. Dark, violent things from her past. Weird stuff in her present. And then there were fae warriors and dragons and dwarfs stalking her in the future. It was all strangely disjointed. Some nightmares were her running from a pack of wolves. Some were her trapped in Faerie with axes flying at her. The fae queen and king seemed to be using her as a pawn in their eternal struggle.

"You have to understand," I continued, "what I do? It's a lot of piecing things together, finding patterns, drawing conclusions based on spotty information and incomplete patterns. I usually don't know the full story.

"The killer we're dealing with now, for instance. I don't know who he is. I have impressions of his personality, what drives him, but I can't tell you what he looks like or where he lives."

"Frustrating," he murmured.

"Bloody useless is what it is." I pounded my first on my knee. "I can tell cops where to find a victim but not where to find the killer before he takes more victims."

Declan turned to me, his expression somehow lighter. "*Bloody?*"

"I lived in England for almost two years while I sculpted the chess set and then waited for her to come claim it. Certain words and phrases have stuck with me." I shrugged. "I like bloody."

"Okay, but if you knew she was in San Francisco and you're in Monterey... That's what? A two, maybe three-hour drive up the coast. Why did you move to England and then wait for her there?"

I threw my hands up in frustration. "How the hell do I know? My visions pointed me there. That cursed fetish under my studio pushed me away. Could I have made the chess set here? Probably, but it would have been different. Something as basic as the stones I chose would have been different here than there. England is closer to the heart of Faerie and so I felt the connection between each piece and its corresponding fae person more strongly there.

"I could have sculpted a beautiful chess set here, but a magical one required I be there. I think. It's not an exact science. Also, though, if I hadn't been there, I wouldn't have been abducted—"

"You mentioned something about that before. What the hell? You were kidnapped?" Declan had taken off his seat belt and was turned in the truck cab, his back to the door.

"Oh, yeah, okay. This was such bullshit, but it's like domino pieces. They all have to line up to work. I think my abduction had to happen in order for me to help Sam Quinn down the line."

Declan stared at me, waiting.

"Right, well, I'd finished the chess set, had sent it to a local agent who consigned it to an art gallery in Canterbury. Before you ask why that one, I had a dream of Sam listening to choir music in the Canterbury Cathedral, so I knew she'd be there to see and buy the set."

"But how did you know?" he grumbled.

"Dude, I'm psychic. I knew. Shut up and let me tell the story."

He shook his head but remained silent. Good enough.

"Even though I'd completed the set, it didn't feel like it was time to go home. It was an odd time. The thing that had driven me for so long was done. There was nothing pressing or pushing me. The nightmares were less intense and kind of my greatest hits, rather than new ones. I was able to work on whatever struck my fancy. My new art pieces sold quickly and for good money, so I was comfortable as I waited in Kent.

"One morning, I'd left the house to walk the half mile to the town center and get breakfast. The house I was renting was on its own, at the edge of the woods. It was adorable and had an attached barn that had been rehabbed into a studio. The light was magical. I loved that place.

"Anyway, the first part of the walk is on a narrow lane with forest on both sides. That morning, when I walked across a short bridge over a fast green river, two fae goons appeared on either side of me. They grabbed me and slid between the realms, using Faerie to slingshot us to the north of Wales."

Declan flinched as though he wanted to interject but thought better of it.

"As you can see, I'm fine."

"No. I mean, you had no problem spelling me out the door and into the ocean. Why didn't you spell them?" he asked.

"Oh, I did. The fae are made of magic more powerful than

mine. Mom probably would have held her own. My spells slid right off them. Mind you, I was able to hear their every thought, knew the plan, who had sent them, and what was about to happen, but I couldn't hurt them, which really pissed me off.

"Anyway, they brought me to this huge old brick manor house owned by a vampire. The fae were working with this vampire who liked to drink from supernatural creatures.

"They threw me in a cell in her dungeon because being part fae, I qualified as dinner. They didn't pick up on the wicche half, because goons, fae or not, aren't the brightest of the bunch. Anyway, every time they grabbed me, shoved me, smacked me, I was picking up information through their touch. By the time they locked me in, I understood the operation and wasn't going to wait for nightfall when the vampire came.

"It was all more of the fae king's bullshit. He was using the vampire to destabilize Faerie, thereby weakening his wife." I shook my head. "Just divorce already. Why drag all these innocent people into your marital issues?

"Anyway, I waited until the guards moved to a different part of the dungeon, cast a spell on the lock, and walked out." I rolled my eyes. "Dumbasses."

Declan's grin was infectious, and I laughed.

"I know. Of course, then I was lost in Wales, but I eventually made my way to a farm house and a phone. The goons knew enough to crush my cell phone, but they hadn't bothered with my wallet, so I called for a car to pick me up and drive me home.

"I added a shit ton of protections to the little house and studio, and they never came back. Honestly, though, they probably just forgot about me. It didn't feel as though it was target-specific, more that they'd just happened upon someone half fae, so they took me."

"Unbelievable," he said, shaking his head.

"And yet all true." I checked my phone. What was taking Mom and Gran so long?

"How does that relate to the Quinn wolf and the chess set?"

"Oh," I began, returning my phone to my hoodie pocket, "she was like a fae chew toy they were fighting over, the king grabbing and trying to kill, the queen sort of helping—though, honestly, just leaving it up to Sam to rescue herself. Anyway, Sam and her vampires were hunting the bad vampire—and really, aren't they all?—because she'd apparently been doing a lot of evil vampire shit. Sam and her crew were trying to rescue the bloodsucker's prisoners—one dragon in particular—and my information from the abduction helped them know who was involved and where to find them."

"Nice," he said, sounding impressed.

"Thanks, but they'd already discovered some of it. My help hopefully got them there faster. I don't know, but that dragon didn't have much longer to live. "

My phone finally buzzed in my pocket. I grabbed it and hit *accept*.

"We're ready," Mom said.

Declan turned on the engine.

"We're on our way. Thanks, Mom."

"Mhmm."

Not *you're welcome*, just *mhmm*. Mom had drummed proper etiquette into me from an early age. The fact that she'd given me a sound of vague agreement instead of the words meant something was up. They weren't doing this out of the kindness of their hearts. This was a negotiation.

As I gave Declan directions to Gran's, I hoped I was reading it wrong, that she was just distracted. I didn't think so, though.

Declan surprised me by seeing the break in the trees and pulling in. Gran and Mom, expressions stony, stood in the center of the small circular driveway. Declan reached for the door and then stopped, looking back and forth between my family and me.

"What am I missing?" he asked.

My window was still rolled down, so I raised my voice, staring my mom straight in the eyes. "Nothing at all. Just two cold-hearted women who would leverage my safety to get what they want."

"Not just *your* safety, darling," my mother responded.

17

Blackmail Is Such an Ugly Word. Accurate, but Ugly

The message could not be clearer. They'd be more than happy to deal with our dark presence situation and to keep Declan from being investigated by the cops. What they wanted in return, of course, was for me to take my place on the Corey Council.

I got it. They were trying to take care of the family and keep the magical influence from leaking into the mundane world. Today was a good example of what they were trying to stop. If I'd joined with them years ago, it was doubtful a cursed fetish could have sat under my home without being noticed.

The miasma of evil clinging to me meant Christopher's killer probably wasn't a garden variety psychopath. If I had been working with them on the Council, it was possible Christopher and his mom would still be living happily in their hidden home.

"You won't be happy until I'm dead, will you? Just like the rest that came before me?"

Declan, having no idea what was going on, reached over and laid a reassuring hand on my arm.

"Don't be so melodramatic. You're nothing like those poor girls who came before you." Mom waited a beat and then added, "I was on my way to the hospital when you called. Sylvia's in a coma."

I hopped out of the truck and stalked toward them. "What do you mean she's in a coma? No she's not. She's healthy. I just saw her. There was nothing wrong with her." Aunt Sylvia often felt more like my mom than my mom. Sylvia was the one who checked on me, dropped off soup if I was sick, took me shopping just because. My eyes filled with tears. "No." It was all I could get out.

Mom cleared her throat. "This is what we've been telling you. There's only so much your grandmother and I can do without you. If this was a peaceful time, we could wait for you, but it's not. We both feel it. There's something poisonous within the family and it's bleeding out into the mundane world."

Declan had stepped out but was hanging back by the truck, unsure of the family drama being played out.

I blew out a breath, angry at the world—Mom and Gran most of all—for stripping away the semblance of choice and leaving me with only one path, the one that led to insanity and death.

I blew out a breath, my heart sinking. "You win."

"Wait," Declan interrupted. He might not have known what was going on, but he got the gist and sounded concerned.

"Stay out of this, wolf," Gran warned.

I pulled off my gloves, closed my eyes, and lifted my arms to the heavens, allowing all my mental blocks to slide away. Voices, emotions, visions swirled around me, but I cloaked myself in the light of the Goddess and vowed, "I, Arwyn Cassandra Corey, accept my destiny, maiden to your mother and your crone. I will share the power and the responsibility. I will protect this family and rout out, by whatever means necessary, those who would endanger my people. I offer, without reservation, my power that it might be used for the safety and betterment of the Corey coven."

I'd smelled the sage as soon as I lifted my arms. Mom and

Gran had been circling me while I spoke, chanting to remove the evil stalking me. I felt them move off and knew they were cleansing Declan and his truck.

When they came back, I lowered my arms and opened my eyes. They each took a hand, and we stood in a triangle. Without me, they'd been off balance, a corner left open, inviting evil to creep into the heart of the family.

Gran began the incantation that brought me into the triad of power. I felt the spell bubbling inside me, as though my organs were made of Champagne. Soon Mom added her voice to the spell and the bubbles multiplied. When at last it was my turn, their voices thrummed inside me like the beat of my heart. Our voices, our magic, each of us a thread woven with the other two, creating a tapestry of power forever intertwined. Our magic, ourselves, more powerful together. The chant ended on a shout as fire raced through my veins, sealing our promise.

A little girl is coloring in a book on her back porch. She looks up, intrigued, and follows, her crayons forgotten, as she moves deeper into the woods, a smile of wonder on her face.

Detective Hernández sits with another sobbing mother.

My cousin Serena and her shop are in the news. Eleven people have been poisoned by her tea. Seven dead. Four in critical condition. Headlines call her a witch, a murderer. Her sister Calliope makes a statement, assuring people of Serena's innocence.

A man in a bar is bumped by a hapless guy carrying four beers. The man growls, his rage immediate. He backhands the bumper, sending him sprawling, beer glasses shattering. The angry man picks up the other from the floor and drags him outside. Muscles bulging, spittle flying, he beats the other man to death. When the police cars arrive, the aggressor, whose eyes have lightened to wolf gold, rushes them before he's shot dead.

My gallery is consumed in flames, a pyre upon the water. Burning planks fall into the ocean, floating on dark water. The posts beneath heat, flames dancing down the wood to Charlie and Herbert, to Cecil. The roof collapses, crushing my home, my heart.

A ring of a dozen wolves surrounds one. Growls shake the earth. They slink forward, readying for the attack. A black wolf stands in the middle. Though they outnumber him, they are no match for him. A gunshot cracks through the silence. He's hit. They see he's weakened and leap, trying to take him down. He tears them apart. One by one, they fall to the side, bloody, panting, as their lives drain out of them. A man steps out of the woods, white fangs glistening in the moonlight. Eyes black, he holds out a hand and a tan wolf, standing apart from the bloodshed, trots to him.

Gran lying on her flagstone patio, foaming spittle on her darkened lips. Magic, power, light, knowledge, love, experience, all gone. Just her lifeless body discarded. On the table a teapot and two cups. Someone she knew, someone she trusted, took tea with her on her back patio, overlooking the ocean. Mom screams.

"Arwyn!"

I heard Declan's shout, the pounding of his boots across the drive to me, but I couldn't move. I couldn't feel my body, though I was sure it was still there. I stared up into the canopy of trees overhead.

Declan's handsome bearded face blocked out the trees. "What happened? Are you okay?" He looked over where Mom and Gran laid and then back to me. "You're not all dead, right?" He ran a finger down my cheek and I felt it, both the physical touch and the concern.

He seemed to have broken the paralysis because I blinked.

"Oh, thank God," he murmured. He glanced over again. "Does that mean they're okay too?"

Damn, my whole body hurt. I started to get up and Declan was there, lifting me to my feet. He held on to my elbow while I tried to regain my balance and use of my limbs. Geez, someone should warn a person what happens in these ceremonies.

I lurched to my mother and Gran. Both were staring up into the trees as I had been. "We should just drive off and leave you two here." *Fuck.* I bent over, almost tipping onto my head before Declan—who was apparently walking behind me as you would an unsteady toddler—grabbed me around the middle.

I reached for both their hands and felt a charge run through me. They blinked and I felt—as I wasn't wearing my gloves— what they'd been going through. They'd been hounded, battered, as they waited for me to fill the void. We had a sorcerer in the family. This wasn't the work of a black wicche. A sorcerer and their demon had been wearing away at my mother and grandmother for years, trying to worm their way in, to siphon off the power, and these two women had been holding the line. No wonder they were always annoyed with me.

"Can you pick up Gran and carry her into the house?"

"Don't curse me," Declan said to my grandmother. "I'm helping at your granddaughter's request."

I went to Mom and rested my bare hand against her cheek. "I'm sorry. I didn't realize how bad it had been for you two."

Blinking, she brought me into focus. "Of course you didn't. We worked hard to block it. From everyone." She lifted a hand for help up and then saw my bare hands.

"Oh. Wait." I always carried an extra pair, sometimes two. When I reached for Mom, I saw that she'd pulled on her own pair. She might have driven me nuts much of my life, but I never doubted she loved me. Deep, deep down.

"I got her." Declan jogged out Gran's front door and reached for Mom.

"Nonsense. I'm perfectly able to stand on my own." Mom waved him off.

I grabbed her arm, steadying her as she stood, and held on until she regained her balance.

She brushed at her clothing and then addressed Declan. "You may go now. We have family matters to discuss."

He nodded, taking a step back, his gaze finding mine. "Are you good, or do you need a ride?"

"I'm fine," I assured him. "You can take off. Mom'll give me a ride home."

"Good enough." He headed back to his truck. "I'll keep working on the deck."

Mom and I moved to Gran's porch so he could turn his truck around and leave.

"Let's go check on your grandmother. If I'm feeling beat up, she must be worse." She held open the door for me.

We walked in and found Gran sitting in her usual chair by the fire, the tea cart next to her. Apparently, she wasn't feeling too poorly to brew us tea. That was a good sign.

I poured us each a cup and sat in a club chair. Mom took the couch, so we were again arranged in three triangle points in the room. I took a sip and let Gran's tea, a restorative, work its way through me. By degrees, the imbalance ebbed, along with little aches and pains.

"Welcome, Arwyn," Grandmother said. "I believe your mother and I were witness to that last vision." She looked at her daughter and Mom nodded.

"It was dark and hazy," Mom explained, "not clear the way you've described them. My guess is since we were listening in on a vision that wasn't ours, our reception was faulty."

"More like one of those dark arty-type films where you spend half the movie wondering what's going on and why no one will turn on a light," Gran said.

We talked through each part of the vision and what I thought it meant. They gave their own opinions, and it was nice to have people to bounce ideas off of. They, of course, had the most to say about Serena and Gran's chapters in the vision.

"This didn't feel like one of my normal visions, though. This felt like it was sent to me because of our joining." I wasn't sure how to explain it to women who didn't have visions, why this felt so different to me. "It wasn't something that's happened or something that will. It felt more like these were the things we needed to focus on. If we didn't intercede, this is what would happen."

Gran said, "A harbinger," just as Mom said, "a warning."

"Yes," I agreed.

"The tea bar in Serena's shop is small compared to all the

shelves of lotions and perfumes and soaps, but we can't make her throw it all out. We don't even know if it's been poisoned yet. The poisoner could strike a couple of days from now. The news scene we saw might not take place for months." Mom shook her head in annoyance. "This is so frustrating, Arwyn. How do you reconcile yourself with not knowing?"

"I don't. Nightmares wake me up. Endless interpretations and the guilt of not knowing how or even when to help keep me up. It's probably why the ones before me checked out early."

Mom and Gran made almost identical moves with their hands, warding off my words, not wanting me to travel that well-worn road. I appreciated the spell but knew the path that lay before me was not in their power to choose.

18

Actually, I Do Know a Demon

"We have potion makers in the family," I suggested. "Maybe one of them—Wait. Do we have any who are sensitive to poison who could check out her tea jars?" Serena and my mom both kept their teas in oversized glass containers with airtight lids. They were labeled and stored in lightless storage rooms. They both had smaller jars out in the shop for brewing each day, as well as special foil-lined packets of their most popular blends to sell to customers.

I was given the vision so we could stop it. Therefore, there had to be a way to intervene.

"Perhaps," Mom said, lost in thought.

Gran nodded. "Yes, we'll talk with Bracken. He's not a Corey—"

"Or terribly stable," Mom interjected.

"—but," Gran continued, "he's quite skilled and he owes me a favor." She turned to her daughter. "Leave this one to me. He knows me, and his instability will work in our favor. Serena will hate him, but once given the task, he'll sit in her storeroom, checking the teas over and over. No one will be able to tamper with them. No one will die."

Gran took another sip of tea. "The child coloring. I didn't understand that one."

"Is it related to where you were today?" Mom asked.

I nodded. "Yeah." I explained what had been going on, my visit from Detective Hernández, Christopher, the killer, and what might have been driving him.

"Do they have ties to the magical community?" Mom asked.

I shook my head. "Not that I know of."

Mom and Gran wore matching expressions of consternation.

"Why the boy then?" Gran pushed her rocking chair into motion. "Or the girl in the vision, for that matter?"

"We'll come back to that," Mom said. "You need to call Phil and have him add fire alarms and sprinklers to the outside of your cannery. Now. Call him." She looked and sounded angry, but I knew she was just worried.

When she continued to stare at me, I got up and walked to the kitchen to make the call. I went through Gran's refrigerator while we talked. Phil obviously thought it was a strange request, as we'd already installed smoke detectors and sprinklers inside the gallery. As it meant more money for him, though, he agreed to start that project soon.

Not finding anything to eat, I went back to the living room. "I'm ordering a pizza. Do you guys want some?"

"You can't order delivery here," Gran said. "The delivery people can't find me."

I thought about that for a minute. "When they get close, I'll run out to the road and wave them down."

"Check the freezer," Gran said. "I usually have one of those French bread pizzas you like in there."

"Score." I turned back around and hit the freezer. Yes! I put it in the oven to bake and then went back to the refrigerator for a soda.

When I returned to the living room, Mom and Gran were deep

in discussion of how to test and keep her teas safe as well. Mom and Serena had different shops in different areas. Serena catered more to the tourist trade, her shop being on Cannery Row. Mom had a very loyal following that drove into Carmel to visit hers.

"It was so sweet of Calliope to speak to the reporters, to try to clear her sister. She's a good girl," Gran said.

"Hey, can't you get the poison guy to test Mom's place too?" I sat down and opened my soda.

"We're going to try," Gran said, "but he may consider that two favors."

"Call me crazy, but could you just offer him a lot of money? That usually does it for most people."

"What a novel approach," Mom snarked while Gran shook her head.

"He won't do it for money. He's quite wealthy already." Gran held up her empty tea cup.

I hopped up to fill their cups. "Okay. Do any of us have something he wants?"

"Well," Gran began, "he's always been quite partial to your mother."

I sat back down on a laugh. "Sorry, Mom. Looks like you're taking one for the team."

"Yes, quite amusing." Mom drummed her fingers on the arm of the couch. "He's always been interested in divination. We might be able to tempt him with Arwyn."

The oven dinged and I went for my lunch. "Stellar parenting there, Mom. Pimping out your only child." I found a plate and an oven mitt. Grabbing the cooking sheet, I slid the French bread pizza onto my plate, put the pan on the stove top to cool, and took a paper towel. When I returned, the women were suspiciously quiet.

I tore the paper towel in half and used part of it to hold the hot bread. Blowing on it, I looked over the top of steaming tomato sauce, cheese, and pepperoni at the women staring back at me. "What? If you wanted some, you should have said something."

"We think we've hit upon an angle," Mom said, "but we want your input."

"Okay." This all seemed very suspicious. Mom and Gran loved telling me things, not consulting with me. This was either great and showed we were equal points on this triangle or they were looking for me to agree to do something that was going to suck for me in order to alleviate their guilt. As much as I hoped for the first, I was bracing for the second.

"Bracken has a child and we know he's very concerned about him. Desperate to know anything," Mom said.

"Why doesn't he know anything?"

"Bracken went through difficult periods in his life," Gran explained. "During one of those periods, he drank a great deal and was abusive to his young wife. She took the child and left one night. He's tried to find them ever since. If you gave him that information, we'd have him as a resource as long as he lived."

I'd already taken a bite, so I shook my head.

"Now, Arwyn, he'd be an incredibly valuable resource," Mom said. "His gratitude to the family would help us all. This is what we do. As Council members, we need to put the welfare of the family above our own ethics."

The pizza burned on the way down, so I took a swig of soda. "Sorry. Let me explain my position. Hell and no. You want me to help an abusive drunk find the woman and child who ran in the middle of the night to escape him? No. Good on her for getting away. I'm sure the child's life is better without him."

"His son is an adult now. It isn't as though you'd be endangering a child," Gran said.

"As the only person in this room who has never met her father, I can tell you I'd much rather live out my life not knowing than be confronted with an abusive drunk. What is his son supposed to do with this crazy old guy on his doorstep?

"And don't even try to backpedal. I've heard the way you've been referring to this Bracken guy. He's rich and nuts. You want the son to deal with some random weirdo he doesn't know trying to step back into the role of his father—a role he abandoned for a bottle? No. I'm not sacrificing someone else's peace and safety to make my or anyone else's life easier." I shrugged. "You two can be as disappointed as you want. As over a decade of avoiding this job has shown, I can ignore your disapproval just fine."

"You act like your grandmother and I are heartless, unconcerned about taking advantage of others." Mom stood, folded her arms across her chest, and moved to the large windows overlooking the ocean. "We're trying to keep innocents from being killed. We have a sorcerer, one in this family." She paused, shoulders tense and high. "Sorcerers and their demons create chaos and bloodshed. The more pain and suffering, the better."

Gran stared into the fire. Like Mom, she appeared defeated before we'd even started. Guilt ate at me. If I'd joined when they'd first asked, we might not have a sorcerer. We might have been able to divert the wicche when they'd first turned to black magic on their journey to sorcery.

"You know what? I know a half-demon. I did a job for him a little while ago. Maybe he can help us." It was worth a try.

Gran looked positively scandalized. "You did a reading for a demon?" She glanced over her shoulder at Mom. "Did you know about this?"

"Stop. I said a half-demon. He was a decent guy looking for his wife. A full demon had abducted and imprisoned her. I charged him an exorbitant amount of money to find her."

"And did you?" Gran asked.

I finished my pizza. "I'll try not to take offense at that. He ended up sending me ten times the agreed-upon fee, so he doesn't hate me." I looked at my phone, thinking. "Not sure how to contact him, though."

"How did he contact you in the first place?" Mom asked.

He'd busted in on a reading and started talking to me in my head, but I wasn't about to tell them that. They'd freak out. "That won't work. Let me think." I swiped open my phone and went into my money transfer app. I found his payment and clicked on it. The app sent me to the screen to send him money. Okay. I sent him one cent and in the message field, I asked him to contact me and gave him my phone number.

I put down the phone and finished the soda. "I'll let you know if he responds. Now what?"

"There's nothing we can do about the child until we know who the killer is, which requires your demon," Mom said. "And the wolves?" She threw her hands up. "How did they become our problem?"

"We haven't had a connection to them since Bridget." Gran pointed at me. "Now this one has a wolf driving her around and building her deck. If you want to know why a Corey vision includes wolves, I don't think we have to look too far for an answer."

"I don't think I like your tone," I said. "The real problem in that part of the vision was the vampire."

Both women gasped. "Vampire?" Mom repeated. "What vampire?"

"The man at the end. He called the tan wolf to him. His fangs glistened in the moonlight."

Mom turned to Gran. "Did you see a man? I didn't see a man, only wolves."

Gran shook her head. "No man."

That was concerning. "Okay, let me start at the beginning and tell you exactly what I saw. You guys let me know if what you experienced was different."

I went back over it all with them and was glad I did. They were missing parts, but what I found more interesting were the things they heard and saw that I didn't. It was my vision. How were they experiencing things I wasn't?

In the first part with the child coloring, they saw a woman in the window behind the child waving into the forest. In the second part, they saw a sign reading Post Creek Roadhouse over the bar. In the section of the vision related to me, they saw multiple flaming arrows hit the side of the cannery. And in the last chapter, they didn't see Gran. They saw a woman dead on the patio but couldn't tell who she was. They recognized the back patio, though, and assumed that was the problem. Gran would have a visitor who died.

Mom went to Gran and held her hand.

"Remember," I warned them, "this wasn't like one of my normal visions. I think this is what we together as a Council need to work to stop." I went to my grandmother and took her other hand. "Now you know to be wary of anyone suggesting you have tea together out there." I gestured with my free hand toward the back windows. "Forewarned is forearmed and all that."

Gran held on to us both and stood. "I need to think about this. You girls go on now." She gripped my mom's hand. "Are you going to see Sylvia?"

"Yes," Mom responded. "Right now."

Gran nodded. "Good. Give me some time. I'll sit with her this afternoon." She walked down the hall, looking more frail than I'd ever seen her.

"Am I dropping you off?" Mom asked.

"Nope. You're taking me with you. I need to see Aunt Sylvia."

19

I Was Going to Need a Nap After This

Mom and I were quiet on the drive over, both dreading what we were going to find. Sylvia was alone in her room, a large spray of flowers on the table beside her. Mom's hand flew to her heart as she crossed the room to her sister. Taking Sylvia's hand, Mom's lips twitched with a healing incantation.

I wanted to wait until Mom was done and no longer holding Aunt Sylvia's hand before I took one in mine.

A nurse walked in and seemed surprised to see us. "Well, isn't this nice. It's good to have visitors." She checked Sylvia's vitals, did a round with the pressure cuff, and made notes on the white board near the door. "You should let her hear your voices. I think it helps."

"I thought her family would be here with her," I said, pulling up a chair. "I mean besides us."

"They were," she said. "Her husband and daughters." She looked between Mom and me. "You're family too?"

Mom nodded. "I'm her sister and this is my daughter, her niece."

"It was strange. I couldn't get them to leave the room for

coffee or breakfast, and then they up and left, one by one. She's been here by herself for hours now."

A code blue announcement came over the loudspeaker and the nurse hurried off.

"I don't understand," Mom began. "Why would they all leave her like this?"

The door opened and Calliope hurried in. When she saw us, she stuttered to a stop and then burst into tears, running to hug my mom.

"Auntie Sybil, it was so awful," she moaned, a tiny trembling thing in Mom's embrace.

"What happened?" Mom asked.

Cal sniffled, trying to stem the tide. "We don't know. She went to her room to get ready for work. Dad stopped to say goodbye and then I heard him shout. I was in the kitchen, making us breakfast. I ran and found Dad picking her up off the floor. He put her on the bed and held a hand over her head, casting a healing spell. He tried so hard, but nothing worked."

Sylvia's husband was a healer and a damned good one.

"What did your dad say he felt with her?" I asked.

Cal flinched at my question. She must not have noticed me. "Arwyn, it's so good of you to come. I know how busy you are at the gallery. Mom'd really appreciate that." She gave my mom one fierce hug and then stepped back, wiping at her tearstained face. "What did you ask—oh, Dad." She shook her head. "He said he couldn't reach her. He didn't sense anything broken or ruptured. He believes she's cut off from herself and therefore him."

She grabbed my mom's hand. "I've never seen him so upset. You know how much he adores Mom."

"Where is everyone? Why is Syl alone?" Mom asked.

Tears sprang to Calliope's eyes again. "Serena had to run to work and I pushed Dad out the door. He was so upset, I was afraid he'd make himself sick. I told him to try to rest, that I'd sit with her. It took some convincing. Once I was alone with Mom, though, I just kept thinking about how none of us could do without her. I was a sobbing mess." She wiped at her face again. "You wouldn't think I'd have any tears left in my body."

Mom rubbed her shoulder and gave her another hug.

"I decided to go to the chapel to ask the Goddess to intervene." Cal checked her watch and blinked. "Oh my goodness; I didn't realize I'd been gone so long." She leaned over Aunt Sylvia and kissed her cheek. "I'm sorry I left you alone. Look who's here, though." She held her mother's hand and summoned some fake cheer. "Auntie Sybil and Arwyn are here for you, Mom. We all love you so much. Please come back to us."

When Cal broke down again, Mom walked her out of the room.

Once they were gone, I pulled off a glove and took my aunt's hand. The pressure was immediate. I couldn't breathe. A weight was sitting on my chest, stealing my air. Voices swirled around in my head, racing each other, overlapping. I couldn't separate them, couldn't breathe. Explosions went off in my head. I needed air. The voices made me dizzy, racing faster and faster. And then I was able to tease out one phrase that got louder and softer as it moved in close before slingshotting away again, the words creating a Doppler Effect of sound. *Just die already, you sanctimonious bitch.* I almost recognized the whispered voice. Almost.

As it all went dark, my body starved for air, a deep, guttural voice silenced the others. *And who do we have here?* The scent of sulfur was the last thing I noticed before I was out.

When I came to, my head was on the side of the bed, pounding so horribly, I felt like my brains were dripping out of my ears. Stomach clenching and spinning, I was on my feet and dashing for the toilet.

Once my stomach contents had been emptied, I stayed hunched over the bowl, panting. I had to get out of here. I tried to stand up, but my head was too messed up, my balance gone.

Falling back, I sat on the tile, my head resting against the wall. Pulling on my gloves, I took out my phone and texted Mom.

> Me: I need to go home. Can you take me?

It took a while, but she finally responded.

> Mom: I was counting on you to stay with Sylvia. I can't take you home right now. Calliope needs me.

I tried to get up again, but my head swooped and I was back on my butt. Damn it. I could call for a ride, but how would I get out of this bathroom and make it to the front of the hospital?

I couldn't believe I was tapping his name, but he was the only person I could think of who knew what was going on and wouldn't ask too many questions.

"Hello?" Declan answered, his voice deep and comforting.

"I'm sorry. I need your help again." I paused, my stomach rolling.

"What do you need?" The sound of the surf in the background helped to settle me.

"Can you pick me up from the hospital?"

"Are you hurt?"

I heard him moving and it settled my writhing stomach even more. When he gunned the engine and spun out, I breathed easier. "I'm here visiting my aunt."

"Oh." His voice lost its urgency. "That's right. You need a pick up?"

"Yes, but more than just a ride. I read my aunt to try to find out what happened to her." I blew out a breath and tried to stand. This time, I tipped so hard to the left, I almost landed in the toilet. "We have a sorcerer in the family, one whose demon attacked my aunt. He did quite a number on me and I'm now in the bathroom of my aunt's room, unable to stand up. I need you to find me, help me up, and then get me the hell out of here."

When I heard tires squealing again, I knew he understood the situation.

"Room number—never mind. I'll find you," he said. *Click.*

While I waited, I tried to get my eyes to focus so I could text my uncle. There was no way he had left my aunt's side of his own free will. That demon was pushing her family away. It wanted her alone.

> Me: Uncle John, I'm with Aunt Sylvia right now but need to leave. Can you come back and sit with her? I'm worried about her being left alone.

> John: Alone? The girls were staying with her while I

> John: ...

> John: I don't remember

> John: I'm on my way right now

> Me: Thanks

Eventually, I heard the hospital room door open. Shit. If this was someone sent to finish off Sylvia, I had to get in there. I was just getting onto my hands and knees when the bathroom door pushed open a few inches.

"Arwyn?"

"Oh, thank goodness." I was listing to the left again when Declan pulled me to my feet and kept an arm wrapped around me so I didn't fall. My legs were shaky, but I could lean well enough.

"Can you walk or should I carry you?"

I looked up at the concern in his voice. He really did have very kind brown eyes. "Can you hold on to me while I use the sink?"

He shuffled me over and then wrapped both arms around

my middle. I did my glove shuffle, leaning forward and turning on the tap, letting the cool water run over my hands. When I brought them to my face, I let out a sigh. The throbbing in my head, while still painful, was no longer debilitating. I let my head fall back against his chest and just breathed.

"Better?"

Nodding, I tapped his arm. "I think I can stand now."

He let go but kept both hands hovering by my sides, ready to grab me if I started to go down, which I appreciated.

I put my gloves back on and opened the bathroom door. Uncle John was leaning over the bed, gently kissing Sylvia.

"Hi." This was going to look mighty odd.

John glanced over. The smile that had appeared at my greeting disappeared when he saw who was standing behind me.

John stared a moment too long, during which I was sure he was checking Declan's aura. "Wolf?"

I walked unsteadily toward John, still listing to the left, and then Declan was there, holding my elbow, keeping me upright and pointed in the right direction.

When I got to John, he hugged me while Declan moved to stand against a wall, ready to help but trying not to intrude.

John whispered, "Did you read her?"

I nodded. "That's why I was sick in the bathroom. First, though, this is Declan. He's a wolf, yes, but also a good man who's my friend."

Declan stood a little taller.

"And, Declan, this is Sylvia's husband, my Uncle John."

The men nodded to one another, neither comfortable.

I turned to Declan, still holding on to John. "Would you mind waiting for me in the hall? I need to speak with my uncle for a minute."

He nodded once more and then left. I knew he'd hear everything we said, but I doubted John did. As Mom had mentioned earlier, we didn't associate with the wolves, especially after Aunt Bridget married one and everything went to hell.

"How are you really doing?" I asked.

His expression crumpled. "What are we going to do? I can't find anything wrong with her. I don't know how to heal her."

Sylvia and John were two of the kindest people I'd ever met in my life. I'd accuse myself of sorcery before either of them. I whispered in his ear, "We have a sorcerer in the family."

He jolted in shock, shaking his head. "No. Not another one."

"I held her hand. It's true."

He took my gloved hand in his. "You saw?"

"Someone did this to her. Mom, Gran, and I are working on it. Don't do anything, okay?"

Tilting his head, he studied me. "You took your spot on the Council?"

I nodded. "Don't confide in anyone. We don't know who the sorcerer is."

His brow furrowed. "But then why did you tell me?"

I kissed him on the cheek. "Because if there's one thing I know in this world, it's that neither you nor Aunt Sylvia would ever turn to black magic, let alone sorcery."

He patted my back. "Well, that's something anyway." When I started to move away, he caught my hand. "You'll tell me, won't you? When you know?"

"I will. In the meantime, though, talk to her. Remind her of your lives together. Tell her how much you love her. She's got a lot of hurtful words circling in her head right now. You need to drown them out with true words of devotion."

He squeezed my hand and then let it drop. Pulling up a chair, he sat down and took her hand, holding it against his lips. "I was just thinking about the time we met," he murmured. "Do you remember that?"

While he reminded Sylvia of their lives together, I made my way to the door, happy when I reached the handle without tipping over. Happier still that Declan was there when I opened the door.

"Good job," he murmured. "Hold on and we'll get you out of here."

I didn't know where Mom and Cal were, but Sylvia was covered and I needed to get home and crawl into a soft bed in a dark and quiet studio.

20

You Might Want to Look Away

The drive was thankfully quick and uneventful. I kept my eyes closed. Monterey's weather was mild year-round, but the May sun was still bright. Declan loaned me his sunglasses, which helped.

"Declan!" The shout came from the gallery steps as soon as Declan turned off the truck's engine. "Where have you—oh, Ms. Corey."

I squinted my eyes open and found Juan. "Sorry. I got hurt and called him for a ride. It's my fault he wasn't here."

"Oh, okay. I'm glad he was able to help you."

There was a charged silence between the men and then Declan said, "Let me get her inside and then I'll get back to work. I can stay until the sun goes down." He walked me to the front door.

Juan followed us. "Yeah, okay. You're doing a good job back there, but we're concerned about timing."

"Understood."

"We're taking off now. We'll see you tomorrow," Juan said. "And I hope you're feeling better soon, Ms. Corey."

"Thank you. I appreciate that." Once we'd entered the gallery, the pounding in my head lessened.

Declan kicked the door closed and then picked me up.

"I'm okay. I can walk." But this was nice.

"I know you can, but no one's watching and you're still unsteady. I don't want you falling down your stairs when you start tipping to the left again."

He juggled me to open the studio door and then he was taking the stairs two at a time up to my loft. I'd expected him to just drop me on the bed, but he was incredibly gentle, laying me down and then pulling off my sneakers. When I rolled to the side, he flipped my comforter over to cover me.

"I'll close your shutters. It'll help with light and sound."

"Thanks," I said, burrowing in. "Oh, can you make sure the front door is locked?"

"You bet," he replied, jogging down the stairs.

I hadn't expected to fall asleep, not with my head pounding and Declan hammering, but I did.

Declan parks his truck next to other cars and trucks out in the middle of nowhere. He followed the directions he was given to the Big Sur Pack grounds. He's late, though, wanting to get as much of the deck finished as he could. He figures Logan and his buddies want to scare him. They'll be disappointed.

He puts his keys, wallet, and phone in his glove box before stripping out of his clothes, slamming the door and shifting to his wolf form.

Unlike with bitten wolves for whom the transformation is painful and lengthy, Declan, a born Quinn wolf, shifts with a thought. One minute a man, the next a wolf. He dances from foot to foot, shaking his fur, shrugging off the magical buzz along his limbs.

Leaving the parking lot, he trots onto pack land, feels the power of it thrum through his system. A pack has a magic all its own and this land recognizes he is not pack.

He sees a cabin a hundred yards to the north and heads in that direction, alert to the sounds around him. It's unnaturally quiet and he begins to doubt he'll make it to the cabin before they attack.

When he's halfway between the truck and the cabin, his ears flick back and forth. Softly, growing steadily louder, is the thumping of many paws hitting the ground. He stops and turns. It was bound to happen. With the Alpha's insecure posturing and Declan showing up late, they've clearly decided he needs to be taught a lesson.

He runs, tearing off across the open field. A dark forest looms ahead. A crack punches through the rhythmic pounding of his pursuers' paws tearing up the field. A figure silhouetted in the distance holds a rifle.

He sprints to the edge of the forest closest to him, bounding over a fallen, rotting tree, another crack ringing out and shredding the bark of a tree to Declan's right. Weaving between the trunks, circling in the forest, he plans to come up behind the shooter.

Insanity. That's what this is.

When he's had to deal with other packs, he's kept his head down and left town as quickly as possible. He intended to do the same here, but something's itching inside him, a need to show them exactly who they're dealing with. The reaction is new and unusual. He's tired of keeping his head down. Tired of moving on because some puffed-up wolf is threatening him. Unbidden, an image of Arwyn, expression defiant, green and purple curls blowing in the wind, comes to mind and he has a hard time shoving it aside.

He doesn't want to be the Alpha, doesn't want to kill wolves in a dominance match. But, he realizes, he doesn't want to leave her more. So, fine. He'll engage. He'll meet the challenge. It's time to stop moving on.

Wolves are crashing through the woods behind him. Sloppy. They've been ordered to hunt down and kill an outsider but not trained to pursue silently? Irresponsible.

Noiselessly, he pads through the soft underbrush, moving up behind the gunman. The man is standing too close to the edge of the woods. Stupid. His desire for a speedy escape makes him that much easier to take down.

The pack has made the turn, their loud pursuit headed his way. The shooter turns to his left as Declan slinks up on his right. The scent of fear is intoxicating as Declan emerges from the woods, leaping to take down Logan, the pack's Alpha.

The rifle is knocked out of his hands as he goes down. Declan's claws tear into the Alpha's shoulders; his jaws snap around his neck. One hard shake of Declan's head and Logan would be dead.

The ground jolts as the pack materializes from the forest, alert, heads down, muscles bunched. They form a semi-circle around the outsider threatening their Alpha.

Declan growls, deep and low, the sound vibrating through the pack lands. He's angry. Not only because they intended to kill him but because their weak Alpha has failed to train them properly. They've allowing a drifter to dismantle the pack. They should have attacked as one. Yes, their Alpha would be dead, but so too would Declan.

He doesn't blame the wolves. He blames the Alpha squirming beneath him, trying to shift but too scared to complete the transformation. He sent his wolves to do his dirty work while he hid behind a rifle.

Declan could leave. Should leave. Can't understand why he hasn't already. This isn't a well-trained pack. These are humans who get furry once a month and run around. They haven't allowed their dual natures to become one.

It's a dangerous practice, othering their wolf. Their second nature will make itself known in moments of great emotion. If one has not learned to listen to his wolf, to accept him as part of the whole, accidents happen and innocents are hurt.

Declan gives a little shake and draws blood, reprimanding Logan for being such a piss-poor Alpha who is more of a peacock than a wolf.

Anger, frustration, and perhaps something else gets the better of him. Before he can think too deeply about it, Declan shifts in front of the pack, picks up the rifle, and swings for Logan's head, knocking him out. He snaps the weapon in two over his knee.

The reaction is immediate. Some drop to the ground, cowering. Some roll to their backs, showing their bellies in submission. A few growl and snap their powerful jaws. Two, however, leave the rest of the pack to flank Declan, each standing on either side, their teeth bared at the other wolves.

"I won't punish you for following your Alpha's orders. But know," he says, allowing those razor-sharp claws of his to slide from his fingertips, "if you ever try to come for me again, there will be no second chance."

One of the growlers who has yet to submit to Declan takes a step forward.

"Kill him!" Logan grounds out.

The wolf charges and Declan's powerful arm swings, his claws tearing *through the wolf's neck. Blood sprays and the decapitated wolf's body drops beside Logan. Two more wolves take a step forward, their legs tensed beneath them. Declan, though, doesn't have the heart to kill more. He stares them down with the force of his will, the authority of the one true Alpha, the Quinn.*

When they finally submit and hit the ground, Declan nods.

Shifting once more, Declan lopes off toward his truck. His two guards stay with him, putting themselves between Declan and the pack. He goes to the passenger side of the truck and shifts, opening the door, pulling out his clothes, and dressing. The wolves stay with him, sitting on either side, facing the field, not Declan.

He steps into his boots, not bothering to tie them, and walks around the front of the truck. "Thanks, guys, but I'm not your Alpha." He glances back over at the meadow. None are coming. "If you can, find another pack. This one isn't training you. It won't protect you. It's broken."

He climbs in and starts the engine, wiping blood from his face. When he spins the truck around, a shot cracks the air, sending glass flying.

I shot up in bed. What time was it? I checked the clock as I jumped out of bed and ran down the stairs. Maybe it was just a nightmare and I'd find Declan still working on my deck.

I flung open the back door and found a tennis ball sitting in the middle of my beautiful, partially completed deck. "Declan!" I ran down the deck and around the side of the cannery. Tools gone. Truck gone.

Smacking my pockets, I located my phone and called. Voicemail. *Damn it.* "Declan, it's me. Please call me as soon as you can." The full moon reflected on the water and I remembered. "When you're done. If you can."

I could see and chat with Charlie and Herbert again. He'd completed a third of the deck, understanding the rest wasn't as urgent. He'd even changed the line of the deck so it wasn't a long, straight rectangle along the ocean side of the gallery. He'd made the edge rounded, with dips cut into the wood that were designed to cradle my tentacles. He'd created exactly what I needed, but I'd been too busy being pissed that he'd questioned my abilities to appreciate it. Jeez, sometimes I was a real asshole.

And now I might not be able to tell him how amazing his design was, depending on the path of that bullet.

On my way back in, lost in thoughts of claws and guns, I scooped up Wilbur's ball and flung it out into the ocean. Stopping just inside the door, I pressed the button, lifting the shutters. I needed to see and hear the ocean.

I went straight to the kitchen, donned thin rubber baking gloves, and took out my mixing bowls. No more sleep for me. The phone was in the middle of my worktable, the ringer turned all the way up as I willed it to ring.

I was spooning batter into a muffin tin when my phone pinged. It wasn't a ring, but I'd settle for a ping. Wiping my gloves on my apron, I dove for the phone, opening my text app. Nothing. I went to email. Nothing. What the hell had pinged?

Then I saw a little red *one* in the corner of my cash app. I tapped it open and found a one cent transfer from Dave with an attached note reading, *Why?*

What did *why* mean? Oh, right. I'd asked him to contact me. Jeez, demons were the worst. I transferred a penny and wrote back, *Because we have a sorcery problem in the family and I could use your help identifying the sorcerer.*

Again?

Yes, fine. You're right. Coreys have a predisposition for the dark arts. Sick burn. Can you please help us? We will, of course, pay you.

Hello, Arwyn. This is Maggie. Thank you for helping Dave rescue me and he will, of course, help you in return. I just got a grudging nod, so it's decided.

Thank you! And I'm really glad he found you. In case he didn't tell you, he was out of his mind with worry.

If you want me to help you, I suggest you shut up.

Fair enough. No more penny messages from me. I replaced the phone in the center of the table and finished filling the muffin pans. Okay, come on, Declan. It's your turn to check in.

I was pulling my second batch from the oven when the seabirds started making a racket. I looked out the windows at the dark blue-gray sky and darker water. The sun would be rising soon. Pinpoints of light moved across the water. Fishing boats heading out for the day.

Mug empty, I was reaching for the teapot when I heard heavy boots on the deck. The pot clattered back to the table when I dropped it and ran. I rounded the door and there he was. Alive. I flew to him and jumped into his arms. Legs wrapped around his waist, I turned his head this way and that, looking for blood.

"Whatcha doing?"

"I saw the rifle, heard the shot and breaking glass."

"Ah, you got all that, huh?" He laced his hands together under my butt so I wouldn't fall. He tilted his head, trying to get a better look at my expression. "You saw what I did?"

"I heard you warn them and then I saw you defend yourself when that wolf attacked anyway."

"Yeah. Not his fault. He was following his Alpha's commands. I had to do it. Had to take one out so they'd stop. I didn't want…" He turned to the ocean and watched the seagulls fly in circles around the fishing boats, his expression a mixture of sadness and guilt.

21

Muffins Alfresco

"Okay," I said, smacking his shoulders. "My exuberance at finding you alive has now been played out. Let me down."

He chuffed out a laugh and put me down on the deck.

"By the way, I love this." I tapped my foot against the gray planks. "What is it, though? This doesn't feel like wood."

Reaching over, he pounded his fist on the rail. "It looks like wood, but it's a manmade composite that's waterproof. No more rotting lumber. The ocean can splash up against it all day long and it'll look just as good fifty years from now as it does today."

Nice. "And you gave me these perfect cutouts for my tentacles." I shook my head. "Brilliant. Can I still nail them to these planks?"

"You can," he said, "but I don't recommend it. The deck'll be fine, but your tentacles will start to rust and rot with the holes made by nails. I'd recommend a boating epoxy. Something specifically made to adhere in saltwater. And then once they've been placed, you can decide if you want a railing to go around them or if we should keep the railing breaks."

Nodding, I waved him in. "Good call. Let's see where we are

after the tentacles are attached." Hopefully, I'd finally be able to finish sealing the current tentacle and start a new one today.

"Something smells great in here," he said, nose tilted up.

"This is what happens when I can't sleep." I grabbed two muffins. "In celebration of you not being dead, I offer you the classic lemon blueberry or what I like to call a Neapolitan. It has a chocolate bottom, a vanilla bean top, with a strawberry compote filling."

Hands on his hips, he studied his choices. "I'm going to surprise absolutely no one by saying I'll have both, please."

"That was, of course, the correct answer." I placed two muffins on a plate with a napkin. "Would you like coffee, tea, milk? What'll you have?"

"A tall glass of cold milk sounds great." He scratched his beard and scanned the artwork I had out.

"You got it." I poured the milk and then handed him both the plate and the glass.

He motioned to the couch with eyebrows raised in question.

"Let's eat alfresco. I'll be right there." I grabbed a lemon blueberry muffin, a napkin, and filled my teacup.

When I stepped out, I found him leaning against the rail, a glass balanced on one side of him, the plate on another. He took a big bite, eating half the muffin in one go.

"Mmmm, delicious," he said once he'd swallowed.

I put my napkin-wrapped muffin down on the deck with my teacup beside it, and then sat down, my legs dangling off the edge. The rail that ran halfway between the deck and the top rail was exactly the right height for my breakfast. Perfect.

I leaned over the rail and looked down. "Good morning, Cecil! Charlie, Herbert, it's lovely to see you again." Cecil's tentacle splashed at the water's surface. It was high tide, so I was only able to see the tops of Charlie and Herbert's stars, but I was sure they heard me. The waves splashing off the posts were leaving droplets on my shoes. Luckily, I was in too good of a mood to care. New deck and not dead new friend. It was a good day.

"Oh my God," Declan moaned.

When I looked up, he had his eyes closed and was chewing. His enjoyment tickled fizzy bubbles in me.

"You're a baking artist too. Those were amazing," he said before downing his milk.

"Oh, all right. You can have more." I gestured to the door. "They're cooling inside. And there's more milk in the fridge."

He'd moved back into the studio at the offer of muffins, but I knew he'd heard the rest. When he returned with two more muffins and a full glass, he sat beside me on the deck.

"How much are you going to charge for these things?" He took a normal sized bite of the lemon blueberry and closed his eyes again.

"I haven't worked out a pricing schedule yet. I'm thinking five, though. They're oversized muffins with big tops. Of course, you just demolished one in two bites, so maybe I'm wrong."

"Five's fair and I'm not your average customer."

"You got that right." I broke off a piece of muffin and popped it in my mouth. Mmm, good. Just the right amount of bright tartness to complement the blueberry. I took a sip and then balanced my cup on the rail.

"I love the soft weathered gray you chose for the decking."

"Good," he said, starting on the second—well, fourth— muffin. "When they didn't have exactly what you asked for at the lumberyard, I started looking around. I know I should have checked with you first, but you were pissed off at me at the time, so I went for it. I knew what you'd planned to do with the tentacles, so I wanted the deck to blend in, to almost disappear, so your tentacles would stand out."

I thought about that for a moment. "You built this gorgeous deck, but purposely designed it to fade into the background so my art would shine." I turned, throat tight. "Thank you for that."

"Sure. And I'm glad I guessed your height right. I wanted the middle rail to hit you just right, so you could sit like this and talk with your friends."

I took another bite of muffin and turned to watch him finish off the second glass of milk. He was lighter now. Some of the darkness he'd carried with him from the pack grounds had slid off him. When he grinned, I couldn't stop myself from grinning back.

"Are you charming me?" I asked. "Is that what this is? Charm?"

His eyes crinkled at the corners. "I don't know. I am pretty charming, though, so probably."

Shaking my head, I grabbed the top rail and pulled myself up. "Okay, breakfast is over." I crumpled up my napkin, going back into the gallery with Declan following. I hesitated to cause him pain, especially since he seemed to be feeling better, but I needed to know. The bloodsucker in my vision hadn't been in last night's dream. Had Declan's decision not to run changed the outcome or were the events in the vision still to come? "I'm sorry to have to ask, but could you tell me exactly what happened last night? I woke up when Logan shot at you. Was that the end? Did I miss something?"

He let out a deep breath. "Can I ask you something first?"

I waited.

He pointed to the water painting. "This is someone drowning? Is that right?"

Retracing my steps, I studied the painting with him. "Yes. I saw a young woman with a man on the beach. It was late at night. She was happy and in love. She looked up at him and the face he showed her was not the one she'd seen before, the one she'd fallen in love with. This one was filled with rage and disgust, a kind of—I don't know—lust for violence.

"She froze when she saw it, recognized it, and was unable to process the change. He grabbed her by the neck and dragged her into the water. She kicked, scratched, punched, but he was just too big, too strong, so she was no match for him. He held her under, choking the life out of her."

"Why?" Declan's voice had taken on a tone, as though he wasn't just asking about this murder, but about all the horrible things we did to one another every day.

I shook my head, unable to answer the unspoken question. "Is there a reason that would justify what he did? He did it because he wanted to, because he could. I think she's one of my cousins. Pearl was maybe twenty. Apparently, she didn't come home after going out on a date with a new boyfriend. Her mom hadn't met him yet. The relationship was all very secret and romantic." I flopped down on the couch and closed my eyes. Poor thing. Her life was just beginning.

Declan sat down beside me. "That's not romance."

Rolling my head on the back cushion, I opened my eyes to find Declan staring back at me.

"Hiding who you're seeing isn't romantic," he repeated. "It means at least one of you is unsure, embarrassed, ashamed, cheating. You know how hard it is to hold in good news. You just jumped on me and gave me a hug, checking my head for bullet wounds and scratches when you found out I wasn't dead." The lightness of a few minutes ago was gone. This topic had hit a nerve. "Secrecy is about having someone on tap when you want them and then being able to dump them without getting your hands dirty. No one will ask, *Hey, Arwyn, how's the new guy*, if no one knows he exists."

"Or doesn't exist anymore," I added.

"Exactly."

Closing my eyes again, I sighed and became one with the couch. Maybe I'd just stay here all day. "Sometimes it really gets to me." I scrubbed my hands over my face. "Why can't I have visions of happy people living their best lives? Puppies and kittens chasing toys?"

"Happy people don't need your help," he said simply.

I opened one eye and pinned him with it.

He shrugged. "I get that it sucks, but the desperate, scared, hurt; they're the ones that need help, not the happy ones with their lives going great. I don't understand it, but you can connect with people who are lost and alone, who would disappear without a trace, if you hadn't found them"—he tapped my temple—"in here." He adopted my posture, scrunched down on the couch, his head against the back cushion. "These people aren't dying alone. They have you and that makes you pretty damned special."

"Charm. You're doing that charm thing again, aren't you?"

"Who me? Nah. I'm just trying to sweet talk my way into more baked goods."

Chuckling, I tipped over and rested my head on the arm of the couch. "I'm so tired."

"Me too," he rumbled. "Listen, Phil won't be here for at least another hour. Let's just take a nap until then."

Yes, please. When I sat up, I saw him skooched down, legs crossed at the ankles, arms crossed over his chest, eyes closed. He almost looked restful, if you didn't notice the furrowed brow. He was still thinking about last night, even after successfully steering the conversation away from it. What had happened?

He opened one eye and stared back. "You're thinking awfully loud. Come here." He patted his chest. "Let's get some shut-eye."

I leaned over, rested my head on his chest, and felt myself begin to relax. When he wrapped a heavy arm around me, I felt safe and secure as I never did. Within moments, I was out.

22

Does Everyone Have a Cousin Who Can Get You What You Need?

"Arwyn?" I felt a hand slide from shoulder to elbow. "Arwyn, the detective is back."

I blinked and found Declan's handsome face looking back at me. Wait. I thought… I sat up and looked to my left. Nope. He wasn't serving as my pillow anymore. When I looked back at him, he was grinning.

"I got up about seven hours ago, when I heard Phil's truck pull up."

Pushing my curls out of my face, I said, "And I slept through that?"

"You did. You were out." He grabbed my gloved hand and pulled me up. "Come on, sleepyhead. You have a visitor."

I checked the time on my phone. "Eight hours? I napped for eight hours?"

"It probably stops being a nap at that point, but you did. Quite soundly. I checked on you a couple of times to make sure you were still breathing. One thing, though. You might want to brush your teeth before you talk to her."

I slapped a hand over my mouth, mortified. When he started laughing, I elbowed him in the stomach, a move I knew he barely felt. I, on the other hand now had a sore elbow. I ran to the half bath I had in the corner by the kitchen. Face red, I brushed my teeth and tongue.

Emerging a few minutes later, I found Detective Hernández in the studio, standing in front of the same painting that had caught Declan's interest. Her dark curly hair was tightly pulled back into a bun at the nape of her neck and she was wearing what was apparently a uniform for her: black trousers, a white button-down shirt, and today a slightly rumpled brown herringbone jacket.

"Hey, I was planning to call you today."

Hernández tore her focus away from the painting. "Why's that?

"Vision. He's going to take another one, or maybe already did. A little girl."

The detective pulled out her notebook and started scribbling. "Did you get any names?"

"No. No one spoke. Her house has a backyard that turns into woods as well. She was little, younger than Christopher. She was coloring on the back porch. Heard something, I think. She'd been concentrating on the coloring book and then looked over her shoulder into the woods. Whatever she saw there delighted her. She stood, left the coloring behind, and walked toward the woods, joy and wonder written all over her."

I waited for Hernández to finish writing. "She may have had a mother or some adult woman looking out the window and waving at whoever was drawing the girl away from safety and deeper into the forest."

"May have? You didn't see her?"

I shook my head. "It's like noticing something in your peripheral vision. I had an impression of her. My focus was on the little girl because it felt like she was being lured by Christopher's killer." Also, I never saw the woman. Gran and Mom did. I didn't want to get into a shared vision explanation, so this was the simplest story.

"No names, huh? Okay, what did the little girl look like?"

"Latina, I think. She was dressed in a pretty, soft yellow dress, with white tights and white patent leather shoes. She has long, dark hair pulled back into two high braided pony-tails." I motioned to my head where they were on the little girl. "Big brown eyes, long eyelashes. She was a doll. Just a perfect, adorable little girl. The kind that makes your heart hurt."

"Any distinguishing marks that could help us identify her?" The detective waited, pen poised.

I closed my eyes and recalled the vision, trying to find anything I might have missed. I was shaking my head when I remembered. "She had a dimple—just one— in her left cheek. And a thin gold bangle bracelet on her right wrist."

"Did it look like it was made for a child or was the bracelet large on her?"

"Oh. Was she playing dress-up or was it her own jewelry? Let me think…it was hers. She was so tiny, a woman's bracelet would slide right over her hand."

"Good. Anything else?"

I shook my head. "That was all I saw. If it's already happened, see if I can visit the porch or her bedroom. Maybe I can get something there that'll help us identify him."

"I'll check and let you know." She put her notebook away and turned her attention back to the painting beside her. "There's something about this one." she said.

"Do you want to buy it?" I went to the kitchen to brew tea.

"God, no," she blurted. "Sorry," she quickly corrected herself. "I just mean it's sinister. I had a nightmare about it."

I turned at that. "You dreamt about my painting?"

She nodded, glancing at it warily. "I couldn't breathe. I was trying to break the surface but I couldn't get there. I woke up gasping for air."

Hmm, either Detective Hernández had some psychic blood in her family tree, or I'd inadvertently created a curse with the painting. As Declan hadn't woken up gasping for breath, I was hoping for door number one. Until I could be sure though, the painting was going into a cabinet.

I picked up the easel and turned it around. "There. All gone. So what's up?" I went back to the kitchen for the tea tray and then set it on the table in front of the couch.

"Tea?" When she nodded, I poured her a cup and then filled my own.

She sat on the couch, reached for the cup, and took a sip. Whereas I kicked off my sneakers and curled up in my chair, the steaming mug warming my hands.

Brooding, Hernández put down her full cup and sat silently for a moment. "It was exactly like you said, down to the anatomy drawings ripped from books and tacked to the wall." She shook her head. "Even after you told us what to expect, I still froze. A lot of the guys bolted back out to vomit. At least I gutted it out, but it was the worst thing I'd ever seen in my life."

"And hopefully it'll stay that way."

She looked confused, so I added, "I hope you never experience anything worse."

Understanding, she nodded. "How do you do it? How do you see these awful things all the time and get out of bed, create art, bake?" She shook her head, looking lost. "I've got to tell you, a couple of days ago when you were giving me a hard time, not wanting to help, I thought you were an over-the-top fake and this was all a waste of time. Now I seriously don't understand why you agreed to it."

I took a sip. "In my defense, I tried to refuse but you were super pushy." When she only waited, I tried to give her a better response. "Here's the thing: There are a lot of horrible things in the world, a lot of horrendous people who do heinous things."

"The three Hs," she murmured.

Nodding, I said, "Exactly. But there are also really amazing people who go out of their way to be kind and generous. And there are all those regular people that mostly try not to cause trouble or be assholes, although sometimes they fail at either or

things anyone's ever offered to do for me." I walked back to my chair. "I've been thinking about getting a pet to keep me company. Maybe a little kitten. I'm putting down roots here. Me and my gallery are staying put, so possibly. I'll need to think on it some more."

"I fully support the pet plan. We have the sweetest mutt. She goes running with me every morning and then snuggles with us on the couch in the evenings. But a pet's not a good replacement for a person."

I stretched out my legs and rested my feet on the coffee table. "You've already forgotten our horrible people doing heinous things conversation. A kitty is by far preferable to a psycho creep."

"There's that." She returned the notebook to her pocket and checked her watch. "Okay. I need to get back at it. Thank you for seeing me and for the muffin. I feel better."

"Good. I'm going to finish sealing my tentacle and then get started on another. Hey," I said, standing back up, "come look at my beautiful deck in progress."

When I walked her out, Declan had another third of the decking complete. "How are you doing this so fast?"

He stood, wiping his sweaty brow. "It's all framed out. All I'm doing at this point is nailing down planks." He turned and pointed to the edge. "I still need to do the rest of the cutouts for the tentacles. That takes longer. So do the railings." He scratched his beard. "I'm getting there, though."

"It looks great already," Hernández said. "I can't wait to see it with the tentacles attached."

"Soon! I want to get them all done first so they can go up at once." Hopefully, I'd freak out a couple of the fishing boats.

23

The Dreaded Three Naming

"Is it okay if I visit again?" the detective asked.

"You bet." Huh, a mundane friend. Well, she already knew a lot of what I could do, even if the wicche part was still a secret. I pointed to the end of the deck. "You can go that way. Save yourself from walking back through the gallery and the construction obstacle course. In fact, I'll walk with you. Our conversation made me realize I need a garden over here." We stepped off the dock and turned right, following the side of the cannery toward the road.

There was a dirt path by the building and then a swath of dirt patches, sand, and tufts of grass maybe ten feet wide, running from the road, alongside the cannery, and ending at the ocean. I was pretty sure the area past that was over my property line. It had tall grass, ice plants, and rocks along the water's edge.

"What do you think? What should I do with this space?"

The detective scanned left and right before staring at the huge wall itself. "I guess it depends on if you're painting a mural here."

A mural? How had I not thought of that? I moved back to take in the whole wall in context with the rest of its surroundings. "Hell yes, I'm painting a mural." I thought about it, saw it. "It'll be a continuation of the sea monster story. I'll paint the side to look like the cannery is old and deteriorating, windows broken, boards weather-beaten and rotting. I'll have tentacles bursting out of the rotting wall, climbing up the side to envelop the whole building." Yes. That would look amazing and would stop cars. They might even visit the gallery. Which meant I needed to blow some glass sculptures of octopuses for the tourists to buy. Hmm.

"Thank you," I said, absently patting her shoulder. "I love this idea."

"In that case, you don't want pretty flowers and bushes. Maybe some tall decorative grasses. Maybe just some deergrass or reedgrass. There's one that's kind of a burnt orange. What's it called? Uh…sedge! Orange sedge. The great part is decorative grasses are low maintenance, low water. Spray from the ocean would probably be enough for them, and they'd fit in with an old, overgrown feel."

"Perfect. If you know any florists or growers you'd recommend, let me know." She was looking better, less haunted. She'd found lighter thoughts to occupy her brain. Trust me, I knew how important those respites were.

"I'll ask my cousin. He's a landscaper. He'll know. I'll get back to you." She was drawing a quick sketch in her notebook and then scribbling down ideas.

"Maybe I could just hire your cousin to do the work," I began.

"Oh, no. You can hire me. I want to do this project." The gleam in her eye relieved some of the guilt I'd been feeling. Returning the notebook to her pocket, she waved as she headed back to her car.

I knew none of this was my fault. It was illogical, but there was something so—I guess—embarrassing having someone else experience even a portion of my trauma. I felt exposed and I hated it.

When I turned the corner, Declan was leaning against a rail, watching me.

"You taking a break?" Why was he looking at me with such concern?

"Yep." When I drew close, he asked, "Can I borrow your phone for a minute?"

"My phone?" I reached into my overalls pocket. "Why do you need my—hey!"

Declan grabbed it and slid it into his back pocket.

"What gives, bub?"

Before I had a chance to cause a little mayhem, he seized me around the middle and threw me over his head, right into the ocean. Having werewolf strength, he flung me far. I really only had time to think, *What the fu—Well, shit.*

With a splash, I dove deep, dolphin kicking along the bottom, startling fishes. As I was swimming back to the piers under my cannery, a certain seal with a tennis ball in his mouth swam alongside me before circling me and bolting ahead.

When I came up for air, I found my mom moving to the railing beside Declan.

"Did I just see you throw my daughter in the ocean?"

Damn, this was about to get ugly.

"Yes ma'am, you did. She was having some dark thoughts and needed a reboot," he replied, grinning down at me.

She bristled. "How in the world would you know what she's thinking?"

"More like I overheard a conversation and scented what she was feeling." Still watching me, he pointed to the finished end of the deck. "I added a rope over there to make it easier to get back up."

"Nice," I called. "I'm going to say hi to Cecil first, then I'll be up." I flipped over and swam between the posts, looking for my octopus buddy. Dang. He didn't seem to be home. Bummer. When I looped around a pier to head back, I saw movement out of the corner of my eye. It wasn't Cecil, but there was another octopus down here. *Cecil, you dog! Who are you shacking up with down here?*

I was almost out from under the deck when a tentacle wrapped around my ankle and tugged. I turned to find Cecil emerging from the sand and silt along the bottom. *You little sneak. You got me.*

His tentacle slid from my ankle as he settled once more on the ocean floor. An empty-mouthed Wilbur shot past me, making sure I hadn't forgotten our game.

Bye, guys. I'm going up. Both octopuses raised a tentacle and Wilbur shot past me again. I swam to the last post and found a thick rope with knots at handy intervals for climbing. When I go to the top, Declan was leaning over the rail, his arms extended.

"Give me your hands."

I did and he lifted me over the rail, depositing me back on the deck.

"Feel better?"

I wasn't sure if the glint in his eye made me want to punch him or kiss him, but it was definitely one of the two. "You know you can't just chuck people into the ocean," I said, feigning indignation.

"Only you," he said, strolling back to the far end of the deck and resuming his work.

"Well, really, darling, you can't go inside like that. You'll trail water wherever you go." My mom took Declan's spot. "And we really need to talk."

"Can you go in and grab a towel from the downstairs bathroom? I'm pretty sure I have one in here."

"Oh, all right, but try to wring out your hair or something while I'm gone."

"Shit, shit, shit," I chanted under my breath while I thought frantically.

Declan put down a plank and strolled back. "What's the matter? Here. Wait. Let me get that." He rolled up my hair into a long snake and then started squeezing out the water, being so gentle, I almost teared up.

I whispered, "Mom doesn't know about my tattoo, and I really don't want a lecture."

"It's your body," he whispered back. "This goes past your butt," he added, awed.

"Try telling that to her. And only when it's wet. It gets shorter as it dries. The curls pull it up."

"Here," he said, dropping his flannel shirt over my shoulders. It reached my knees.

"This'll help, but—"

"Here we go," Mom said, walking out the studio door. "I couldn't find a towel in your downstairs bath, so I took one from the upstairs."

"Perfect; thank you." I wrapped the towel around my waist and turned my back on both of them.

"I think we have this now." Mom was trying to get rid of Declan.

"I'm sure you do, ma'am, but I'm invested in the story now. I just need to see how this all plays out."

I kicked off my sneakers, unlatched the buckles on my overalls, and let them fall in a heap on the deck. I held the towel under his shirt, low on my hips, so it reached my ankles. Hey, this might actually work. "Give me a few minutes, Mom. I need to take a quick shower."

I ran past the two of them and then heard, "Arwyn Cassandra Corey! Why is there a tattoo on the bottom of your foot?"

I just kept going, ignoring Declan's laughter, straight into my bathroom. I lifted my foot and found my tattoo hiding on my heel. "Poor thing," I said, rubbing it. "You tried."

I dropped the towel and clothes, kicked them to the mat by the washing machine, and stepped into the shower. I don't know what my mom was so worked up about. I'd talked about getting a tattoo ever since I was little.

Fae blood made me stand out as a child. It wasn't just that my hair changed colors in salt water—which is how I knew my father must be ocean fae, rather than river or lake—it was that I had a swath of iridescent skin on my back. It ran from my right shoulder to my left hip before it swirled around my left thigh.

Mom used to buy me one-piece bathing suits with matching shorts. We thought it was concealed, but little Calliope saw. She was very sweet, wishing she had such pretty colors in her hair and on her skin. She thought I looked like a mermaid. She was a year younger and not a strong swimmer, so she stayed right by the shore. I, of course, was born to the water, but she looked so small and sad, I often sat at the edge of the waves so she'd have someone to talk to and play with.

She was only a year younger, but it felt like more. She was a chatterbox and loved having someone to talk with. She was the first one to notice the hair color issue. It wasn't obvious. Wet hair was generally dark. Purple and green highlights are hard to notice in wet hair. She did, though, and was so excited about having a mermaid cousin, she called the others over to see.

When a particularly large wave had knocked little six-year-old me over, my shorts drifted up for a moment and she saw my skin. I'd jumped up and ran to my mom, wanting to go home, but it was too late. She'd told them and they'd all crowded around, wanting to see. The adults shooed them away, but the damage had been done. Some of my shittier cousins had spent the next ten years making my life a misery.

I studied ancient grimoires for years, trying to find a spell to make my skin look like everyone else's. Finally, when I was fifteen, I found one that created a magical tattoo. I'd been worried I'd screw up the highly complicated spell—written in spindly, faded handwriting—and make the problem worse. I then spent weeks working on the image I wanted, perfecting, shading, painting.

When I was finally ready, I'd performed the spell while Mom was at work. I'd worried about being interrupted. I supposed I needn't have worried so much, as I'd overshot what I'd been aiming for. Instead of the octopus I'd wanted on my back, my iridescent skin enhancing the tattoo, I'd created an animated tattoo that grew bigger and smaller and moved around my body.

When I was scared, she enveloped me, tentacles wrapping around me. Today, when I was worried my mom would see her, she made herself small and hid under my foot. I'd named her Ursula.

I felt her moving while I showered, wanting to be in the water, no doubt. She was back in her usual spot now, resting almost like a backpack with one tentacle barely reaching over my right shoulder and another running down my left hip and wrapping around my thigh. The other six swirled around me, some holding on to my waist, some just resting on my back.

I dried and dressed in another long-sleeved thermal top and overalls combo before dealing with my hair. Declan was right. It was extremely long. I'd tried cutting it numerous times over the years, but it always grew back quickly to this exact length. I didn't know for sure but figured it was a fae thing and so stopped trying to change it. It was a shit ton of hair, though, so I went through lots of conditioning products, some for use in the shower, some leave-in.

After working product throughout my hair, I used my diffuser to start the drying process, blotting the dripping ends. A few minutes later, I used a soft terrycloth headband to keep the hair out of my face while it air dried the rest of the way. Long hair was a stupid amount of work.

As I knew I'd have to prove I had no tattoo on the bottom of my foot, I slid into flip-flops, grabbed a pair of gloves, and went downstairs, where I'd expected to find my mom drinking tea and staring at my home with a judgy expression. Instead, the joint was empty.

And then I heard raised voices out the back door.

24

Mom's Meltdown

"... **B**ecause I don't know anything about you and I don't like the way you look at my daughter."

Uh-oh.

"How do I look at her?" Thank goodness Declan didn't sound angry. I didn't want my mom mauled this afternoon. We had stuff to figure out.

"Like you're thinking about eating her." Mom's indignation was palpable. She wasn't used to people not jumping to do her bidding.

"It sounds like I need to do a better job of schooling my features because I would enjoy eating your daughter, but probably not in the way you mean."

I slapped a hand over my mouth. He *did not* just say that to my mother.

"Crass. The fact remains that you're some kind of itinerant worker and nowhere near good enough for my daughter. You see this big shiny gallery, the wealthy family, and the naïve artist who doesn't have enough experience with men to recognize a user when she sees one."

My mouth dropped open, anger and embarrassment making my face flame.

The deck shuddered with the intensity of his growl. *Oh shit.* I ran out the back door and stood between the two.

Declan grabbed me around the waist and picked me up, depositing me three feet to the right. Out of the splash zone.

Mom shook her head at me. "You barely know him and you're trying to protect him from me?" Yeah, she was pissed all right.

"Well, I heard the tail end of that, and you were being rude. Also, I have no desire to see my mom talk herself onto the receiving end of lethal claws."

Declan blew out a breath and moved back. "I wasn't going to hurt her."

"I'd like to see you try," she snapped back.

"Mom! Stop being a dick and wait for me inside, okay?" I wasn't sure what was going on, but this was out of line.

"I won't be spoken to like that." Spells were about to explode out of her.

I held up my hand, trying to stave off a meltdown. "Declan is out here doing his job and you're insulting him."

"Is it his job to insert himself in our conversations or to throw you off the deck?" Mom was so brittle, I thought she might crack.

"We're becoming friends." I paused, trying to figure out what was really going on. This was so out of character for her. Imperious? Sure. Ready to throw down? No way.

Behind me, I heard Declan blow out another breath. "I don't have a permanent address. Not because I'm untrustworthy or evading the law, but because I'm not a pack member. I move on before the local Alpha comes knocking."

When she just stared, her gaze hostile with a side of homicidal rage, he continued.

"I didn't grow up in a pack. My father was Alexander Quinn. He and my mother were murdered when I was a toddler. My aunt took me in and raised me in the mundane world. I didn't know what I was until I shifted the first time.

"My aunt moved us around so no one asked too many questions. After she passed away, I stayed on the road. I don't have a home or people to speak for me. I get that that makes me seem sketchy to you. I have my own money. I don't need yours or your daughter's. I like working with my hands, enjoy building furniture and the occasional deck."

"I didn't know you made furniture," I interjected. "Do you have pictures of your pieces?"

He nodded and pulled out his phone, swiping through it to find his photos. "Here you go." He handed me his phone before returning his attention to my mom. "As for today, I heard her say that a swim in the ocean usually brightens her mood. Since she seemed to need it, I tossed her in."

"These are really beautiful," I said, scrolling through. "You have a gift."

He looked over my shoulder. "Thanks."

"This headboard and footboard? I must have them." He'd carved an incredible forest scene into them. They were works of art.

"Can't have those. They were a commission and I've delivered. Besides, that set isn't right for you. If you want a bed set, let me think about it. I'll come up with a sketch and show it to you."

"Perfect," I said, excited about my future bed.

"No," Mom said. "It's not perfect. None of this is perfect!"

I turned back to Mom, handing Declan his phone. "What's really going on here? Why are you acting so crazy?"

She looked like she was about to scream and then her eyes got shiny. "Sylvia is trapped in a coma and now another Quinn wolf is sniffing around this family. Bridget disappeared, Arwyn. My sister. She married that wolf, and then he was killed and she's been on the run ever since, trying to hide herself and my niece from whatever is hunting them. Is it a wolf? This sorcerer? I can't lose you, not my daughter *and* another sister. I won't!"

Oh. I was an idiot. "Declan, would you excuse us, please."

He walked back to the end of the deck and resumed nailing in planks.

"Come on, Mom. Let's go inside." I closed the door after us and walked her to the couch. After she sat, I went to the kitchen to brew a new pot. I wanted to give her time to settle while I futzed around. I knew my mother. The loss of composure was killing her right now, especially in front of a strange wolf.

Once the pot was ready, I added two cups and carried the tray to the table. I poured hers, placed it between her cold hands, and then poured one for myself. Instead of my chair, I sat beside her on the couch.

I took a sip, put the cup down, and then turned to her. "I'm not going anywhere. This is my home." I gestured to the whole of the studio. "Look at this place. It's what I've always wanted. And this cannery; you know I've always felt a connection to this place. The gallery is my dream.

"Plus, I just took my place on the Council. You think I'm going to finally agree to that and then take off? I know Bridget is a strong wicche, a gifted one. She was supposed to be the third on the Council, but remember something, Mom. Are you listening?" When she met my gaze, I said, "She's not me."

Mom turned to look at me and then let out a breath. "No, she isn't. She's strong, you're right, but she isn't you." She shook her head, the ice starting to melt. "No one is."

"Right? And we're not going to let that demon have Aunt Sylvia. I got a hold of my demon and he said he'd come."

Mom brightened at that news. "When?"

I shrugged. "No idea, but his girlfriend promised he would, and I got the impression she'd push him if he stalled."

"Okay," Mom said, finally raising the cup to her lips. "Okay. He'll come and we'll tear Sylvia from their grip." She blinked rapidly.

"We will."

She put down her cup, looking out at the setting sun. "I should probably go. Let you get back to what you were doing."

I waved that idea away. "Stay and have dinner with me. Then if I hear back from the demon, you'll be with me and we can break him into the hospital room together."

Still emotional, she nodded and then looked over at my kitchen. "Do you have anything that resembles dinner over there?"

Hmm, good question.

There was a knock on the back door and we both turned. Declan opened it and stepped in. "I'm going to call it a day out here. If you'd like, I can run and pick up dinner." He pointed at me. "This one only had a muffin early this morning."

"Thank you," I said hurriedly, not wanting Mom to be rude again. "In fact, you should stay and eat with us."

Declan raised his eyebrows and waited a beat. "I wouldn't want to intrude."

Mom, seeming to be back in control again, exhaled and then stood, turning to Declan. "I'd like to apologize for my behavior earlier."

He shook his head. "Don't. I'm not made of glass. You didn't break anything."

Some of the stiffness left Mom's shoulders.

"How about if I get food and give you guys time to decide if you want company or would prefer to be on your own?" At my nod, Declan said, "Good," and closed the door behind him.

Mom waited a few moments and then said, "I still don't like him."

Laughing, I filled our cups with the tea still steaming in the pot.

"Why is that easel pointed at the wall?" she asked.

"It was freaking out Detective Hernández." I walked over and turned it back around.

Nodding, she said, "Oh, I see. This is Pearl's death?"

"Her murder, yes. Assuming we're right about it being Pearl." I sat down in my chair, slipped out of my flip-flops, curled my legs under me, and sipped the tea.

"Who else could it be?" She sighed and took a sip. "Poor child." She turned to me, her judgy look back in place. "And since when do you have a tattoo?"

"Who, me? Why would you think that?" I hid a smile behind my cup and then took another sip.

"Don't play with me. I saw it on the bottom of your right foot."

I put my cup down on the side table and straightened my legs, pointing the soles of my feet at her. "You know, I read somewhere that showing someone the soles of your feet—or maybe just shoes—is considered a horrible insult."

"I don't care," she countered. "Where did the tattoo go?"

"Tattoos don't just move around your body, Mom," I said, twisting my legs under me again. "And as you've seen, there's nothing on the bottom of my feet. Maybe it was a shadow or I stepped on a wet leaf or something. I'd just come out of the ocean, for goodness' sake."

Mom stared with squinty-eyed suspicion and I pretended not to notice.

"How's Gran feeling today?"

Mom gave me one last look and then let it go. For now. "She spent the day with Sylvia and John. I brought them lunches, though none of us ate. We tried to work together to push the thing squatting in her out, but we couldn't reach it. Or her, for that matter."

"I'm sorry."

"It's torturous, this waiting. Your grandmother and I are used to fixing the problems, casting the spells, banishing the evil. This time, we can't even reach the problem. We have to wait for someone else. Someone we neither know nor trust." She stood and began to pace, stopping now and then to study one of my pieces.

"What you should have that wolf make you," she finally said, "is a dining table. Where are we supposed to eat this dinner he's supposedly fetching?"

"Mom, you know he's getting us dinner and don't use the word *fetch*. It's rude. He's not a dog. And since when do you have a prejudice against wolves?"

She paused her pacing to say, "Since one became interested in you."

He was nearby. How odd that I would know that. "Shush," I whispered. "He's coming back."

His boots sounded on the deck and then he was knocking on the glass door again.

"Come in," I called. Mom was right. I needed a dining table. Hmm…

Declan brought in two large bags of food and shut the door, blocking the chilly wind off the ocean.

"Give me a minute." I moved the tentacle that had dried from yesterday but still wasn't finished. At some point, my life would return to normal and I could get back to work. I went into the pantry closet and pulled out a tablecloth—still in its package because what am I going to do with a tablecloth? My mother, who gave it to me, tutted and unwrapped it, throwing it over the worktable.

"Almost," I called and went into the gallery for the two folding chairs I had at the card table for readings. I placed them at one end of the table and then ducked into the fire room for a stool, placing it near the chairs. "*Et voilà!*"

Mom had gathered plates and utensils while Declan unpacked the bags. "I considered seafood," he explained, "but I wasn't sure if you ate that. I hope Thai works for everyone. There's shrimp in the mango salad, but I ordered pad thai with chicken, beef and broccoli, a red curry with pork, cashew beef. Uh, I skipped the calamari—"

"Good call," I said.

"But I got satay chicken and imperial rolls. Brown and white rice—I wasn't sure which you preferred—and a pork fried rice." He put down the last box from the bag and grinned. "Sound good?"

"That is a considerable amount of food for three people," Mom said.

He claimed the stool before I could, which was kind, as it wobbled. "Not if you're me. Besides, I like leftovers. It takes the guesswork out of tomorrow's lunch."

"It all sounds great," I said. "Let's eat."

25

Unexpected Visitors

Dinner was delicious, if awkward. I asked Declan about his woodworking and where he apprenticed. Mom asked him about his schooling and his plans for the future. What killed me, though, is as much as she was trying to scare him off, he just smiled and calmly answered her questions. I would have bagged up the food and left, but he had a much longer fuse than I did.

When we were done, we put the leftovers in my fridge. He was working here tomorrow anyway. There was no point in taking the food for a drive. And if some of the food fell out of the cartons and on to my lunch plate, who would be the wiser?

A knock sounded at the back door. Declan growled, clearly taken by surprise. The outdoor lights were on a motion sensor but hadn't turned on. As I didn't think Wilbur had grown hands, I flicked my fingers, casting a spell to turn on the lights.

Mom flinched, but I remembered that grumpy face. "It's okay, Mom," I said, patting her shoulder.

Declan stood and walked me to the door.

When I opened it, I realized there were three people, not one.

After a long pause during which we stared at one another, the demon said, "You asked me to come. Are you letting us in or what?" Dave, dressed in all black, stood with his arms crossed over his chest.

He wasn't the problem, though. The ridiculously good-looking vampire behind him was. And it wasn't the chiseled features, the stormy gray eyes, or the thick dark blond hair that pissed me off. It was that he and two of his bloodsucker buddies had broken into my house when I was in England, threatening to drain me dry if I didn't give them the information they wanted. Assholes.

"You, I remember," I ground out, "and there's no way I'm inviting you into my home."

"About that," he said in a perfectly polished British accent, "I do apologize for threatening you."

Declan moved up directly behind me and growled, the floorboards reverberating. "Bloodsucker," he rumbled.

"Yes," the vampire responded, "well spotted." His hand flew up in the air and was suddenly holding a tennis ball.

I had to view this around Declan's shoulder because as soon as the bloodsucker moved, Declan stepped in front of me. I patted his shoulder. Hard. And then pushed him aside. I had this.

The fancy British vampire held the ball out to me. "Was this intended for you, or shall I throw it back?"

Wilbur was out of control. I sighed. "Yeah. If you could throw it as far as possible, I'd appreciate it."

"Of course." He spun, chucked it farther than it's ever gone, and was facing forward, wiping his hands on a handkerchief in the blink of an eye. Okay. Maybe Declan had a point. I couldn't move anywhere near that fast. I'd be dead before I could spell him.

The vampire returned his gaze to mine, and I remembered too late I wasn't supposed to look a vampire in the eye, as they can mesmerize their victims. This one, though, didn't seem to be doing that. "As I believe we explained at the time of our intrusion in your lovely cottage, my wife"—he had an arm wrapped around a woman who he pulled into the light—"had been abducted, had been gone for a week, so I was beside myself with worry and, unfortunately, not at my best."

The woman elbowed him. "Apologize."

Declan crowded me again, suddenly very interested in the third person on the deck.

"I do, of course, most grievously regret frightening you." The vampire bowed his head in a strangely antiquated mea culpa. "I'm afraid I don't recall if we even introduced ourselves at the time. I'm Clive and this is my wife Sam. She was quite determined to meet you once she learned from Dave"—he patted the angry-looking demon on the shoulder—"where he was headed this evening. The lateness of our arrival is all my fault, I'm afraid."

The woman was beautiful, though her long brown hair kept flying into her face. The vampire brushed it back and held it, his hand becoming her ponytail holder. She had killer cheekbones, green eyes, and a cleft in her chin. Huh. The eyes and chin were so much like...

"Holy—" I breathed.

"Hi!" She gave me a little wave and said, "Sorry. We didn't mean to interrupt your evening. I just really wanted to meet you and thank you for the chess set."

"Mom!" How? How did I not know? How did I not make the connection?

Her smile faltered when I shouted, but she continued, "It's saved my life more than a few times. Oh, hi." She cautiously greeted my stern-looking mother while leaning more firmly into her husband.

The vampire moved so his shoulder was now blocking her from Mom and me. He was clearly concerned about our reaction to her.

"Mom, this is Sam, the woman I made the chess set for. Sam," I repeated to her. "Quinn. Who has Bridget's eyes and chin cleft."

Mom's eyes went wide and then glassy. She stepped past the men and cradled Sam's face in her hands. Both the half-demon and the vampire were on high alert. Mom wasn't paying attention, but I was. If she made one wrong move, she'd be dead. Twice.

"Are you really Bridget's?" Tears ran down Mom's face.

Sam's startled gaze darted all around before settling back on my mom. She nodded. "My mother was Bridget Corey, yes."

Mom wrapped her in a tight hug and sobbed. All these emotions weren't like her, but in her defense, she'd been dealing with a lot. She pulled Sam into the studio and turned her to me. "Look, Arwyn, she has Bridget's eyes. I'm looking into my sister's eyes." Mom held her hand to her mouth, trying valiantly to stop the tears.

Dave walked in behind her and leaned against a wall looking bored, like he was waiting for the family drama portion of the evening to come to a close. Only the vampire remained on the deck.

The tennis ball bounced across the deck and he spun, kicking it halfway across the ocean. Wilbur gave a happy bark and sped away.

"We have a puppy," he said. "This one seems rather similar."

"Okay, fine." I waved him in. "Apparently, you're family."

"Very gracious," he murmured, moving past me to stand beside his wife.

"Where have you been all these years?" Mom asked, glancing back toward the window. "Is Bridget with you? But… no. You said *was* didn't you? *Bridget Quinn was my mother.*"

Sam looked like a deer caught in headlights. She twisted her wedding ring—a gorgeous blue diamond Art Deco design—shifting her focus between my mother and me. "Sorry, I'm a little turned around. I didn't know Mom had more sisters. I only knew about Abigail."

At mom's stricken look, Sam quickly added, "But she never

talked about her family. When I asked, she teared up and wasn't able to speak, so I stopped asking." She glanced at all of us again. "I have to admit, I wasn't sure if you'd be all that happy to see me. I was a little worried you might try to kill me. Truth be told, I'm still on edge about that."

Clive kissed her forehead, whispering something to her.

"You know what," I interrupted, "let's all sit down and try to untangle this."

Mom had yet to let go of Sam, so they sat on the couch together, with the vampire on Sam's other side, holding her other hand. I was struck all at once that I couldn't do something so simple. It was a stupid thought, out of nowhere. I looked at those joined hands and my own gloved ones and wished—not for the first time—that my gifts had been different ones.

Feeling off and strangely separated from the drama unfolding, I took my chair, leaving Declan and Dave to pull over the folding chairs. They looked like mirror images, both sitting with their muscular arms crossed over their massive chests, monitoring the situation.

"Arwyn's very first vision was about you," Mom said to Sam.

"What?" I didn't know that.

She kept her gaze trained on Sam while she answered me. "You were three, I believe. Bridget had become engaged. She'd brought Michael to meet the family. The reception was cordial, if a bit chilly. I thought he was charming and so very handsome."

Sam hung on my mother's every word.

"You'd been playing outside with the other children. Abigail had been watching to make sure no one tumbled over the cliff and into the ocean. You all came in while the champagne was being poured. You walked straight over to where Bridget and Michael were sitting. You took both their hands and your eyelids fluttered. A moment later, tears ran down your face and you said —so seriously for a three-year-old—*I'll miss you*. Then you laid a tiny hand on Michael's cheek, shook your head, and said, *Ouch*.

You turned to Bridget, squeezing her hand in both of yours, and said, *Wolf-girl live. Big and strong.*" Mom glanced at me. "You were only three and having trouble finding the right words."

Mom continued, "You said, *She lost and sad. Alone. Ouch, ouch. Then big happy.*"

Sam turned to Clive, a wistful smile on her teary face, before returning her attention to Mom.

"Bridget and Michael looked so confused, but Arwyn wasn't done. She said, *I miss you, Auntie Bridget. I like your baby. She queen and men bow.* Then my girl moved to my side, looked down at her hands, and asked for mittens.

"Bridget assured everyone she wasn't pregnant, but the family kept eyeing her the rest of the afternoon, looking for clues." Mom wiped her face again. "I always knew my daughter would be a Cassandra. Now the rest of the family knew too."

"You never told me that story." How had no one ever told me?

Mom looked down into her lap, at Sam's hand in her own. "I think we all wanted to pretend it was fanciful baby talk. To accept your vision meant my sister and her fiancée would die soon, but not before they conceived and gave birth to a daughter, a wicche-wolf who would someday be queen, who men would bow to.

"We discussed it in small groups and hushed tones. We had planned for Bridget to take a seat on the Corey Council when your great-grandmother passed, but we understood after your vision that would never happen. Then the talks began as to whether one of you two should take a place on the Council. Some felt that since neither of you were pure wicche, that disqualified you. Others—the clearer thinkers—realized that more powerful wicches meant more strength overseeing the family.

'But"—Sam cleared her throat—"but that means my parents knew the danger of their path. If they'd split up, they might still be alive."

"True, but then you wouldn't be here."

When Sam sniffed, Clive handed her a clean handkerchief and kissed the side of her head.

"Besides, if Arwyn told you you'd have a much better chance of surviving if you dumped your husband—"

"She's already been warned," Dave muttered.

"—would you leave him?" Mom finished.

Sam smiled, wiping her eyes and nose. "Never."

"And there you go," Mom said.

"Oh, sorry." I needed a moment to regroup when I realized something was bothering me but couldn't figure out what it was. I'd play hostess until I'd solved it or shaken it off. I went to the kitchen and brought back a plate of baked goods. "What would everyone like to drink?"

Mom cleared her throat. "Tea, darling."

"I'll have a beer, if you've got one," Dave said.

Declan nodded, seconding Dave's order.

I looked between Sam and the vampire.

"Um." Sam swiped at her nose again. "Do you have a soda?"

"Just orange or grape," I offered, waiting for the inevitable *no thanks*.

Her eyes lit up. "Grape, please!"

The vampire shook his head. "Nothing for me, thank you."

Declan followed me to the kitchen area. "I can help." His gaze, though, was trained on Sam, the long-lost Quinn.

"Perfect. Here, take these." I pushed the beers and the soda into his arms. "I'll brew another pot for Mom and me."

"Try one of the lemon things," she heard Dave suggest.

A moment later, Sam groaned. "Oh my—you have to learn to make these things."

"I've been trying. I can't get it right," the demon said.

I returned with a magically brewed fresh pot—the spell brewed the tea leaves quickly, but the taste wasn't as rich—and poured for Mom and myself.

"If you can help us in any way," I said to the demon, "I'll give you my recipe."

He nodded. "Good trade."

"Okay," I said, curling up in my chair. "I think the person who needs to start this conversation is you, Sam. It's been twenty-something years since you and Aunt Bridget left. What happened?"

26

In Which Sam Learns She Has Family Who Don't Want to Kill Her

S am clutched Clive's hand but she'd angled her body toward my mother, addressing the one woman in the room who needed the story the most. "Some of this, I remember. Some I've pieced together. Mom's younger sister—"

"Abigail," Mom interrupted. "She's so worried about your mom. She's constantly scrying, trying to find her. When she thinks she's located her, she runs off, only to come back a few days or a week later, dejected that she's missed you again. It's been months now and she's not answering her phone." Mom shook her head. "Sometimes I think Abigail took Bridget's disappearance the hardest of us."

Mom ignored the tea, both of her hands wrapped around Sam's. "We all wanted you back. Desperately. We would have protected you from the wolves"—her eyes darted to Declan—"or whatever had killed your father and was hunting you."

Sam held Mom's hand and gave her an overview of the last twenty-plus years—and it was insane. Bridget was dead, had been for almost eight years. Sam had been attacked, her body left covered in scars, before she'd been abandoned in San Francisco. At seventeen, she opened The Slaughtered Lamb Bookstore & Bar, an establishment on the ocean's edge that catered to supernaturals only

She'd run her business quietly, without too much fuss, until this past year when all hell had broken loose. She'd been trapped in visions, attacked by wolves, pulled into vampire wars, abducted into Faerie, met the queen, had beef with the king, and visited Hell. Somewhere, through all that, she'd fallen in love with a vampire and eventually married him.

I leaned forward to get Sam's attention. "Did I hear that right? You're a necromancer?"

Sam nodded. "It was that pendant I told you about. My mom made it for me when I was little. It tamped down and hid my powers—even from myself. I'm sure my mom would have explained it all if she'd had more time. I didn't know I was a born wolf either; didn't understand Quinn held any special meaning. Once the pendant was destroyed, though, things started changing."

Clive and Dave chuffed laughs as though that was an understatement.

"When I learned I was a wicche, I tried to do simple wicchey things but was an embarrassing failure. And then ghosts started popping up to talk to me and I discovered there was a reason I couldn't do a lot of normal wicchey stuff."

"No," I said, shaking my head. "We're very rare, you and me, and the fact that we're both alive at the same time"—I checked with my mom—"that's never happened, has it?"

Mom wiped her face dry of tears. Thinking it was possible her sister was dead was different from knowing it. And the news about Abigail had knocked her off balance. "No. True necromancy and precognition are extremely rare. Wicches with those abilities only show up every couple hundred years. I've never read any histories about them ever being alive at the same time."

"No, that's not right," Sam said to me. "You and Martha

overlapped. Though she did say it was really strange that she and I, two necromancers, overlapped."

"My Aunt Martha?" Mom asked. "She left town when she was in her late teens, early twenties and we never heard from her again. How in the world did you meet her?" Mom glanced over, checking with me. "Did you know that Martha was a necromancer?"

I shook my head. "No, but I do remember having a dream about her when I was little. She lived in a foggy forest, in a hollowed-out tree with a woman who had long, silvery hair."

"Yes!" Sam confirmed. "That was her wife Galadriel. She's an elven warrior. The fog was the hazy ghosts all around her. Martha said she dealt with a lot of cruelty growing up because she didn't manifest magical talent when others did. Later, when she started showing signs of being a necromancer, family members were suddenly interested in her. She'd said they'd already shown their true faces and so she'd left. She and Galadriel were together for over fifty years.

"Once it became clear that I was a necromancer, we tried to find someone to train me. My friend's mom did some sleuthing and took me to meet this old woman who owned a fae bar in Colma, south of San Francisco. She lived in a massive tree, part of it in this world, part in Faerie." Sam shook her head. "I thought she was the only family I had left, on either side. When she was killed—"

Mom flinched.

"Oh," Sam said, "I'm so sorry. I shouldn't have said it like that. That was thoughtless."

"No, no," Mom said, waving a hand. "It's just—this has all been a lot to take in. I barely remember Martha. I'd been building up hope to see her while you spoke but then, well, I suppose not." Mom caught my eye. "But she grew to an old woman. That's good to know."

Sam looked confused, so I explained, "Necromancers often die young."

"We do?" Sam asked.

"Not just you. Cassandras or precognates do too," I explained.

"I mean, don't get me wrong," Sam said, "everyone and their uncle *has* tried to kill me. I just didn't realize it was a fated thing."

"It's not," Clive said before I could respond. "You're not going anywhere. You two will be the ones who break those old patterns."

"Yes," Declan murmured, which was nice.

"Remember too that times were very different when the Corey family last produced a necromancer before Martha, or a Cassandra like you," Clive added.

"He's right," Dave said. "Even a hundred years ago, talking to ghosts or knowing the future would be considered signs of demonic possession. Some of your predecessors were probably killed by ministers and neighbors for assumed sins."

"Sadly, that is pure truth," I agreed. "And if their neighbors didn't get them, they got themselves. Most of the Cassandras before me went crazy and took their own lives."

"No," Mom stated, shooting to her feet. "You're not like all of those others. Your fae blood makes you stronger, gives you gifts they didn't have."

Sam rose a moment later, taking my mother's hand again. "Can I ask a favor of you, Ms. Corey?"

"Sybil, dear," she said, absently patting Sam's hand, her worried gaze still on me. "I'm your Aunt Sybil."

"Can you tell me other stories of my mother, please?"

Mom's attention returned to Sam. "Of course, dear."

"You could show her the gallery while you discuss Bridget," I suggested.

"If you wouldn't mind," Sam added.

I think it was obvious to my mother that she was being handled, but she seemed to accept that she needed to settle, and a gallery tour discussing Bridget was as good a way as any to do that. "It's right through here," she said, opening the door between the studio and the gallery.

"Holy crap!" Sam said in awe.

Once the door closed, we all seemed to relax. Mom's agitation was getting to all of us. Well, maybe not the vampire, who looked entirely at ease. Or the demon, for that matter. Fine, Declan and I relaxed.

"So," Dave said, "we all got that her mom chose a fae father for the sea wicche over here because she'd be stronger, right?"

"Yes, indeed," Clive agreed.

"We don't know that for sure," I countered.»

The vampire and the demon remained silent, letting me maintain my illusions, if I wanted them.

Declan leaned forward, resting his elbows on his knees. "Arwyn, we may not know for sure, but he's right. It was pretty clear she was terrified you'd be like all the other Cassandras and so made sure you had fae blood to make you stronger. If you think about it, it's a huge gift."

"But how did she know?" Dave said, lost in thought.

"That *is* the question," Clive said. "If Miss Corey is the first Cassandra in hundreds of years, how did her mother know she'd bear one and would therefore need a fae father for her child?"

"She didn't. That's crazy." Except I wasn't sure it was.

The vampire nodded easily. "Of course."

We sat in an uncomfortable silence and then Dave turned to Declan. "So what's your story?"

Declan held out his hand to shake. "Declan," he said.

Dave shook it. "Werewolf."

Declan nodded. "Demon," he countered.

The corner of Dave's mouth turned up. "Only half."

"No one ever asks you about the other half, do they?" I wondered.

He raised his eyebrows and shook his head. "They do not."

"I feel like they should," I said.

"Probably," he agreed.

Weird tension seemed to have formed between Clive and Declan while Dave and I spoke. I wanted to kick Declan because he was staring Clive in the eye. When Declan began to growl, a small smile formed on the vampire's lips.

"No challenge intended," Clive said. "I was merely studying your bone structure. You remind me of someone I love quite dearly. Could you tell me your last name?"

I could see Declan struggling. The question was politely asked. It would appear weak and churlish not to answer so basic an inquiry. It was almost imperceptible, but I saw it, the moment Declan owned his birthright.

"Quinn."

"What?!" The shout came from the gallery right before the sound of running feet. The door flew open, and then Sam was standing in front of Declan.

"You're a Quinn?" she asked.

He nodded, standing up to face her.

She held up a hand and five long, sharp claws slid out of her fingertips.

He watched, a smile hidden in his beard, and then held up his hand, claws sliding out.

"Is this some kind of fucked-up werewolf bonding moment we're witnessing here?" Dave asked.

Sam bounced on the balls of her feet and then spun to see Clive, her eyes glassy with tears. "Coreys and a Quinn!"

"I know," Clive said, the smile on his face so gentle, I never would have pegged him for a vampire if I hadn't already known.

"I have family! That don't want me dead!" She turned to Declan and me, her expression suddenly serious. "You don't, do you?"

We both shook our heads.

"See? They don't hate me," she said, grinning ear to ear.

"Give 'em time," Dave grumbled.

"You, shut it," she said to the demon. "Oh, sorry! I left your mom in the other room. Be right back." She ran off and returned soon after with my mom.

Sam said something to her, and my mom responded, "Not at all. I needed a few minutes to compose myself."

"Why don't we talk about why you asked me to come here," Dave said.

I gave them a bullet-point version of the last few days, visions included.

When I finally finished, Dave nodded. "It's not just about what the sorcerer does. Having a demon actively working with a sorcerer bleeds into the community. Dark shit starts popping up that isn't even connected to the demon and sorcerer. The evil was always there, the sociopath walking a tightrope between socially acceptable behavior and serial aggression. The darkness the sorcerer and demon create can tip people, who have no direct connection to them, over the edge.

"It's why you often hear about sick shit happening in clusters or multiple serial killers working in the same general area."

My mother, who had been quiet since returning from the gallery, turned to Dave. "Do you really think you can get rid of that evil toad squatting inside my sister?"

"Well, I really do want that lemon bar recipe, so I suppose I'll have to."

27

Demicche

S am had apparently recently learned to drive, so she got behind the wheel of a sleek silver blue roadster with Clive in the passenger seat and sped off. Dave took his own car, scoffing at the idea of carpooling. The three of us climbed into Mom's sedan and went to the hospital together.

Declan dove, as he was too tall for the back seat. Mom sat in the passenger seat, so I was relegated to the back. I liked the quiet and the dark of the backseat, though, staring out the window as Monterey slept.

"What are your impressions of these three, darling?" Mom half turned in her seat to see me.

"I haven't read them, but I get the impression they're on the up and up." I was pretty sure, anyway.

"My goodness, Arwyn, you can't adhere to these self-imposed privacy rules. We need to know if this demon has the power to help, and what he expects in return." She turned back around, her jaw set. "I love my sister dearly, but I won't allow a demon access to our family in an effort to save her. Better she die than we produce more sorcerers."

As much as I wanted to disagree with infringing on another's right to privacy, I had agreed when I joined the Corey Council to put the family first, to protect them. Dave wasn't here with me, but I thought back to when he'd first visited me, when he came looking for his imprisoned banshee wife. I'd held his hand then.

Putting myself in that mindset, I slipped one finger out of my glove and slid it into the other glove, trying to connect to the memory within myself… He was driving to the hospital, thinking we didn't seem like complete assholes, which was a surprise. Someone cut him off on the road and he flicked his fingers off the steering wheel, giving the car a flat tire. Wait. Was that a demon thing or was the other half wicche?

Get the fuck out of my head!

Oops. That last thought was a little too loud. *Quid pro quo, buddy. You did this to me when you were trying to find your wife.*

Girlfriend.

I rolled my eyes. *Girlfriend? What are you waiting for? You should lock that down before she comes to her senses.*

Hilarious. What do you want?

Can you really do this, and what do you expect in return? We don't want any of our family members in league with demons.

Yes, and I already told you. I want the lemon bar recipe. And none of that leaving out a key ingredient so yours can be better bullshit. I'm pulling into the hospital. Now fuck off.

He pushed me out with an ease that was honestly embarrassing.

"I trust him. He says he can do it and just wants the recipe." If this worked, I'd give him a few extra recipes as a bonus. "Also, the half not demon might be wicche."

Mom turned in her seat again to stare at me and take that in. "Really?" When I nodded, she smiled and settled back in her seat. "I feel better about him now."

Declan pulled into a spot beside Dave's muscle car. The demon was leaning against the driver's door, arms crossed over his chest. We got out and looked around at the mostly empty parking lot.

"We should get moving before security spots us on the cameras," I suggested.

Dave led the way to the doors, saying, "The cameras are experiencing some technical difficulties right now."

We followed him through the entry, walked right past an empty desk, a deserted water feature, down a few twisting halls. When we filed past the nurse's station a few doors down from Sylvia's room, none of the nurses looked up from their work. Dave pushed open the hospital room door and then held it for us.

Once the door closed, Mom moved to stand between Dave and Sylvia. "What's your family name and how did you know this was her room?"

"Feels a little late for questions like that, don't you think?" He walked around the bottom of the bed to the far side. He took Sylvia's hand in his and closed his eyes. "Everybody, shut up now."

Mom gave me a pointed look, expecting me to do something about this. Considering, I moved the blanket from Aunt Sylvia's foot. She had little socks on, so I removed a glove and touched her ankle.

Fuck off.

I'm not bothering anyone.

You're bothering me.

Oh, stop being such a baby. I won't cause problems. I'll just be your quiet little shadow.

You might want to work on the quiet part. Now, shut up.

I waited in the dark and silence for what seemed like a very long time. Oh, my legs and back stopped hurting. Someone must have slid a chair under me, so I wasn't leaning over the end of the bed.

Finally, after what seemed an eternity, I heard Dave's perpetually pissed-off voice, *Leave this one.*

Oh, it's you. Come slumming, have you?

Why this host? Did she summon you?

That's nothing to do with you.

I think you'll find you're mistaken about that.

I don't answer to you and I don't care who your daddy is. You don't scare me.

I should.

Pain, like nothing I'd ever experienced, burned through my body for a moment and then it was gone. Something was different, though. Nothing felt or sounded as it had moments ago. I tried to locate the demons again and heard only my own thoughts echoing inside me. He'd trapped me in something, hadn't he? Damn it! *Let m*—

A loud hiss reverberated around me.

Fear was new for me. Horrible images preyed on me, but I always knew I could protect myself. I wasn't feeling that way now. I'd been trapped by a demon in something similar to what had trapped his girlfriend. If he did not get me out of here soon…well, clearly nothing. How the hell do you escape from a demon box? Asshole.

And then I was blinking my eyes open, my head on the side of the bed, my hand still wrapped around Sylvia's ankle. I lifted my head to find Mom and Declan watching me.

"Are you okay now?" Declan asked. "You got really agitated there for a while."

"Yeah," I said, sliding back into my glove. "He and the demon were trash talking and then this one hit the demon with a ton of pain. It was horrendous for the blink of an eye and then he put me in a mental box, keeping me safe from their spat."

"Did you hear who the sorcerer is?" Mom asked, her hands wrapped tightly around Sylvia's.

I shook my head. "No idea. Maybe Dave knows, but I didn't get anything from the demon. He was just a voice for me."

A nurse walked in, and we all froze. Thankfully, she didn't seem to notice us, so the spell was holding. She checked Sylvia's chart, took a small vial and a syringe from her pocket, and injected the medicine through the port in her IV. She checked the IV line on the back of Sylvia's hand, secured the tape, and then walked around the bed to where Dave was standing.

I was afraid she'd walked right into him on her way to the EKG display. Instead, she stopped, pulled back her right arm, and punched Dave in the jaw. Mom and I threw spells at the same time, knocking the nurse to the ground.

"What the hell was that?" Declan demanded.

Just then Dave—who'd barely flinched at the punch—opened his eyes as the heartbeat line on the EKG went flat. An alarm sounded in the hospital and footsteps pounded down the hall.

We all got out of the way of the nurses and doctor as they began working on Sylvia. The medical personnel were doing their jobs while also shooting us confused and angry looks. They knew we weren't supposed to be here and were no doubt thinking we'd done something to cause this.

"Call the cops," the doctor shouted when a nurse ducked his head in the door. "We have a nurse on the ground and this patient is coding."

Before the nurse could leave, I added, "Ask for Detective Hernández." I'd been helping the woman. The least she could do was keep us out of a jail cell tonight.

Mom, Declan, and I watched them work on Sylvia. Dave leaned against a wall, his eyes on the downed nurse.

After what felt like either hours or seconds, they stopped what they were doing, took a step back, and the doctor checked the wall clock, declaring my aunt dead at 12:03 in the morning.

Two nurses rushed to the nurse sprawled on the floor and checked for a pulse. One of them gasped while the other glared at us, her eyes filling with tears.

Hospital security stepped in to stay with us while we waited for the police. When the nurses started to move the dead nurse, both the doctor and the security guard told them not to. This was a crime scene now.

Sooner than I would have expected, the door swung open again and this time it was Detective Hernández with a very large man. Declan and the man stared each other down for a moment and the man then blew air out of his nose while Declan crossed his arms over his chest, adopting the same stance as Dave.

The detective was almost as tall as Declan—who had to be at least six and a half feet tall—but had even broader shoulders, if that was possible. Like Hernández, he wore a jacket and slacks. His button-down shirt was blue. He was a Black man with close-cropped hair and eyes a light, golden brown.

While Detective Hernández came to talk with us, the large man prowled the room.

"Arwyn, you want to tell me what happened here?" she asked, taking out her small notebook.

"We came to see my aunt—"

Hernández glanced over her shoulder at the hospital bed. "This is your aunt?"

I nodded while Mom cried silently beside me. "Mom was having a bad night, thinking about Aunt Sylvia here all alone, so we came to sit with her, talk to her like the nurse yesterday told us to do."

"It's after hours," the detective reminded us.

I shrugged. "We wanted to try and no one stopped us, so we came in to see her."

The male detective put gloves on and reached down to roll the dead nurse onto her back.

"Sir, wait," I said. "She has some kind of medication in her pocket. She came in while we were talking and filled a syringe with whatever's in that vial. Then she added it to the IV. Less than a minute later, Aunt Sylvia's heart had stopped and alarms were going off."

"This is Detective Osso," Hernández said. "Arthur, could you check her pockets?"

He nodded, checked the pockets and came up with a vial.

He walked to the door and asked the security guard to get the doctor. His voice was a deep baritone rumble that called up visions of dark cozy places and long rests.

Wait. I caught Declan's eye and tried to ask the question I was thinking through my WTF expression. He kept his focus on the detective but eventually nodded.

I knew Detective Hernández had asked me something but my mind was buzzing with excitement. A bear shifter? Seriously? How did I not know there was such a thing. *Damn.*

"Arwyn?"

"Right. Right. Sorry. What was that again?"

"Do you know this nurse? See her last time you were here?" Detective Hernández glanced at her partner and scribbled a quick note.

"No." I turned to check with my mom.

Mom shook her head, wiping her face, and said, "She wasn't one of the nurses I've seen going in and out."

The guard pushed open the door and the doctor was back. Detective Osso took the evidence bag out of his pocket and showed the doctor.

"Is this the medication this patient should be receiving?"

The doctor's annoyance at being called back morphed into confusion with a side of fear. "Of course not. Where did you get this?"

28

Just a Little One?

"So this isn't something commonly given to coma patients?"

The doctor glanced at us and then said, "If I could talk with you in the hall?"

Detective Osso walked the doctor out.

"Let's go over this again. Exactly what happened?" Hernández asked.

"Barbiturate, neuromuscular, terminal patient," Declan mumbled, clearly forgetting we had a mundane in the room.

Detective Hernández pinned Declan with a look. "What about barbiturates?"

Declan's face went blank. I think he was shocked to have slipped so badly. He pointed at the door. "I have excellent hearing. The doctor just told your partner that vial contained euthanasia medication."

"Is that so?" she asked, clearly not believing him.

"It is," Detective Osso said, as he walked back in. "He's like me, Sofia, when it comes to hearing and scent."

Hernández's brow furrowed as she looked back and forth between the men. "Exactly like you?"

"Not exactly," he said, crouching down by the dead nurse a

moment before looking up at Dave. "Who are you and what do you know about this?"

"Dave."

Detective Osso waited a beat and then pushed, "Dave what?"

Dave pulled his wallet out of his pocket and flipped it open, showing his ID.

Osso copied down the info and then stood, waiting for Dave to answer the second half of his question.

"Sorry, just one thing, Detective Osso." I walked across the room to stand directly in front of him, my back to Detective Hernández. I mouthed, *Does she know about you?*

After a charged moment, he tipped his head in a way I interpreted as yes.

I threw a muffling spell at the door and then, eyebrows raised in question, I checked in with everyone assembled. Dave shrugged. Declan nodded. My mother dried her face with a tissue in her bag and said, "I trust your judgment."

"What's going on? Arwyn?" Detective Hernández was looking decidedly nervous.

"Okay. I think we need to stop trading in partial truths," I began.

"What does that mean?" she demanded.

I really hoped I was making the right decision. "Cards on the table. You already know that Detective Osso is a bear shifter." I turned to him. "Am I using the correct term?"

He nodded. "Close enough."

Hernández looked panicked for only a moment before her expression smoothed out. "I don't understand."

"It's okay," Osso said. "These two are wicches"—he gestured to Mom and me—"that one is a werewolf, and judging by the scent of sulfur, I'd say this one is a demon."

Dave nodded.

Hernández looked like she might stroke out, so I hurried on to explain. "A wicche who works with demons to gain power and cause pain is called a sorcerer. They're evil. Normal wicches, like Mom and me, have been around for millennia. We're born with our powers and do no harm to the mundane world. A demon—not this one—was working with a sorcerer to pull my aunt into a coma."

Hernández crossed herself and stepped away from Dave, almost backing into Declan. You could see it on her face. She remembered what Declan was and took another step to the side.

"Sorry," I said. "I know this is a lot. I'm trying to give you the quick version. Our own healers couldn't help Sylvia, which is how she ended up in this hospital. We don't normally come to places like this for fear of our true natures coming to light.

"I met this demon," I said, gesturing to Dave, "a little while ago. He seemed decent enough, so I contacted him to see if he'd be willing to come here and try to figure out who the sorcerer and demon targeting my aunt are."

"And did you?" Hernández asked Dave.

"Yes and no," he responded. "Yes, I know the demon, but that's no help in this situation. He wouldn't name his symbiot, which isn't surprising. I caught a glimpse of her in his thoughts, when his defenses were low."

Hernández scribbled a few notes and then flinched.

"It's best not to take notes on any of this," Dave said.

The detective stared a moment longer at the now blank sheet of paper and then put the notebook in her pocket.

"The woman he's working with has big green Corey eyes. She was in shadow, huddled behind Abigail."

"Abigail?" my mom repeated.

"That's what I saw. Abigail's not involved in this, but someone who worked with her is."

"But Abigail's a magical tutor. She worked with most of Arwyn's cousins, helping them strengthen their skills. I don't understand how…"

Mom and I were lost in thought when Detective Osso asked, "What does any of that have to do with the dead nurse?"

"Oh, sorry," I replied. "While Dave was on another plane of existence, roughing up the other demon, trying to get a name, the demon apparently possessed this nurse. He walked the nurse in, had her kill Aunt Sylvia with the drugs in that vial, and then had her walk around the bed and punch Dave."

"I was wondering why my face hurt," Dave murmured.

"Mom and I spelled her to stop her, but then she hit the floor dead. Our spells would have frozen her, not killed her. We don't do black magic."

"When the demon left the nurse, he took her life," Dave said. "That's usually how possession ends for the host."

Hernández looked at Osso. "Are you buying any of this?"

He slapped his small notebook against his palm and rumbled, "Yeah, I am."

"Damn it," she said. "So am I." She rubbed her forehead. "How the hell do we investigate demon possession? How do we write that up?"

"You don't," Dave said. "The doctors don't know why she fell into a coma. Why would you, if they don't? As for the nurse, let the doctors figure it out. Demon possession often kills brain cells, mimicking stroke. She could have been in the early stages of a stroke, grabbed the wrong medication, accidentally killing the patient before she herself died."

We all stared at him a moment.

"Damn, you're good at this," I said, more than a little concerned at how easily he came up with a completely believable story that would fit all the evidence.

He flashed a smile that made my insides turn liquid.

The door opened again and Sam and Clive slipped in.

"Stop," Detective Osso commanded. "You're not authorized to be here."

"Where's the guard?" Hernández asked, her arm out, trying to usher the late arrivals back out the door.

"I sent the guard on his way," Clive said. "If you can relax a moment, my wife has some information for you."

"What? You have no right to send the guard anywhere. This is a crime scene." Hernández looked like she was starting to lose it. Her hand rested on her gun as she waited for Sam and Clive to leave.

I opened my mouth to try to smooth this over, but Sam moved to the detective's side.

"I know this is all crazy and I'm so sorry that you're being forced to not only learn about the supernatural world, but are having to do it on the job, with little preparation. I know you don't know us and therefore have no reason to trust us, but Arwyn sort of knows us and Dave knows us well."

"Aligning yourself with the demon in the room probably isn't your smartest move," Dave grumbled.

She tipped her head from side to side, weighing his words. "Good point. My name is Sam. This is my husband Clive. We have some information we wanted to share, but if this is a bad time, we can go." She turned to me. "Does he need to wipe their memories?"

"What?" Hernández squeaked.

"Sorry, sorry! That came out wrong," Sam said. "That wasn't a threat. No one wants you to have to deal with more crazy stuff than you can handle."

"She's fine," Osso grumbled.

"Good. That's fine, then." She tilted her head, her brow furrowed as she studied him. She breathed deeply and then broke into a huge grin.

Osso rested his hands on his hips, glaring down at Sam, looking stern as hell.

Clive moved forward, put his hands around her waist, picked her up, and moved back to the door. "Let the nice man be, darling."

"But," she pleaded.

"No," Clive said, keeping an arm around her.

Osso continued to glare, but Sam was nothing but delighted.

"Just a little hug?" she wheedled.

Osso's growl shook the room.

"Okay, okay, jeez," she mumbled. "Try to get a little bear hug…"

"You can hug me," Clive said.

She sighed dramatically, resting her head on her husband's shoulder. "It's just not the same."

"I know."

"What information do you have?" I asked.

"Oh, so I was talking with your aunt—Wait. Shouldn't we do something? It feels disrespectful to just leave them lying here while we chat, especially Marcy, the nurse on the floor."

Sam moved to the bed and patted Aunt Sylvia's arm. "She wants to make sure her body is released to her husband so he can prepare her properly for burial."

"She's with us now?" Mom asked. She moved to her sister's other side and clutched her hand.

Sam nodded. "Marcy's with us too," she added. "Unfortunately, she's terrified and confused, so she's crying. Right in my face." She tipped her head back. "I'm worried I'm going to accidentally inhale her. Marcy, come on. You have family waiting to see you. Let me help."

Sam sighed. "Damn. She's seen herself and is now freaking the heck out." She squinted at Osso. "I sure could use a hug."

"No."

"Oh, all right." She focused again three feet to her left. "Sylvia, your family's here. Is there something you'd like me to tell them?" She was silent for a few moments. "She's moving on, which is good, but she's flickering. Something about the ring you wanted…Take it…Her daughters…protect th—no her. Protect her…something about—It's all Abigail's fault. She taught her—something…She loves you both…John…forever…she'll wait."

Sam blinked. "She's passed on now."

I went to Mom and we joined hands, singing the song of death, our magic carrying Sylvia off this plane and on to the next. Tears streamed down our faces. It was hard to breathe, the pain in my chest overwhelming. The world was a colder, lonelier place without her.

"Detectives," Clive said, "the rest of the family is arriving. I think it would be best if this poor nurse didn't remain on the floor."

Detective Osso nodded and left the room. A few minutes later, a gurney was rolled in. The attendants put Marcy on a stretcher and then lifted her to the gurney and wheeled her out.

John and Calliope rushed in. He went to Sylvia and pulled her into his arms. Cal was distracted by all of us.

"Oh, you got here first." She dabbed at the wetness under her eyes. "That's so good of you. Mom loved you both so much. I don't know if you knew this, Aunt Sybil, but Mom looked up to you her whole life. She used to joke that whenever she was faced with a difficult situation, she'd ask herself, *What would Sybil do?* and then she'd do that."

She took my mom's hand before turning to me, adding, "And she's always considered you one of her daughters."

I nodded, throat too tight to speak.

She laughed, eyes sparkling with tears. "It made me so jealous when I was little because, I mean, look at you. You already had all this power and beauty and my mom thought of you as one of hers too?" She shook her head, eyes wide, tears dripping prettily from her long eyelashes. "And then I grew up and understood my mom's heart was just too big to limit herself to a few. She loved without measure, without bounds." Covering her mouth with a trembling hand, she asked, "How will we go on without her?"

Mom pulled her into a hug. I turned to the side to wipe my face and caught Declan's scowl. Sam and Clive slipped out of the room, giving us privacy, but Sam wore an expression matching Declan's.

What had I missed?

29

Thanks, Dad!

W hen Serena, Sylvia's oldest, arrived, I went for a walk. My own grief was already overwhelming. Standing in that room, though, I was drowning under the combined mourning. I was halfway down the corridor when I realized Declan had followed me.

"Okay if I come with you?" he asked.

I thought about it a moment. "Yeah. The company is... appreciated."

Pushing through the front door, I breathed deeply and tried to clear my head. Sometimes, often really, I wished I could teleport back to my cannery.

"Arwyn?"

I turned at my name and found Sam and Clive sitting in their car.

"We were going to head out but then Clive heard you coming." She stepped out of the car and then Clive was suddenly beside her. The man moved faster than my eye could track. "I'm just so grateful. I wasn't sure what kind of reception I'd receive here, and you've all been so incredibly kind and welcoming."

I stuffed my hands in my pockets, suddenly cold. "I can't

believe that in all those visions I had of you, I never got that you were a Corey." I rubbed my forehead. "Maybe I have a Corey block. Dave said the sorcerer has Corey eyes, but I couldn't see her when I touched Sylvia. I'm not seeing her in visions."

"I would imagine," Clive began, "that for one who can see so much, having a blind spot would be incredibly frustrating."

"You got that right," I grumbled. "Apparently, I knew at three what was going to happen to your parents but not that their killer was standing twenty feet away from me." The wind changed directions and my hair flew into my face, the chill making me shiver.

"Perhaps it's not a Corey block," Clive suggested, "so much as a demon or sorcerer block."

If he was right, how the hell was I going to find the one responsible for all of this?

"You have such beautiful hair," Sam said. "I can't do fancy stuff, but I can braid it to get it out of your eyes if you'd like."

"Oh." I waved away the need. "I got this." I pushed my hair back, gathered it all into a handful and then started twisting, creating a long, thick rope, which I then coiled up and shoved down the back of my jacket. Once I buttoned it up to my chin, I had essentially imprisoned my hair.

"Is it okay if we visit again?" Sam asked, still obviously unsure of her footing in Corey Country. "And you're always welcome at The Slaughtered Lamb. All of you," she added, looking at Declan.

Clive reached into a pocket and came out with two cards containing their contact information. He gave one each to Declan and me.

The wind changed again and Declan went on alert.

Clive said, "Fire."

Declan shifted and tore off, his clothes and shoes left in a trail after him. It was so sudden, I jumped.

"He's right," Clive said. "I think it's your place. It's the right direction and the right combination of scents. You two drive," he said to Sam. "We'll meet you there." And then he was gone too.

Sam and I picked up Declan's things and jumped into her car. Thankfully, the streets were near empty this late at night.

My insides churned. The cannery was miles away. I was sure they were wrong, but then I remembered the vision about my gallery consumed in flames. My heart lodged itself firmly in my throat. No. Not my gallery. My art. All lost.

While I'd been eavesdropping on a demon, his sorcerer had been setting fire to my home. They knew who I was and that I was looking. Then I remembered the fetish under the old deck. They'd always known what I could do and wanted me gone. First pushing, then burning. What was next?

Sam screeched to a stop in front of the gallery a few minutes later. It was dark. No fire. Two silhouettes came around the side of the cannery, one wolf-shaped. I jumped out of the car, leaving Declan's stuff on the hood so he could shift and dress if he wanted.

"It's okay? It wasn't me?" Relief was just out of reach as the fiery vision kept playing over and over in my head.

"No. It was," Clive said. "I had just arrived when I witnessed the most extraordinary thing I've ever seen." He shook his head in wonder. "The deck and the back wall of your gallery were engulfed. The flames were moving up the roof. Come." He beckoned both Sam and me to follow him around the corner.

"See? You can see the blackening of the walls." He led us past where I'd planned to paint a mural, to the edge of the water, looking at the back of my gallery. "The deck is gone," he continued. "The walls have some fire damage, but it doesn't seem too bad. Do you know why?" He looked out to the ocean. "Because a massive wave—had to be forty feet high—swamped the gallery and put out the flames."

"What?" I followed Clive's gaze out to the ocean. "That's impossible. The waves never get that high here."

Declan walked up to join us, his clothes looking a little worse for shifting. "I think your dad was looking out for you."

Clive turned at that. "Is your father water fae?" He pointed to the gallery. "The Sea Wicche? That's you?"

I nodded. "I've never met him, but I have an affinity for the ocean, so I assume so. I didn't think he knew about me, though." How odd to think he'd known and been watching. I wasn't sure how I felt about that.

Charred boards floated in the water. Oh, shit. Cecil! I took off my jacket and stuffed it in Declan's hand. When I ran to the water's edge, I heard, "Phone!" I fished it out of my pocket and threw it over my shoulder—one of the three of them would catch it—and then dove in.

The water was warmer than it should have been. I swam to Charlie and Herbert first. They were attached to piers that had been on fire. Starfish die from heat. Swirling my hands in the water, I cast a spell, cooling it. That would help, but it wasn't enough.

I went to Herbert, as he was closest, and laid my hand on his body. He was trying to push the heat into the five star-points, away from the central disc that held his heart, stomach, and nervous system, but it was too much. This wasn't an unseasonably hot day. This was fire.

Placing my other hand on the pier, I spelled both Herbert and the wooden pole, siphoning the heat through me and then out into the ocean. The water around us continued to drop in temperature. It looked like Dad was still lending a hand.

Once Herbert seemed to be doing better, I swam to Charlie. His normally bright orange body was looking decidedly pale and dull. The colder water was helping, but he was in extreme distress. Like with Herbert, I pulled the heat from him and the post, experiencing a flash of heat before releasing it into the cold water.

There was movement above me, but I ignored it. Charlie needed my full attention. Once I felt his system was evening out,

I went in search of Cecil and his friend. Did I need air? Sure. It would have alleviated this pounding headache, but it wasn't necessary. The ocean wouldn't kill me.

I swam under the cannery, looking for my octopus friends. I didn't see them, which was good. Unlike the starfish, they were mobile and hopefully got away before the ocean started heating up and fiery boards started raining down.

After checking on Charlie and Herbert once more—still recovering—I surfaced, filling my lungs and clearing my head.

"Holy crap!" Sam shouted. "I was holding my breath while you were down there. Not realizing it. Just doing that weird sympathetic thing and Clive had to shake me when I started to pass out." She went to the edge of the water and gave me a hand, pulling me up the rocks. She was ridiculously strong.

I surveyed the blistered paint on the back wall of my gallery, the remnants of the charred deck, and then noticed Declan in the water. He was fishing out the burned boards, tossing them to Clive, who moved easily from post to post before throwing the boards on the grassy area beside the gallery. They were cleaning the ocean, and it eased some of the pain I was feeling.

"Deck again," I murmured.

Sam dropped my jacket onto my shoulders, and I tucked my arms in and wrapped it around myself. "What about the deck?" she asked.

I'd forgotten how good everyone's hearing was. Even with the roaring of the surf and the wind, she'd heard me mumble. "When Declan was tearing out the old deck, he found a fetish."

Sam's face was screwed up in confusion. "Some kind of sex toy? I don't understand."

Clive laughed as he leapt to another post. "Wrong usage, darling. She's referring to an object imbued with magical powers."

"Exactly," I agreed. "In this case, a curse created to push me out of my home, to make me want to go away."

"This was arson," Sam informed me. "They smelled gasoline when they got here."

Someone tried to burn down my beautiful gem on the water. My stomach twisted in knots. "I'm surprised the windows didn't blow out," I mused.

Clive threw more boards onto the ground beside Sam and me. "Had the wave not hit when it did, they probably would have."

"Is it safe for her to sleep here tonight? Is the building itself okay?" Sam turned to me, "We can take you wherever you want to go."

Oh, shit! I ran back toward the front of the building, fishing my keys out of my wet pocket. The gallery and my studio were probably under water. The fire outside had no doubt tripped the sprinkler system inside.

I flung open the front door, expecting the worst, and then stopped, confused. Everything looked as it had and was dry. On one hand, great, but on the other, what the hell? It was a newly installed system. Why didn't it work?

The smell of smoke was horrible in here, but the alarms hadn't been tripped. I ran over to the windows, wanting to throw them open and get fresh air. I touched the lock and drew my hand back with a hiss of pain. It was scalding metal. Sam tucked her hand into the sleeve of her coat and then started opening windows to air out the gallery while I went into the studio.

Again, dry. I looked up at the high ceiling and stared at the useless sprinklers. The smoke started me coughing. Sam jogged in and went to the back door, opening it. Clive was suddenly there, balancing on the edge of the doorsill, most of his body over the open water. He gave her a kiss and she stepped back, letting him in.

Clive looked up at the sprinklers, just as I had. "Malfunction," he asked, "or spelled not to turn on?"

I trusted my contractor. Phil would have double and triple-checked the system. We knew we had a sorcerer, so spelling my alarms and sprinkler, hoping to burn down the whole cannery, was the most logical answer.

I was about to flop into my chair when Sam shouted, "Stop!"

I caught myself and spun, readying a spell.

"Sorry. No threat," she said. "It's just that you're sopping wet. I assumed you might not want to sit in your chair like that."

I shook my head, feeling like an idiot. "I don't. Thanks."

"Maybe you should go take a hot shower and get cleaned up. We'll mop the floors while you're gone," she volunteered.

"No need." I swished my wrist, drying the floors and then the steps as I climbed them. Could I dry myself? Yes, but I hated the gritty feel of sand and salt on my skin when I did a quick dry. "Be right back." I stopped at the top of the steps and looked down. "Declan's okay, right?"

"Perfectly well. He went to his truck to get a change of clothes," Clive responded.

I nodded. "Good." I took a step and stopped. "He didn't have my phone in his pocket when he jumped in, did he?"

Clive pulled a phone out of each pocket. "I have them right here."

I held up a hand and he threw it, smacking it directly into my palm. "Thanks." I checked and saw a message from Mom. Sighing, I called her back. I needed to tell her what had happened and what I thought it meant.

30

Nightmare Negotiations

"Where did you go?" Mom asked, her voice a strained whisper.

"Home. It was too much. I couldn't stay."

"You should have told me." There were footsteps, and then the background noise changed. "Do you know who the sorcerer is?"

I tapped speakerphone and peeled off my wet clothes. "No. Dave said Corey eyes. I didn't even get that. I'm wondering if I have a blind spot when it comes to Coreys." I considered what Clive had suggested. "Or maybe it's just sorcerers I can't see."

"I hope not. That would be decidedly less helpful for the Council." The background noise changed again, becoming quite still. Mom was still walking, though. I could hear it in her voice. "I'm going to your grandmother's house. I need to tell her about Sylvia."

"I'm sorry, Mom."

"Me too." The hitch in her voice made my throat tighten.

"Before you hang up, I need to tell you about tonight. First, I'm fine." I gave her the shortened version, as she wouldn't particularly care about Cecil, Charlie, and Herbert. We ended the call when she reached Gran's. I was fine. She had to go break the news to Gran that one of her daughters had died tonight, and another years ago. And that both had been killed by sorcerers within the family.

After I finally got cleaned up and dressed in my soft black loungewear, I went back downstairs, only to find Declan watching a ballgame on the projector system and Sam and Clive nowhere to be seen.

He'd taken off his boots and sat with his feet up on the coffee table, a beer in his hand. When he turned and smiled, bubbles filled my insides. "Sam and Clive had to go. They said goodbye, left another contact card in case the other one went in the ocean, and again invited you to visit or call."

"Damn." I settled into my chair. "I was hoping to thank them before they left."

"You can text her. I think he was driving. It's close to three in the morning and she was looking tired. They had to go, though. You know, vampire, dawn."

"Right." The back door and all the windows were still open, which was helping to air out the gallery. "Good game?" I nodded to the basketball game being projected on the wall.

He shrugged. "I'm not paying much attention. I turned it on to try to drown out your conversation with your mom."

At my no doubt confused look, he took a sip. "You forget. Werewolves, vampires, demons, we all have excellent hearing. You can't use a speakerphone around us, even upstairs, behind a door. I hate to break it to you, but we can usually hear both sides of a conversation without a speakerphone too. Honestly, I'm pretty sure Clive would have heard both sides even if you'd been talking normally in a car parked across the street with the windows rolled up.

"Nice enough guy, I guess, but he had me on edge. I kept waiting for him to fang out and kill someone." He fake-shuddered and took another sip. "Bloodsuckers creep me out."

I thought back over my phone call with my mom. Had either of us said anything we shouldn't have in front of an audience? I didn't think so. Although when I had turned down Mom's invitation to stay at her house tonight, she told me to make sure the wolf stayed for protection.

"Do you want anything to eat?" It was the middle of the night, but he was a werewolf, so I wasn't sure of his food requirements.

He gestured to the fridge. "I hope you don't mind. I already pulled out some leftovers from dinner. Shifting takes a lot of energy and hollows me out."

"Mi kitchen es su kitchen. And thank you so much for going in the ocean and collecting all the burned boards."

"No problem. We can't have planks dropping on Cecil or bouncing off Charlie and Herbert." He winked and it wasn't smarmy or creepy. I'm not sure how he winked in a way that created more bubbles instead of making me cringe, but he had.

"Do you want to take a shower?" I shivered and Declan grabbed the throw blanket I had folded on the back of the couch and tossed it to me.

"I'm out of clothes to change into, but thanks." He pointed up the stairs. "It's okay. You can go to bed. I'll keep watch down here while the doors and windows are open."

"Better idea. You go get the wet clothes and I'll put them in the wash with mine. In the morning, you can take a shower and have clean clothes to change into." Laundry and beer were the least I could do. The guy didn't have a stake in any of this, and yet he'd stuck around to help.

He saluted me with his bottle. "I'll take you up on that one. Be right back." He went through the door to the gallery and out the front.

While he was gone, I walked along the back wall of my studio and gallery, spelling the windows and doors to not let anyone or anything in. I realized my mistake a moment later when the wind stopped blowing. I tweaked the spell to allow wind and light, while blocking psycho killers and curious seals.

A moment later, I heard the satisfying thunk of the front

door lock and heavy footsteps returning. As the footsteps neared, I worried I was being stupid and readied a spell just in case this wasn't Declan.

Thankfully, Declan walked in. The unease, however, hadn't left. "You didn't see Hubert out there, did you?"

He stopped, brow furrowed. "Hubert? I thought the starfish was Herbert."

"He is," I said, taking the pack he'd made by wrapping his wet clothes inside his dry flannel shirt like a hobo's bindle. "I got worried you weren't you after going outside, so I was testing you."

"I wasn't—oh, yeah, still me. No demon hitchhikers."

"That you're aware of," I corrected, taking his clothes upstairs.

He chuffed a laugh. "Thanks. I was hoping to never sleep again, so this works out well for me." He dropped back down onto the couch, kicking off his boots.

I threw his wet clothes in with mine and then turned on the washing machine. Stopping by my bed, I considered just crawling in and falling asleep, but decided against it. I'd get an hour or two up here if I was lucky. Downstairs with Declan, I had a better chance of actually falling asleep and staying that way.

Grabbing my favorite blanket, I went back downstairs, surprising Declan, who'd already stretched out on the couch with a silent basketball game on the screen. This didn't work. The poor guy's legs were hanging off the end.

"Can I ask a favor?"

Declan sat up.

"Sorry. I want to ask something that benefits me and is uncomfortable for you, which is shitty." I'd fallen asleep on the couch twice with him and both times, I'd slept without nightmares waking me. I really wanted that again, especially after today.

He waited to hear what I wanted. I liked that he didn't jump to agree to the favor before he'd heard it.

"I feel stupid asking this, but I told you I'm a terrible sleeper, right?"

He nodded. "You do all your baking in the middle of the night."

"Right. Well, I don't know why, but when I touch you, I can't read you. And when I fall asleep touching you, I don't have nightmares waking me up."

He slid to the end of the couch and patted the cushion beside him. "Do you know why that is?"

I shook my head. "I have no idea. It's never happened before." And I was scared to delve too deeply into it. Was Declan the perfect man for me or was I trying to remold him into that because I was lonely and wanted it to be true? I didn't trust my reactions to him. I'd been wrong before.

"Hmm, I guess we'll have to figure that one out." His gaze bore into me. He wasn't a pushover, not under some inadvertent spell. He was just as wary of me as I was of him.

Relief flooded through me. "Sitting up on the couch isn't a comfortable way for you to sleep, so—I'm not propositioning you—we can also sleep on my bed."

He glanced up the stairs and then out the windows. "I won't be able to relax that far away from all these open entrances. Someone's trying to make you go away and the pack isn't happy with me. As much as I'd love to go up those stairs with you, I don't think that's a good idea." He patted the cushion beside him again. "We've made this work before. We can do it again."

I gave him a pillow to put behind his head when he slouched down, his legs straight out, crossed at the ankles, his hands interlaced over his stomach. I threw the blanket I'd wrapped around myself earlier over him. I knew werewolves didn't really mind the cold, but it was especially chilly in here tonight.

Placing a second pillow against his hip, I lay on my side, head on the pillow, legs bent so I fit, and then threw the blanket

I brought downstairs over myself. "So, what's happening with the pack? Logan doesn't seem like the type to take his humiliation and let it slide."

He chuffed out a breath. "No." He was quiet for a while. "I don't know. I've got pack members following me around. I don't know if they have plans for me or are just keeping track of the lone wolf in their territory."

"Aren't you concerned about an ambush?" I snuggled deep into the blanket. The wind coming through the windows and doors was biting.

Declan pulled a corner of the blanket up, so it covered the top of my head. "Nah. And you shouldn't be either. You've got enough going on. Pretty blanket," he said, clearly changing the subject.

"Yours or mine?" His thigh muscle flexed under the pillow. If he didn't want to talk about it, I wasn't going to force him. For now, anyway.

"Both. I meant yours, but the one you gave me smells like you, which is nice."

"This one was given to me by Aunt Syl when I moved in here, as a housewarming gift. The yarn is soft and every color of the ocean. I think she commissioned a woman who's a master weaver. Look, she even added waves to her pattern."

"Hm, beautiful." He rubbed the blanket between his fingers and then turned off the muted basketball game so we could sleep.

After a few minutes, I began to drift.

"You—"

I flinched.

"Sorry. Never mind," he whispered. "Go back to sleep."

"It's okay. I'm awake. What were you saying?" Moonlight shone through the windows, giving us a night-light in the dark.

"Nothing. I was just thinking. That's important to you, isn't it? Commissioning artisans, rather than buying in a store?"

"I'd be a hell of a hypocrite if it wasn't important to me. I make my living as an artist. So, when choosing what to buy, I make sure other artists can make a living as well." I shrugged one shoulder. "Plus, I like unique things. There's something to be said for the ease and speed of ordering things through big online companies, but interesting and unique are more important to me than speed and ease."

"Hmm."

"It must be the same for you, right? You don't order mass-produced furniture. You make it yourself." And he had a gift for it. "You seem to have a real affinity for wood."

"That was my aunt's doing. She wanted me to have a male influence in my life and there was an old man who lived next door to the little house we were renting. He was retired, no kids. A little grumbly, but you could tell that under that was kindness. He'd had a career in woodworking and still tinkered in his garage. My aunt asked him if he'd be willing to teach me some basics.

"I could tell at first he wasn't too keen on the idea, but after a couple of Saturday afternoons, he started planning projects for us that would require my coming over more often. I made a mail sorter and a birdhouse, a skateboard and a bench. Eventually, he taught me to cut mortise and tenon joints, dovetail joints, so I could graduate to tables and chairs.

"I loved the planning and building. And hanging out with Edgar—he insisted I called him by his first name." While he spoke, he began to absently coil my damp curls around his finger.

"Anyway, I used to get in trouble in school. A lot. Talking, constantly getting out of my seat, not focusing on classwork. No one was thinking werewolf then—I hadn't shifted yet—but my energy level and metabolism pointed to maybe ADHD. When I was feeling down on myself, because of poor teacher reports and grades, my aunt reminded me that I had no problem focusing on woodworking.

"I'd worried I was too dumb for school, but she insisted no.

She said school was too sedentary for me, that I needed to run. Thankfully, I had a second-grade teacher who watched me run and play every chance I got. She told me when I was having trouble concentrating and needed to run, I should go take a quick lap around the school and then come back ready to work. She even made me a special pass that hung by the door.

"It was amazing. The first time I did it, I couldn't believe how much easier it was for me to do the classwork afterward. I used to run laps three or four times a day and my grades steadily improved.

"And I'm not sure why I told you all that."

I smiled in the dark. His voice was a comforting rumble that made me feel safe. "You've learned a lot about me today. Maybe you decided it was time to share something of yourself."

"Hmm…that doesn't sound like me."

31

The Siren and the Werewolf

I slept soundly for about an hour and then startled awake. I wasn't sure why. Declan's breathing was still deep and slow. He wasn't awake. The moon was setting, so the studio was darker than before.

Not wanting to wake Declan, I tried not to move too much as I looked around. Had something slithered through my spell at the windows and doors? The unease I'd felt earlier was back and stronger than ever. Even with Declan beside me, I wouldn't sleep again.

I glanced up as I tried to figure out how to stand without waking my guard. There, in the skylight, was a shadow with yellow eyes staring back at me. My heart stopped and then galloped. That wasn't a man. That was a demon. Watching me while I slept.

Tearing off the blanket, I stood and threw a spell at the skylight, turning it opaque. I turned and found Declan still asleep. A dry, papery laugh filled the room and then a horrible high-pitched shriek, like nails on a chalkboard.

I looked back up and saw lines being scraped in the now black skylight. An eye peered at me through the thin scratch.

More scraping and the word *run* appeared, along with a dry cackling that had the blood draining from my head.

All at once, footsteps pounded on the roof, racing toward the back of the gallery, to all the open windows and doors. "Declan!" I screamed.

He slept on while I ran to the back, spells racing to my fingertips. I waved both hands, slamming closed the windows and doors. Staring out into the dark, I scanned back and forth. And then there he was, standing atop a post right outside the glass door, something wriggling in his hands.

He held it up, shadowed tentacles curling against the dim moonlight reflecting on the waves. When I stepped forward, he smiled and then tore the octopus in two, flinging the halves in opposite directions.

"No!" I cried. Not Cecil, not my Cecil. I threw a spell at him, my strongest, but he barely flinched. He wagged a finger at me in admonishment, the maniacal smile slipping.

He disappeared and for one moment, I thought it was done, but then he reappeared with two giant starfish in his fists. He slapped them against the glass door. They slipped a few inches and then held.

"Don't," I breathed.

"Don't what?" His voice was in my head, mocking me. He pulled a long, serrated knife from his belt. "Don't do this?" he asked.

I barely saw his arm move before one of Herbert's star points was separated from his body, dropping into the ocean below.

"Please don't," I begged.

Never breaking eye contact, never dimming his grin, he cut off each and every arm until only the center discs remained. Then he stabbed each and flung them over his shoulder into the water.

I understood the threat. This was what he'd do to me.

Wilbur barked and the demon's eyes lit up. He disappeared again. *No. No. No.*

I went to the back door, my hand hovering over the knob. This was what he wanted, me letting him in. I couldn't. I knew I couldn't, but neither could I stand here and watch him kill Wilbur.

I stripped off my gloves, rubbed my hands together, and called on the combined power of the Council, of my mother and grandmother. The power built in me and when I threw the spell, I had a moment to worry it still might not be enough. The demon held up Wilbur to take the hit in his stead. My little fetch buddy was there, his eyes wide with fear, and then he was blown to bits, like he'd swallowed a grenade.

I screamed and the demon laughed, his harsh papery voice filling my brain.

"Arwyn! Wake. Up."

Blinking, the shout caught in my throat, I stared into Declan's concerned brown eyes. His hands caged my upper arms and I realized he must have been shaking me, trying to extricate me from that nightmare. Had it been a nightmare, though?

Head swiveling, I tried to take it all in. The skylight was clear, gray morning light trickling through. The windows and doors were open.

"Is the word *run* scratched into the skylight?" His eyesight was perfect. If the scratches were there, he'd see them.

Thankfully, he didn't throw off the question. He stared at the skylight a moment and then jogged up the stairs to get a better look. He shook his head. "No," he said, looking over the railing at me.

I shook off the blanket and stood. Okay, good. Good. Maybe it was just a dream. Maybe—but I'd felt the uneasiness before he appeared. I'd felt it while I was awake. Had it found a way into my home? Had the fire messed with my protections?

Or had I become his unwitting host? Was he rattling around inside of me? A chill ran down my spine.

When I turned in my pacing, I bounced off Declan's chest. He grabbed me before I lost my balance.

"Can I ask another favor?"

He nodded warily.

"Can you check on Charlie and Herbert for me?" If it was all a nightmare, they'd both still be on their posts.

Declan nodded before stopping at the open door. "Can I get through?

I waved a hand, dismantling the spell, and he leapt through, landing on the top of the closest post before hopping to the next. Once he was on the last one, he leaned over, pulling his phone from his pocket and taking a picture to put me at ease. "They're fine," he called.

My heartbeat slowly returned to normal. "Cecil? Wilbur? Are you okay?" I didn't know if either were in earshot, but I hoped.

"A tentacle splashed the water over here," Declan called, returning his phone to his pocket. A moment later, when a soggy tennis ball flew straight at his face, he caught it easily and sent it sailing out over the early morning gray surf.

"Thank you." I moved out of the doorway so Declan could jump back in. "Really," I said, grabbing his wrist. "Thank you. I was so scared it was real."

He looked down at my gloved hand on him and then let his gaze travel to my eyes and my mouth. My body combusted, but I didn't move.

He reached for the long curl hanging in my face. He rubbed it between his fingers, his eyes never leaving mine. "Soft," he murmured before pushing the curl back, out of my face.

"I'm going to bake, but you can go back to sleep. You have a few hours before Phil and the guys show up." I headed to the kitchen and then remembered. "The dryer." I jogged up the stairs to move our clothes.

Once I was done, I brushed my teeth and dealt with my hair. I needed to put it up before I started baking. No one wanted my hair in their food. I flipped my head over, gathered my hair, coiled it up, and then flipped up to secure the sloppy bun with a super strong band.

When I came back down, Declan was still standing at the open door.

"Everything okay?" I went to the pantry to start collecting ingredients. Ever since meeting Detective Osso last night, I'd been thinking of making something with honey. I'd pretty much decided on brown butter honey cookies, although honey vanilla pound cake was a close second.

"No," Declan said.

It took me a moment to remember I'd asked him a question. I put down the flour, sugar, and honey on the counter and turned. "What's the matter?"

He walked toward me, his stare intent. "Are you attracted to me?"

"Oh, um." My whole body went up in flames every time I looked at him, but I was pretty sure I wasn't supposed to tell him that. I cleared my throat. "Yes. Yes, I am."

He blew out a breath. "Good." He came to a stop directly in front of me. "I don't know how to reconcile feeling this way about you if nothing can ever happen between us."

"Oh," I said again. I was having a hard time thinking when he was looking at me like that.

"So I propose an experiment. Before either of us go too far down this path, we should kiss. If you can't be with me, I need to find a way to stop thinking about you naked."

"Oooh" seemed to be the only word I was capable of.

"What do you say?"

The fire in his eyes melted my resolve. "Okay."

He took each hand, slowly pulling my gloves off and dropping them onto the floor. He held my hands in his own, his thumb brushing circles in my palms. "Still okay?"

Was it? I didn't hear his thoughts, so I nodded.

"Good." He leaned down, his lips hovering over mine until I couldn't take it and leaned forward, taking his mouth with my own.

It was electric. Groaning, I went to my tiptoes and wrapped my arms around his neck. He grabbed my butt and hiked me up around his waist so the height difference wasn't so problematic. He tilted his head and his tongue was sliding along my own.

And then I was sitting on some surface I could care less about because his hands were gripping my hips and his lips were on mine. I had my legs wrapped so tightly around him, he was never getting loose.

After a few hours or a few minutes, he leaned back and looked down at me, a finger caressing my cheek. "Do you know what I'm thinking?"

"I hope to hell it's what I'm thinking," I said, flexing my legs, bringing him in closer so we lined up just right.

"But you don't know for sure?" he asked.

"What? No, I—oh! No. I don't know what you're thinking. It's something nice, though, right? Please don't be thinking I have a huge ass and you can just close your eyes and pretend I'm someone else."

His growl filled the room and stirred up the bubbles inside me. Leaning in, he kissed my neck before nibbling on my ears. "If you remember his name, I'll go rip his throat out. I won't even feel bad about it."

He ran his hands from my hips to my thighs and back. "He was clearly a moron. You are"—he studied me from the top of my head down to my feet—"a work of art, one created to drive me mad." His hands moved up, barely brushing the side of my breasts.

I was going to combust. Here and now. Just go up in flames, immolated on the altar of lust.

"You're a siren, calling men to die at your feet, no room in their thoughts for anything but you." He kissed me again, long and deep. His hands gripped my hips, pulling me to the edge of the counter and then tipping me back, the bulge in his jeans hitting me just right. When his hips began to move, my head dropped back on a groan.

"Arwyn!"

Declan and I stopped and stared at each other a moment. Did we both hear that?

"Oh, darling. It's so much worse than you said." Shit. Mom.

"You have got to be kidding me," I groused, pushing Declan back and straightening my clothes. "Come to the front door, Mom. You can't come in that way."

I turned back to Declan and ran my hand down his chest. "Sorry."

He nodded, scrubbing his hands over his face.

I rested my hand on the bulge in his jeans. "Hold that thought."

"Seeing as you're coming back with your mom, that's probably not the best idea," he grumbled.

32

Jeez, Is This the Real Corey Curse?

W hen I came back into the studio with Mom, Declan was gone. Weird. I supposed he could have used the posts out the back door for a quick exit. I wouldn't have blamed him. Men with hard-ons rarely want to chat up moms who didn't trust them in the first place. Understandable. Still bummed me out, though.

"Did you have these windows open all night?" Her concern rightly focused on the fire, not the absent suitor. Paramour? Beau?

"The sprinkler system didn't go off, which was good in the long run, but—"

"They were probably spelled not to," she interrupted, placing her handbag and keys on my worktable.

"Right, but the smoke in here was horrible. It needed to be aired out." I pulled out my mixing bowls and then butter and eggs from the refrigerator. Sometimes my mother was easier to deal with if I didn't give her my full attention. "Have you had breakfast?"

"Yes. I had some yogurt and granola before I left home. Could you brew some tea, though, dear?" She paced the room, checking everything out before folding the blankets on the sofa. "Did you sleep down here?"

"If you can call it that," I said. "I slept for maybe an hour before I had a horrible nightmare." I set the kettle to boil and then added Mom's favorite loose leaf tea to the infuser.

"Ergo, the baking." She sat on the sofa and watched me collect the rest of the ingredients.

"How's Gran doing?" I dropped four sticks of butter into a saucepan, lit the fire under it, set a timer on my phone, and then turned to Mom.

"Mourning, of course, as are we all."

I just realized we were both dressed all in black.

"That's the blanket Sylvia gave you, isn't it?" Mom stared at the folded blanket she'd left on my chair.

"It is."

She nodded. "We're planning an informal get-together this afternoon. It will take time to plan the funeral. We need to be together now. Gather around your grandmother."

"Of course," I said. "What time?" I poured the boiling water over the tea infuser and let it steep in the pot. I then held my hand over the pot and pushed it along.

"Why are your gloves on the floor?"

Thankfully, I was looking away, checking on the butter browning, so she couldn't see my face flush. "They must have fallen out of my pocket. I usually use thin rubber gloves for cooking. No one wants fuzz in their baked goods."

"But then why aren't you wearing them?"

I stared down at my hands, confused. Normally, if I touched a carton of eggs or a bag of flour without gloves, I'd tap into the person who stocked the shelves in the market or the cashier or someone. "Maybe my brain is just too frazzled." But I worried about why it was different today.

I went to my worktable, snapped on the thin blue gloves, and set a tea tray for Mom, including the last lemon bar. "Here you go."

"Thank you, darling, and four o'clock. Bring whatever you're making this morning. I'll have a simple buffet catered, but your desserts are always better than whatever they can come up with."

"Sylvia loved key lime pie. I'll make that for this afternoon. Individual tartlets with a shortbread crust."

Mom nodded, but I could tell she wasn't listening, her thoughts no doubt consumed by the two sisters she'd never see again.

My alarm went off, making us both jump. I added the brown butter to brown sugar, granulated sugar, and honey in the large bowl of the stand mixer and set it to mixing on medium.

"Did the wolf stay with you last night?"

Damn. She waited until I was facing her for that one. Luckily, I'd spent my life schooling my expression when I saw things I really wished I hadn't. "Yeah, he did. Poor guy. He maybe got an hour of sleep before I was waking him up with a nightmare." Always stick as close to the truth as you can when telling a believable lie or, in this case, omission. "I'd spelled the windows and doors so I could be safe while airing it out. The problem is I have no idea what demons are capable of. I wasn't going to leave Declan down here on his own to deal with whatever walked through that door." I turned around and began adding eggs, one at a time.

"I see." She gave a long, suspicious pause and then said, "Well, it's good you had backup, if you needed it."

I added vanilla to the mixer and then poured flour and baking soda into a bowl and whisked them together. Footsteps sounded above in the loft. Oh, so that was where Declan had got off to.

"Darling, is someone here?" Mom wasn't fooling me. She thought naughty things were happening with Declan. Granted, if she hadn't shown up so early, that probably would have been true, but as it hadn't, I didn't enjoy getting the vocal equivalent

226

of a side-eye when I hadn't done anything. Not that it was any of her business!

"Arwyn?"

Oh, right. I was too busy arguing with her in my head to answer her. "Yeah, Declan. I just told you he stayed to help me guard the windows and doors. He jumped in the ocean last night to fish out the burned boards. I washed his clothes while he slept, so he could get cleaned up before work."

"So he slept here naked while you cleaned his clothes?" The shock and horror in her voice were over the top.

I scrunched up my face. "Don't be ridiculous. Like I'd have anyone's naked ass on my couch. That's my napping spot."

"I had another set of clothes in my truck," Declan said, coming down the stairs. When he got to the bottom, he watched me for a moment. "Thanks for letting me use your shower. It feels great to finally wash the sand and grit away." He had the clothes he'd slept in under his arm.

"Oh, go put those in my washing machine. I'll do another load today. You don't have to take dirty clothes home with you."

"Thanks. I appreciate that." He turned and jogged back up.

When Mom thought Declan was out of earshot, she said, "Not today, but soon, the Council needs to meet and cast as one. We must try to find the sorcerer."

"Okay." I looked longingly at the giant tentacles. It looked like they'd be put off a bit longer. "When I'm done with the cookies, I'll start on the key lime tartlets for this afternoon."

"Good." She came and gave me a kiss on the cheek, just as Declan was descending again. "Mr. Quinn, would you escort me out?"

"Of course." He went to her and offered his arm.

"That won't be necessary," she said, striding past him through the door to the gallery.

Eyes rolling, I slowly mixed the dry ingredients into the mixer, definitely not wondering why she'd waylaid him. I was pretty sure I knew why. She blamed Michael Quinn for her sister's death, even though that was obviously untrue. The Coreys were to blame for Bridget. We'd produced yet another sorcerer.

We had a reputation for it. We were one of the most powerful wicche lines in the world and were, quite tragically, one of the most interested in black magic and sorcery. Coreys had been killing each other off for millennia. In fact, it became so bad, a Corey Council ages ago created a curse.

Be warned. If hand is raised and Corey slew
Powers, born and learned, shall be stripped
from you
Treachery, like a poison, has weakened our clan
We, the three, have enacted a plan
Once great, we are too few
Slaughter and you will be unmade. We spake
true.

As children, we memorized it. We had it drilled into us that we should never turn from the light and that we must never endanger one of our own. Yet, here we were. With another damned sorcerer doing whatever it took to gain more power.

When Declan returned, I asked, "Everything okay?"

"Sure," he said, crossing to me and leaning against the counter, watching me mix in extra honey—I had a feeling I'd be seeing Detective Osso today. "She hates my guts and wants me to leave town now, but other than that, all good."

I turned to go get into a hell of a fight with my mom, but Declan grabbed me around the waist, spun me around, and kissed me instead. Oh, all right. I'd leave off for now. He really was an excellent kisser.

Sometime later, we heard, "Kee-ryst, would you look at this." Again, we stopped and stared at each other. This time, though, Declan's hand was up the front of my top, cradling my breast. It was nice. My left boob totally wanted to make friends. He hugged me to him, grabbed my ass, and then blew out a breath.

"You're killing me, Ursula." He untied the flannel shirt from around his waist and then put it on. Untucked.

"Phil," he called. "I'll let you in the front door."

After he left, I used my scooper to make perfect cookie balls, filling up baking sheets. I put them in the oven and started another timer before going out to talk with Phil and the guys. Declan had already filled him in on the fire and they'd begun to discuss what needed to be done.

"Ms. Corey, we'll check, but we're probably going to need to tear out part of the roof, replace any burned timbers, and then re-tile. Have you called the fire department yet? You'll need their report to submit to your insurance."

I nodded, only half listening. The asshole who set that fire not only almost burned down my home, they'd also created chaos and headaches and expense. What was the point? I'd originally thought it was retaliation for eavesdropping on Dave's conversation with the demon, but now I wasn't so sure. The sorcerer, or someone the demon possessed like the nurse, had come over here with gasoline. They'd sprayed it around and lit a match. Timing wise, though, it couldn't have been in retaliation. Most people don't have full gas cans lying around for arson emergencies.

So, was it planned? No one would have guessed we'd be in a hospital room after hours, after midnight. Was the plan to kill me in the inferno? Was that the goal?

"Ms. Corey?"

"Sorry, Phil." I shook my head, annoyed with myself. "I'm a little out of it today. What did you ask?"

"We're discussing how safe this building is." He scratched his forehead. "We also have another big job starting when this one was supposed to end, so I've got some rearranging to do. I don't want to leave you with no back wall or roof, but…" He rubbed his fingers over his mouth. "Could you maybe live somewhere else for a while?"

"Yes," Declan said just as I said, "No."

"I'll call the fire department," I said. "I'm pretty sure I have an uncle who's a firefighter. Doesn't matter; I'll get that started. We don't need to wait six months for insurance. I can pay for your work while I wait for the check."

Phil let out a relieved breath. "Okay, well, that's good. Uh, Declan said most of the piers looked okay. There was minimal damage, which is great. He can get started rebuilding right away." He turned to Declan. "I can call in a lumber order."

Declan nodded.

"Okay. I'm going to climb up on the roof and see what we're dealing with," Phil said.

"Oh," I began, not sure how to phrase it. Phil was in his late fifties, early sixties. He should not be climbing around a peaked roof like a mountain goat.

"I can do that, boss," Declan cut in.

Phil looked relieved but said, "You'll be building a deck."

"Not yet, and I won't be working on the roof, just giving a damage assessment."

If I hadn't already wanted to jump him, that would have done it. He was letting Phil save face while still getting the job done.

"Well, okay, but be careful up there."

"I will. I'll be fine." He walked toward the front door. "I'll grab the big ladder from your truck and then go around the side to hop on."

When he opened the door, Detectives Osso and Hernández were standing on the porch.

"Jeez, don't you two sleep?" I asked.

They stepped in as Declan went out. "We could ask you the same," Osso responded.

The alarm on my phone went off. "Come on back. I had a feeling you might be visiting today."

"What am I smelling?" Detective Osso asked, sniffing the air.

33

Never Get Between a Bear and His Honey

"Let me just get this taken care of and we can talk." I pulled out the baking sheets and lined them up on the stove top, then I began to fill my second set of baking sheets. "Detective Osso, do you prefer your cookies chewy or crisp?"

"I like both. Why?"

I almost jumped at his deep voice. Almost. I hadn't realized he'd moved directly behind me. "Half the batch is for you."

He let out a gust of air and remained directly behind me.

"After meeting you," I elaborated, "I started thinking about honey recipes. I added a little more than the recipe called for, but I didn't think that would be a problem." Sliding the new trays into the oven, I reset my timer, and then transferred half the batch to the cooling racks, leaving the other half on the baking trays. "The ones I leave on the cookie sheets for a few more minutes will be chewier."

He made a soft grunt and nodded.

"If you'd like a couple right away, before they coo—"

"Yes."

I hid my smile by getting a plate from the cabinet. I moved four from the rack to his plate and then handed it to him.

He sniffed and then threw one in this mouth and savored it

a moment before swallowing and throwing another in. Had he chewed? Eh, whatever.

I glanced around Detective Osso's huge frame to find Hernández once again staring at my paintings. "Detective Hernández, would you like a couple of cookies?" At Osso's strange, growly sound of disapproval, I added, "Hers will come from my half of the batch, not yours."

He threw the last two into his mouth on a nod.

I slid a cookie onto a folded paper napkin and brought it to her. She nodded her thanks, still staring at the underwater painting.

"I couldn't sleep. The—" She looked at the open door and whispered, "demon you talked about last night, the one who possessed the nurse, is he involved in this stuff too?" she asked, gesturing to the paintings.

I walked to the adjoining door and shut it. Phil, Juan, and Mike couldn't hear through walls and I didn't want the detectives to have to whisper or speak in code. "Dave, the nice demon you met last night"—I thought about that a moment and then shrugged—"I guess he's nice. I don't know. He's only half demon. Maybe that makes a difference. Anyway, he explained that when you have a demon and sorcerer working together in a particular area, bad things start happening around them. It's not directly related, except it is.

"The demon and sorcerer aren't out encouraging people to kill each other. It's more that what they do allows evil to seep into the community and then those individuals who were just barely clinging to appropriate social behavior are pushed over the line. All those horrible impulses that they've been able to suppress up to that point are now set free. The reins have snapped and they're acting out in ways they'd only ever fantasized about."

"Shit," Detective Osso grumbled.

"Exactly," I said. "Have you had an increase in violent crimes lately?"

"Yes," Hernández responded. "It's been increasing over the past couple of years, but in the last six months, maybe, it's gotten so much worse." She looked at Osso for confirmation and he nodded.

Hernández stared down at the cookie in her hand as if confused as to how it had appeared. Shaking her head at whatever she was thinking, she took a bite and stopped, closing her eyes. "Oh my God. Maybe you should be opening a bakery instead of a gallery."

"I excel at many things," I said, strangely annoyed that she'd prioritize my baking over my art.

There was a thump outside the window and we all turned. Declan, balancing on one foot on the post outside the door, leapt in. "I can vouch for that. She excels at a great many things."

"Where the hell were you?" Detective Osso demanded.

"Roof." Declan pointed up. "Arwyn hasn't mentioned it yet, but she had a visit from an arsonist last night while we were all at the hospital."

"What?" Hernández strode to the door and then grabbed the frame. "The deck's gone."

The alarm went off in my pocket. "Don't remind me." I pulled out the cookie sheets and then loaded up two more with the last of the batter. "Hey, do you know the name of an arson inspector I can call?"

I went back to my pantry and looked for a carrier to loan Osso. Top shelf. As I felt uncomfortable using a spell in front of the cops, I started to drag over a chair. Declan was there, putting the chair back.

"What do you need?"

"Oh, good. Top shelf. I need both those carriers." I turned to the very large detective hovering possessively around my oven. "I can loan you my cookie carrier, but I need it back, okay?"

234

He nodded, his focus on the cookies. "What kind of honey do you use?"

I went to my pantry and pulled out four sealed jars. "I have a cousin—there are a million of us, but not all magical—who's a beekeeper. She makes her own blends. In the cookies, I used a fig honey. I also have clover, pomegranate, and an apple-pear I particularly like. Today, though, I thought you'd like fig best."

"Yes," he nodded, studying the jars.

"Would you like a taste of these?"

"Yes," he said, reaching for the jars.

I put them down on the worktable we'd eaten off of last night and grabbed four spoons from a drawer. When I turned back, he already had all four lids off and was sniffing.

"Arthur, someone set fire to the gallery." Hernández watched Osso with disbelief. "You know, police work."

"I can do both," he grumbled before savoring the first spoonful, one so full, I knew I'd need to order more honey.

I think watching Detective Osso's fixation on honey was making the rest of us uncomfortable, so Declan suggested taking photos of the damage for the cops. While Declan hopped from post to post, taking pictures and Osso took a honey break, I started loading cookies into the four-tiered carrier.

When I finished, I scribbled my cousin's name and web address so Detective Osso could buy himself some honey. I put the card on top of the carrier and placed both on the table beside him. There was one moment of tension when I thought for sure I was about to be swatted by huge bear claws because I took the honey jars back—far emptier than when I'd pulled them from the pantry.

Declan was back, showing Detective Hernández the images. "Arthur, come look at these."

He put the card in his wallet and then picked up the carrier of cookies, taking it with him across the studio.

"Can you send me the photos and I'll contact someone I know in Fire who should be able to help. Let her do her inspection, though, before you start repairs." Hernández then started texting. "Arthur, why don't you explain to Arwyn why we're here this morning."

A rumble rolled through the room, but it didn't seem directed at anyone, more frustration in general. "A little girl disappeared into the woods yesterday."

"Yellow dress?" I asked, the vision racing back to me. "She was coloring on the back porch, wearing a yellow dress?"

"Yes," he grumbled.

"Was there a woman with her, inside the house?" I hadn't seen her, but Mom and Gran had. That had to be significant.

"Yes. A girl, but yes. The babysitter was in the kitchen, by the back door to the porch. She was texting with her friends and didn't hear or see anything."

"How old is the babysitter?" I asked. I was getting a funny feeling about that wave Mom and Gran had seen.

"Uh." He checked his notes. "Fifteen. Why?"

A little older than I'd anticipated. "I think the babysitter knows the killer. The age isn't quite right, so maybe not a friend. Maybe just knows him. He's a neighbor or the younger brother of a friend."

"You think she knows something?" He started scribbling in his notebook.

"No," I said slowly. "It isn't that. I don't think she's covering for him or anything. I just think you might find him through her."

He nodded. "Can you come with us to her house? Touch things. Whatever it is you do?"

I looked at my unfinished tentacles that would remain unfinished a little longer and sighed. "Yeah, sure. I need to be back by one, though. I have desserts to make for my aunt's sort-of wake."

"We can get you back by then," Hernández said.

Declan shook his head. "I'll drive her. Then she can leave whenever she needs to." He turned to find my eyebrows raised.

The presumption was strong in this one.

"If that's okay with you. I can't get started until the inspector's been here and the materials have been delivered. Besides, I'd like to help if I can," he said.

I turned and headed for the stairs. "Give me a minute to get changed."

Rummaging through my closet, I grabbed jeans and a sweater and changed before pulling on my hiking boots. Taking the band out of my hair, I let it fall but kept the tie in my pocket in case I needed it later. I stopped in the bathroom, put on some mascara and lip balm, and called it good enough.

When I went back downstairs, I found Hernández studying the painting of the woods and Declan and Osso outside balancing on the tops of piers, studying the fire damage.

"Was this intentional?" she asked. "Right here?"

I stood beside her to look where she was pointing.

"Do you see it? It looks wet and muddy, under the leaves and this bush, but there's yellow. You used yellow paint. You can barely see it, but there's one thin, yellow brushstroke right here."

Peering closely, I saw what she did. The edge of a yellow dress. "I don't remember painting that." I tried to shake off the unease but couldn't. Glancing up at the skylight, I found it demon-free and told myself to relax. "I was in the zone, just trying to get everything out of my head and onto the canvas."

"I took pictures of them both," she said. "Hope you don't mind. I want to study them in detail. There may be more in there you didn't realize."

Nodding, my eyes wandered the whole large canvas. What else had I missed?

Detective Osso and Declan hopped in the door and shut it, both moving to the painting. They'd clearly heard our conversation. Declan pointed at the wisp of yellow, Osso nodding.

I was about to remind Detective Osso not to forget his cookies when I saw he already had the carrier in his hand and was chewing.

Declan swung by the stove top, picked up two cookies, and bit in. He sighed and shook his head. "Damn," he breathed. "Oh, and can I have one of the key lime tarts? I love key lime."

Detective Hernández looked around. "Where?"

"She hasn't made them yet," Declan responded.

Hernández raised her hand. "May I, too, request one? Please."

After pulling butter out of the fridge to soften for the short-bread crust, assuring all assembled they would get one and making up a plate of cookies for Phil, Juan, and Mike, I finally climbed into Declan's truck. Phil had assured me he'd keep an eye out for the arson inspector.

"Osso gave me the address," Declan said, putting it into his phone. He glanced over. "You okay?"

"Yeah," I said. "I just can't get my hands warm." I rubbed my gloved hands together, confused. It wasn't a cold day.

He took my left hand, wrapping his right around it. He radiated heat and I began to thaw. "Do you want to take the gloves off? It'll probably warm you up faster."

I was just about to do it and then stopped myself. I didn't know why but my heart sped at the idea, not in excitement but in fear. Something was telling me not to do it. But what and why? I pulled my hand out of his as a horrible thought occurred to me.

"It's just around this bend. We're maybe a mile from the last house. Christopher's," Declan clarified.

"Okay." I needed to get my head in the game. A child had been taken. People were relying on me. The Council and therefore my family relied on me. If what I was thinking was true— and I desperately hoped it wasn't—it meant I had to choose between my own happiness and everyone else's safety. Why did the universe hate me so much?

34

Too Bad You Can't Eat in a Vision

"You okay?" Declan asked, glancing over. "You seemed to get sad all of a sudden."

"What?" How could he know that?

He tapped his nose. "Wolves can pick up emotions, smell lies. Not always, but often."

"Oh. Cool." I wasn't ready for this conversation. I needed to find my resolve before I discussed it.

Declan pulled up behind a patrol car and shut off the engine. For the first time in my life, I worried my gift wouldn't be there. I'd wished it away a million times and now here I was, desperate for it to work. This was who I was. I didn't know how to *not* be the sea wicche. Finding this little girl, keeping Gran from being murdered and Serena out of prison relied on my being the sea wicche, on my having the powers I was born with.

My mind kept going back to this morning. I'd been cooking without gloves. I'd rummaged in the pantry, picked up packages, cookie sheets, measuring cups, all of it and hadn't felt anything. If Declan was a magical null, it meant I could have a partner, a lover. I could hold his hand or kiss his lips, but doing so would strip my magic away.

He opened his door and then paused. "Are we still doing this?"

Osso and Hernández were waiting outside the truck for me. I couldn't think about this now. I opened the door and jumped out. What if it didn't work anymore? Was I still a Cassandra?

"It's this way," Detective Osso said, leading us up the short walkway to the front steps of the small house in the woods. It was similar to Christopher's, small, neat, and butted up against the woods. This one, however, had a stream running along the back of the house. There was no fence around the house, so I could see a bit of it from the porch.

I followed mutely, terrified I'd fail. With an audience. Other aspects of my life might have been in shambles, but the one thing I could always count on was my gift. It felt like I was marching to the gallows. My mind should have been on the missing girl and instead I was panicking that I'd touch her belongings and feel absolutely nothing.

"Are you okay?" Declan whispered, putting his hand on my shoulder. I cringed away and he reeled back like he'd been slapped.

I held up my hands. "Sorry. I need a minute. My head's all messed up." I stepped off the small porch and cut across the struggling lawn to the narrow, empty road. I knew they were probably talking about me, but I couldn't care about that. People had thought I was crazy my whole life. A few more weren't a big deal in the grand scheme of things. My magic not working was.

Sending up a prayer to the goddess, I took off my gloves, joined my hands, and searched my mind for what was hidden inside me. Images flashed, so many it felt like a water hose of visions had been unleashed, taking me out at the knees. I heard a low curse and then I was out.

I woke up in the cab of Declan's truck in his lap. Scrambling away from him, I plastered myself against the opposite door.

"Whoa. Wait. What just happened?" he asked.

"You can't touch me." I heard the panic in my voice as clearly as he did.

He held up his hands like he was dealing with a skittish wild animal. "I won't, but why?"

I didn't want to do this now. A little girl needed me, but I wanted him to understand. "I have to give them whatever information I can about this little girl."

He nodded. "Right. That's why we're here."

"This morning, I kissed you. Touched you—"

"You said you didn't read me." His brow furrowed, trying to understand the problem.

"I didn't, but afterward when I was cooking, I forgot to put on my gloves. I touched a dozen things and didn't see anything. At all." I waited for him to understand but he clearly didn't.

"Declan, if the reason I can kiss you is because you're a magical null—"

"A what?"

"A person or thing that strips away magic. If you're a null, then I can't do what I need to do in order to find this girl. When I joined the Corey Council, that vision I had that knocked us all out—I have shit I have to do to keep my family safe. I'm afraid that being with you strips away my magic and without it"—I shook my head, overcome by the thought—"I'm nothing."

"No. That's not true." He moved and I flinched. Deflating, he sat back, staring out the windshield. "I don't believe that. I don't believe your gift only exists in isolation. You're stronger than that." He crossed his arms over his chest. "I won't touch you until you say I can, but we're going to figure this out. Okay?"

"Not now," I responded.

"Of course not now. You have a little girl to find. Later. Arwyn," he said, waiting for me to look at him, "I'll leave if you ask me to, but let's not make decisions based on partial information, okay?"

Hope could devastate, but a small, warm spot in my chest

began to hope. "Okay," I said, slipping out of his truck again. I looked down and realized my gloves were on again. "Did you put my gloves on me?"

He nodded. "I was trying to protect you from more visions."

"But then you had to touch my hands."

He nodded.

Shit. I might not be able to read anything in this girl's house.

Osso and Hernández waited for us on the porch, talking in hushed tones when we returned.

"Sorry. I'm ready to try now." *Try.* Who was I? I didn't try. I did. My stomach twisted, terrified that now I did not.

The dimensions of the house were similar to Christopher's, but the furnishings were quite different. Christopher's house had been sparse and tidy. This one, however, was full of life, sneakers left by the door, magazines on the coffee table, headphones and an empty glass on a small dining table, and lots and lots of books. They had two overstuffed bookcases along one wall, with more piled up on the floor beside them. In the short hall to the bedrooms, pictures had been hung of the girl through the years.

The detectives waited at the door, letting me go in alone. It was a tiny jewel box of a room. The walls were a lemony yellow like her dress. Her favorite color. The comforter was an airy white with a fringe of lace around the edges. Her pillowcases bore a lush, floral design.

A small table draped in yellow fabric sat beside her bed, with a big-eyed stuffed elephant standing atop and staring at the empty bed. Colorful construction paper flowers adorned the walls. White lacy curtains hung over her window.

I pushed the curtain aside and looked out over the backyard, stream, and woods. Turning, I studied the bureau and the bed, the little table and the bookcase stuffed with picture books, trying to decide which one would be the most meaningful, which one would give me the strongest vision—assuming I saw anything at all.

Gaze resting once again on the elephant, I decided to start

there. Crossing to the bed, I sat and gave myself a moment to breathe. Slowly, I slipped off the gloves and placed them on the table beside me. Taking a deep breath, I blew it out and then picked up the elephant. No immediate jolt. *Fuck.*

Glancing over my shoulder at Declan, who stood at the door with the others, I shook my head. He strode out of view and I tried again, digging deep. Still nothing. Stomach jittering, I moved one hand to her pillowcase while the other held tight to the elephant.

Spits and sputters, flashes. A birthday cake. Presents. Crying. Crayons. A coloring book. Balloon animals. Face paint.

It was clearly a birthday party, but I couldn't see enough of any flash to know why it was important. Suddenly something cold and wet touched me. My eyes flew open to see Declan, leaning over me, holding something to my forehead and the back of my neck.

"Wha—"

"It's not salt water," he said, "but it's from the stream out back. It's fresh water." He nodded encouragingly. "Go on."

Taking a deep breath, I closed my eyes again, hands on pillow and elephant. Water trickled down the back of my sweater and the sides of my face, and I felt better, more myself. Lifting my hands to my cheeks, I touched the water and then the pillow and elephant again.

I was falling backward in slow motion, plummeting into a vast nothingness. Dim lights like lightning bugs zipped around me. I'd been falling so long, I stopped worrying about hitting bottom. I was in a bottomless freefall as pinpoints of light bobbed around me.

One in particular, a persistent little bugger, hovered at the end of my nose. When I swatted at it, it disappeared. A moment later, it was back. I tried again, intent to catch it, and I did. I held the fluttering light tight in my fist and then I was standing outside in the creek.

I was barefoot, the water to my shins. Extraordinary. I

glanced around, something deep in the woods calling to me. A laugh broke the silence and then noise rushed back in, disorienting me. No longer falling in a soundless void, I was dropped into the middle of a five-year-old's birthday party.

Music blared from a speaker. A man was barbecuing ribs, chicken, and ears of corn. A table nearby was laden with a feast: tamales, enchiladas, beans and rice, guacamole, salsa, a pot of pozole, and a pink and white birthday cake with a unicorn on top.

The adults were trying to gather the children to sit and eat. A woman in a pirate costume made balloon animals for the children while another painted faces. The birthday girl, in a dress of pink frills, came running, out of breath, having eluded the three children chasing her.

She had a face filled with flowers and vines, a balloon unicorn under one arm and a stuffed elephant under the other. Her mother picked her up and swung her around before balancing her on a hip.

Whispering in Ana's ear, her mother asked, "Are you having fun, mija?"

"Yes!" Ana bounced, wanting down. "Can I play some more, Mama?"

Her mother tried to find a spot on her daughter's face not covered in paint. It wasn't easy, but she found a clean spot for a kiss. She put her daughter back on the ground and called, "Come back to eat soon!" but knew her daughter had already put food out of her head and was rushing back for another balloon animal.

The longer I watched the family and friends talking and laughing, running and shouting, I knew I was looking in the wrong direction. A chill ran down my spine, a prickling between my shoulder blades.

I turned my back on the light and love, instead staring into the gaping maw of death—the forest—or more precisely, the hunger within the forest watching the children.

Much like Hernández studying my paintings, I scrutinized the wooded area before me. Towering trees created an ever-gloom, with saplings, bushes, and vines growing thick amongst them, hiding secrets, and a killer. He was here, watching, imagining. Vile thoughts cycled through his brain. He hated them, hated them all, with their birthday song and candles, the brightly wrapped presents and hugs. Blocking out the party, he imagined each of them dead by his hand.

Studying people as one would animals in a zoo, he'd learned how to mimic, how to behave as they did. He practiced expressions in the mirror. No one ever really paid him much attention, but if they did, he knew how to look confused and innocent. He was just a kid, after all.

No, sir. I never saw a little girl. I'm in sixth grade. Why would I be playing with a kindergartener? And a girl?

Yeah, that was the right tone. Respectful but uninterested. Even when adults looked at him, they never saw him. He liked it that way.

He eyed the birthday girl greedily, watching her father spin her through the air. It wouldn't be long until those squeals of laughter turned to screams. He couldn't wait.

I heard his thoughts. I didn't see him, but I also didn't turn away. Like that brushstroke of yellow hidden in the painting, he was hidden in this forest. I was standing in this stream for a reason. There was something special about this perspective. I was sure of it.

Leaves were fluttering in the wind. My eyes, though, were drawn up, to a spot that moved out of sync with the wind. Finally, I saw it. Blue eyes peeked out from behind obscuring tree branches. So young. How did one so young become so irretrievably twisted?

And then he moved forward and I saw his face, the empty eyes and the feral grin. I had him. Opening my hand, I released the lightning bug that had found me in the void.

35

Unicorn Deception

Blinking, I looked into Declan's eyes. He was crouched in front of me, still holding wet towels to my forehead and the back of my neck. "How messed up are your legs right now?" They were shaking, poor guy.

He fell back on the bedroom floor with a pained groan.

"How long was I in it?" I glanced at the detectives before turning back to Declan, who had moved, trying to find space in the small room to stretch out on the floor.

"I'm fine," he said, though the strain in his voice said anything but that.

"Far too long for him to be stuck in that position," Osso clarified. "I tried to take over but none of us wanted to do anything that would interrupt the vision."

I stood, putting the elephant back on the table and slipping my gloves back on. "Stay there," I said to Declan. "Can I get paper and a pencil?" I asked Detective Osso. "I have his face."

I hadn't brought a sketch pad and charcoals—which I really should, if I did any more police consulting. I felt like a horrible intruder, walking through their lovely home, their daughter's death fresh in my mind. Sitting at the dining table, I waited for supplies. Osso came back in the house a few minutes later with a memo and a dull pencil.

"Good enough." I scrubbed the side of the lead back and forth over the memo, slowly rolling the pencil, sharpening it without a sharpener, and then turned the memo over to the blank side and got to work.

I wasn't sure how long I was sketching, but when I'd finished, I looked up to find all three of them sitting at the table watching me. I slid the sheet across the table to Detective Osso.

"That's him. If you show that to the babysitter, she'll be able to identify him." Standing, I checked my phone for the time.

"Wait," Osso said as he and Hernández rose as well. "Where is she? Is she still alive?"

I blew out a breath and shook my head. "I didn't get it all. Parts were muddy or incomplete, I guess. I was just getting flashes before Declan used the water—good call, by the way—so I'm not positive." Both detectives had their notepads out. "Again, this is based on feelings and images I saw for less than a second, okay?"

"We get it," Osso grumbled. "Go."

"We understand this isn't an exact science. Your impressions could help direct our investigation, though," Hernández elaborated.

"Okay." I went to the back door. "Let's go outside." Stopping at the edge of the stream, I tried to gauge where I'd been standing in the vision.

When I sat down on the grass and began to unlace my boots, Declan moved beside me. "What are you doing?

Once I'd removed my boots and socks, I pulled up the hem of my jeans and offered him my gloved hand. He pulled me to my feet easily.

I paced back and forth over a six-foot area until I was sure and then stepped into the stream. Unlike the ocean, I felt the cold here. I walked out to the middle, water rushing by my calves.

"He knows you found his lab," I told them as I peered into the dark depths of the forest. "He came back while you were processing the scene. He was angry. He'd been using that spot for over a year and now everything he'd built was being carried out by techs. After a while, though, he just enjoyed watching the work. All of those adults were out there working, running around, taking pictures, talking to each other about what he'd done. A kid. They were awed by what he'd accomplished."

My feet were going numb, which was probably for the best. "Maybe a month ago he went for a walk, checking up on potential victims. Drawn to the music and laughing, he arrowed through the woods to Ana's party." I looked over my shoulder at the three on the shore. "You know her birth date. It was a Sunday." I turned back around to the forest. "He watched and eventually zeroed in on Ana. She was so happy, loved her unicorn cake and her stuffed elephant, loved the way her dress flew out when she spun. He wanted to take it all away, to strip away the security and introduce fear. He considered taking her mother briefly, wondered what she might whisper to him, but decided he wasn't ready for adults yet. He had more training to do first.

"He came back often on his rounds. There were a few people he was watching, including Christopher. When he saw his lab had been found, Christopher's body taken before he was done recording his findings, he was irritated. The cops thought they were so smart. He'd do it again. Right under their noses, and there was nothing they could do about it.

"He came straight here and found her alone on the back porch, coloring. He stood right over there." I pointed. "He knew that spot would be hidden from the window in the back door. He asked if she'd seen a unicorn. She shook her head no. She knew better than to talk to strangers. He told her he was sure he'd seen one. He'd been following it in this direction.

"She shook her head but then looked over her shoulder at

the woods, eyes wide with hope. He started to move off but she stopped him, asking if it was true. Did he really see one? Was it really coming here? He said yeah and waved her to him while he pretended to look down narrow paths, where a unicorn may have got off to.

"She hesitated on the steps, even called to the babysitter, but when she called out, he moved farther into the woods. The babysitter didn't come, and he was going to find a unicorn without her, so she ran, splashing through the stream—she knew where the shallow part was—before stepping into the woods.

"She couldn't see where the boy had gone, so she searched down what wasn't quite a path, overgrown with trees and bushes. A branch snapped and when she turned, a rock hit her in the forehead.

"When she woke, she was bound, her mouth taped. He didn't have his soundproof lab anymore." I wrapped my arms around myself, shivering uncontrollably.

"I don't want to talk about what he did. Your doctors can tell you. I will say it was a quick death, which is, I suppose, some comfort." Finally, I saw it. I pointed to a branch maybe ten feet off the ground and in the crook of the branch and the trunk was a black plastic garbage bag. Like in the vision, the wind changed directions and the leaves moved, revealing a sliver of shiny black.

"She's in that tree. He used a rope thrown over the branch to pull her up there and then climbed the tree to untie the rope and wedge the bag into the crook. Much like with the super-heroes watching Christopher die, he thought it was funny that the family would go crazy looking for her while she was right here, hidden out of reach."

"Okay, come on." Declan reached out a hand for me. "That's enough. You guys know where to look."

I took his hand and let him steady me so I didn't slip. When I got out, I saw he had a dry towel in his hand. "Thank you."

Detective Osso was talking into his radio while I sat and wrapped the towel around my frozen feet.

Hernández dropped into a crouch beside me. "Are you okay?"

I nodded, knowing I'd be waking in the middle of the night screaming for little Ana for years to come. "The dress is under the bush at the base of the tree."

"Okay. Thank you," she said.

I nodded, pulling on socks and stuffing frozen feet into boots, suddenly exhausted. "We're going to go now."

"Sure. We'll come to you if we have any questions."

I nodded. "Not today, though, okay? No more today." My eyes filled with tears and I scrubbed them away. The poor baby was chosen because she was happy and loved. "The babysitter knows his face. You go get him, okay? Prove it's him. He won't stop on his own. He needs to be stopped."

Hernández nodded. "We will."

We walked around the side of the house to Declan's truck. I didn't want to walk back into that nice house with her death playing over and over in my head.

Once we were in and buckled, I gestured to the house. "Where's the family?"

"The cops asked them to go."

Confused, I turned to Declan as he started the engine and swung his truck around. "And they did?"

Glancing over, he continued, "I asked the same question. They told the parents they wanted to bring in a psychic. The house was filled with family and friends getting ready to go search the woods again. At first there was some pushback. A few people heard and were giving the cops a hard time about grasping at straws. Osso ignored them and explained to the parents that this was the woman who had just found another victim.

"The parents agreed after that and their whole group moved

to another house a mile or so away to wait." Declan turned onto the main road and headed back to the gallery.

"It's good that they have each other. They thought the day she disappeared was the worst day in their lives. It wasn't. Today is."

36

Cookies & Milk

W hen Declan pulled up in front of the gallery, there was
a new truck parked at the curb. I knew Phil, Juan, and
Mike's vehicles. This wasn't a construction vehicle. It was big
and shiny, not battered and dusty.

Two brawny men stood shoulder to shoulder, arms crossed
over their chests, leaning against the side of my building. They
didn't look alike or dress alike, and yet they gave the impression
of being the same. One was Latino, wearing a plaid flannel,
jeans, and boots like Declan's. The other was Asian and wearing
a dress shirt open at the collar, with suit trousers and shiny black
shoes. He looked as though he'd just taken off his tie and jacket
before commencing to lean menacingly.

Declan went on alert. "Stay here. I'll deal with this." He
slammed out of the truck and strode over to the two men, who
instantly came to attention.

Not one to be told what to do, I hopped out and came
around the front of the truck. I tapped my magic and relaxed
my eyes so I could see their auras, know what we were dealing
with. Werewolves.

"Looks like you had some trouble here last night," the
almost-suit wearer said.

"That's right," Declan responded. "Did you put your stalking to good use and see who it was?"

"We're not stalking you, boss," the casual one said.

"I'm not your boss," Declan ground out.

"Yet," the dressy one added.

"Ever," Declan shot back.

"I don't know about that," the casual one said, scratching his cheek. "Ever's a long time."

In my vision, when Declan had revealed his true nature, his Quinn lineage, to the pack at the moon run, two wolves had moved to flank him, seemingly to protect them. I was assuming these were those two wolves. If their goal was to watch out for Declan, they were okay in my book.

Stepping forward, I held out a gloved hand. "Hi. I'm Arwyn. This is my gallery you're loitering in front of."

Both men relaxed their stances. The well-dressed one reached for my hand and shook it. "Kenji, ma'am."

Casual man then offered his hand. "Daniel." Returning his focus to Declan, he said, "We can help you rebuild the deck, do whatever repairs are needed to the walls and roof."

"Actually," I interrupted, "Phil's my contractor." I studied Kenji's very expensive-looking clothing. "And you don't appear to be dressed for scut work."

A grin split Kenji's stern expression, transforming him from forbidding to gorgeous. *Damn.* "I'm a lawyer now, but I used to work for my parents' construction company." He gestured to Daniel. "This is the guy who's cosplaying a construction worker."

Daniel looked down at himself. "What? It's what he always wears," he said, nodding to Declan. "And those other guys working inside, they dress like this too." He looked down at his feet. "I like the boots."

I grinned in spite of myself. "So what do you really do?" I asked our faux construction worker.

Kenji laughed. "He's a money guy, a financial advisor."

Declan blew out a breath. I could see the dilemma he was having. Help would be great so we could get the repairs done as soon as possible, but accepting help from these two felt wrong as he was *not* the Alpha.

"Would you guys like some cookies?" This was my place, after all, and I had visitors.

The wolves were clearly surprised by the question, but after a shared look, Kenji said, "Sure."

"Great. I'll go get them while you guys hash this out. What would you like to drink?" I was pretty sure I saw Declan give me an eye roll, but too bad. My place. My rules. And guests were offered baked goods and beverages around here.

Kenji shrugged. "Soda?"

"I only have grape or orange soda." I really needed to pick up a couple of cans of the normal stuff.

"Orange," he said with a grin.

"You got it." I looked at Daniel and waited.

"Do you have milk?"

"I do. Cookies and milk. A traditionalist. I'll be right back." I glanced at Declan. "Play nice."

I went into the gallery and talked with Phil. The arson inspector had been by and confirmed that the fire had been set with an accelerant. Like Clive and Declan, the inspector said gasoline. Phil was amazed at how quickly an inspector had showed up. He had been afraid construction would be stalled for weeks, at least.

"I guess those detectives that keep visiting put in a good word for you," he said.

"Thank goodness. Does that mean Declan can get started?"

"Possibly tomorrow. The inspector will send a report you can then send to your insurance company, but we're still dealing with a burned building. That requires specific safety measures for workers and inspections of the work. They want to make sure we're not, you know, throwing up some paint and calling it good. This place is going to be open to the public, so they need to make sure we're following code.

"Come look," he continued. "We finished the café area."

Throat suddenly tight, I swallowed. It was perfect. The display case was beautiful and so shiny. The wood I'd chosen for the cash wrap, the long counter behind, and the shelves was the same soft driftwood gray that I'd had them install in my studio. Perfect.

I went behind the display case and opened the cupboard doors beneath the counter. Each wooden shelf pulled out for easy access. "I love it," I said. It made me so happy to focus on the progress inside instead of the ruin outside.

"Good. We also finished the shelves your mom asked for. Juan said you approved it after the fact. The guys now understand to never let someone who is not the owner dictate what we do." He was clearly embarrassed about that one.

"Thank you. I do appreciate that, but I also know my mom can be a force." And an unfairly magical one.

"I need to get to another job, but Juan will text me if any more official types show up today. I won't be far."

"Sounds good. Thanks." I then went to the studio, as I'd kept my guests waiting long enough. I returned moments later with a glass of milk, a plate of cookies, and two cans of soda in the crook of my arm—in case Declan had relaxed enough to want something to drink.

The men still seemed in a standoff when I returned. After handing Daniel his milk, I made Declan take the cookies so I could hand Kenji the soda. I took the plate back from Declan when it became obvious he wasn't going to offer any to the men.

"Thank you, ma'am," Daniel said.

"Thank you," Kenji echoed.

Declan remained silent, shaking his head at the offered soda.

"Okay, guys, the cookies aren't going to eat themselves." I held out the plate and Daniel and Kenji each took one, quite obviously trying to appease me.

Daniel stopped chewing, cocking his head to the side. Kenji grinned broadly and reached for more, Daniel following suit a moment behind him.

I turned, offering the last two to Declan. The struggle was clear. He wanted to maintain his hard-ass silence, but he also wanted the cookies. Which would win?

Declan grabbed them while I asked the guys, "What's going on with the pack? Is Logan still gunning for this one?" I jabbed a thumb in Declan's direction.

Their expressions sobered. Kenji said, "Officially, we left the pack. We still hear things, though."

"That's none of our business," Declan broke in. "You don't have to share anything."

"You," I said to Declan, "shut up." I turned back to our guests. "I want to know if people are trying to kill him." And I couldn't just touch Declan to find out.

Daniel shrugged. "After they shot out his tires, dumping him into a ditch—"

"What?" I turned back to Declan. "After *what* happened?"

He ran a hand down my sleeve. "It was nothing. I have spares. I changed them out easily and I was still here on time for work."

He gave the men a look and then both were assuring me it was no big deal.

"No," I said, shaking my head. "I won't be lied to or protected from the truth. If you can't be honest, you can all leave." I held out the empty plate, waiting for my glass and soda cans to be returned. Daniel and Kenji put theirs on the plate with a look of apology. I waited for Declan.

"Arwyn," he began and then stopped.

I flicked my fingers and everything disappeared, including the can in his hand. I'd opened up to him and I never did that shit. I'd begun to trust him, and he couldn't even tell me people were trying to kill him? This is what being vulnerable got you. Lies.

I walked away. I had baking to do. My aunt was dead and I had a wake to prepare for. They had werewolf business, which was apparently none of mine. Fine by me.

Striding through the gallery, propelled by anger, I was annoyed—mostly with myself—for giving him the power to take the shine off the work being done in here. I'd been so pleased with it only moments before. Stupid man.

I went to my studio and closed the door. I was done people-ing for a while. Opening cupboards, I pulled out ingredients, moving them to my kitchen counter.

"Sorry."

I jumped at his voice.

"For scaring you too." He was sitting on the loft stairs, watching me. He'd obviously gone the back way while I'd been stomping through the gallery. "I didn't tell you what was going on because we'd been busy—"

"Don't. There's always time to say, *Hey, somebody just tried to kill me*." I took out my mixing bowls, measuring cups, and tartlet pans.

Scratching his beard, he nodded slowly. "That's true." He came down the stairs and stood beside me. "I was uncomfortable that you'd had a vision about me. That you'd seen what I'd done on the pack lands. You saw me shift, saw my other nature. I was ashamed you saw me kill a man I didn't have to."

"He was the one who attacked you," I said, in spite of myself. I wasn't planning to help him explain why he'd lied by omission.

"Yeah, but I could have put him down without killing him." He stared out the window and sighed. "I did it for a lot of reasons. If I killed him decisively, I hoped no one else would try me; no one else would get hurt in a battle they couldn't win. Part of me, though, was so damned sick of keeping my head down and moving on when wolves far weaker than me came at me. My whole life has been like that. At first I did it to placate my aunt. She worried so much. When I was eighteen, I ran into a pack in Idaho. Assholes trying to cow me, trying to get me to break and turn tail. I was a man—or so I thought— and I wanted to fight back.

"I did fight back, humiliating a few of the members, including the Alpha. They didn't come for me, though. They went for my very human and fragile aunt, tearing her apart while she was jogging in the park."

"Oh, Declan, I'm so sorry."

"Me too. The authorities chalked it up to a mountain lion, since one had been spotted near town a few days earlier." He shook his head, silent for a while. "I was trying to keep you away from it all. I didn't want someone else I cared about dying because of me."

"Not because of you," I protested.

"Close enough." He blew out a breath. "I was going to leave again when that pretty boy Alpha showed up here, but I'd met you at that point and I didn't want to leave." His gaze traveled over me before returning to the ocean. "I still don't."

37

So, We're Doing This?

"What's going on with Logan? I don't know much about werewolf packs, but doesn't beating the Alpha make you the Alpha?" I needed to pick up some kind of *Werewolves for Dummies* book.

"I didn't claim it." He shook his head. "I don't want it."

I checked the time. I had to get baking, but I wanted him to admit this first. "I think you do."

Brows furrowed, he gave me a dark look. "No. I don't."

I pretended to think about it for a minute. "Not buying it. When you stepped foot on pack lands, you felt the power thrum through you. When you took down the Alpha, the land moved. An Alpha had been deposed and a new one ascended."

He shook his head, but it felt more thoughtful than an outright denial.

"Daniel and Kenji moved to you, recognizing their Alpha. The others were confused but submissive to you. I caught your thoughts in that vision. The pack was weak and poorly trained. You could fix that. They hadn't learned to fully integrate their dual natures, making some of them dangerous. Again, you could help them do that.

"And a part of that prophetic vision I had when I joined the

Council was about the wolves." At his stern expression, I continued. "It was a bar, kinda divey. A man accidentally bumped another man and the bumpee went nuts on the bumper, beating him to death. Cops showed up and he rushed them before being shot. The thing is, his eyes had turned wolf gold while he was beating the poor bumper."

He cursed viciously and then gave a quick shake of his head. "I'm not Alpha."

"But you could be," I reiterated. "There's no reason not to. You said you wanted to stay, right?"

He turned to study me again before nodding.

"Okay, then. They need a strong Alpha and you no longer have someone you need to protect."

He raised an eyebrow at that.

"Do I need to throw you out and dump your ass in the ocean again? Not for nothing," I continued, checking my phone—where was my grocery order? I needed limes and condensed milk—"you're looking at one of the most powerful wicches this line has ever produced. Like I need your help dealing with some mangy wolves." I rolled my eyes to make sure he got the point. I wasn't his fragile aunt. I took care of myself and always had.

I needed to make the shortbread crust first anyway, but I really needed those limes. I liked to add lime zest to the shortbread. I pushed a finger into one of the wrapped butter packages I'd left on the counter to soften. Yep. Soft.

A knock came from the gallery door. When I opened it, I found Mike holding out a grocery bag. Finally! "Thank you." I closed the door and looked in the bag. Perfect, the limes looked fresh and healthy. "Oh, no wonder it took so long. That little go-getter found me actual key limes too. I need to up his tip."

"There are key limes?" Declan asked. "I thought the *key* part was just something you did to limes to make the pie."

"Nope." I held one up. "They're more yellow than regular limes." I held up one of those too for comparison. "I have key lime juice in the fridge in case he couldn't find fresh key limes, but he did. Huzzah."

He walked to the back door, opened it, and then sat on the threshold, his legs dangling over the ocean.

"Good call. Commune with the ocean and figure it out. I need to bake." I got a grunt in response.

A little while later, shortbread crusts made and the first tartlets in the oven, I brought Declan a beer and a shortbread cookie. He needed fuel for his deep thinking, even though it was quite obvious he should be the Alpha. I supposed the same could be said for me and the Corey Council and look how long it took me to finally agree. So, okay, we both fought against fate.

When my alarm went off, he got up and closed the door.

"They still need to cool," I explained, pulling one set of trays from the oven before replacing them with a second set.

"Do they?" he asked, leaning over me and sniffing.

I elbowed him. "You're as bad as Detective Osso."

Peering into my mixer, he asked, "What's this?"

"Marshmallow. Once they cool, I'll add a fluff of marshmallow and a bit of candied lime zest." I pointed to the wire rack where I had the zest cooling and drying.

"I'm begging you," he said.

"Fine, fine, fine. Go sit over there. You're crowding me." I put together two tartlets—before they were chilled and ready—on a plate and brought them to him.

His groan of pleasure made me grin and caused bubbles to fizz in my stomach. When my alarm went off again, I was sliding the first tray of assembled tartlets into the refrigerator.

"Are Daniel and Kenji still out front?" How many people was I feeding now? Detectives Hernández and Osso wanted some of these too.

"Nah. I told them to go back to their real jobs. I didn't need them." He returned with the empty plate, rinsing it off in the sink and then placing it in the dishwasher.

I checked the time again. "I need to go get cleaned up.

Don't touch anything. Nothing cooling on the stove top and nothing chilling in the refrigerator. Nada. If you're hungry, I have chips in that cabinet," I said pointing to the one beside where I kept my baking stuff. "I mean it."

"Got it," he replied, pushing me toward the stairs. "The ocean and I still have some things to work out." And so saying, he went to the back door, opened it, and sat back down.

I returned almost an hour later. My hair takes a ridiculous amount of time to deal with. I wore black trousers with a V-neck black sweater, and high-heeled black ankle boots. In general, I don't wear jewelry. Too many emotions and memories can be attached to jewelry—even after a thorough cleaning—but I wore the pearl earrings Aunt Sylvia had given me at my high school graduation.

A beautifully lustrous white pearl sat in the center, with fiery light-blue-green opals surrounding it, almost like petals. Serena had seemed upset that her mother had given me a gift far more precious than what she had received. Calliope had said they looked perfect on me, but I'd seen resentment in her gaze. When I'd asked my mother, she'd looked shocked I had them and seemed to disapprove, so I'd kept them in the box, never taking them out.

The sound of my heels on the stairs echoed in the studio. Declan, sitting on the couch, turned and watched me descend.

"I, uh." He cleared his throat. "As I was sitting here, it occurred to me that I could just go home. I see now I was waiting for this. To see you again before I left. And to say I'm sorry about your aunt."

I nodded, the grief hitting in unexpected waves. "Could you stand up?"

He did. No hands. Just stood from a couch only using his leg muscles. Show off. I stood before him, closer to his height with the heels, but let's face it, not really. "Can I hug you?" I held up a hand. "Don't touch me. I may be going to a wake with a sorcerer, so I'd like my magic to work, but I could really use a hug."

He opened his arms and waited. I walked into them, rested my head on his chest and slid my arms around his waist. Just this. Even just this was so much. I'd spent my life avoiding touch, missing this warmth and comfort. He crushed me to him and I tensed.

"I'm only touching your sweater," he said, the deep rumble making me want to cry.

Why? What was wrong with me? I was grieving my aunt but his voice made me tear up. Burrowing in, I never wanted to let go. But I had to. Now. In a couple of minutes. Probably.

"Do you want to come with me?" I asked out of nowhere.

"I can, if you'd like, but I'm not dressed appropriately."

Leaning back, I took in his worn jeans, work boots, dark brown t-shirt, and brown plaid flannel shirt. "You look okay." That was a lie. He was gorgeous and his grin said he knew it.

"If I can swing by my place, I can grab a decent shirt to wear."

I let go of him and went to deal with the tartlets. "Thank you." I added the marshmallow and candied zest to the second batch and then swapped out the ones that had been chilling in the fridge. "My cousins can be dicks, so apologies in advance." While the second batch chilled, I used the bigger carrier to load up the tartlets to take to Gran's house.

I made short work of it and then we were in his truck on our way. It turned out Declan's apartment wasn't too far away. While he ran in to get changed, I texted my mom, letting her know I was bringing him.

Her response was immediate: Why?

Luckily, he was back in under five minutes, saving me the trouble of responding. He was coming because I wanted him there.

He started up the engine. "Your grandmother's, right?"

I nodded and he took off. Damn, he cleaned up nice. He wore black trousers, a white button-down, and black dress shoes.

"You look nice."

He nodded his thanks. "I was aiming for better than okay. We can't have your date looking like he wandered in from a construction site looking for a bathroom."

"Date? Who said anything about a date?"

He reached over and held my gloved hand. "I did."

"So," I said, uncomfortable with the sweet talk, "what did you and the ocean decide?"

"We decided I was too old to still be making decisions based on the family I *used* to have." He turned onto a narrow road. "I think, in the back of my mind, I assumed I'd someday return to the Santa Cruz Mountains where my father was Alpha and take over."

He was quiet for a moment. The only sound was the truck's tires on pavement. "I realized I don't want to go back there. Ever. My mother and father were murdered there. The pack fell apart because of more murders." He shook his head. "I don't want that. It'd be like buying a haunted house so you can be near the dead.

"I like it here," he continued, "on the Pacific Ocean. I could use a little peace, you know?" He glanced over and I nodded. "Don't worry. I'm not making this decision because of you. Even if you throw me off your deck again and tell me to get lost, I'd still want to be in this area. It feels right. So I texted Logan and formally challenged him."

He turned down the road to Gran's. "The last time was a failed ambush. It needs to be a fair fight. That's the only way the pack will accept me. Next full moon, we'll meet on pack lands and battle for Alpha."

He pulled into Gran's driveway and parked next to Mom's car. There were already quite a few cars here. "You want to hear something funny?"

"Hmm?"

He turned off the engine. "As soon as I'd made my decision, a stray wave hit the post in front of me, sending a fine mist of sea spray into my face. It felt like a sign."

I hid a smile, sliding out of his truck. I was pretty sure that was Dad's seal of approval. When I leaned back in for the carrier, it was gone. Declan slammed his door, came around the truck, and offered me his free hand.

I knew what he was asking. Were we going to really do this and if so, were we telling people? I took his hand, pulling him down so his ear was close to my mouth, whispering, "I need you to watch and listen. Chances are our sorcerer will be here. I have history with these people. I won't see them with clear eyes. I need you to."

He nodded, moved my hand to his elbow, escorting me to the door. "I'm on it, Ursula."

38

My Cousins Suck

G ran's living room was already crowded with family in various stages of mourning. Mom saw us and gave me a look I knew quite well. It was the *Why, Arwyn? Why are you doing this?* look. I nodded in greeting, pretending her disapproval went right over my head. I'd been pretending not to notice her disapproval for most of my life. It was our thing.

I heard the word *earrings* hissed within seconds of entering. Oh, good. We were starting right away. Declan stuck with me as I made my way to the refreshments table. I wore a small black patent leather crossbody bag on a delicate silver chain. Sylvia had given it to me years ago, but I rarely ever did fancy, so it had remained in tissue paper in my closet. Today, since I had no dressy black overalls with big pockets, I used the bag for my phone, wallet, keys, and gloves.

I took a pair of plastic gloves out, pulled them over my regular ones, and transferred the tartlets from the carrier to the empty serving plate Mom had left for me. Once empty, I stowed the carrier under the table, hidden by the long tablecloth, and then looked for Gran so I could offer my condolences.

She was sitting on the patio, watching the ocean alone, which was odd. Why wasn't anyone with Gran? I pulled on

Declan's arm again. When he lowered his head, I said, "I want to talk to Gran. Can you stay in here? Watch and listen?"

He nodded, turning back to the table and taking a tartlet.

I'd only taken a few steps, though, before my cousin Colin appeared in front of me. "I heard that old cannery finally burned down."

"Nope." I tried to move past him. "It's good to see you, Colin." Although, seeing you in Hell would be better.

"Wait," he said, grabbing my arm, keeping me beside him.

I can't tell you how I knew this, but I absolutely knew Declan was watching, waiting to see if I needed his help. It could have all been in my head—my back was to him, after all—but for the first time in ever, it felt like someone had my back at one of these cousin things.

I stared down at Colin's hand until he reluctantly removed it. "Yes?"

"I can't believe you!" he whisper-shouted. "They've lost their mother and you just have to rub it in, with those fucking earrings, that Sylvia loved you more than her own daughters." He shook his head. "You're such a freak."

Is that what they'd thought? "Aunt Sylvia loved everyone, but no one more than Uncle John, Serena, and Calliope. Don't disparage her like that. I'm wearing them because she gave them to me and I miss her."

When he reached for me again, I sidestepped his hand and had taken two steps to the patio door when Serena slid in front of me.

"It's always about you, isn't it?" Tears gleamed in her eyes, but she was pissed off. That was clear.

Over Serena's shoulder, I saw my cousins Cat and Mia staring and whispering behind cups of tea. "I'm very sorry for your loss. You know how much I loved your mother. The world is—"

"Shut up. Why are you even here?" Apparently, whisper-shouting insults at me was the theme of this event. She shook her head, disgust written all over her face. "You show up late—with a date," she sneered, "and parade around in those stupid earrings."

"I don't parade."

"She was *my* mother. Not yours. You have your own, cold bitch that she is." Her gaze was over my shoulder, where I assumed my mother was talking with someone. "Why is my mom dead? She was fine! A couple of days ago, she was perfectly fine. And then she's in a coma, a fucking *coma*? Dad can't heal her, can't even reach her, but there you are. You and your mother are in her room in the middle of the night and she dies? No. I'm not buying it."

"Mom had a feeling about her sister," I explained, "and needed to see her. She was at my place, so I went with her. That's all." We weren't saying *sorcerer* yet. It would cause a panic and we needed more info first.

"A feeling. Right." Serena looked like she was about to throw a punch and then Calliope moved in and wrapped an arm around her sister's waist.

"Sorry," she said, wiping tears off her cheek. "We're all drowning in grief right now."

I nodded my understanding. "I'm very sorry. I feel it too." I ran my fingers over the handbag chain, trying to figure out how to offer condolences while still getting to Gran.

"That's my bag. You bitch, how did you get my bag?" Serena's eyes narrowed. "What? Are you going through my closets when I'm not around?"

I looked down at the beautiful little bag that I'd never worn because it seemed too special. "Your mom gave it to me for my birthday years ago."

"Liar," she spat.

Leaning in, voice low, I said, "I'm very sorry about your mother. You'll never understand just how much I'll miss her, but I'm done taking your shit. E-nough. Do you hear me? Enough. I'm not this family's goddamn punching bag."

I moved around the sisters and Serena reached out, grabbed the bag, and yanked hard. The chain bit into my neck and then snapped.

"Do you like it, honey? I thought it was so pretty." Sylvia waits for Serena's reaction.

"Uh, yeah, it's nice. I was just hoping for the sparkly red one I showed you in the store window. I'm just not really a black bag kind of person." She looks at her mother's crestfallen expression. "I mean it's super cute, but you should keep it. It would look good on you."

Sylvia nods, taking the little black handbag back. "When I went to get the red one for you, they were sold out. They had pink and green. I just thought the black was nicer."

"Pink? I didn't see pink. Perfect. Let's take that one back and exchange it for pink, okay?" Serena's face glows at the thought of a little pink bag.

Sylvia isn't going to exchange this one, though. She realizes she's made a mistake. She was thinking about Arwyn when she bought it and her niece has a birthday coming up. "Sure. We'll go tomorrow."

"Arwyn, honey, are you okay?"

My eyes fluttered open. Uncle John. Oh, thank goodness I wasn't on the ground. He was tall, like Declan, though not as broad. I wrapped my arms around him, resting my head on his chest. "I'm so sorry, Uncle John. I loved her so much."

"I know you did, sweetie," he said, rubbing my back. "And she loved you like you were her own."

I squeezed him and stepped back, wiping at my eyes. "And she loved you with her whole heart."

He nodded. "I know it. She always made sure I knew it." He wiped at his own eyes and then he smiled. "Hey, you're wearing the earrings. She worried you didn't like them since you never wore them."

"Oh." I looked around the room. People had moved back, thankfully. "I love them. They're the nicest, most meaningful thing I own."

He smiled more broadly at that.

"It's just"—I gestured around the room—"other people

were upset that my gift was so much more expensive than what others received at graduation."

He laughed and shrugged. "Well, the fae aren't known for being poor."

"The fae?" What did the fae have to do with anything?

"Your dad wanted you to have those. Sybil wouldn't pass them on, so he approached Sylvia, asking her to give them to you. I'll tell you," he said, glancing around the room. "Sylvia was nervous about going against her sister's wishes, but she firmly believed you had a right to gifts from your father."

I touched them. "These were from him? Aunt Sylvia met him? He was checking up on me, giving me a gift ten years ago?"

His smile slipped. "She didn't tell you?"

I felt just as confused as he looked. "No. Everyone thought they were from Aunt Sylvia."

Eyebrows raised, he said, "We couldn't have afforded anything like that." He glanced around the room, realizing people were watching and listening. "And that's why everyone was so hostile when you walked in wearing the earrings." He sighed. "Including my girls." Patting my shoulder, he added, "I'll explain it to the girls."

Gran was still alone and I wanted to get to her, but he stopped me again. "Honey, you're bleeding. Here. Let me help with that." He knew not to touch me, so his hand hovered over the skin of my neck as he chanted soundlessly.

A teapot was on the table by Gran's elbow. A teapot. Gran. On the patio. The vision came swimming back, sluggish and dark. *Damn it!* That demon was fucking with us, causing all this drama, getting people to step in front of me, trying to get me to forget why Gran alone on the patio was dire. Fucking demons!

I ducked under Uncle John's arm and ran for the door. Gran was just picking up the teacup. I grabbed the doorknob and tried to turn it, but it was locked. Mia and Cat moved in to start some shit with me.

I don't know what made me do it. I'd never tried anything like it before, but I turned, pulled off my gloves, held up my hands, and yelled "Stop!" with as much magical force as I could muster.

And they did. Everyone froze in place. Spinning, I spelled the door to unlock and tore through it, just as Declan came running around the back side of the house and hit the teacup out of Gran's hand.

Gran blinked, as though waking from a dream, and then looked down at her lap, where a few drops of tea had fallen. "What's going on?' she asked, a strange mixture of confusion and annoyance.

"How did you know?" I asked Declan.

"Smell. The tea smelled different than what everyone else is drinking. It smells like nightshade." He looked down at Gran. "Sorry about that, but the tea was poisoned."

I looked back through the picture window at all the frozen people.

"What did you do to them?" Declan asked, awed.

"No idea."

Gran stood and studied her frozen family. "One of them is the sorcerer?"

"I think so," I said.

"Well, get in there and touch them. We need to know who it is." She brushed the beads of tea off her black skirt and then looped an arm through Declan's. "This young man can be my bodyguard today."

"My pleasure, ma'am."

I went back in, picked up my gloves, and started with the ones I trusted least. Could it be my mom? Possible but doubtful. Uncle John? No. I began by relaxing my vision and pushing on my magic so I could see their auras. Most were exactly what I'd assume a white wicche's to look like. Some, like Uncle John, were so bright and shiny, they hurt to look at. My mother's was a little gray around the edges. She was a woman who did what had to be done.

Sylvia had said that Abigail had tutored a number of the cousins. I'd start there. As Cat and Mia were right by the door, I started with them. I didn't want to hit the ground. I just wanted to do a psychic glide over. If anything stood out, I'd go deep. As I had no idea how I'd frozen them, I had no idea how long the spell would last.

I tried something different. Instead of resting my hand on Mia's skin, I barely brushed a finger over the back of her hand. I needed to check as many people as possible and I didn't want to know their life stories. I just wanted to know if they were trucking with demons.

While Mia was unpleasant, she wasn't a sorcerer. On to Cat… And so it went as I grazed over their lives, not wanting to invade their privacy but needing to know who had taken up sorcery. As my work with Detectives Hernández and Osso proved, what the wicche and demon plotted had mundane as well as magical world repercussions and I didn't want to have to look for any more dead children.

39

Gran Brings the Hammer

"Dec," I called.

A moment later, he and Gran were at the patio door.

"I don't know how long this spell is going to last. While I do this, can you sniff around? See if anyone smells like nightshade?"

"I can." He walked Gran to a chair and helped her sit.

Gran was nowhere near that fragile. She was milking old age for all it was worth now that she had a hot young bodyguard. When he walked away, she winked at me. I knew it.

I'd always hated Colin, so I wasn't looking forward to this, but I moved to his side and swiped his hand.

"Gran?"

"Yes, dear."

"The first order of Council business is magically castrating this one. He's been using his magic to spell women into his bed." He'd been the main instigator growing up, encouraging everyone to mock and shun me. I knew he was an asshole. I hadn't realized he was evil.

Gran stood easily and came to me. "A rapist, is he?"

"Yes."

"I can take care of this right now." She put her hand on his chest, her lips twitching with a silent spell. She looked pained for a moment and then she let out a breath. "This time, darling girl, I really could use help getting to that chair."

I put my arm around her and slowly walked her back. "What did you do?"

"I've taken his magic. I'll hold it until the Council is able to meet. And if he tries to harm a woman or coerce a woman on his own, the harm will visit him threefold."

"Only three?" I helped her down.

"I tried for higher, but I'm not as young as I used to be." She patted my arm, careful not to touch my ungloved hand.

"Still stronger than most of the people in this room, Gran."

She smiled weakly. "True. I'm going to need a nap, though. Hurry up, now. The feel in the room is changing. I don't know how much longer you have."

"Hey, Ursula? You might want to come over here." He was standing beside Serena.

Shit. I really didn't want it to be Serena. She was vain and difficult, but she was also hard-working and loyal to her friends. She might have hated me, but I never thought she'd hurt her mother. Sylvia would do anything for her girls. I felt sick swiping her hand.

"No, I—" Declan began, but I was already gliding over Serena's demon-free life. She was beautiful and used it to her advantage when she could but didn't rely on it. Hard work and dedication were how she had built her shop into a success. She didn't like me, but she also gave me very little thought, which was good. She loved her mom, though it annoyed her when Sylvia made too many suggestions. She was frustrated that everyone thought Calliope was the sweet one. It was all pretty normal stuff. She didn't have a hand in killing her mother.

I looked at Declan in question.

"She has two different nightshade scents on her. Her right hand has an almost imperceptible aroma. She has a much stronger, more pure scent around her waist."

Her waist? And then I remembered. "Where's Calliope?" I scanned the room but didn't see her. She was just here. She had to have run when I went for the patio door.

"Gran?"

"Oh, child. Tell me they weren't doing this together. Not both of them." She sounded so tired.

"I don't think so. When I read Serena, there was nothing that indicated a hatred of her mother or an interest in sorcery. I heard the voice racing around Aunt Sylvia's head when she was in the hospital. It wasn't Serena's."

Staring at my mother, who was frozen in conversation with her brother Joe, I wondered what it would take to kill your own mother and then I remembered the Corey Curse. Calliope couldn't be the one to kill Gran. She'd lose her powers.

"I bet the demon pushed Serena to deliver the poisoned cup to Gran. Cal couldn't get her hands dirty because of the family curse. Serena, though, the older, prettier, more successful one, well, if we accused her of being the sorcerer, that might just brighten Cal's day. Serena would have her magic stripped from her and she'd be banished. She'd lose it all and guess who could step right in and take over?"

Gran was lost in thought. "I don't remember walking out to the patio. I have no idea who brought me the cup of tea." She pounded the arm of the chair. "A demon used me like a puppet, and I didn't realize, didn't stop it." Her gaze found mine and I felt her fear.

"It might have been the same for Serena," I suggested. "The nightshade is strongest around her waist, which is where Calliope wrapped her arm when Serena was going at me. And she's not here anymore."

Declan held his hand low on his chest. "Is she the little one, short black hair, wearing a dark purple dress?"

I nodded.

"Oh, I believe it."

"Yes," Gran sighed, "unfortunately, so do I. Young man, would you walk me to my room? I need to lie down."

"This is Declan. Remember? You met him before." Gran usually had a mind like a steel trap. I wasn't ready for her to start forgetting things.

"I'm aware," she said, getting up and leaning her narrow frame against Declan. "If he proves to be an upstanding young man who sticks around, I'll use his name."

He patted her hand, watching me. "I'm not going anywhere, ma'am."

She nodded as they moved to the hall entrance. "It'll be nice to have an Alpha in the family."

"Gran," I warned. One kiss. We'd only had one incredible, earth-shattering kiss, and we were still working out if his touch was hazardous. We were not getting married. Damn pushy woman.

She tapped Declan's arm and turned around. "They're coming back. The energy in the room just changed."

And then people were blinking, rubbing their foreheads, looking around.

"We had an incident," Gran proclaimed, her voice strong. "Hear me now," she said, and every gaze not already pinned to her found her. "We have a sorcerer in our midst again."

There were a few mumbles of denial but mostly what I was seeing was pained expressions of acceptance. Not again.

"Arwyn." Gran held out a hand but people misunderstood, gasping, thinking I was the killer. "Don't be idiots," she continued just as a spell hit me in the shoulder. It was weak, like I'd been hit with a rubber band, but still. Rude. I took Gran's hand, standing on her other side.

"Arwyn and her young man saved me. This sorcerer attempted to kill me, poisoning my tea. We will not allow that evil in our family. Is that understood? I don't care if you love her, if you believe this must be a mistake. Know that it is not."

She stared down everyone in the room. She put Declan and

me at her side for a reason. She was telling the family that we were with her and to be believed. She was sheltering us under her umbrella of fearsome power and respect.

"The sorcerer is Calliope."

Eyes wide, they looked around the room and didn't find her. Serena clapped a hand to her mouth and shook her head, tears running down her face. Uncle John bowed his head, his shoulders slumped. He'd lost his wife and now his daughter.

"We will find her and we will deal with her. As of now, she is dead to you. You will not meet with her. You will not offer her aid. Sorcery will not be overlooked because you want to believe her to be who you always thought she was. The mask has dropped. This is who she is, a woman who killed her mother, who attempted to kill her grandmother. For power.

"Comfort one another if you must, but then go home. The Council must decide on next steps." She turned to go and then stopped. "And Colin, you've been stripped of your magic and are summoned to appear before the Council when we have time for you. Until then, the women of Monterey County will hopefully be safer around you."

Declan and I walked with Gran to her bedroom.

"I really do need to rest," she said in a hushed tone. "Could you stay to make sure everyone leaves?"

"Of course," Declan responded, making me smile. She already had him wrapped around her little finger.

When we returned, quite a few people had already left. Mom tried to move past us, but I held her up.

"Gran needs to rest. She'll talk with us afterward."

Her head lifted as she pulled herself up, preparing to unleash her wrath on me for barring her from her own mother. Instead, though, she whispered, "Is it true?"

When I nodded, she sagged. "How?"

I understood. She'd been there Calliope's whole life and had never seen it. And now a niece she loved had killed a sister she adored. It was all too much.

"Why don't you lie down in Gran's guestroom," I suggested.

Mom nodded listlessly and went down the hall.

When I turned, Frank and Faith were there with Aunt Elizabeth and Uncle Robert. Elizabeth was the quiet one of the family. She had the black Corey hair and dark green eyes, though hers were far kinder than most. There were five girls and two boys in my mom's generation. She and Elizabeth had now lost three of their sisters.

Elizabeth leaned in and gave me an air kiss close to my cheek, knowing not to touch me. "Thank you for saving my mother. If there's anything we can do to help in your investigation, you only need to ask." *We have unique abilities you might be able to use*, she said directly to my mind.

Her husband, Uncle Robert, was from a prominent East Coast wicche family. Like Uncle John, he was a healer, though he chose to help the mundane world as a pediatrician. He was a handsome Black man, just beginning to gray at the temples. *Whatever you need from us.*

Holy crap, they could both do it. How had I never known this? "I'm sure I could think of something I'd like to learn," I said, making them both smile.

I didn't know Frank or Faith well. They were much younger, perhaps late teens, but I'd always gotten a good feeling from them. "Perhaps you all can come to dinner and we can discuss some things. Catch up."

"Yes," Robert agreed. "I think that would be a good idea."

Frank shook my hand, which seemed oddly formal until I felt something fluttering through my glove. I looked into my palm and saw a tiny, fire-breathing dragon pacing across the black knit of my gloves. I barely had a moment to appreciate his shiny, ruby-colored eyes before he disappeared with a soft pop.

When I looked up at Frank, he was grinning, and Faith looked to be holding in a laugh. "I'll show you what I can do later," she whispered.

Nodding, I waved goodbye, excited for that dinner and to learn what Faith's gift was.

Once we finally got everyone out—and that was a chore—Declan led me to the kitchen. "Do you smell it?" he asked.

I shook my head but was distracted by my bag with the broken chain. It was sitting on the counter by the sink. "What's this doing here?" I opened it and all my stuff was there except for the blue rubber gloves I'd used to transfer the tartlets to the plate.

"I don't know," he replied. "It was sitting there when I smelled the nightshade and walked in here."

I opened the door beneath the sink and looked in the trash. There were the gloves. I tore off a paper towel and picked them up. The fingertips were stained with a dark, purplish juice.

Declan leaned over me. "That's it. That's the scent."

I pulled off one of my gloves. I was sure we were right, but we'd just branded Calliope a sorcerer, so I felt the need to make sure. "Don't let my head hit the floor, okay?"

I'd meant *please catch me before I crumple to the ground*, but Declan swung me up into his arms and then nodded, waiting for me to proceed. Hmm. This was kinda nice.

Touching the glove, I was sucked in. *Hands mixing white powder from an unlabeled vial into a bowl of water. Tea leaves drop into the solution and are swirled with a wooden spoon. I can't see the person, but I know that ring. She was wearing it tonight. The light green peridot sparkled against Serena's black dress when Calliope wrapped her arm around her sister.*

After the tea leaves soak, they are laid out to dry.

A deep voice makes me jump. "Use this. Add it to the tea before you serve it." A branch with small dark berries appears on the counter. "There will be healers nearby. If you want to make sure she dies quickly, use both."

A soft laugh. "I'd love to draw it out and make her suffer the way she's made me wait for that Council spot, but you're right. Faster is better. And with another position soon open, I might have a shot on the Council after all."

"We get rid of the freak," the deep voice rumbled, "and the mother will be so grief-stricken—losing sister, mother, daughter—that you can sail in and take over."

"And we'll be able to harness all that power. Abigail explained it to me. The triad on the Council is connected to every Corey so they can police their own, but the connection can be used to draw power from each of them as well."

"With great power," he began.

"Comes great fear and ultimate control," she finished on a laugh.

40

Unexpected Messengers

Grandma's house was already Fort Knox, but I added my own unique enchantments to the doors and windows. No one was getting in while Mom and Gran slept. One of the things we discovered when I was little was that no one could counter my spells. The elders could counter other children's early spell attempts, but not mine. We assumed it was because they were full wicche and I was part fae. My magic was just a little different. What that meant now was that Calliope couldn't break through the additional wards I set. Of course, who knew what the demon could do.

Declan and I cleaned everything up, put the food away, mopped floors, wiped down counters, but still neither woke. He said he could hear their heartbeats—and only theirs. No one was hiding— and they were both strong, so we decided to let them sleep and go home.

As I climbed into his truck, I wondered, "Did you hear a car start? I mean when Calliope escaped, did you hear her go?"

Reversing, he shook his head. "And I would have. She had to have walked."

"Or the demon muffled the sound." I shook my head. "I

need to take a class on demons. I have no idea what they can and can't do."

He pulled out onto the road and headed back toward the gallery. "We could go to San Francisco. See The Slaughtered Lamb and ask that Dave guy to help us out."

Nodding, I considered. "Yeah, let's do that. He already way overpaid for my help in finding his girlfriend, though. And then because she pushed him, he came down to help when I asked. We need to go see him, but I also need to bring something as a form of payment." What, though? What would he dig?

"You could make him something," he suggested.

"Yeah, that's what I'm thinking too, but what?" Something related to his girlfriend, as that was who he obviously loved. He'd mentioned something about a new house, so maybe a glass piece? I'd think about it.

I turned in my seat to watch Declan. "When I said the sorcerer was Calliope, you described her and said you believed it. How did you know who she was?"

He scratched his beard, made a turn, and then glanced over. "After you left me at the food table, she appeared at my side, saying how good it was that I was with you for moral support, what a good friend I must be. She was saying the right things, but they were all lies."

He tapped his nose. "It's clear you guys don't spend much time around wolves. The lies were flying in that room."

"You can really smell lies?"

"Essentially. It's more that we can sense emotions. Deception gives off a sour scent. The person has to know they're lying though. It doesn't work if they're just mistaken or if they're psychopaths devoid of emotion. Mostly, though, I can tell."

He looked at me again. "Part of why I changed my mind about you. I could see what you could do, but I could also sense your absolute sincerity and felt the insult when I questioned your integrity."

"Yeah, you were a dick." I looked down at the broken chain

on my handbag. I had jewelry-making tools at the studio. I could fix this.

"Also, about Calliope. She was coming on to me."

"What?" I shifted in my seat to study him again. "We came in together. I was holding your hand. What the hell?"

Grinning, he shook his head. "Why do you seem more outraged by this than her killing people?"

"I'm not! Don't be ridiculous." Was I? No, of course not. "It's just"—I threw my hands up—"she's plotting world domination and she stops to steal my boyfriend?" Who does that? Jeez, was she picking pockets on the way out too?

"Boyfriend, huh?"

"What?"

He had a smile that could light up a truck. "You called me your boyfriend. No take backs," he warned.

I couldn't help it. I laughed. "Are you sure she was coming on to you and not just trying to get info out of you?"

"Please. I know when people are coming on to me." He gestured, from his gorgeous face down his incredible body. "Are you under the impression I don't own a mirror?"

Snickering, I smacked his arm. "So what did she say?"

"I told you. All the right stuff, but they were lies. She kept touching my forearm, running a hand over my biceps. It could have come off as sympathetic, but we'd never met and there was intent behind the touch. The weird part was I didn't smell lust on her. It was just that sour deception scent. If I had to guess, coming on to me was more about the conquest of taking what she saw as yours. Did you take something of hers?"

I shook my head, confused by the whole damn conversation. "No. I actually used to look out for her when she was little. She wasn't as much of an asshole to me as the other cousins were and she often played alone, so if I was around, I'd go sit with her, keep her company."

"When she ran her hand down my thigh," he said, "I looked

her dead in the eye and said *No*. She got flustered and wandered away."

"And what did you do?" I asked.

"I ate another tartlet. Honestly, I ate most of them. Probably a full pie and a half of them. I would have eaten more, but one of the aunties gave me a dirty look. I figured some of them probably already had a bad opinion of werewolves. I didn't want to be the animal tearing through the food table when everyone around me was grieving, so I stepped away. It was hard."

"There's more at home."

"Knowing that was the only thing that allowed me to step away. Just to spread my gluttony around, I tried one of the brownies."

"Ooh. Sorry."

"It was a brownie. What the hell did someone do to the brownie to make it taste that bad? I mean, how? It's a brownie."

My heart clutched at his befuddlement; nay, his sense of betrayal by a brownie. Why this touched me, I have no idea.

"I mean, sure, it's not going to be as good as one of yours. No one expects that. But it's a damn brownie. Just a basic, straight from a box, brownie is better than whatever that was."

"I know. We've all made that mistake exactly once. I don't know how she does it—Aunt Sarah is my mom's brother Joe's wife."

"I think I'm going to need a cheat sheet on all these people."

"I don't blame you. There are a lot of us. I'll make you a Corey family tree. Anyway, my whole life, her brownies have been inedible, but she insists on bringing them. I've actually tried a bite a few times, trying to figure out what she puts in them. I can't. It defies logic."

"Mustard?" he guessed.

I thought about it. "Pickle juice?"

"Do you think her cookbook has pages stuck together and

she's starting the recipe for brownies but then skips a page and finishes with the recipe for a loaded hot dog?"

I laughed. Couldn't stop laughing. Everything was hitting at once, yes, but also having someone to share this with, helping me talk trash about my family, was the best. My stomach hurt and I was gasping for breath. Declan reached over and patted my thigh. He got it.

When he parked, the sun was just setting. It was late spring, early summer and the sun set around eight at night. It wasn't late, but I was exhausted.

"I realize this is overstepping, but I don't feel comfortable driving away when we have a sorcerer on the run and everyone knows you're the one who found her," he said.

"It could have been Gran," I countered.

He shook his head. "They were all looking at you. They know who saved your grandmother and uncovered the sorcerer. Someone tried to burn down your gallery last night."

"Are you looking for a sleepover invitation?"

"Yes. I'd feel better if I could stay on the couch and you stayed in your loft. You can consider me your guard wolf."

I hated to admit it, but I felt safer when he was around too. "Okay, you can sleep on my couch, but this better not be a ploy to clean out my refrigerator while I'm sleeping."

He crossed his heart and held up his fingers in a Scout salute.

"All right. Let's go." I slid out of the truck, holding my bag by its broken strap. Declan carried in the empty baked goods carrier and a duffle bag. After we entered, I relocked the gallery door and set my own magical ward. We crossed the gallery, our footsteps echoing in the huge, empty room.

I put another ward on the studio door once we were through it. "You're not hearing any heartbeats other than our own, right?"

We both stood still a moment and his brows furrowed. I

began to prepare a spell for whoever was laying in wait when he pointed at the back door.

"No. You do, however, have a naked guy standing on a post out there."

I huffed out a relieved breath and then realized he was serious. I went to the back door, spell ready, and stared at the slight man with almost translucent hair and very familiar eyes. Declan tried to stop me when I reached for the doorknob, but I patted his hand away.

Wind blew the door out of my hand, the sound of the surf a comforting roar.

"Wilbur?"

He bowed his head. "You may call me that, mistress, but my name is Emrys."

I nodded, unable to speak. A selkie? Wilbur was a selkie?

"My master is pleased you are wearing his earrings. He hopes this means you will someday be willing to meet with him."

I nodded again.

"Lovely. I'll let him know. In the meantime, he wanted to make sure you were aware that if you touch those earrings without gloves, he will know you need him and will listen."

Holy—"Seriously?"

"Absolutely."

I wasn't sure why, but it felt important that he knew this. "Can you tell him that I didn't know these earrings were a gift from him. I thought they were from my aunt, and they seemed to cause so much strife in the family, I left them in the box, looking at them often. They are the most beautiful and precious things I own."

Emrys-Wilbur smiled and bowed again. "I will pass this message on to my master. It will mean a great deal to him."

"Good. Um, should I stop throwing the tennis ball? I thought you were a harbor seal. I didn't mean any disrespect."

"I travel back and forth between the realms. My master gave

me the task of watching you to make sure you were well. When I'm in this world, I enjoy the ball game and would like to continue it. In fact"—he opened his hand and there was the soggy yellow tennis ball—"you're it." He threw the ball over my head, donned his seal skin, and dove into the ocean.

41

In Which Arwyn Comes to Terms With Her Life Being a Bit Too Interesting

D eclan and I looked at each other and then back out the door.

"So, that happened," I said.

He went and grabbed the ball, wound up, and let it sail out over the darkened ocean. A seal barked as Declan closed and locked the door. His hand hovered over a switch to the right of the door. "Does this put the shutters down?"

I nodded.

"Okay?"

"Good call." I flicked my fingers at the back door, making the glass opaque before I did the same with the skylight over my bed.

I didn't know what to do. I should probably eat something, but I knew my stomach would rebel. Maybe I should take a shower. Or just go to bed. I stared at the tentacles. I was so behind on that. I could pull an all-nighter and work on the tentacles. I wasn't feeling it, though.

My father gave me these earrings. I'd denied myself a gift from my father because I knew the cousins would throw a shit fit. Why didn't Aunt Sylvia ever tell me? And why didn't Mom want me to have them? He wants to meet me and sent me Wilbur to keep an eye on me.

I needed aspirin. My head was killing me. I also needed to get changed. Oh, I should fix the chain on the handbag. I needed to find my tools first, though. I haven't made jewelry in a while. I also needed to figure out what to make Dave as a thank you for a demon tutorial.

"Hey, Ursula?"

I turned to see Declan standing with his arms open.

"You look like you could use a hug."

I walked into his arms and wrapped mine around him. "I don't know what's wrong with me," I mumbled, my words muffled by his shirt.

"I do. You don't get anywhere near enough sleep. Your aunt just died. Your father..." and he proceeded to list everything swimming around in my head. "It's a lot. Now, how about this?" He dragged his hands down my back, palmed my butt, and hiked me up so I had my legs wrapped around his waist. "I'll carry you up and you try to sleep. Tomorrow, we'll regroup and you'll figure out what needs to be done first. Okay?"

I nodded, exhausted yet ridiculously aroused. "We need to figure this out," I said, running a gloved finger down his nose, over his cheek. God, he was gorgeous.

He growled low and deep, and I felt it vibrating through certain parts of my body. Oh, my.

"The universe could not be this cruel, to place a siren in my path and then not let me touch her." He kneaded my butt, dropping me down so I rubbed against his bulging zipper.

At the top of the stairs, he crossed to the bed and laid me down. He grabbed one of my legs, lifting it over his shoulder as he leaned down, hovering over me, skin not touching. "We're going to figure this out real fast, okay?"

I nodded, not breaking eye contact. When he tried to get up, I wrapped my other leg around him. He moved his hips, hitting just the right spot. Supporting his weight over me with one arm, his other hand slid up my side before settling on my breast. I let out a gust of breath, squirming to get closer as his thumb found my nipple, brushing over it, back and forth. "So beautiful," he breathed.

It didn't take long before both of us were breathing heavily, wanting to kiss but knowing we couldn't, not until we figured out how to touch without muting my power. When I flew apart, he slumped forward on a long groan.

He kissed my sweatered breast and stood. "Go to sleep. I need to get cleaned up and changed. I'm a light sleeper. If you need me, call."

"Do you want to use my shower?"

"I'll be fine," he grumbled, heading down the stairs. "I haven't had to do this particular type of cleanup since I was a teenager, but I remember how it's done."

I grinned in the dark, loose, happy, relaxed, achy. If that was how he could make me feel fully clothed, with no skin involved...

I undressed and crawled into bed. Thankfully I fell asleep almost immediately.

He's out, wandering the woods, looking for a new workshop. The excitement of the cops investigating his old workshop is fading. Now he's just pissed off. He worked hard to make sure he had everything he needed down there. He needs to start again. And he hasn't found a place anywhere near as good as his last one. He hates that he had to rush with the girl. He needs more time with his experiments.

Stupid cops. While he's out, he looks in on a few he's had his eye on. He might have chanced it, made his move tonight, but he doesn't have a good place to take them and all his tools are gone. No. He'll wait. Collect more tools and have them ready before he grabs another one. He really hates waiting, though.

He isn't paying attention as he walks out of the forest and up the path to his back door. Scrolling through pictures of Christopher and then Ana, reliving it. Maybe he won't wait.

Bright lights flash in his eyes. "Down! Get down. Face down. Hands to the side."

Hernández and Osso walk out of the dark into the stark light. A uniformed cop handcuffs the kid and then pulls him up to his feet as Detective Osso uses an evidence bag to pick up the dropped phone, an image of Ana glowing on the screen.

The kid starts crying. "I didn't do anything! You can't prove it. I'm just a kid. You can't arrest me." *He struggles against the restraints, trying to kick the cop who holds him in place.*

Detective Hernández leans in. "I'm afraid you'll find that isn't true. We've already spoken to your grandmother. She gave us permission to search your room. We have your maps and your diaries. We have your phone and the pictures you took as you tortured and killed your victims." *Her voice is low and weary. None of them are gloating about catching this particular killer. They look, all of them, sick to their stomachs.*

"That wasn't me. I didn't do anything." *Tears glisten in his eyes but it's impossible not to see the calculation hiding behind them.* "He made me. This guy. He kidnapped me and made me do it. Made me take pictures. He had a gun."

Osso steps up. "You found them, researched them, stalked them. We've seen your notes. Your findings on your experiments. It's impressive what you did. No one would have guessed someone your age could've accomplished something like this." *He shakes his head as though awed in spite of himself.*

The kid has a thin, angular face, sandy brown hair, and dead blue eyes. Bony shoulders poke at his t-shirt. If you saw him riding his bike down the street, you wouldn't look twice. Up close, as Osso is, he sees the sociopath lurking behind the innocent façade.

"I know what you're doing. I'm not stupid, you know. You can't trick me into confessing something I didn't do." *His chin tips up defiantly.*

"I wouldn't try that. Not with you. Not with a kid who created a torture chamber like that." *He shakes his head, subtly moving his huge frame to the side, blocking the kid's view of Hernández.* "Just between us," *he adds, leaning in.* "How'd you pick them? Is there a commonality we're not seeing? Or did you pick them because they were different?"

The kid glances at all the activity around him. It's like when they'd found his workshop, exciting and scary. "Hypothetically?"

Osso nods. "Sure."

"Maybe. I don't know, but maybe because they were there and stupid enough to walk into the trap."

Osso nods again, like he's giving this response his full attention and finds it fascinating.

"I mean, I don't know, right? It was that other guy, but I bet they were annoying little babies who couldn't even imagine their lives not being perfect. I—that guy just helped 'em grow up. I told him to stop, though. I thought he was just kidding around. I didn't think he was going to kill anyone."

"Uh-huh." Osso drops the faux interest. The fierce expression on his face makes the kid lean back, unable to move farther away because of the cop standing directly behind him.

"I don't care if you believe me. It's true." He shrugs one of his bony shoulders. "I'm just a kid," he says again. "It's not like you could throw me in prison."

"That's true," Osso responds, his voice a deep rumble.

"And even if I was convicted for the stuff that guy did, a couple of years in juvie and I'm out." He looks around Detective Osso at Detective Hernández, his gaze moving up and down. "Some people should worry about me getting out in a few years and maybe not liking the cops who made up all this stuff about me."

The kid returns his attention to Detective Osso. "My life has been tough. Doctors will tell the judge I was too young to know right from wrong. And I don't have parents, just that old bitch in there. I never knew my dad and my mom got sick and died. See? You should be helping me, not arresting me for stuff that isn't even my fault."

Detective Osso nods to the uniformed cop to take the kid to the car, to bring him to the station and then turns his back on the kid. Detective Hernández does the same.

"Hey, wait. Wait!" The killer is escorted away. He continues to look over his shoulder, trying to get the detectives' attention back on him, where it belongs. When they go around the side of the house toward the driveway, he stops struggling. Seems pointless. He sizes up the officer with him. "Can you get me my phone back? That's my phone. He doesn't have the right to take it. It's mine." He'd feel better if he could look at the pictures on it, relive them. He'd feel better if he could just do that.

On a gasp, I sat up in bed and then let out a long, slow breath. They got him. Dropping back onto the pillow, I stared up at my ceiling. This was normally when I'd go bake, but I couldn't because I didn't want to wake up Declan. *Damn.*

"You okay up there?" he called.

Jeez. His hearing was ridiculous. "They arrested the killer."

A moment later, he was standing beside my bed. "How do you know?"

"Saw it." I pointed to my head.

"You sure it wasn't a nightmare or something? You said you always have those." He sat on the edge of the bed.

"I'm sure. This had the clarity of a prophetic dream, like when I saw what happened with you and the wolves. My night-mares are a jumble of a million horrible things I've seen, relent-lessly trying to swamp me. This was different. Hernández and Osso will come tomorrow"—I checked the clock—"today to tell me about it."

He let out a breath, patting my knee beneath the comforter. "You did it. Because of you, that guy won't kill anyone else."

I nodded, sitting back up. "Christopher was already gone before Hernández came to me. Ana, though, she was taken after. I wish I could have—"

"Don't. You did everything you could. You found her and her killer. And I'm sure he had his eye on other kids who will get to grow up now because of you."

That sounded nice, but I wasn't there yet. "Could you sleep up here so I can go down and bake? I'm not going to be able to fall asleep again."

He studied my bed. "Lie down on a comfortable bed instead of a too-small couch? I don't know…"

"Ha ha," I said, jumping out of bed. I slept in a tank top and panties, but it was particularly dark up here with my skylight blacked out. I went to my closet and grabbed a pair of sweatpants and a hoodie. I found my slippers and was toeing into them when Declan cleared his throat.

"I feel honor-bound to tell you that werewolves have excellent night vision and now I won't be able to sleep either, as I'll never get the image of you in your underwear out of my head."

I checked the clock again. "Good. I'll make you a big breakfast and then you can get to work on my deck."

He fell back on the bed with a groan. "I'll be there in a minute. First I need a cold shower."

"Do what you need to do," I said, jogging down the stairs. Instead of the kitchen, though, I went to the back door, opening it on the cold and wind. Sunrise was still hours away, but I called, "Good morning, Charlie! Good morning, Herbert!" I looked down into the water directly beneath me—I missed my deck. "Good morning, Cecil. I hope you and your friend are doing well." A tentacle broke the surface and then slipped under the waves again. And there, three posts away, was the tennis ball.

We still had a sorcerer to catch, but my friends were okay. I had a hot guy upstairs and a possible visit from my dad. The detectives would be showing up in a few hours for their key lime tartlets and I was pretty sure they were bringing me a new case. I didn't know how it had happened, but my life had become insane…and I didn't hate it.

Excerpt from Wicche Hunt: The Sea Wicche Chronicles #2

Keep reading for a sneak peek of
WICCHE HUNT: THE SEA WICCHE CHRONICLES

1
I Fortunately Know a Little Magic

Seagulls dove and wheeled over the roaring ocean. Spray misted the air as I closed my eyes and breathed it in: the salt, the pine, the hot dude next to me.

"Did you remember to send that demon your lemon bar recipe?" Declan, a tall, broad-shouldered, all-around-jaw-dropping werewolf, jogged beside me down the steps to Lands End in San Francisco, holding my gloved hand.

I'm Arwyn, the sea wicche of Monterey, and I was on a demon fact-finding mission. "Of course I did. I even sent a video of me making them." I didn't want him thinking I'd reneged on a deal. "In fact, I sent a few more recipes to butter him up for tonight."

"Good thinking." Glancing down the stairs, he ushered me off the path, out of the line of tourists.

The sun was setting over the water, waves splashing on the rocks below. We were at the spot where the ocean met the bay. We waited for a large family to pass us on their way up. It wouldn't do to disappear into a magical bookstore and bar right in front of non-magical folk.

I pulled out my phone and took a panoramic photo. The gloves I wore had connective threads at the fingertips so I could use touch screen devices. You might be wondering, *Arwyn, why not just take off the gloves?* Well, I'll tell you. I'm a wicche, specifically a Cassandra. Our gift is prophesy. I wear gloves because I also have a—I guess we'll call it a gift—for psychometry, meaning I glean information by touching things.

On the one hand, useful. On the other, a nightmare for most normal human interactions, especially dating.

After the family passed us, I put my phone away and Declan grabbed my hand once more. "I'm hanging on to you," he said as the stairs turned. "If her wards try to block me, I'm hoping you can drag me through with you."

"She said she'd tell the wards you were coming." *She* being Sam Quinn, the owner-operator of The Slaughtered Lamb Bookstore and Bar and a newly discovered cousin of mine. Sam was part Quinn wolf, like Declan, and part Corey wicche, like me.

Between one step and the next, the glorious purpling sunset and crashing waves disappeared and we were in a dark stairwell, lit by flickering wall sconces. I experienced a moment of panic and realized Declan must have too because we'd both clutched the other's hand hard.

"I guess it worked." The rumble of Declan's voice in the dim light put me at ease.

Within a few steps, I heard the low murmur of conversation. I pulled up short two steps later, though, when I heard growling.

Grinning, Declan urged me along. "It's a dog."

Light from the bar hit the landing below and there we saw a black wolfhound growling up at us—well, Declan really. Clive, Sam's vampire husband had mentioned they had a puppy.

"Fergus! Don't growl at customers. That's not polite puppy behavior." At the sound of the woman's voice, the dog sat and stopped growling. Mostly. He raised his lip on the right side of his muzzle—away from the bar—showing us half his teeth.

Ha. I loved the little shit already. When Declan and I reached the landing, we both sat on the stairs and waited to pass inspection. Fergus, which was apparently his name, leaned forward and sniffed at us both. Declan got a wary look and a low growl as the dog positioned himself between us, his back to me, protecting me from the werewolf.

Declan shook his head as I laughed and kissed the top of the pooch's head.

"See?" I murmured, getting up. "He knows you're sketchy." Fergus kept to my side down the remaining steps and into the bar. Holy—I'd seen it in my visions, but those had been pale representations of the real thing.

Waves splashed against the wall of glass, the sky going indigo over the North Bay mountains. The sea level was about five feet above the barroom floor. Kelp bobbed and fish slid through the dark water.

The voices around me were so much white noise. I skirted around tables until I was in front of the window. I knew I was surrounded by wicches. I recognized the buzz of their magic. As I didn't feel hostility from them, though, I sat on the floor, placing my hands on the glass. Almost at once, a tentacle reached up from below and slapped the window, its suckers separated from my hand by a half foot of aquarium-grade glass.

"Hello, you," I whispered. Three more tentacles hit the

window as she rose from under the bar. Resting my forehead against the cold, slick surface, I watched the octopus undulating in the waves, one rectangular eye on me. "You I shall name... Violet." The gray tentacles turned a lovely purple. She approved.

Two seals swam in loops, each coming a bit closer with every swoop. "Thank you for the welcome." They surfaced, barking their greetings and making me laugh.

I saw movement out in the depths but couldn't make out what was there. Chairs scraped the floor around me as people moved away. The bar had gone silent. Why—oh, now I saw. My focus had been too narrow.

Violet slipped down below The Slaughtered Lamb again and the seals shot off toward the Golden Gate Bridge.

"What are you doing out there? It's late in the season for you." A massive gray body, fifty feet long, swam close to the glass, his huge black eye on me. Magic gathered around me. I held up a hand to the wicches behind me who were readying spells. "Don't."

He moved closer. I returned my hands to the glass and whispered, "Safe travels, my friend." Breaching the surface, he flipped onto his side, swamping the window with a tidal wave of water. Vocalizing, he made a croaking sound that was dangerously close to a laugh. Cheeky bastard.

"As you were," I said, standing up. "He was just passing by and detoured to say hi." I went to Declan, who stared out the window in awe, Fergus held under his arm. "I want glass panels in the new deck so I can see down into the water."

He shook his head, breaking the spell. "You can just look over the edge of the deck. And Cecil and Wilbur might not appreciate you spying on them." The gangly pup, who was all legs and huge paws, wriggled, so Declan put him down.

Hmm. That was a good point. "New thought: glass panels, but I paint the bottom so you see tentacles that are pushing up out of the water to crush the Sea Wicche art gallery."

"I can't believe that just happened." Sam, The Slaughtered

Lamb owner and recently discovered Corey cousin, was behind the bar. Shaking her head, she asked, "What can I get you two?"

"Beer. Whatever you have on tap." Declan took the empty stool in front of her. He'd thought he was the last of the storied Quinn line of werewolves. Like me, he'd found out that he, too, had a relative, one who had been hidden most of her life.

Taking the seat beside Declan, I said, "We've worked it out. Declan here is your uncle. And I'm fine with water."

Sam grinned and it lit up the bar. There was something about her that made you feel safe, cared for. I couldn't explain it. "Was your dad Alexander?" she asked. At Declan's nod, she said, "I'm his son Michael's daughter." Shaking her head, she glanced over at her ridiculously handsome vampire husband. "This is my Uncle Declan."

He ran a hand down her back. "So I heard." He had a beautiful English accent, chiseled features, thick dark blond hair, and gray eyes that went soft whenever he looked at his wife. I'd seen him in a rage, eyes black, fangs descended, so I knew just how terrifying he could be. Now, though, here with Sam, he was a different man.

"That," he said, gesturing toward the window, "was the most extraordinary thing I've seen in my very long life. Do whales often drop by your gallery in Monterey?"

"Depends," I said, tipping my head back and forth. "If it's their migratory season and I'm out on the deck, I often get a few visitors. Not close like this, though. The water's too shallow for gray whales right next to the gallery. They're maybe thirty yards away. I've taken some great shots of them, though. Once the renovation is complete, I'll have a wall for my photographs."

"Oh," Sam said, like a thought had just occurred to her. Clive smiled and nodded, almost as though he'd heard her thought. "Can you do a portrait of Fergus for us?"

I glanced around the bar, looking for him, and found him once again on the landing, keeping a suspicious eye on all of us. I took out my phone, fiddled with the settings, and slid off the stool to take a few. "I'll see what I can do now. If I don't get anything good, we can schedule a session."

Sam bounced on the balls of her feet. "Perfect." She looked past me into the bookstore. "Fyr?" she called.

Out of the bookstore strode the most Thor-looking mountain of a man I'd ever seen. He had long blond hair, dragon-green eyes—you know what? Just picture Thor and you've got it.

"Can you watch the bar?" Sam asked Thor. "We need to go back and have a chat with our guests."

He nodded, grabbed a bar towel, and folded it into his waistband. It was nothing, the most basic of movements, but most of the people in the bar—including me—couldn't tear our eyes away from him.

Fingers snapped in my face and I startled, finding Declan staring at me, eyebrows raised. *Oops.* I shrugged. It wasn't my fault the gorgeous man walked in front of me. I'd been minding my own business, framing dog photos. I can't be held account-able for noticing gods walking among us.

I caught up with Sam. The kitchen was remarkable. Her countertops were like my floors, concrete stained the blue-green of shallow water. The dark floor gave just a bit with each step. "Cork?" I asked.

Dave, Sam's half-demon cook, looked over his shoulder and nodded. He wasn't wearing his usual glamour, that of a tall, muscular, bald Black man. How freeing The Slaughtered Lamb must be. No humans could get in, so supernaturals could be themselves. In Dave's case, he was still tall, muscular, and bald, but he was now also red-skinned and black-eyed.

"Yeah," he replied. "Cork flooring is easier on the knees and feet." He tilted his head toward the counter to his left. "Wolf, I put a cheesesteak aside for you, if you want it."

Declan grabbed the plate and followed Sam through a dark doorway. I paused, taking off my backpack and pulling out a gift cocooned in Bubble Wrap.

"Thank you for meeting with me again. As a token, I made Maggie a little something for your garden."

Dave wiped his hands on a dish towel and then tossed it onto the nearby island. Leaning against the counter, he studied what was in my hand. "This is for Maggie?"

I nodded.

"Can I open it?"

"Please do." Hopefully, he'd like it too. "It's glass," I warned. I didn't want it broken before it made it to her.

He unwrapped an eight-inch-long glass hedgehog. I'd remembered he'd said his girlfriend wanted a pet hedgehog but couldn't have one, as they'd been living in an apartment. Once he rescued her, they were going to look for a house with a backyard.

"I'd never tried to make a hedgehog before." I thought it had turned out well, though. I'd pulled and snipped the ball of hot amorphous glass, shaping sparkling brown quills, and I'd made the sweet, tapered face a color somewhere between tan and pink. When Dave came close to smiling, I thought my payment had been accepted.

"Go on," he said, waving me toward the door.

Before stepping through, I looked back and saw him gently placing it on his desk. The world went dark again, like when we'd went through the ward on the stairs, and then…oh, it was an apartment. The living room was cozy, saddle brown walls, mahogany wood, and beautiful green leather couch and chairs. They'd moved one of the wooden chairs from the bar in as well.

Declan was sitting on the couch, chatting with Sam and Clive, who were in the matching chairs. Declan patted the cushion beside him. Instead of sitting, though, I went to a painting hanging on their wall.

It was Paris, unmistakably Paris at night, the Eiffel Tower lit up in the distance. This wasn't the painting of a street artist cranking them out for the tourists. This packed an emotional punch. The colors, the brushstrokes, the dreamy quality of the moon glowing behind snow clouds...

"Do you like it?" Clive asked. I hadn't seen or heard him move. If I thought too much about it, he'd scare me, and I didn't want to be scared of him.

"I do." I scanned the corner for a signature and recognized the name. He was a master.

"It's the view from our hotel room balcony," he said. "We went to Paris for our honeymoon."

"Clive hired the artist and then booked him into the suite we'd stayed in so he could get the view exactly right," Sam explained. "I love it so much. Sometimes I just sit here, fall into the painting, and visit Paris in my memories."

Dave walked in a moment later, carrying a plate of lemon squares, placing them on the coffee table. Clive and I took our seats.

"Well?" I asked the grumpy demon. I hoped he was happy with the recipe results.

"You tell me." He handed me a pair of chopsticks before sitting in the wooden barroom chair.

He'd remembered. Gloves made eating finger foods tricky. I used the chopsticks to pick up a lemon bar and place it on a napkin, before using them again to pluck off a piece and pop it into my mouth. *Mmm.* "They're delicious."

He waited, clearly wanting a better critique than that.

"This is a taste thing, okay? I like a little more lemon zest in the shortbread crust and sprinkle a little less sugar on the dough before you bake." I turned the bar over to study the bottom. "I'd go another minute, maybe even two before you combine the crust with the lemon filling."

Nodding, he crossed his powerful arms over his chest. "Okay, good."

Declan put his empty plate down and grabbed a lemon bar. He took a bite, *mmm*ed, and said, "Excellent."

Sam took a bar and then sat, her legs curled up under her.

"So," she said, glancing between me and Dave, "what questions do you have for our former resident of Hell?"

I took another bite and then put the napkin with the bar on the coffee table. "How do we find and stop a sorcerer?"

Dave blew a gust of air through his nose. "Good luck. We were hunting our own for quite a while. I can tell you that sorcery bleeds over into the mundane world, so sometimes you can track the incidents of bloodshed or death to the sorcerer's doorstep."

"Yeah," I said. "We've been seeing that. The detectives I spoke with said violent crimes have been getting worse and more frequent the last couple of years."

He nodded. "Which tells us this isn't a new arrangement. See if you can get them to map it for you."

"According to you guys and my mom," I began, "my aunt— the sorcerer causing you all those problems—trained Calliope, my cousin and our latest sorcerer. Mom says Cal began studying with my aunt when she was young, at maybe eight or ten years old, so seventeen-ish years ago."

"And you never saw any black in her aura?" he asked.

When I shook my head, he paused, staring into the middle distance. "So why haven't there been violent crimes the last seventeen years? Hmm. Has she changed locations, moved closer to Monterey?"

I shook my head. "She's always lived with her parents."

"Ask your police to check nearby communities. She doesn't practice sorcery in the bedroom of her parents' home. She has to have a workshop someplace where she has privacy and isolation. It wouldn't do to have neighbors hear chanting in the middle of the night. Maybe also check records of proper-ties owned by Coreys, your aunt, Calliope, long-lost relatives you've forgotten about. She needs a place to work that isn't too far so she can be there when a family member calls for her."

I reached into my backpack, pulled out a small notebook,

like the one Detective Hernández used, and began jotting down what we needed to do.

"I haven't worked with a sorcerer in a while," he continued, "but I did it for a very long time. Most of the wicches I worked with tried to hide the marks of sorcery. I've only known of one, though, who was able to do it."

He scratched his jaw, thinking. "He was a Corey. I'm almost positive. Maybe four or five hundred years ago. Maybe Ireland." He shook his head as though trying to jostle his memories into place.

"I didn't work with him, but I remember hearing mumbles about a spell that could wipe an aura clean. I know who your cousin's demon is now and I don't believe he was the one working with that sorcerer either." He shrugged one large shoulder. "My guess is there is a Corey spell, maybe even a black magic grimoire with many spells, that's passed down from one sorcerer to the next."

As soon as he said the words, I felt the truth of them. "That may be why there are so damned many of them in my family tree."

"Our family tree," Sam said, pointing to herself, Dave, and me.

"Yeah, *our.*" I knew that should have made me feel better. I wasn't alone in all this. Unfortunately, hunting down and stopping Calliope felt very much as though it had been laid squarely on my shoulders.

Don't for get to pre-order
WICCHE HUNT: THE SEA WICCHE CHRONICLES
out April 16, 2024

Dear Reader,

Thank you for reading **Bewicched: The Sea Wicche Chronicles**. If you enjoyed Arwyn's first story, please consider leaving a review or chatting about it with your book-loving friends. Good word of mouth means everything when you're a new writer!

Love,
Seana

Acknowledgments

Thank you to my family for putting up with me as I raced to finish this book. I just put in the retirement paperwork at my day job, so as of June, I'll be a full-time writer! After so many years of writing early mornings, weekends, vacations, I can't quite wrap my mind around being a full-time author. Amazing. Scary. Somebody pinch me.

Thank you to the best critique partner ever: C.R. Grissom. Throughout the writing of this book, she sent me video clips of octopuses, seals, sea turtles, surfing manta rays (look for them in the next book). She kept me inspired, cheering me on one chapter at a time, and I love her for it.

Thank you to Peter Senftleben, my extraordinary editor. He has the enviable knack of getting to the heart of the story and then helping me to see my own work through a different lens. He said this was his favorite of my books. Here's hoping readers agree. Thank you to Susan Helene Gottfried, my wonderful proofreader who always knows exactly where the commas go (unlike myself).

Thank you to the outstanding team at NYLA! You've made every step of publishing a little easier with your compassion, commitment, and expertise. Thank you to my marvelous agent Sarah Younger, the fabulous Natanya Wheeler, and the incredible Cheryl Pientka for working together to make my dream of writing and publishing a reality.

Want more books from Seana?

If you'd like to be the first to learn what's new with Arwyn and Declan (and Sam & Clive), please sign up for my newsletter *Tales from the Book Nerd*. It's filled with writing news, deleted scenes, giveaways, book recommendations, first looks at covers, short stories, and my favorite cocktail and book pairings.

The Slaughtered Lamb Bookstore & Bar
Sam Quinn, book 1

Welcome to The Slaughtered Lamb Bookstore and Bar. I'm Sam Quinn, the werewolf book nerd in charge. I run my business by one simple rule: Everyone needs a good book and a stiff drink, be they vampire, wicche, demon, or fae. No wolves, though. Ever. I have my reasons.

I serve the supernatural community of San Francisco. We've been having some problems lately. Okay, I'm the one with the problems. The broken body of a female werewolf washed up on my doorstep. What makes sweat pool at the base of my spine, though, is realizing the scars she bears are identical to the ones I conceal. After hiding for years, I've been found.

A protection I've been relying on is gone. While my wolf traits are strengthening steadily, the loss also left my mind vulnerable to attack. Someone is ensnaring me in horrifying visions intended to kill. Clive, the sexy vampire Master of the City, has figured out how to pull me out, designating himself my personal bodyguard. He's grumpy about it, but that kiss is telling a different story. A change is taking place. It has to. The bookish bartender must become the fledgling badass.

I'm a survivor. I'll fight fang and claw to protect myself and the ones I love. And let's face it, they have it coming.

The Dead Don't Drink at Lafitte's
Sam Quinn, book 2

I'm Sam Quinn, the werewolf book nerd owner of the Slaughtered Lamb Bookstore and Bar. Things have been busy lately. While the near-constant attempts on my life have ceased, I now have a vampire gentleman caller. I've been living with Clive and the rest of his vampires for a few weeks while the Slaughtered Lamb is being rebuilt. It's going about as well as you'd expect.

My mother was a wicche and long dormant abilities are starting to make themselves known. If I'd had a choice, necromancy wouldn't have been my top pick, but it's coming in handy. A ghost warns me someone is coming to kill Clive. When I rush back to the nocturne, I find vamps from New Orleans readying an attack. One of the benefits of vampires looking down on werewolves is no one expects much of me. They don't expect it right up until I take their heads.

Now, Clive and I are setting out for New Orleans to take the fight back to the source. Vampires are masters of the long game.

Revenge plots are often decades, if not centuries, in the making. We came expecting one enemy, but quickly learn we have darker forces scheming against us. Good thing I'm the secret weapon they never see coming.

The Wicche Glass Tavern
Sam Quinn, book 3

I'm Sam Quinn, the werewolf book nerd owner of the Slaughtered Lamb Bookstore and Bar. Clive, my vampire gentleman caller, has asked me to marry him. His nocturne is less than celebratory. Unfortunately, for them and the sexy vamp doing her best to seduce him, his cold, dead heart beats only for me.

As much as my love life feels like a minefield, it has to take a backseat to a far more pressing problem. The time has come. I need to deal with my aunt, the woman who's been trying to kill me for as long as I can remember. She's learned a new trick. She's figured out how to weaponize my friends against me. To have any hope of surviving, I have to learn to use my necromantic gifts. I need a teacher. We find one hiding among the fae, which is a completely different problem. I need to determine what I'm capable of in a hurry because my aunt doesn't care how many are hurt or killed as long as she gets what she wants. Sadly for me, what she wants is my name on a headstone.

I'm gathering my friends-werewolves, vampires, wicches, gorgons, a Fury, a half-demon, an elf, and a couple of dragonshifters-into a kind of Fellowship of the Sam. It's going to be one hell of a battle. Hopefully, San Francisco will still be standing when the dust clears.

The Hob & Hound Pub
Sam Quinn, book 4

I'm Sam Quinn, the newly married werewolf book nerd owner of the Slaughtered Lamb Bookstore and Bar. Clive and I are on our honeymoon. Paris is lovely, though the mummy in the Louvre inching toward me is a bit off-putting. Although Clive doesn't sense anything, I can't shake the feeling I'm being watched.

Even after we cross the English Channel to begin our search for Aldith—the woman who's been plotting against Clive since the beginning—the prickling unease persists. Clive and I are separated, rather forcefully, and I'm left to find my way alone in a foreign country, evading not only Aldith's large web of hench-vamps, but vicious fae creatures disloyal to their queen. Gloriana says there's a poison in the human realm that's seeping into Faerie, and I may have found the source.

I knew this was going to be a working vacation, but battling vampires on one front and the fae on another is a lot, especially in a country steeped in magic. As a side note, I need to get word to Benvair. I think I've found the dragon she's looking for.

Gloriana is threatening to set her warriors against the human realm, but I may have a way to placate her. Aldith is a different story. There's no reasoning with rabid vengeance. She'll need to be put out of our misery permanently if Clive and I have any hope of a long, happy life together. Heck, I'd settle for a few quiet weeks.

Biergarten of the Damned
Sam Quinn, book 5

I'm Sam, the werewolf book nerd in charge of The Slaughtered Lamb Bookstore & Bar. I've always thought of Dave, my red-skinned, shark eyed, half-demon cook, as a kind of foul-mouthed uncle, one occasionally given to bouts of uncontrolled anger.

Something's going on, though. He's acting strangely, hiding things. When I asked what was wrong, he blew me off and told me to quit bugging him. That's normal enough. What's not is his missing work. Ever. Other demons are appearing in the bar, looking for him. I'm getting worried, and his banshee girlfriend Maggie isn't answering my calls.

Demons terrify me. I do NOT want to go into any demon bars looking for Dave, but he's my family, sort of. I need to try to help, whether he wants me to or not. When I finally learn the truth, though…I'm not sure I can ever look at him again, let alone have him work for me. Are there limits to forgiveness? I think there might be.

The Viper's Nest Roadhouse & Café
Sam Quinn, book 6

I'm Sam, the werewolf book nerd owner of The Slaughtered Lamb Bookstore & Bar. Clive, Fergus, and I are moving into our new home, the business is going well, and our folly is taking shape. The problem? Clive's maker Garyn is coming to San Francisco for a visit, and this reunion has been a thousand years in the making. Back then, Garyn was rather put out when Clive accepted the dark kiss and then took off to avenge his sister's murder. She was looking for a new family. He was looking for lethal skills. And so, Garyn has had plenty of time to align her forces. When her allies begin stepping out of the shadows, Clive's foundation will be shaken.

Stheno and her sisters are adding to their rather impressive portfolio of businesses around the world by acquiring The Viper's Nest Roadhouse & Café. Medusa found the place when she was visiting San Francisco. A dive bar filled with hot tattooed bikers? Yes, please!

Clive and I will need neutral territory for our meeting with Garyn, and a biker bar (& café, Stheno insisted) should fit the bill. I'd assumed my necromancy would give us an advantage. I hadn't anticipated, though, just how powerful Garyn and her allies were. When the fangs descend and the heads start rolling, it's going to take every friend we have and a nocturne full of vamps at our backs to even the playing field. Wish us luck. We're going to need it.

Bewicched

The Sea Wicche Chronicles, book 1

We here at The Sea Wicche cater to your art collecting, muffin eating, tea drinking and potion peddling needs. Palmistry and Tarot sessions are available upon request and by appointment. Our store hours vary and rely completely on Arwyn—the owner—getting her butt out of bed.

Hi, I'm Arwyn, the sea wicche, or the wicche who lives by the sea. It requires a lot more work than I'd anticipated to remodel an abandoned cannery and turn it into an art gallery & tea bar. It's coming along, though, especially with help from a new werewolf who's joined the construction crew. He does beautiful work. His sexy, growly, bearded presence is very hard to ignore, but I'm trying. I'm not sure how such a laid-back guy got the local Alpha and his pack threatening to hunt him down and tear him apart, but we all have our secrets. And because I don't want to know his, or yours for that matter, I wear these gloves. Clairvoyance makes the simplest things the absolute worst. Trust me. Or don't. Totally up to you.

Did I mention my mother and grandmother are pressuring me to assume my rightful place on the Corey Council? That's a kind of governing triad for our ancient magical family, one that has more than its fair share of black magic practitioners. And yes, before you ask, people have killed to be on the council—one psychotic sorceress aunt stands out—but I have no interest in the power or politics that come with the position. I'd rather stick to my art and, in the words of my favorite sea wicche, help poor unfortunate souls. (Good luck trying to get that song out of your head now)

Wicche Hunt

The Sea Wicche Chronicles, book 2

I'm Arwyn Cassandra Corey, the Sea Wicche of Monterey. Want a psychic reading? Sure. I can do that. In the market for art? I have all your painting, photography, glass blowing, and ceramic needs covered in my newly remodeled art gallery by the sea. Need help solving a grisly cold case? Unfortunately, I can probably help with that too.

After more than a decade of being nagged, guilted, and threatened, I've finally joined the Corey Council and am working with my mother and grandmother to hunt down a twisted sorcerer. We know who she is. Now we need to find and stop her before more are murdered.

The evil the sorcerer and her demon are doing is seeping into the community. Violent crimes have been increasing and as a result Detectives Hernández and Osso have brought me another horrifying case. I'll do what I can, because of course I will. What are a few more nightmares to a woman who barely sleeps?

Declan Quinn, the wicked hot werewolf rebuilding my deck, is preparing for a dominance battle with the local Alpha. A couple of wolves have already left their pack to follow Declan, recognizing him as the true Alpha. Declan needs to watch his back as the full moon approaches. The current Alpha will do whatever it takes to hold on to power, including breaking pack law and enlisting the help of a local vampire.

And if Wilbur, my selkie friend is right, I might just be meeting my dad soon. Perhaps he'll have some advice for this wicche hunt. I'm going to need all the help I can get.

Content Warning: Wicche Hunt: The Sea Wicche Chronicles is a contemporary fantasy novel with suspense elements about a clairvoyant witch who, among other things, helps detectives hunt a killer. While there are light, funny, romantic moments, there are also dark ones that may be disturbing for some readers. Warning for: visions that include graphic or explicit violence, murder

Titles by Seana Kelly

The Sam Quinn Series

The Slaughtered Lamb Bookstore & Bar

The Dead Don't Drink at Lafitte's

The Wicche Glass Tavern

All I Want for Christmas is a Dragon (novelette)

The Hob & Hound Pub

Biergarten of the Damned

The Banshee & the Blade (novelette)

The Viper's Nest Roadhouse & Café

The Sea Wicche Chronicles

Bewicched: The Sea Wicche Chronicles

Wicche Hunt: The Sea Wicche Chronicles

About Seana Kelly

Seana Kelly lives in the San Francisco Bay Area with her husband, two daughters, two dogs, and one fish. When not dodging her family, hiding in the garage to write, she's working as a high school teacher-librarian. She's an avid reader and re-reader who misses her favorite characters when it's been too long between visits.

She's a *USA Today* bestseller and is represented by the delightful and effervescent Sarah E. Younger of the Nancy Yost Literary Agency

You can follow Seana on Twitter for tweets about books and dogs or on Instagram for beautiful pictures of books and dogs (kidding). She also loves collecting photos of characters and settings for the books she writes. As she's a huge reader of young adult and adult books, expect lots of recommendations as well.

Website: www.seanakelly.com

Newsletter: https://geni.us/t0Y5cBA

twitter.com/SeanaKellyRW

instagram.com/seanakellyrw

facebook.com/Seana-Kelly-1553527948245885

bookbub.com/authors/seana-kelly

pinterest.com/seanakelly326

www.ingramcontent.com/pod-product-compliance
Lightning Source LLC
LaVergne TN
LVHW060302161224
799208LV00033B/633